WOMAN OF PROPERTY

Mabel Seeley

WOMAN OF PROPERTY

GARDEN CITY, NEW YORK

Doubleday & Company, Inc.

1947

This is a story of hungers which seem to propel much of humanity, and something of humanity must therefore be reflected here. There is no intention, however, to portray any actual person, living or dead, and any similarities arise wholly from coincidence.

For any good there may be in this book, much credit must go to my husband for his ideas, collaborative assistance, and advice, to Isabelle Taylor for her four years of encouragement and most practical advice and assistance, to Jacob and Franklin Hodnefield for their help in research and criticism, to Eugenie Heger for her meticulous checking of detail, to Josephine Lush and Ann Jolly for excellent criticisms and suggestions. I also am grateful to the staff of the Minneapolis Public Library, for being so endlessly co-operative, and also to the staff of the newspaper room of the Minnesota Historical Society. Most of all, though, I thank those four women who consecutively helped tend my lively small son—without them I'd have written no book at all.

Contents

Part One
FIRST SIGHT

In the United States, in that year which was called 1889, only small pockets of frontier were left, but the people still pressed outward. Oklahoma, that year, was settled in what seemed like a day; newspapers, that year, trailed brilliant courting plumage before Canada—Canada, they said, could never Fulfill her Destiny, except in Union with her Sister Country to the South. A man named Harrison, that year, moved to the White House; park bands played "Tara-ra Boom-de-ay"; small children died (each family with its vacant chairs) from scarlet fever, measles, summer complaint; across an impressed countryside the Women's Christian Temperance Union labored laboriously "For God and Home and Native Land." Charges of political corruption and bribery in the major parties grew so loud, that year, that leaders on both sides (they, naturally, the loudest) cried for remedial legislation; while the whole of American Industry, other Ezekiels warned, was being walled off into Trusts.

For the most part, however, for most people in most places, the great business of living, as always, was mostly a matter of getting up in the morning and of going to bed at night, of sweating at some kind of work, of relaxing a bit in the evening, of loving a little, planning a little, trying for some goal. Like all other years, this one, too, was a link between what had gone by and what was to come. Some people died in the space of its twelve months, others were born——

CHAPTER I

AT HIS desk on the balcony, Junius B. Hake turned the pages of his credit ledger to Mrs. Mathew Drake's account. "Saturday, June 8, 1889," he wrote, his hand moving in large negligent arcs to form the small and even script, "16 yards French Foulard, $21.60, 4½ yards sash ribbon, $5.63." Nothing in Mrs. Drake's account, nothing in any of the credit accounts, explained his indolent light pleasure; credit, he thought, had only one advantage over piety— you needn't die to find out your returns.

No, it was the girl downstairs, the girl sweeping out the darkened store, who furnished his enjoyment; he'd been assured of that for several weeks. It was so easy to know, from her activity, the vehemence of her otherwise concealed emotions. Now at ten, late shoppers and his four other clerks gone, her clatter was furious at the far side, as if she beat out there against counter and cheese cask a storm of angers and resentments. The fury of these encounters would subdue as she came down the dry-goods aisles, but ferment somehow would be there, coupled with tightening anxiety. Finally would come a slow, repeated swishing at the foot of the stairs, before she climbed to his balcony office to complete her night's task.

Naturally she stood in awe of him. But what entirely made her reluctance? Almost he was tempted to make some approach. Nothing definite or certain, of course—after all she was only fourteen—just something to awaken her to the possibilities in herself—and in him. Most men—certainly the bumpkins of West Haven—would see nothing in her; his son Palmer, for instance, would consider her far beneath his scorn. Palmer, at eighteen, was confining his sheep's eyes to well-bred lilies like Cecilia Amiot. Palmer had none of that calm acceptance of one's quality which could lead to the savoring of a condescension.

This girl, though, had something. Vigor, perhaps. And strange eyes—narrow, small, elusive, pale. Her unawakened mouth was small too. Small and moist.

A tingle in his fingers served only to speed his posting of the credit accounts; some such outside leaven was just what he needed to make this first half of his nightly reckoning bearable. Not until the credit ledger had been pushed aside did his faculties bear on the task at hand.

The four brown waiting tills were old and scuffed, but on this Saturday evening they were full. Separately he took them in his spatulate pale fingers, weighing them, guessing at their sum, before he spilled them out upon the desk. Then as he moved his palms against the pile, compressing it, he felt a flooding pulse. This was where power and glory lay, right here in the money. This was what kept him at storekeeping, past all the tedium, the smells of kerosene and mice, the dependence on a custom he disdained. Trying to shut out every exterior thought, concentrating all perception in his hands, he began sorting, absorbing the delicate skin-soft crinkled feel of paper, the cool, smooth, solid weight of silver.

Almost at once, however, he had to suffer the division which broke such moments of sharp relish. In spite of all he could do, his hands became intactile, automatic, his mind lifted outward, disengaged, until without contact or emotion he looked in on himself from the outside, seeing the dark disordered balcony hemmed with racks of garments, heaped with boxes, seeing the shaded gas mantle that spread a bell of light shaped like a woman's skirt, seeing the roll-top desk beneath and the tired, sardonic, shirt-sleeved man who dealt cash as if he dealt at cards—tens to one pile, fives to another, ones in a small drift.

Near the periphery of darkness on the desk, the light picked out the cold gleam of his Colt Peacemaker. Uncontrolled, his mind swung out across the past; again he stood at the window of this same balcony looking down upon the daylight shapes and dust of a September thirteen years before; again through glass he knew activity all in and out of reason—galloping horses and careening riders, shouts, shots; again he heard the sharp bee whine of a bullet past his ear. Once more, as so often, his effortless right hand reached holsterward; again he took aim, and saw his kill. How easily and gracefully that foremost horseman had slid forward! That had been Jesse James's last raid, the last raid of the famous James and Younger brothers, the one that broke the gang. Out of all West Haven men he, Junius Hake, had been the first to return fire. That had been his day, when he had been alive and whole, when he had lived completely in the personal interchange of death.

All this, however, was an immersion from which, presently, he drew himself; there would be other times when he would need that refuge more. Now there was this other—even if trumpery—thing, the girl.

Senses reawakening, after complete lapse, he heard the susurration of her sweeping, near the stair. Movement had softened to decorum, now; it sounded as if she brushed, over and over, the same strip of aisle. And when her ascent of the stair began, she waited on each tread as if she were poised to fly if he—or was it some poltergeist of darkness that she feared?—should burst upon her. Yet finally when she rose from the stairwell to his sight she showed neither fright nor any other turbulance. Wordless, and with sulky, cast-down glance, she reached to sweep the large litter on the floor.

Abruptly chilled, repelled, he flung repugnance at her in cold, almost hating words.

"Don't feel I'm in your way, Miss Schlempke. I'm soon done."

How under heaven, he asked himself, feeling even through his back her blundering thick formlessness, her crudity, had he been led to think of her? Cruelly now he saw her snarled and frizzled dark hair, for all the world like a Zulu's, saw the dark freckles on her nose, her high color, her slackness in the limp, cheap cotton challis. Schlempke, her impossible name. Frieda Schlempke. He'd hired her only to get peace at his barber's; her father was in the town's one decent shop. She had grown, in the year she had been in the store; conical small breasts pushed against the lavender challis, but she stood too loosely, without pride or consciousness; her calves—why didn't her skirts cover them?—were heavy; she wasn't even corseted.

Yet two seconds after he had been swept by this digust he knew what his approach would be, and that he would make it now.

He rose, turning to fling the banded packets of the bills, the docketed bag of coins, into his safe. So abrupt was his movement that he caught her unaware, her broom and sulkiness alike forgotten, her light eyes for the moment not elusive as she stared.

Not at him. *At the money.* Of course, he thought, with a release of wild upspringing laughter in his breast, it was the money. That hadn't been awe of *him*—though as possessor he too must represent some power—that had kept her mowing and scraping at the foot of the stairs. Men composed their faces, before banks, and entered softly, hushed.

Still shaken by his soundless quiver of perception, he watched her while she caught and startled, her glance sliding past his in its blurred recovery, before she was recaptured by a deeper blankness, and her untidy head bent again above the broom.

"Why, you——" he said softly. And then more surely, swiftly and extemporaneously: "Did you ever think how easy it is to throw this stuff around, Miss Schlempke? See, like this——"

He said it too loudly, he thought; not easily enough. But he could put fluid careless arrogance into the gesture with which he tossed packets of money here and there about the balcony, not even watching as the bands broke and the bills spilled, not looking toward the girl who pressed back against a rack of ladies' cloaks, her face drawing close as if against attack.

Some of the money landed at her feet.

"Now it's yours to gather up," he said. "The safe locks when you slam the door."

Swaggering, knowing he swaggered, he took up gun, hat, coat; casually as he passed he raised his hand to bump her chin, letting his knuckles graze, delicately, the blunt tip of her left breast.

"Someday it might be yours," he said, letting each word fall with meaning, before he went on down the stairs, across the store, pausing only to check the night latch as he left.

Feeling the smile still on his lips, the current of amusement still at ebb and flow, he indolently moved on toward his night of poker at the Benson House. To throw the money—how had he thought of that? Theatrical, of course, but somehow right, exactly right. Fools would say it wasn't safe to leave her with it; that was the feel of the gamble, but actually there was none. The girl might, when she woke to herself, lie for the stuff she picked up, cut throats for it, plot for it, perjure or sell herself for it, but she wouldn't steal it—not the actual cold cash. A stolen host bestows no benison.

He could sit back now, and for a long time make no further gesture, watch the coil he'd started, play a waiting game, his favorite, with cards close to his chest. He'd impressed her, all right—impressed her as he never had impressed anyone. But also he knew, and this with an increase of amusement, that he had impressed himself. Even in his brush with Jesse James he hadn't felt more glorious and drunken power.

Obscurely Frieda knew the incident as a beginning. All her life it was to stay in high relief, so that at any moment she could live it over, feeling the press of coats at her back, seeing Mr. Hake—his tired indifferent eyes, his drooping lids, the momentary strike of light beneath them when he swung upon her—and then the money falling, thickly and forever, as it seemed, the separate bills lying on the air for moments, weightless, sailing slowly, settling like leaves come to earth.

All her life she still breathed heavily, remembering how at the time she had been numbed and suffocated.

After Mr. Hake had gone, after she heard the night latch fall and knew she was alone, she scrambled quickly, trembling, smoothing out crumpled bills, restoring them to the safe's sanctity, hunting and rehunting, stacking and restacking, retrying the safe door once she had it shut. Even after she at last left the store, to bump against her outraged and forgotten father, to hear his hissed "SSSo! Here I wait like I am notting!" to take his open slap across her face, she had lived, continued to live, only in what had happened on the balcony.

Yet afterward she found that other lineaments of that evening, too, stayed sharply fixed. Earlier and later memories might slip back to a dark insentient limbo, but even years later any mention of her father could evoke the light *spat* of his feet as he bounded home that night, like a small angry bull, before her; she again could see his hunched back, his outthrust head, hear his mutterings; once more she experienced the rush of yellow lamplight as the kitchen door jerked open, once more smell chicory coffee from the range, once more see the white cups and the coffeecake on the blue-checked cloth, once more feel that tight expectancy which was the concomitant of her father's home-coming. The two younger children, Ernst and Lotte, rubbed shiny after bathing, hunkered on the rug before the stove in night-gowns. Viktor and Gottfried, her two older brothers, the white dust of the flour mill still powdering them even though they'd washed and changed, lounged in their usual remoteness, hands in pockets and heavy backs against the sink, eyes flicking one glance like a snake's tongue at the opening door. And between sink and door her mother waited, in a usual attitude of humble, strained apology.

"Coffee is ready—I go now to pour it in the cups." Immediately the father's step was heard, Ilse, the mother, broke into her stiff English, her tone stricken by despair as she saw how things were, yet rushing in as if she might, by haste, ward off the inevitable.

"Coffee! Coffee! Coffee!" From a first shout just inside the door, Otto Schlempke's voice rose to a scream; here at last he was at home where he could let himself go. Rushing forward on his neat light feet, he caught at Ernst and Lotte as they scuttled for the angle between stove and wall, knocking them about until they fell sprawling. Then he rushed back toward Frieda.

"*Coffee,* they say, when I stand hours, *hours* waiting while this Fräulein—this is how she has been brought up, this respect she has for Papa—keeps me waiting like I am a lamppost in the street. Hours I stand. Hours, hours, hours!"

Blows knocked her head to this side and that, bumping it against nails set in the door for coats, until in his blind rage his hand glanced from her face to rake across the nailheads. Dazed then by a different injury, he held up a hand from which blood dripped.

"This you do by *Papa?*" he asked piteously. "Blood pours out, and no one helps. I may be dead, and no one says notting."

Falling upon a chair, rolling his face in the arm of the uninjured hand, he stiffly held out the injured member.

"No one is to blame but yourself." It was Ilse who finally and wearily made answer as she stepped forward to assist, filling a washbasin and tearing up a towel for bandage. Frieda did nothing but slide along the wall to join with Ernst and Lotte. Against her father's abuse she had raised only the savage inchoate emotion, too formless to be rebellion, which had been her response since infancy. What she had just taken had been simply the punishment that always followed on angering her father; this was the way life was. She was almost as tall now as Otto Schlempke, but she had had no idea of defending herself; she had expected no one to interfere in her behalf, any more than she would have interfered if it had been one of the others who had been attacked. Yet on this evening she had to know, dimly, that there was a difference. Previous punishments such as this had been right, acceptable, but this one, someway, had been wrong, an outrage.

Morosely enclosing a surge she did not dare express—had no idea of knowing how to express—she later made one with her mute brothers and sister as, her father's hand now bandaged, she was brusquely ordered to table. In German her father now recited a saga of his martyrdom. He worked, they played. He massaged bestial faces, he washed filthy heads, he cut hair and trimmed beards for those impossible to please, while here at home his wife and children lived like kings, they ate, they drank, with no thought for the coming day; he, he alone, bore the burden and the heat of labor.

Restored almost to good humor by this fiction, lordly and relaxing, he waved the bandaged fingers, resting against an adulation which, if it could be elicited from no one else, at least came surely from himself.

He was, he might have said, a handsome man, far handsomer than any of his children; he might have expressed grief that none of them had his attractiveness, his virile, almost oriental masculinity, his closely curling crisp black hair, his gray flashing eyes, his bold straight nose. (A small pink mouth, speaking of feminine petulance, was a feature he ignored.) He, his manner said, was worldly; he could go anywhere, be accepted anywhere, while they were peasants like their mother. Before their doltish glumness he might flash his spirit, but without hope of answer.

The faces about him did not, indeed, show more than a cautious hope, as he first drained, then pushed back his cup. This was the moment toward which the evening, like the week, had verged.

"Now, Viktor." He was winning, gracious. "You have something for the papa, no?"

In a stolidity so entire it was close to violence, Viktor pulled from his breast pocket a small fold of bills, the product of six ten-hour days at the Amiot Flouring Mill, laying them in unbroken impassivity before his father.

"One, two, three, four, five." As if in surprise Otto counted. "This is nice. Five dollars, all from Viktor. Five dollars is nice money. And Gottfried?"

In duplication of his brother, Gottfried produced a smaller fold, a single coin.

"One, two, three. And fifty cents. We buy two horses, maybe, and a carriage." This was persiflage, so to be taken. "But there is one more —Frieda!"

As wordless as her brothers, Frieda bent to insert a hand under her skirt, removing from her stocking the money she had hidden away when she was paid, that day at noon.

"One dollar, fifty cents. Rich we are, now!" Still in the vein of affable pleasantry, he looked about him. "Viktor looks," he teased, "Viktor thinks tonight he will buy beer, he will play cards, he will be big boss, throwing out money. Gottfried looks, he too will treat the boys; Frieda looks, she thinks she buys silk dress, she will be fine girl, too fine for her papa. Mama looks——"

He paused, his voice grown thin and fine, his mischievous glance now on his wife, whose short, thick body quivered silently.

"Papa is generous," he went on, "Papa gives here, gives there, Papa gives to all, even to Ernst and Lottchen. *Nicht wahr,* Ernst? *Nicht wahr,* Lottchen?"

"One time a nickel," whispered Lottchen through stiff lips, her eyes mesmerized.

"*One* time a nickel," he chided. "Many times a nickel." This night he prolonged the teasing, returning again and again to each member of his family, repeating their wants, repeating former instances of his liberality, in which he had given as much as two dollars to each of the boys, and swept the rest of these earnings into his wife's hand with permission to spend them as she pleased upon herself and the younger children, gloriously ignoring the fact that from that sum they all and he too would be fed.

Tonight it seemed he never would be done, and in agonized desperation Ilse at last broke, her small round blue eyes strained and hopeless, like those of a wild animal plunging toward a hunter, knowing danger yet powerless to prevent self-destruction.

"How motch I get to buy the food?" The words fell tremblingly. This was what he had awaited.

"*Mautch* I get," he mimicked. "Mautch-I-get, mautchiget, mautchiget!" Springing to his feet, he swept the money—all of the money—into his pocket.

"All the time *mautchiget!* What for you need money? You think I'm made from money? You think money runs? You think I dip my hat in the river and it comes up money? You think I pick up money from the street? You think it falls down on the floor like hair? All the time—money, money, money, money!"

With a last windmill gesture, which brought his hat into his hands from the doornail where it had been hung during the bandaging, he charged out through the door.

It wasn't too different from any Saturday. Yet while Ilse stormily, now the father was gone, swept Ernst and Lotte off to bed, while Viktor and Gottfried slouched out like heavy shadows for whatever penniless Saturday night pleasures they could find, while Frieda bathed in the soap-scummed tub behind the stove (Father, who bathed on Sunday mornings while the family was at Mass, got fresh water, but she didn't) she again sensed difference.

Vaguely she was able to discern that, since this difference was not in her father nor in any other aspect of her family, it must lie in herself and in what had happened on the balcony.

"*Someday it might be yours.*" For the first time since their impact on her ears, those words emerged shakingly, so that her hands, for reality and support, pressed hard against the tub's soft, slithery bottom. Mr. Hake had said that, not of a small pile of money such as her father had had on the table, money which hitherto had been the wistful height of any hope, but of a thick rain of money.

Someday it might be she who stood in Mr. Hake's place, throwing money.

Dream-walking, once her bath was done, she got herself upstairs to the bed she shared with Lotte.

"*Someday it might be yours.*" That was what made the difference. Through all the fourteen years of her life—and it seemed to her then, looking back, as if those fourteen years were complete now, thrust aside—she had been mostly something on which other people acted: a passive, helpless, inert, smarting object to be pummeled, punished, bewildered, commanded or ignored, as others willed. Now, staring forward at a future dark but untrammeled as the night around her, she looked at the possibility that she might *own,* and so herself be an agent, acting on others and on life.

Mr. Hake, in addition to throwing the money, had also touched her, touched her in a way strange and disturbing. That too, somehow, was moving, but not to the extent the money was. What she felt about the money could not be put into words; there were no words to fit the wide yearning which possessed her. All she could know was that she felt stirred and wakened, that there was something she now strained toward, with her heart and lungs and viscera.

Someday she might have money. Mr. Hake had said so, speaking to her as a person.

CHAPTER II

She had long known she bore two stigmas: foreignness and poverty.

The Middle Western valley town in which she lived was one to which her family had moved when she was nine; they had no roots in it, little standing, few countrymen, no real friends. Of West Haven's four thousand inhabitants, half had come—or were descended from people who had come—from New England and New York, who had laid out wide tree-shaded streets, who had built porched and fretted white New England houses, who had founded Amiot College, and who called their town, nostalgically and blindly, "New England in the West." Of the rest, by far the greater portion was Norwegian, a com-pact close community which stood rigorously on its worth, and so was half accepted. The Norwegians had their rival college, St. Ansgar's, the fathers taught there or the children went there; together with the New Englanders they joined in scorning all "aliens"—the few German families, the Irish, Balik, the Hungarian photographer, and Pallini, the Italian in whose tonsorial parlor Otto Schlempke worked.

West Haven schools, as the *Independent* boasted, "opened their doors to rich and poor alike," but in them the children of these foreign families were alternately baited and ignored; teachers who, because the immigrants spoke a clumsy English, suspected their bodies of smelling and their minds of being turgid, seated them in rear corners and considered a righteous duty well done when they were allowed to listen while the fortunates were taught. At work they found open only such jobs as were socially unacceptable—house drudgery, rail laying, ditching, milling. Even before God they were separate—Catholic in a town which otherwise was solidly Protestant.

That the Schlempkes belonged to this outcast fringe they themselves did not question more inside the family than outside. All five children were American born, but both Otto and Ilse had emigrated from Bavaria; Otto, for all his quickness, could not manage a *th* sound; Ilse, under stress, lost her English entirely. And if the family's foreignness was thus fixed and immutable, so was its poverty. True, Otto Schlempke sometimes boasted he made twenty dollars a week in tips and wages—more than many a professor in the colleges—but this made no difference; it made no difference that Frieda and her brothers worked. Of Otto's income, almost the whole was spent on, or at least by, himself, squandered on drinks, gambling, cigars and those Benson House dinners to which he stormed out when he found the household fare uneatable. *He* was no peasant, as he frequently reminded himself and the rest of his family; his mother had been an officer's widow, the gayest and prettiest of Nuremburg; as a boy he had had everything he wanted; he had been raised (this was vague) to be banker, financier or diplomat; he had come to America to enter on a life of flowers, ease, wine, servants, rich clothes, admiration, perfume and the opera. It was only because of an incomprehensible and bewildering blindness among Americans, only because he had been dogged by bad luck, only because while still so young he had burdened himself with a wife and family, that he had been held from his birthright.

He might, as he did, grandiloquently order home the newest in ropework settees and rockers, and in ornate cupid-supported lamps; in the parlor these incongruous luxuries, together with the marble-top table, the Brussels carpet, the fringe-heavy scarlet curtains, sat tended and aloof, awaiting those few occasions when they were on display. But even these carried no weight against the humbling, shameful sparsity at every angle of their lives. Often there were no pennies for the collection plate at Mass, Lotte and Ernst filched paper and pencils from their mates at school, Viktor and Gottfried, at seventeen and sixteen, wore shirts and trousers rebuilt from Otto's. It was Ilse who held the family together, she who had induced Otto to learn barbering, she who maneuvered with limitless fierce patience until they had a cow and chickens, she who cleared weed-tangled wastes for gardens, she who sewed and preserved, she who bargained with the mill foreman for discolored flour, she who sold eggs, milk and vegetables to get the quarters and half dollars which bought staples and their meager clothing. Chickens could be eaten only when they got too old for laying; if they had other meat it was only because, perhaps once in a fortnight, Otto picked a butcher shop as the scene of his spending.

"Beef roast for my family—the best," he would say richly, hunching his shoulders to indicate his plight as the provider for so exigent a crew. "Nothing will do them but the best." At table afterward, reserving for himself the choicer portions of his purchase, he would continue to eulogize his provisioning, but even while his family ravenously ate, it kept the memory of all the evenings it had fared, and knew it yet would fare, on milk mush, on radishes with bread, or on a single egg for each.

This was the background with which Frieda was permeated; the background she knew as her own. And, looking about her at eight o'clock Mass, on the morning following the incident of the balcony, she had to feel—though this again was not in words—that here too, in what, except for her existence at the store, had been almost her only social contact, she was held within what was low, beggarly and alien.

The church structure enclosing her had been built for a scant twenty years, but already wall plaster was falling, revealing the rough laths and chinking; the ceiling above the rickety ash-gray stove was deeply grimed; the altar, though hung with an elaborate cloth, was unmistakably a pine kitchen table; the picture above it, of the Holy Family, was a rude lithograph in blues and reds; the benches were unvarnished and unpainted pine; the rough plank floor uncarpeted.

And of the congregation that jerkily creaked to stand, sit, kneel and genuflect within this edifice, most of the older generation, like her parents, wore the harsh stamp of Europe. Of the men, by far the greater number were farmers who had arrived in mud-caked lumber wagons and buckboards from a settlement near by, farmers who displayed the round bristled heads, thick necks, barrel chests and stumpy legs of peasants. Usually these men were thriftier than Frieda's father, most of them lived spartanly, working ten, twelve, fourteen hours a day, that in the future they might be rich, but there was something of Otto Schlempke in them nevertheless. No matter how humbly they might walk before the world, at home they were often overbearing and oppressive. Sentiment for a wife did not keep them from thinking of her as a servant; pride in a son did not prevent that son's being used as a source of labor and revenue through his minority.

This cult of the dominant male was one that had been brought from Europe, intact; it was one that in their lifetimes would never be broken. And if the men were like Frieda's father, then the women were even more like her mother: publicly silent, kerchiefed, wide-cheeked and cow-hipped, staring out with a blank passionate bleakness at a world in which they were given so little importance.

Between these parents and their children existed little but incongruity—and a lack of sympathy as deep as the oceans. The generation born on American soil might at home breathe the smog of Europe, might eat European cooking, might go almost as ill nourished as its parents had on those starved handkerchief plots that in Europe were called farms, might in addition bear through its impressionable youth the hated obloquy of being foreign. But still the newer generation was American, the young boys breathing and glancing like colts brought only resistantly and rebelliously to harness; the girls, even those as sullen and repressed as Frieda, carrying under their surfaces the gathering forces of ferment. Fathers were determined to press this young life into an old mold; mothers were frightened, before it came, by the inevitable separation; while the children spent themselves in loathing the parental language, the parental culture, the parental way of life—everything that seemed to make them inferior before their fellows.

When Father Doern, desisting from his Latin mumble, turned before the altar to deliver, in alternately shrieking and cajoling German, his usual sermon—a vivid portrayal of the postlife torments awaiting those who did not furnish the Church with one tenth of their gains —Frieda, who knew every facet of this group and her position in it with a dimmer but just as certain perception as that of sight, abruptly reached an overmastering necessity.

All her life she had kept away from those Other People of the town —the Americans, the people who Had Things, the people who made the judgments, the people who set the form. Now, however, she wanted to go where she could see, feel and know what made them different from herself.

She knew, too, exactly where she could go to do so. Between ten-fifteen and ten-thirty, on Sundays, the Best People of West Haven filtered themselves out from the Norwegians and the late-Mass Catholics, also church-bound at that hour, to move by carriage or on foot down Front Street toward the First Congregational Church. She would no more have thought of entering that chaste white-spired edifice than she would have thought of knocking at the gates of heaven, dressed as she was in her ignoble flesh. But across Front Street, under the low-hanging maples, anyone, even a foreigner, could linger and look on.

The thought of doing even so much was paralyzing, but there was a push in her muscles which almost violently propelled her toward it. So far in her life she had usually been alone in her activities: trudging alone to school, withdrawing suspiciously from any friendliness (Ilse taught her children to trust no one) offered by those of her own low caste, drudging by herself at the store. Now, however, she shrank from the thought of appearing under those maples unaccompanied. Yet with her on the short pine bench were only Lotte and Ernst, infants of five and seven, and not only would Ernst and Lotte be no support, but they might also reveal her new blind groping at home.

As uncertain in its quest as a bee, her glance skipped over the heads of girls she knew by name among the worshipers—Miss Klaumeister, the butcher's daughter, who, whatever she might have been christened, was known among her mates as Schatz, or Schatzi; Lise Hetweit; Maria Pallini; twelve-year-old Rozzie Balik. Approaching any one of them was an act of such hardihood that it alone, at any preceding time, would have been incredible. Yet when Father Doern at last rose from his prayers, coifing himself and striding from the altar as a signal that the service was over, she found herself moving with puppet-stiff jerks toward Rozzie Balik.

"I don't suppose you'd want to—go by the Congregational." The hoarse words cut torturously at her throat and burst from her lips, seeming, the moment they were said, to be outrageous and indecent. At once she would have recalled them if she could, but Rozzie's head with its two long red-brown braids had already jerked about, Rozzie's brown eyes had sparkled and her whole angular face leaped to responsiveness.

"You mean stop by there and see the people? I *luff* to go by there; I often go by there." In the hushed words was the exact assurance Frieda cried for—Of course you have a right to see those people, that assurance said, I understand in every way. But even while Frieda was sending Lotte and Ernst—dumfounded by the freedom—home alone, even while she was stepping woodenly with Rozzie from the church steps to the tree-lined walk where in the sun the gum was oozing from the boards, she knew another hot discomfort. Rozzie limped terribly, without repression or concealment, her head rising and falling in a bobbing abandon at the level of Frieda's shoulder, her misshapen body twisting, her shorter leg flirting its foot to the side. At school—Frieda had left the year before, but Rozzie still attended—boys ran past Rozzie, catching with suddenly outshot feet at her good ankle, bringing her crashing to the ground. From these falls Rozzie always rose laughing and good-natured, as if she thought the boys were friendly—Rozzie expected friendliness in everyone. Not that she found much of it. In school the Germans and Irish at least had a few compatriots, but of Hungarians there was only Rozzie. Just as, of Italians, there was only Maria. Maria, cast on Rozzie as an only resource, fitfully accepted and rejected Rozzie's amity.

"Maybe Maria could come too," Rozzie now hinted, but when Frieda silently clopped on she accepted the rejection without argument. "What I luff *most* about First Congregational is the clothes," Rozzie immediately said, slipping into an easy confidence. Rozzie, apparently, could describe every Empire-green ostrich plume, every brocaded polonaise, every embroidered cashmere in West Haven.

While they went up one street and down another (Mass had been over shortly after nine) Frieda had good time to regret what she had started. Mutely and unseeingly, thinking only of her purpose, she followed wherever Rozzie led, past wide white houses set well back behind lawns studded with star and crescent flower beds, with flowers in kettles swung from iron tripods—sign that that family no longer rendered its own lard or made its soap; past cheaper houses set up near the walk, their narrow porches lumbered with rockers, kitchen chairs and dirt-smeared children; down into the business section of the town, past livery stables smelling acridly of ammonia, manure and dusty hay, past the sour-sweet smell of the lumberyard.

West Haven had been settled for a quarter century; it had two banks, a city hall, a Y.M.C.A., a power company; it thrived and bustled, vying with larger cities to the north for the eminence of being a metropolis; it lay pleasantly upon the flood plain of a river, the Cannon; it was surrounded by an undulant rich farm country of clear fields, substantial farmsteads, hardwood patches. Upon a low hill to the south, beyond the river, stood Amiot College, with its six buildings, its thirty acres of grounds, its tended trees and flowers and paths; on another hill to the north were St. Ansgar's fifty-seven acres, its path-threaded woodland, its two tall brick buildings from which the Gothic windows looked over the treetops at the town like brow-arched eyes.

Of this town through which she now passed, however, Frieda knew only what impinged directly upon her: the street where she lived, the Hake Grocery and Dry Goods Emporium where she worked, the river where occasionally she had gone with Ernst and Lotte to wade in the cold, red, bubbling, iron-smelling water.

"You'd look nicer than Nettie Orcutt if you had Nettie's fawn merino; it has stays." Rozzie, as they progressed, continued to babble. Schatz Klaumeister and Lise Hetwiet, seeing them walk off together, had glanced meaningfully at each other and giggled; no one else had seemed to notice, but Frieda felt intolerably that she had demeaned herself. Yet she could not break away, either. The necessity to look on at those Other People had now become a fever in her blood.

"Calico is nice, but it goes *slimp*." With shy fingers Rozzie touched the sleeve of Frieda's green calico, put on that morning for the week. "Someday," she confided, "when I get to sew better, I will make you a dress really *beautiful*."

At the stare which met this, Rozzie flushed darkly, red rising slowly over her wide high cheekbones; when next she spoke it was almost fiercely.

"I don't care. Someday I will do good sewing. See, I make my own dress now. Maybe it is not good, but it makes me look better than I *am*."

The dress of which she spoke was a sheer wool in dark rose, which fitted her smoothly but not closely, the basque rounding at the waistline, the skirt draped in slight U-folds across the front and caught into a puff in back.

"Someday," she went on belligerently, when Frieda's silence continued, "I will be the best dressmaker in this *country*." But then, lightly, she exploded her temerity with laughter. "No, but I will make pretty dresses to wear on Sunday in West Haven, and maybe *you* will get the prettiest."

Be friends with me, the words coaxed, and maybe you need not be sorry.

Deaf to anyone else's purposes, Frieda would have said she did not hear. The two girls were again, for a third or fourth time, across from the narrow, neat New England meetinghouse, complete with white clapboards, porch and spire, which was the First Congregational. This time it was not untenanted: the two big carved oak doors had been thrown open, revealing a dim interior which even across the street smelled richly of decorum, varnish, carpet, paint and plush; about the steps a group of half-grown boys had gathered, indulging in those swipes at hats, those jerks at coattails, those subdued knee-kicks in the pants, which were appropriate to that time and place.

Heart thickly beating, unconscious fingers clamping convulsively on Rozzie's arm, Frieda moved forward until she stood half under a concealing maple, her whole body becoming a medium for absorption and reception. This was the time she had awaited, now.

Halfway down the block a family was approaching, first a father and grown son, each with derby, short cutaway buttoned just below the breastbone, tight striped trousers. Next came four girls in ruffled white, and last the mother with a younger son, the mother toqued and parasoled in pink lilac, rustling in a dove-gray satin polonaise drawn back to reveal its pink-lilac underskirt.

"That's the Leveretts," murmured Rozzie. "Louise has her summer white on. Mrs. Leverett's parasol is nice; it makes her face and dress all rosy." But again Frieda only vaguely heard. It was not—or was it?—for lessons in fashion she had come.

As the parental Leveretts filed into the church, the six children, caught by suddenly imperative conversation, stayed out on the boardwalk. New groups, meanwhile, like the Leveretts but different, came in view—fathers leading small boys with prominent pearl buttons on their prominent anteriors, mothers fussing about little girls in full white lawns or muslins, with bright cascading hair and small round hats held to the backs of the necks by vivid ribbons, or swung swaggeringly from the hand. A young couple came alone, the man with his bowler in hand, bent toward a pert girl who twirled a black lace parasol and laughed up at him. Quickly now the street was full, families driving up in fringe-top surreys from which the men descended gravely to tie horses to the hitching posts, and from which stout women in black silk, some still wearing bustles, with great fuss and flurry got themselves to earth. Bachelors and more young couples dashed up in single buggies, the girls uttering subdued shrieks and giggles as, in the approved manner—hand to the shoulder of the gentleman, gentleman's hand under their elbows—they were helped down, their dainty slippered feet groping helplessly within a foamy sea of petticoats to find the small elusive steps.

"Those are the Cantrells," Rozzie whispered. "That's Mr. and Mrs. Page and their little boy. That's Mrs. Simon and Mrs. Langesley. That's the Coburn family. Those are the Wattses." Some of these figures, dimly, Frieda recognized; the Widow Noble, for instance, was a regular customer of Hake's, and so were the Bacons. When Rozzie, nudging, whispered the name "Amiot," however, her lips opened and all other cognizance faded out. The Amiots were people of such high importance that she scarcely dared look.

On foot they advanced down Front Street—West Haven's first citizen and his daughter. Two terms in Congress had affixed an "Honorable" to Thomas Amiot's name; he owned the mill where

Viktor and Gottfried worked, he also owned the bank, the college honored by its name his generous donations. It was incredible to think that she, Frieda Schlempke, could thus stand to look on at his solid nearing bulk, his high silk hat, his tailed Prince Albert, his gold-tipped cane, his eyeglasses. And as for Cecilia——

Everything about Cecilia Amiot, as Frieda had to see at once, was perfect. Cecilia was dark-eyed and waxen, Cecilia had pale, fringed, ash-blond hair on which rode the tiniest of green-and-pink-plumed hats; Cecilia was dressed in silk of palest green, the basque revealing an incredible slenderness, the skirt a miracle of drapery, panniers and ruffles.

Like other people of his advanced age, Thomas Amiot ascended at once into church, pausing only for a few grave, dignified greetings to those who clustered about the door, perhaps for this privilege. But Cecilia, like the other young people, slipped aside to join one of those chattering and merry-glancing sidewalk groups which, just then, seemed to be suffering an apprehension and a waiting.

"I don't think they'll get here at all!" One feminine voice could be heard, pouting. "They've gone off somewhere, that's what they've done!" But this plaint was broken by a flutter almost of applause.

From the direction of Amiot College appeared a dozen bicyclers, first discernible in the distance as a moving blot of flaming color, later resolving itself into the gay bloods of the town, young men in striped blazers, boaters, forelocks, slender trousers, who wheeled with incredible verve and dash the fashionable contraptions—mostly high-wheelers, but there were a few even of the brand-new safeties—which they bestrode, sitting back with arms folded to let their machines steer themselves, coming to split-second stops and turns, weaving in and out in convoluted patterns, performing miracles of balance as they made their descents.

Forthrightly, in the sun of their self-confidence, these audacious spirits invaded the waiting groups, setting bonnets on the bounce, drawing the chosen up into the church. After them, in a swiftly disappearing ebb tide, went the others. The double doors closed, the porch was empty, the church, to all senses but one, was deserted. From the interior came the sound of voices in a hymn. It was ten-thirty.

On the walk opposite Frieda stood awhile without moving, stood so long Rozzie made an uncertain offer.

"We could stay to see them come out."

"No," Frieda answered without inflection. "I don't want to see them come out." She began to move, taking leave of Rozzie with no more than an abrupt "Good-by now." She had no more immediate need of Rozzie.

What seemed to remain in her mind most blindingly, as an apex and symbol of all she had just seen, was a mental picture of the stocky young man in an orange-and-blue-striped blazer who, skimmer in hand, had stopped to nod his head familiarly and easily at Cecilia Amiot before escorting her into the church. Once a week, at least, that same young man burst into Hake's to do what he called "knocking the old man for a rap." He was Palmer Hake, Junius B. Hake's only son. Mr. Hake didn't go to churches; Mr. Hake said so, with his tired indifferent insolence, even to ministers. But his son did. She had seen him. With Cecilia Amiot.

Her father, as she soon found, was home alone; Lotte and Ernst had chosen a lesser evil by trotting off with Ilse and the grown boys to second Mass. From a bitterly vituperative hangover, when she appeared, her father spat at her her latest sins: she had dared to send Lotte and Ernst home alone while she went off no one knew where, for no one knew what vicious purpose, but obviously to annoy him; she thought she was a clever Fräulein to defy her father and all decency, but she would find out.

As insensitive to his words, since he didn't actually ask where she had been, as to the slaps which punctuated them, Frieda waited until, infuriated by her passive lack of resistance, he at last screamed at her to go. Taking then the steep, curving, triangular-stepped stairway to her room, she dropped upon the patchwork-quilted bed.

She was, still, almost unconscious of herself, filled only by the people she had seen. Cecilia Amiot and Palmer Hake, as they walked up those church steps, had almost visibly exuded that golden haze of richness, self-confidence and impregnability, in which, for her, Those Others lived and had their being. They were the people who knew everything, enjoyed everything, owned everything, were at home in everything. They were the people who Had.

"Someday it might be yours." If she had money, as much money as Mr. Hake had thrown about the balcony, then she too—wouldn't she?—would be one of Those Others. Somehow, in getting money, she must be transformed out of her poverty, out of her foreignness, out of her inconsiderableness, out of this room, in which one small square window looked in at the low sloped ceiling, the rickety short scratched wooden bed, the washstand. She would be transported to an unimagined realm of friends, admiration, Things.

Or perhaps, perhaps——

Heart beating out against her ribs in swelling, thudding bumps, she glimpsed a possible other way.

Perhaps it was by getting to look like those Other People, by walking like them, talking like them, that you got the money. Perhaps it was becoming one of those Other People that *came first*. Somehow you got accepted by them, taken into them, and then you *got the money*.

Into her small, round, scallop-edge mirror she gazed dispassionately. Between herself and the flecked and wavy glass hovered an image of Cecilia Amiot, of Cecilia's fringe, her palely gleaming coils of hair, her pallid skin, her fairy's dress. Through Cecilia she looked upon her own thick, dark, kinked mop—hair which, in spite of Ilse's tired chidings, seldom got much more than a few impatient tugs from the comb. She looked, too, upon the crudity of her color, and then, far beyond the mirror's confines, upon the shapeless ugliness of her unfitted bodice, the shortness of her skirt, the clumsiness of her shoes, the entire sodden nothingness of her person.

Impossible, one part of her mind cried fiercely, while another as fiercely answered, Sometime it might be yours. For a moment she saw another vision of herself—her hair changed not so much in color as in smoothness and luster, her color lessened, her figure tightened and lifted. That vision left, but after it was gone some difference seemed to remain—perhaps a steadiness of regard.

Vaguely she recalled a time when her mother had still brushed and dressed her, and when her father had occasionally called her *"Mein Herzchen mit Lochigem Haar."* After its infrequent washings, her hair still rippled.

Quietly stealing down to her mother's bedroom, as quietly returning, she stood again before the mirror, this time with scissors in her hand.

CHAPTER III

By the time she got to work on Monday, what her skin enclosed was a bubbling ferment.

Foremost had to be an agony which had crept on her overnight—fear that the money Mr. Hake had so rakishly sown about the balcony might be gone, and she be blamed. Mixed with this was an indecisive quaver—how would Mr. Hake now treat her? Would there again be that breath-taking closeness, that *strike* she had felt in him there on the balcony? Imperceptive as she was, ignorantly unknowing of herself and men, she yet had to feel the balcony encounter as incomplete, a seed of action rather than an act itself. And then, finally, there was her new hairdress, which this morning she was for the first time exposing to a larger audience than that of her family.

It was a hairdress which, when she had come down for dinner on Sunday noon, had immediately thrown her father into a slit-eyed alertness. Once started, she had done much more than cut a fringe. Bending until her hair flowed to the floor, she had whacked with a brush until all snarls were gone. And when she had then gone to work with the comb, she had been able to smooth out deep springy crinkles which, trying and retrying, she had rolled high at the sides of her head and coiled low in back. The fringe, cut at the level of her eyebrows, had for a long time refused to be anything but a brush. Only after she had remembered how her mother curled Lotte's hair over her finger had she gotten anything she liked: a close mass of small round circlets.

What she had then seen in the mirror had almost stopped her breath. So brushed, her hair had its own color and sheen—the color and sheen of deeply stained and highly polished walnut. The black-brown mass at her forehead (maybe she had been lucky, after all, in inheriting her father's tight curls!) had seemed, to her, to make her eyes recessed and dreamy; the upsweep from her cheekbones made her whole face look cleaner, burnished and adult. In a quick bloom of elation and success she had seen herself perhaps not Cecilia Amiot, but quite as good-looking as some of the other First Congregational girls. Only when her glance had fallen once more to her dress and shoes had that bloom faded and her shoulders sagged. Against her over-all cheapness and shapelessness, what use was any improvement? It had been in a dull renewed acceptance of her irretrievable impossibility that she had turned aside, not even pausing to undo the new hairdress before going downstairs.

"SSSo!" After a first quivering perception, her father at once had pounced. "Our Fräulein cuts now a fringe—like a lady our Fräulein combs the hair. A man our Fräulein thinks she will get herself, maybe? A man she thinks she finds, to leave the mama and papa, eh?" Then lightninglike, "SSSo! A man she walks with from the Mass! A man she sneaks with, sending Ernst and Lotte to be run over! A man——"

Even her mother, this time, had joined in the uproar, one which enforced finally a partial confession—it had been only Rozzie Balik with whom she had walked after Mass.

"Rozzie said why didn't I cut a fringe like other girls." Somewhere, ready, had been the lie. And no more than half believing, insensitive but suspecting something more, her father had fallen into derision—that was the only friend she could find, was it, a Hungarian, a cripple, whose father was a give-away fool. The scalding intensity of these comments had not moved Frieda; by them she had known her success. It was because of this success that she had repeated her brushing and combing this morning. And, once again, she found tribute.

"Well! Look what combed itself this morning!" One comment, from Miss Gibney to Miss Shatto, might be the sole expressed reaction, but it was enough. Both Miss Gibney and Miss Shatto, immediately afterward, found it necessary to repair to the customers' mirror on the dry-goods side, to pat and pull at their own coiffures.

If other preoccupations had not been so heavy, this matter of her hair might indeed have taken up all of her mind, but as things were it had to be pushed partially aside. While she stood by the sugar barrel, scooping its contents into two-pound sacks, Mr. Hake came in, and if she had thought there would be a noticeable difference in his manner toward her, then she had to suffer a deflation. Mr. Hake, as he walked past her, wore the same apparent inability to see her that he had always had. And then, as soon as he was past, that other eclipsing agitation woke: suppose, when he got to the balcony, suppose when he opened the safe—— The outrage of his "Miss Schlempke! Get up here!" was so audible that she dropped the sugar scoop and turned to obey. Not until ague-shaken old Mr. Ives, her superior on the grocery side, had looked at her over his eyeglasses with a re-proving "We can't have the sugar scoop on the floor, Miss Schlempke," did she realize Mr. Hake had not actually called, and that what she was hearing was only imagined. While she still bent for her dropped utensil, Mr. Hake was back beside her again, pockets bulging and coin sack under arm.

"Bank, Mr. Ives," he acknowledged, nodding.

The relaxing of her muscles was so thorough she had to hold the sugar barrel to keep herself erect. The money was all right then. He had it.

But as he went on out the door a different straining awoke. That wealth with which he walked out had been so allied with herself that when the door fell closed she could feel tendrils breaking. That money he carried was different from other money; he had said it might someday be hers. Even if she got it, there might never again be money of the same quality and power.

If she had had any tendency to think, in her groping, that she herself might somehow *make* the money Mr. Hake had said she might have, that thought submerged quickly. From her father she had heard—with her father it was inevitable she should hear—of people who by miraculous means had "made their pile" and "gotten on Easy Street." Never, in these tales, was there any suggestion of labor or effort on the part of the fortunate. Only luck.

Work, to her, had to be associated with her mother's desperate, hard, cheerless drudgery, toil which, since it did not return money, she saw as unproductive; work was associated with the sweeping, dusting, weighing and unpacking—all heavy, unskilled tasks—which she did at the store; work was associated with the heavy lifting and emptying of grain sacks done by her brothers at the mill. Work was associated with pittances, not with money. Only the poor worked. As was only too well known, the poor had no money. Therefore work did not make money—her own wages could never have fed and clothed her if she were on her own. To her fourteen-year-old mind, this logic was incontrovertible.

Increasingly, instead, she fastened her thoughts to that other way she had glimpsed—that by becoming one of those Other People, the money which was the concomitant of that state must also come. Cruelly now she saw all the differences between herself and Those Others, but beyond the first costless change in her hair she could not seem to get. Of other things she wanted she thought only in vaguest terms: rich clothes, a body radically changed, a metamorphosed manner, friends, surroundings. That there might be anything beyond even this she did not in any way guess; to her the surface was everything.

That materials for a further change lay almost under her hands she also for some time did not see. Merchandise at Hake's, during her service there, had gotten to be simply stuff on which, like grain at the mill, she worked. Only the cheapest calicoes, the coarsest stockings, the heaviest shoes, had had any conceivable relation to herself. Since she had not been hired to wait on trade she had mainly kept herself, during store hours, to that back room where eggs had to be unpacked and individually shaken, where butter tubs must be plumbed, and incoming freight unboxed. Now, however, with curiosity awakened, she began making forays, lurking in nearby aisles to scrutinize customers at first hand. Hake's, she came gradually to know, was patronized by almost all of West Haven. Workingmen and their wives—poorer Americans, Norwegians, even foreigners—came for overalls, cotton gloves and visored caps, calico and challis. But to

Hake's, also, came many of Those Others—proud stout housewives who bought henriettas, foulards, laces; chattering young ladies in striped washing silks and flowered lawns, who came in to buy braided jackets, cordovan boots, parasols and undermuslins, and who cast at each other meaningful cryptic phrases—"Oh, Sophie, aren't you *fly!*" or "We all know what *Edna's* thinking!"

Yet it was as the result of an accident, rather than of any slowly seen accumulation, that she came to realize the store's function. Early one August morning, while dusting, she came upon Miss Shatto behind the garment racks with a surreptitious customer.

"That's why I got here at *dawn,*" the customer was whispering, with heavy stresses. "*No* corsets and *no* petticoats. I thought if I kept my cloak on no one could possibly see. They say that in Meridian they have a *fitting room* for corsets, and I said to myself, 'Now this time I'm going to get corsets that *fit.*' It makes all the difference in the world, I always say, if just your corsets *fit.*"

Frieda stared. The lady was the Widow Noble. At least the face was Mrs. Noble's. As for the rest——

Against Mrs. Noble's figure as she had seen it at other times, the upper portion trim, slim, roundly bosomed, the nether section elegantly draped and full, she now placed a loose slack body, a flat chest, a rounded and protruding stomach, a skirt entirely deflated.

When a shoebox fell from Frieda's hands, the faces of Mrs. Noble and Miss Shatto shattered like thin ice.

"Oh, it's just Frieda," Miss Shatto almost at once gasped, turning. Fittings were given for dresses, in West Haven, in the decent privacy of your own or the dressmaker's bedroom, but no one knew better than Miss Shatto what would be said if it got out that she had fitted Mrs. Noble with a corset at Hake's, *right out in public!*

"Tell her to go away! Go away!" repeated Mrs. Noble, her face too collecting, but still horrified.

Miss Shatto had no need to say anything; Frieda had already backed away.

For quite a while, in the seclusion of the back room, she stood to stare at the sorghum keg.

Mrs. Noble, without her corsets, had been no more than a bumpy beanpole. Mrs. Noble, without her corsets, had had no wasp waist, that long tubular mid-section, coming to a sharp forward point, which more than anything else set one off as being a lady. Mrs. Noble might have been any woman. A foreigner. Might have been Frieda.

Mouth slack, body forgotten, she sat on a butter cask while pieces of something slowly laid themselves out on the plateaus of her mind.

So that was what Hake's was. Hake's was where other people got the things that made them Other People. Silks. Organdies. Gloves and mantles. Parasols. Opera-toe boots. Corsets. She had unpacked these, put them on their shelves and counters. They were right here, close to her.

Her two hands, compressed palm to palm between her knees, ached from her knees' pressure.

Hungers from then on could be sharp and centered. Slipping aside the top of a shoebox she was returning to its shelf, she stroked the soft leather inside, fingered a needlepoint toe. If I could have these, she thought. Rearranging bolts of fabric, she laid her palms secretly along the richer satins, the more elaborately embroidered muslins. This would be the kind of dress. Saturday nights after she was alone in the store (except always for Mr. Hake, as indifferent as always on his balcony with his money) she swept with furtive nervous haste, using the saved time to try before the mirror anything she dared—a Zouave jacket, gloves, a sash. Every week, tensely alert for any sound that might mean Mr. Hake arising from his desk chair, pressed by the necessity to hurry before her father waited and got angry, she tried over her dress at least one of the shoulder-strapped and steel-boned corsets, pulling the strings excruciatingly tight, twisting and turning to see the transformation of her figure. At each new stricture of whalebone and muslin the blood of her compressed body pushed burstingly outward, her breath came in gasps, but that was nothing. What mattered was that, corseted, she had the right outline, her bosom was thrust upward into a round containing case, her mid-section constricted, her hips made elegantly full.

As days passed her desire to be corseted became a fever, an obsession; she thought of nothing else, her hands trembled when she touched the garments, at night she lay awake remembering how she had looked in them. If she could appear before the world so transfigured, she thought, then surely They must see she was worthy, and so take her in to be one of Them—the climax of transfiguration remained vague, but the Hake wares were immediate. Corsets cost $1.89, $2.47, even more—sums to make one despair, but at least finite. If only her father would give her as much money as he sometimes gave Viktor and Gottfried——

On Saturday evenings as the family drank its chicory around the blue- or red-checked table, as her father's temper mellowed toward the pleasant moment when she and her brothers would pay in their earnings, her lips formed words—this way, now that.

"Please, Father, I need——"

"Father, I'm too old now for children's clothes; I need——"

Yet when the moment came her lips would open, but the words would plummet, dropping to some inner reservoir of fear and weakness. Too well she knew what would result.

Against such small sums as her mother had she equally despaired of levying; such sums never stretched to anything that could be considered unnecessary. Between herself and her mother, too, rose barriers on Ilse's side of seclusion and reproach, on Frieda's of impatience and scorn. Yet it was against her mother she made a first attack.

"I got to get me some money."

It was a September evening when she made her try, an evening when Ernst and Lotte were already in bed, her father and the boys out, her mother mending stockings by the yellow light of the kitchen lamp. At the demand, which snapped a long silence during which Frieda had stared moodily at her fists clenched on the table before her, Ilse's needle kept on with its weaving, while her face closed warily in, at bay.

"Everyt'ing I get goes for the food, the clothes. Lotte needs shoes, already Ernst I patch on top of patches——"

"Papa could give it." The words came from a reservoir of storm.

"From Papa you know how hard it is to get."

"I got to get some."

At the writhing insistence, Ilse's needle did slow, her round faded eyes and rounder body stiffening.

"Why? For why you need money?"

At suspicion and probing, the barriers slapped shut, swept higher; she could not tell her mother of the needs that flailed at her, the purpose she had glimpsed. To do so would have been to rip away her clothes, her flesh, to expose the bloody throbbing of her heart.

In her father's footsteps, ever since she was old enough to see a selfish course and grasp it, she had considered her mother as a creature made first for her father's service, secondly for as much service as any other member of the family could wring from her. That her mother was open to pity and understanding she willfully could not see; it was not closeness she wanted from her mother, who, with her untidy flying hair, her bleak blue eyes, her bitter complaints, her thick peasant's body, her thick awkward speech, her helpless labors, represented all those things from which Frieda most wanted to escape. She had never been able to feel quite the same harshness toward her mother that she had toward her father, but that did not mean she was often touched by softness toward her, either.

Turning her head aside, she muttered darkly, "Clothes. I got to get me some clothes."

Sighing as her needle recommenced its glinting passage, Ilse relaxed to a usual troubled anxiety.

"Clothes," she too muttered. "Ach, for a young girl, clothes." Behind the words was the glimmer of her own youth, of days in a Bavarian village which now held a distance-dimmed and golden brightness. Painfully she again sighed. "Clothes—for rich people, fine clothes. For us, we are lucky we do not go naked."

This, as Frieda beat her fists against the table in impotent and inarticulate revolt, was what remained.

Yet, instead of discouraging her, the very act of voicing her desire quickened and emboldened her, made her more doggedly determined. On the next Sunday she again drew Rozzie Balik aside after Mass, to clump silently beside the cripple through the chill mist of an autumnal day, to pause again across from the temple of the elect while the Best People gathered.

But this Sunday her watching grew intolerable. When down the gray-blue street appeared a stout augustness which might be Thomas Amiot, with a graceful violet-blue blur beside it which might be Cecilia, Frieda turned abruptly to walk off in the opposite direction.

"Oh, let 'em go."

Since the time of her awakening she had not seen Cecilia Amiot at Hake's; Mrs. Amiot and Cecilia, like a few other West Haven notables, went to Meridian, the state capital, for much of their shopping. If Cecilia's eyes should fall on her, she felt now, all her humiliating secrets would be bared; Cecilia would know at once that it was her coiffure Frieda copied; the mere thought was stifling. Only when Rozzie caught panting at her arm did her flight slow. She had forgotten her present purpose with Rozzie.

"You walk so—fast!" gasped Rozzie. "I can't go so—fast, I—limp!" As if reminder could be necessary.

"You get money!" It was accusation. "What makes your father give it?"

"Don't you get money?" Rozzie's return held no more than a startled wonder; still panting she tried to draw abreast, where she could peer into Frieda's face.

"No."

After a temporary dumfoundment over the solitary syllable, Rozzie brightened.

"But you don't *need* money; you work. I wish I could work. The minute I can, I'm going to start saving up for a sewing machine——"

"Start saving up!" Frieda stopped short. "How could you save up if you didn't have any?"

They faced each other now as people from two different camps, Rozzie's head with its long brown braids held forward as if in an attempt to peer through deep bewilderment.

"But I *would* have some if I made it. That's why I——" She paused, to gulp. "So often, you know, Papa just gives things away. If people like their pictures, then——"

"But *he'd* have your money." Deaf to cross meanings, Frieda felt only impatience at Rozzie's obtuseness.

"You mean my father would?" Still puzzled, Rozzie gave Frieda another quick look, then grew subdued. "Oh yes, I guess he would, if he needed it. Of course he would. There isn't anybody," she added in quick confidence, "that I luff like my *father*."

On a deep breath, Frieda tried to swallow what welled inside her. What was this talk of love and sewing machines?

"There's got to be something you *do* right now," she returned to her first effort, "to make your father buy you things. *What is it?*"

"Something I do?" Again Rozzie was at sea, her eyes traveling back over an unknown relationship. Whatever she found there was warm and satisfying; her eyes kindled and her voice took on softness. "But of course I don't have to do anything. My papa says, 'Today I make money on pictures—today I take mine Rozzie downtown to buy wool, buy silk, buy finest stuff in the country for mine Rozzie.'" While she mimicked her back straightened, her tones filled, she seemed to grow taller, stalwart. Then, with a light, humble giggle, she deflated.

"If he doesn't say that, then I know he doesn't have any," she added simply. "And of course I don't ask him."

Whatever Rozzie's face held was more intolerable even than what her mother had given her; with an abrupt, wild surge of anger and negation, she pushed away answer and answerer, both. Without looking back to see if Rozzie stood or fell, she rushed away.

Added to her mother's counsel that she was lucky to be covered, she now had for her pains this sore unhealing knowledge: that in some families—how many she didn't know, but certainly in Rozzie's —things were different.

So violently that Lotte whimpered in her sleep, she threw herself about her bed at night, hating Rozzie's father, a strapping, mobile, sweepingly mustached dark man, a widower whom she had seen only at Mass. Hating Otto Schlempke. Nothing would put *her* father in a mood where he would say, "Today I get mine pocket full of tips, today I take mine Frieda out, we buy a dress."

When that next week she went to confession for the monthly communion which Father Doern imposed as a routine, these hatreds bubbled. Kneeling at the curtained slit, whispering her habitual answers to the rapid impersonal mumble, she heard not so much the priest's inexpectant "You have honored your father and mother?" as much as she again heard Rozzie: "There isn't anybody I luff like my father."

With a fresh geysering of the emotions which filled her bosom, she choked out an honest answer.

"Why should I? That's what I'd like to know. If there's anybody I *hate,* it's my father."

Never since she made her first communion had she answered anything but the stifled obsequious negations, completely unrelated to her life and feelings, which had been the joint fruit of her instruction and her own sullenness; formlessly she expected now that some explosion must occur, some violence to meet her violence; she wanted violence.

Instead Father Doern mumbled in his usual swift and unmoved whisper, "That is very wrong, my child; children must obey and love their parents; I will give penances."

She said the penances, kneeling at the altar platform until her knees were sore and aching. But even while she lipped the words her inner mutiny continued.

CHAPTER IV

Her mother, Rozzie and the priest—from these resources she had been given nothing but a resignation she could not accept, a way of life she could not understand and hence repudiated with loathing, and—from Father Doern—indifferent reproof. Willfully and stubbornly, however, she persisted.

More boldly, as no catastrophe occurred, she now moved in the store, daring to fill orders for the poorer children, who always had to hang about lonesomely until other customers were satisfied, daring to walk as freely as the "high and mighty counter jumpers" while she did her shelf filling, daring to talk back, when she was reprimanded or ordered to some task she did not like, not only to the two men, Mr. Ives

and George Bibbensack, but also to the two ladies, Miss Gibney and
Miss Shatto.

Again no skies fell; Mr. Ives laughed; George Bibbensack favored
her with one or two of those pinches he usually reserved for Miss
Gibney; Miss Shatto and Miss Gibney told her she had become impossible, told her they would complain to Mr. Hake. Before the
incident of the balcony this would quickly have quelled her; now
she hoped they would complain to Mr. Hake; tumultuously she
wanted to break the detachment in which her employer had continued ever since that one break. This unshaped rebellion was given
even sharper impetus when, one October afternoon, Cecilia Amiot
and her mother came into the store.

The hour was five o'clock—a time when early-supping West Haven
mostly kept itself at home. Only Miss Gibney tended store; Frieda
was on the balcony unpacking woolen lumberjacks left from the year
before. Coming down the stairway with a heavy, odorous burden—
the lumberjacks had been sown thickly with mothballs—she blundered
in the aisle against what she thought, since she had not heard the
opening door, must be Miss Gibney.

"Why don't you look out?" she asked tartly, from behind her heap
of clothing. "You can see—I can't."

When in reply two gasps reached her, as well as Miss Gibney's
"Really, Frieda!" she shifted her load to one side. What met her was
Cecilia Amiot's aloof blank stare.

In untouched and untouchable fragility, clasped in a velveteen
cloak of pale lilac, another plumed and feathered carriage hat low
on her fringe, Cecilia stood with brows sweetly lifted, awaiting a
subservient penitence and withdrawal. Cecilia was so shortsighted as
to be, toward any distant object, almost blind, and Frieda was something she did not bother to distinguish beyond a blurred impression
of unfamiliarity, dishevelment and burden. But to Frieda it seemed
that the opaque distant eyes knew instantly, as she had foreseen, the
groveling confession of her hair, the indecency of her untrammeled
body, the hideousness of her dress and shoes. At this moment more
than ever—hair disordered by its contacts with rough garments, face
flushed, hands and store apron grimy—she knew herself an object
to be held in scorn. Yet she was frozen; she could not escape.

Miss Gibney's sharp, repeated "Frieda! At least excuse yourself
and go!" at last broke her immobility. Interposing the jackets as a
screen, she backed away.

With her went one of the careless phrases with which Cecilia
habitually hid her dimmed vision.

"Really!" Cecilia Amiot said. "What an apparition!"

For the woman in the sealskin sacque Frieda had no notice until, above Miss Gibney's flustered apologies, another voice came clearly.

"But what handsome hair the child has—what handsome dark hair! Cecilia, didn't you notice?"

"Oh, Mother." Cecilia's indifferent patience said the incident was closed. "Some foreigner."

"Foreigners are *people*," Mrs. Amiot chided gently, but without lowering her voice.

Once more in the hideaway of the back room, biting down hard on her lip, Frieda dumped the jackets. "An apparition, really." "Foreigners are people." She had never before heard the word "apparition," but she sensed its meaning, sensed the unbridgeable distances which Cecilia and Mrs. Amiot felt existed between themselves and her. "But what handsome hair"—that leaping cross fire threw itself against the burn of the other.

Released by recent ventures into speech, her storm could, to some extent at least, canalize itself in words.

"They'll see," she promised. "They can just wait and see."

Means of making them see, however, remained through that winter distant and unreachable.

Again and again, as the Saturdays passed, she tried forcing herself to beg money from her father; again and again, when the time came, she drew back in despair from an exposure she well knew as useless. To uphold her she had only her hair and her secret life within the store, in which more and more the trying on of garments came to be torture. Wearing things only in her own sight got her nowhere; if she were to advance in the world she must have ownership; the purpose of *things* was to display her.

At Christmas she had one small brief hope; her gift from her father was a fifty-cent piece. This coin, which she saw expanding into all she wanted, she tied in a handkerchief and carried on her person; at any time of day or night it was a joy to feel its shape and know she had it; fiercely she repudiated any suggestions for its spending. In mid-February, however, she was forced to yield it; Ilse, knowing she had it, refused to squeeze money from their food for new stockings.

After this forced parting, she came into a period of black calm, in which it did not seem worth while even to brush her hair. Rising late, she often threw herself together as hastily as she had a year ago, turning sullen ears to a reproachful "You don't look yourself this morning, Frieda," from Miss Shatto, or a "Maybe our Fräulein finds out she is not so smart, eh?" from her father.

So far she had not thought of any of her fellow employees as possible allies, or even as sources of advice. Of her two superiors on the dry-goods side, Miss Shatto was a prim woman devoted to family glory; Flora Gibney a slow-moving cloudy girl of nineteen, who could arrest herself in almost any motion to stay poised, apparently in a trance, for hours. Young, and in sultriness of mood not unlike Frieda, Miss Gibney might have seemed the natural confidante, but it was Miss Shatto who, one day, stepped part way into that position.

"You know, Frieda, I hesitate to mention this——" Replete with three hundred years of family epic, Miss Shatto on that day was generously moved to lift her head from the price-ticketing of a case of ladies' spring union suits, for a look at her assistant. "Really, you should *do* something for yourself. A girl your age, you know——" Delicately, with a cough, she dropped her voice. "How old are you, Frieda?"

"Fifteen next week."

"I thought so. H'm. It's really time you should wear—well, some *support,* you know, Frieda. And *long skirts.* One can't help but notice —you're beginning to fill *out."*

The Shatto history had long shuttered Frieda's ears; closed within her usual miseries, she had, during the afternoon's work, been an automaton at Miss Shatto's bidding. Now, however, as she drew herself out of the packing case, she heard the flat, neat voice as an assault, saw the flat, neat face across the box as rimmed by fire.

"Do something?" she repeated fiercely. "Don't you think I want to do something? Don't you think I want to look decent? How can I when I get no money?"

"No money?" Since Miss Shatto was seated at the marking table she couldn't actually retreat, but at such unexpected vehemence she patently drew back. "I thought—why surely, you must get something——"

"What good does that do me, when he just takes it?"

"Why really, I——" Miss Shatto must have expected some response to her approach, but obviously it wasn't this. Curiosity, however, overcame affront.

"Who just takes it?"

On her side of the gulf, Frieda struggled to throw out a rope of understanding.

"He does. He. My father. And he won't give any back!"

"Your father—well. You poor child. I've heard, of course——" Miss

Shatto, at this point, seemed able only to twitter. "Some men—head of the family—I'm sure I never thought——"

"Every week, all of it!" Once started, Frieda could not hold herself from crying out more of her formless mutiny. "First Viktor, then Gottfried, then me. If Mama asks——"

"Oh yes, yes indeed! Your own mother would surely——"

"If Mama asks, she gets nothing."

"Well, all I can say—really." Having reached a mental wall, against which she flattened like an espaliered pear tree, Miss Shatto gazed out at reality. "Such a handsome man, too. I've noticed him, often, on the street. He must do *something* with the——"

Then, in one quick subsidence, Miss Shatto quit floundering and reached comprehension:

"Oh, you poor child. He drinks."

To Frieda, who had always taken it for granted that her father drank, Miss Shatto's flurry over this conclusion meant less than nothing.

"That's it. Depend on it, he drinks. A man who doesn't even see his family clothed. A man like that isn't—well, isn't responsible. You'll just have to stop giving him your wages, Frieda, for his sake as much as yours."

Only one fact marred this well-meant advice.

"But he'd hit me!"

"Your brothers must then come to your aid."

"They don't dare! He gets their money too!"

"He can't. A thing like that can't go on." Shaken again, but holding tight, Miss Shatto hewed to the line she had taken. "You'll have to stand up for yourself, Frieda; a thing like that isn't even American."

For Frieda, all this meant at the moment was more despair. But afterward she found much food for thought. Miss Shatto had talked as if *fathers had no right to their children's wages at all.* So cataclysmic was this change of view that it took several days for her to become in any way oriented to it.

"All you need is *courage,* Frieda," Miss Shatto urged as Saturday approached. "Stand up to him! Stand on your rights!"

Fevered by this and by her own hungers, Frieda again built up her whole life toward a crucial conflict, imaging a scene in which she would say boldly, "No! It's my money and I keep it," imagining a response in which her father would throw up his hands to cry, "I can do notting!" Even in a dream, however, the pattern refused to take shape; even in imagination she saw her father's leap, felt his blows. And when the moment actually came, when again her father pushed back his cup and turned expectantly to Viktor, she cowered guiltily, fearing that just by looking at her he would guess her presumption.

In the end, it was again an incident which touched off the accumulation.

With both Amiot College and St. Ansgar's in its environs, it was inevitable that West Haven streets should sometimes effervesce. One of these hurly-burlies was an annual Shindy Day, when the burgeoning young gentlemen of Amiot College, dressed as scarecrows in castoff stovepipe hats, tattered tail coats and jacked-up pantaloons, gathered themselves in force, garnished themselves with pennants and streamers of Amiot yellow and violet, advanced across West Haven in a body, charged St. Ansgar's hill, and cast bricks, stones, insults and catcalls at the St. Ansgar dormitory until its expectant male inmates issued forth for a skirmish.

Heroes of the day were those who went down with concussions, broken arms and cracked ribs; fists, feet and brass knuckles flourished; any man above the grade of poltroon emerged almost naked, bloody of nose, black of eye, bruised thoroughly from head to foot. Fighting continued until one side or the other retreated to a year-long ignominy; triumphantly the victors gathered together such apparel as remained, and bore off their wounded to the mothers who waited trembling behind lace curtains for this home-coming. All those who could walk descended on the town for a night of roistering.

It was an occasion when, at the first hint of assembly on the Amiot campus, every girl or young woman of good family shut herself within doors, or—if she daringly ventured forth to see the fun—did so well guarded by at least three brothers or two elderly female relatives. Frieda, however, was as remote from all town and college stirrings as if she lived upon another continent, and when she left the store at five-thirty one Saturday in April for her early supper, she thought only that the streets seemed quieter than usual. Sun lay warm on her back after a day of false, too early spring, old blackened snow crusts had melted into frothy pools and puddles, the boardwalks seeped damp, the air about her was soft but needled with the promise of returning chill. After her hurried meal she started back through what ostensibly was the same sunny quiet, but when she passed the corner saloon, a block below Hake's, its swinging doors split open to emit a surge of college boys.

To a triumphant excitation which had needed no heightening, they had added a round of drinks, and the moment they saw Frieda they whooped and charged.

It was a day when she had not bothered to put up her hair. The coat she wore over her short dress was—as all coats in the Schlempke family were—a black, stiff, shapeless garment made over from a discard of her father's. Bareheaded, bulky, known to them only as "one of those foreigners," she was, to these boys, fair game; they felt no more kinship for her than if she had been one of the unowned dogs they had tormented ten years earlier. Instantly she became the pushball of a howling, milling and demoniac mob.

"Look what I got." "Here, you take her." "God, ain't she awful?" "Hello, elephant." "Naw, she ain't no elephant, she's a rhi-NAW-ceros!"

The last cry, yelled by more stentorian lungs, was taken up, became a chant.

"Rhi-naw-ceros! Rhinawceros! Rhinawceros!"

Impelled by thrusts from this side and that, she was propelled forward. In an instant of clarity before blind panic struck, she recognized a boy against whose solid body she was thrown, and who, as he cast her back to other hands, was the first to cry "rhinoceros." Covered scantily by trousers of which one leg was ripped off just below the thigh, and a coat which retained one sleeve, its collar and its dangling fronts, his face reddened, puffed and frenzied, he was a distortion of her employer's son and Cecilia Amiot's beau.

Abandoned by strength so that she would repeatedly have fallen if they had not held her upright, breathing in great choking gasps, she was rushed onward until, after what to her seemed hours, she was dumped on a doorstep, while her tormentors streamed off to take over, from a confounded farmer, his team of horses and his wagon.

Actually the period of her nightmare had been no more than three or four minutes; from it she rose as if she had been ill for months. Back of her was still the impulse to get back to the store; trying and failing, she at last managed to get to her feet; clinging to buildings, she started to drag herself onward, casting terrified glances at the riotous crowd as it once more came past her, whipping up the farmer's plunging horses, derisively singing, when it saw her, "Bring back, bring back, oh, bring back my rhino to me, to me——"

Only by instinct did she move in the right direction. When at last she reached a store front she recognized as Hake's she clung to it for minutes before she could believe she had reached its haven. Once inside, she fell against Miss Shatto. With the exception of her employer, the entire personnel of Hake's had witnessed her discomfiture but had not gone forth to her rescue. Of the four, only Miss Shatto now was horrified; to Flora Gibney it was "what that bold girl has coming to her." Mr. Ives and George Bibbensack, with the detachment of onlookers at a dogfight, said cheerfully that they had known Frieda could look out for herself.

Even Miss Shatto, while she supported Frieda to the back room, where she fanned, rubbed and supplied drinks of water, had more personal vindication to confer than sympathy.

"Now you see, Frieda, if you'd followed my advice, if you'd *done* something for yourself, this wouldn't have happened. Those boys would never have dared to act in that way toward a girl they could see was a lady."

Out of her raw agony, that too was what Frieda drew. This torture into which she had been thrust, this Gethsemane, this flaying humiliation, had come about because she was so obviously poor, outcast, alien. It was because she was uncouthly dressed, uncorseted.

Otto Schlempke, over his coffee that night, was in a blooming mood. Frieda had not kept him waiting at the store, his day at barbering had been good, customers had spoken to him as an equal, but remembered to give tips. No one less than Thomas Amiot had stepped to his chair for a special haircut, the Senator—a center parting from forehead to nape, the hair brushed sideward toward each ear. Mr. Amiot had been regally satisfied. Pallini's had reverberated with tales of Shindy escapades—those young scapegoats had stolen a farmer's team and wagon, driven all over town, carted an outhouse from Widow Heenan's lot to the town dump, tied the reins and sent the horses home alone, leaving the farmer stranded in West Haven. They'd hustled some girl, too, he negligently added. Girls had no sense, not staying home at such a time.

From this he passed by natural routes to tales of his own school pranks in Nuremberg; it was in a state of great self-pleasure that he pushed his cup away and flicked the cake crumbs from his small, meticulously clipped mustache.

"Now comes the big time of the week for Viktor, Gottfried and Frieda, yes?" he kindly asked, rubbing the palms of plump, small, well-kept hands, gazing beneficently about the table. "Today they show Papa and Mama how smart they are to make the money, yes?"

To Frieda the moment brought no heightening. She had, in the intervening hours, managed to draw herself somewhat together; the only physical remnant of what she had experienced was a slight convulsive tremor which she could not lessen or control; rhythmically it moved downward, beginning with a quiver of her head, a spasm of her neck, a shaking of her body; even her feet, inside her shoes, partook of the agitation. When her father spoke of the girl who had been hustled this shivering increased; she felt as if she crouched, cold and alone, behind a dike which shut her from a darkly rushing river. But when she heard he apparently did not know who the girl was, this palpitation eased. The river sped by on its near course while first Viktor, then· Gottfried, turned in money. Then her father waited pleasantly for her.

Her wages were clenched in one hand. Stumbling to her feet, she pulled herself to her father's place. Inside her trembling existed that life-surrendered quiet in which a man moves up against guns. She put her fist down on the table, closed.

"I got to keep some money." The small voice was a trickle from deep within herself. "I got to keep some for a while, until I—until I get me some clothes."

Otto's face remained indulgent.

"You need clothes," he graciously acceded, with what was more a bow than a nod. "To Mama you go for clothes. Mama is——"

"Mama has no money. I need money."

"Now, Frieda." Out of his good mood he chose reason, patience, coaxing. "Papa is the one to say where money shall be spent, no? Papa gives to Mama, Mama buys for Frieda——"

"She doesn't get me what I've got to get." The stronger passage of her voice was now like water spurting. "This dress—it isn't like other people's dresses—my coat, it's black and terrible—everything I wear is terrible—my shoes, my underwear—*I haven't any corsets!*"

To her own ears incredible, the words came, words she never had meant to say.

"Of such things you speak to *Papa?*" The features of the face before her seemed to fly apart, the lower lip of the small pink mouth flapping violently as the voice grew thinner and higher. "What girl is this I have here, with no shame? Before Viktor and Gottfried, before Ernst——"

"I don't care. I've got to get those clothes. I've got to, got to, don't you understand?" She too beat with her closed fist on the table, her voice too rose; at the sound she felt a sudden breaking, as if the river had swept through its dikes, rapidly sweeping away all defenses, sweeping her with them down its dark and rushing course.

"It was *me* those boys pushed around—*me, me!* Because I haven't any clothes, because I look foreign, because I look poor! Because I haven't any corsets, because I have to wear your old black coat! I've got to have money!"

"So! Now it comes how you tell Papa! Disgrace you bring to this house—shame you bring to Papa!" With a smashing blow of his fist as he rose, he flattened her clenched hand on the table, snatching the money out from under it. "Every night I go by the store when it is late—I wait—I do not let my daughter in the dark alone. For this she throws herself among the college boys—the sports—she makes of me the laughingstock. This I deserve, this I am repaid. 'A fine family,' I say to other men, 'three boys and two girls. For them I would do anything, the best.' And this she does to me!"

She had thrown her arms crosswise before her face; between them and around them, on her head, fell blows heavier than any she had taken before. Still in her extremity calling out her need, she was forced to give ground until she reached the stove.

She did not hear her mother's "No, Otto! She will be killed!" or see her clawing to tear her father from her. When finally she reached the angle where Ernst and Lotte already crouched, her father had flung her mother off to rush back and forth across the kitchen like a tomcat in fits, his face purpled, his eyes starting, in a rage so black that as she looked her own storm grew smaller in the squeeze of awe and terror.

From his moistened lips continued to fall frothily the broken syllables of anger and humiliation; he was now disgraced forever, he could look no man in the eye, call no man friend, he had become the laughingstock of West Haven. He had a daughter who had so comported herself as to fall into the hands of mobs of men. And on top of that she had the temerity to ask him for money.

The forepart of this occupied him during the height of the paroxysm; the last came when, out of exhaustion, he began to slow. In the accents of a broken man he cast himself then upon Viktor and Gottfried, who had stood silently and expressionlessly watching with their backs against the door. Shaking each by the hand, clasping each by the shoulder, he gave each an unprecedented three dollars.

"You, my son, from you I know such disgrace cannot come."

With a last sorrowing and reproaching look toward the stove, still with broken step and bearing, he took up his hat with sad dignity and plowed into the night.

CHAPTER V

It was what she had expected. It was final. From now on, as long as memory lasted—which would be as long as he had any occasion to bring the subject to mind—she knew she could expect nothing from her father.

Dragging herself in a catharsis of spent emotion and accepted failure up to bed, jerking away from her mother's sorrowing and despairing "Ach, Frieda, Frieda," she yet had to suffer another ordeal. After Lotte was asleep her mother stole into the bedroom to sit hunched and awkward on the bed, to stroke her hair in aching hands, and then ask exactly what the boys had done.

From Frieda's sullen, evasive answers Ilse once more drew relief, but instead of leaving she stayed on in an enveloping embarrassment which extended over Frieda like the sticky falling of warm fog.

"Some things you should know." The words came in a blurting whisper. "You get to be a big girl now—it is not safe you should be off with boys alone—they might do something. Like Papa says, always a girl has to take care."

As if she herself found this confidence intolerable, Ilse at once rose to slip away, leaving Frieda to fight off the spongy tentacles of this new incubus as well as what she had before.

Sex was something she knew by short and ugly gutter words; friendless as she had been, there had been boys and girls to supply them. But as yet she had made no connection between such things and herself. For a moment after her mother had gone she struggled weakly in the grasp of something half seen and half known, before it too drowned in the dead sea to which her stream had carried her.

After this there could be nothing more. "It might be yours." Writhing on her bed, she suffered the death throes of her hope and her ambition. As if it had happened in another life she now saw Mr. Hake standing by his desk, the money in his hands, again she saw the money falling, again heard his words. But it had been a false light; she had tried, and for her there was no opening toward the glimpsed fulfillment. She could do nothing but fall back to what she had been— blank, dull, hopeless, sodden. She could do nothing but so benumb her senses that she would no longer see herself as she was, or hear the taunts that would be thrown at her, or feel the jostlings of no one knew how many more Shindy Days. She had been beaten down to nothing but a bloody ooze upon the bed.

But it was out of this surrender her way opened. Opened down an avenue she had not glimpsed—through Mr. Hake.

There was no question of giving up her job. On Sunday she stayed in bed; on Monday when again she did not rise her father came upstairs with a strap and belted her until she did. Each morning after that she crept to work, submerging herself in the back room, performing a minimum of work, sitting for hours in what amounted to a coma. To Miss Shatto's questions and George Bibbensack's rallying she was impervious, her whole attention centered on remaining at as low an ebb of consciousness as possible.

On those occasions when her duties brought her near her employer she was no longer aware of him; she no longer allowed herself to look at what he counted. She had accepted that after one aberrant contact he had cut himself away from her; he had been making fun of her; he hadn't meant it. If she had been capable of any further emotion and humiliation, she might have burned at the way she had responded and been taken in.

On the last Saturday of April, two weeks after her utter demolition, and almost a year after the incident which had fired her useless efforts, she once again climbed to the balcony for its lethargic weekly sweeping. When her employer almost at once spoke she was so unprepared, so deeply sunken in her comatose remoteness that even after she had started, turned, it took awhile before her ears could relay to her mind the sense of what he said, or her eyes see on his brown thin face the shape of laughter.

"What's the matter?" he asked easily, as if he had been in the habit of speaking thus closely to her any day. "No more trying my corsets? I'd gotten so I liked the show."

She could do nothing but gape at him.

"You put your hair up another way, too, for a while. It was quite handsome."

Blood rushed to her face with the flood of knowledge. Those nights when she had tried on clothes, preening and posturing before the mirror, he must have stolen to the balcony railing to stand leering down, this same soundless laughter in his eyes and on his mouth. She had thought she could not suffer further, but now she crouched back, feeling each word draw across her like a razor.

He balanced on the two rear legs of his chair, steadying himself by a hand against the desk edge.

"Miss Shatto tells me," he went on as evenly as if she were making unconcerned, untouched responses, "that your father takes your wages. Money isn't for girls to handle, eh? Well, it's my guess he doesn't know you. Come here and sit down."

He pointed toward the armchair at the desk's end, the drummers' chair. When she remained stock-still, unable, indeed, to move if she had wished it, he rose, impelling her by a light, almost caressive pressure, his arm along her back, his hand squeezing her shoulder, until she sat in the chair, the broom still clutched convulsively in rigid fingers, caught eyes on his face.

"There, we'll be comfortable." Lightly he returned to his own chair. "It seems to me that between us——"

"I didn't hurt them." Her voice came momentarily unstoppered. "Not any of those things. I put them right back. I——"

He waved away her panic. "Try 'em all you want to—I don't care. Loosens 'em up for the women who buy 'em. Now. Miss Shatto tells me you'd like to get yourself fixed up a little. That right?"

Again her voice was suffocated, pushed down by the weight of all she had tried and failed in.

He nodded. "That's all right. I don't see why you shouldn't do it. You were doing well in the store here, for a while. Waiting on children, getting around more, showing an interest."

He paused, expectant. She had nothing to reply.

"How'd you like it if I got in someone else to do heavy work—we're in a busy season—and put you to waiting on trade? Say in groceries? I've got a reason for wanting George Bibbensack out of groceries awhile."

Again she could say nothing; she had opened enough now, could feel enough, to know he was hedging, working around something.

The intentness of his face increased. "I'd pay you more, of course. You're pretty young yet—fifteen; you'd make mistakes, likely, where they'd hit me—in the cashbox. Say two dollars and a half a week. That's a dollar raise."

At the low horizon of her vision the bosom of her dress fluttered from the thudding of her heart.

He went on, "I suppose if you brought home a dollar raise your father would just be very pleased. Well, I think we could fix that too."

Leaning across the angle of the desk between them until his face was close, he let his words fall softly, separately.

"You see, *mein liebes Fräulein*—that's the right term, isn't it?— when you try for anything, it's well to use what we'll call scheming, stratagem, finesse. You tried, didn't you? You threw yourself at what you wanted—asked for it, straight out. You tried to get what you wanted at the expense of someone else, and naturally that someone else —your father, in this case—fought back. That's a very poor system— seldom gets anyone anywhere. There's a word you'll learn. *Manipulate*. Me, for instance. I was here. Why didn't you try manipulating me? Suppose you fixed things this way. Suppose you kept on taking home your dollar-fifty every week, but got your raise in trade."

Significantly his voice slowed and lowered. "One dollar, every week, in trade."

The turbulent flood wall that had hit her at her final failure came back, this time to thrust her upward, lifting her, tossing her upon its dashing crests; galvanically her body jerked, her hands clasped and unclasped on the broom, her dry lips opened to emit some sound; all that would come was a hoarse rasp.

At the sound he threw back his head to laugh aloud. Again tilting his chair, clasping his hands together behind his neck so that the face with the mocking gleam inside it was pushed forward, steadying himself this time by a knee, he spoke again.

"Tell me what you'll do with it," he said.

She was yet incapable of thinking, but now words could tumble.

"I'd—I'd wait until I had enough to buy a corset." Said here, the word carried no wrappings of indecency. "Then I'd—I don't know. Shoes. A dress, I'd need. A coat——" Her hands moved rapidly up and down the broom handle, which felt light and small inside her fingers, like a pencil.

He laughed. "You needn't look at me like that. I'm no god, in or out of a machine. All right. Now get up and sweep this balcony as if you weren't already nailed into a coffin."

That abruptly it was over. Waveringly she stood up.

"You mean it's going to be true?" she asked. "You mean I——"

"I damn well mean." He let his chair return to solidity, spreading his hands over the money, the beautiful money, which she could now again allow herself to see in piles upon the desk. But yet he waited.

"Anything else?"

"No, I—no. I—you said a dollar?"

As soon as she had said no, his shoulders lifted in a shrug. At once shut off from her, intent, he began counting, stacking, tying notes into packets; for minutes longer, stupefied, she stood staring at him as he worked. Within her, with terrible, resuscitated life, throbbed the ambition whose death she had suffered. Now when she had given up, now when everything had been lost, to have hope given back to her was almost more than she could bear.

Still in a stupor, but remembering his last words, she leaped in agitated and erratic labor, returning to swish at sections she had swept before, banging against the garment racks, knocking down piles of boxes, her hands so unsteady that again and again she spilled the accumulations she gathered into the big dustpan. When, still in this state of bemused, uplifted excitation, she started tremulously for the stairs, he stopped her.

"You still haven't anything to ask?"

"It's—it's—if it's going to be true? I——"

"Fiddlesticks. You'll have to do better. How're you going to explain the stuff you'll drag home to your father?"

The dustpan shivered, clattered on the top step, tumbled in a trail of dust and litter down the stairs.

"See? Didn't think, did you?" He now looked coolly, almost contemptuously, across at her. Once more she could not answer; she was too filled by the certainty he had evoked. Her father feigned disinterest in what his family had or wore—that was woman's province—but actually he would know the moment she added one item to her wardrobe—know she was holding out on him.

"Wouldn't work, would it?" her employer asked, still coolly. "I doubt if he'd take your explanation. Now, if you asked *me* to tell him——"

Her lips formed the plea she could not sound.

Abruptly he once more laughed aloud.

"Gad, you're articulate, aren't you? Go on, get yourself out of here."

Breathlessly, through the days that followed, she waited for signs of her father's knowing.

At work, everything went through as Mr. Hake had said it would go.

"Take Frieda with you in groceries, and put George in gents' furnishings and shoes." This, from Mr. Hake to Mr. Ives on Monday morning, had been all that was needed to affix her to a counter. Eddie Noble was hired to sweep, dust and unpack—something in itself astounding, since Eddie, she had thought, was of the Other People, and she now became almost his superior.

After two years she knew weights and prices; children fell naturally to her lot, as did foreigners and farmers; Mr. Ives hustled to wait on town women of any position and style, but if there was a rush even such customers might glance askance at her awkwardness as she cut cheese or ladled butter, might shrug and sigh when she counted change two or three times over, but no open complaints were made. Once more Mr. Hake treated her with nothing but aloofness, but this time she was not fooled; his amusement lay always at her back. In a fervor of painstaking care, each morning, she scrubbed and brushed, curling her fringe over her fingers, trying her side and back hair in new ways. For her elevation Miss Shatto had a congratulatory whisper: "I knew it! I knew he would, after I spoke to him!" Miss Gibney wondered what the world was coming to, and Mr. Ives and George Bibbensack agreed Frieda could do anything she put her mind to.

Yet all this, as she so exigently felt, meant nothing, if she could not retain money for her use. At home, during the past fortnight, her father had held mulishly to his disgrace; actually it was not known in West Haven that she had been the girl molested, but he had not allowed this to alter punishment. In the current week, on the other hand, he was beginning to be revisited by amiability; two Saturdays on which his children had unhesitatingly turned over good money had gone by; it might not be a bad idea, his manner hinted, for Viktor and Gottfried, reaching an age when boys sometimes got restive, to see how unmistakably he was boss.

Visibly, amidst this returning good humor, he was annoyed and mystified by Frieda's revigoration. Subdue herself at home as she tried to, she could no longer creep about with head bent and eyes blankly lowered; insurgent bursts of energy threatened sometimes to burst from her; she alternated between trembling moments when she felt an actual soreness in her body, of senses in too high a state of bliss, and other moments when what Mr. Hake had contrived seemed incredible.

Not until almost a week had passed did what she had awaited come. Her father, on that night, stamped home at half past seven to greet her with a slap.

"Some people think they are smart, eh? Some people think they go to fool the papa, eh? Papa will fix. Mama"—this last was accompanied by a forward-flung arm—"from us our Frieda gets no more the clothes, for her you never again sew the dress or buy the stockings. All these years Papa buys like he is made from money—dresses, coats, hats, finest shoes, perfume—but for Papa she cares nothing."

The family flew to its usual cover, Ilse asked weakly what the girl had done now, her father kept raging, but Frieda knew an unholy joy. Let him hit her, let him belt her, she was well covered and protected. Open to her eyes was the difference between this and his previous rages. In spite of his fire he was baffled, because he could do nothing against Mr. Hake. When on the next night she demurely laid before him her dollar and a half, he fell into new tantrums, but this time the impotence was still more marked; he didn't even strike at her.

Transport could fill her, and vindictive triumph. She had not often laughed, in her lifetime, but thinking of the scene there must have been at Pallini's, she laughed aloud. Transport, however, had to be worn off by impatience. Not only must her corset be secured ($2.49, it cost, two and a half weeks of waiting!) but also a dress. In choosing her understructure—the most waspishly indented of Hake's stock— she could with flaming certainty go directly counter to Miss Shatto, who thought that for a girl of fifteen a Ferris waist would be the thing. In picking the material for a dress, however, she had to find Miss Shatto's advice more worth considering.

"It's hard to do better than a good twelve-cent gingham," Miss Shatto insisted, her forehead rippling like a washboard in the serious- ness of her concentrations. "Especially when you'll be cutting for the first time from a pattern. After all, you don't want to risk *too* much."

It was this last which made Frieda listen; she wanted to risk nothing. Every penny of her money was as precious as hope; silk, even poplin, meant weeks of waiting; in the end she settled on the brown- and-rose plaid gingham, with a crossing green strand, which Miss Shatto, growing wiser, casually but often brought before her eyes.

Even this, in an irreducible twelve-yard length, meant $1.44, a week and a half. In addition she must have a pattern at thirty cents, and at least twenty yards of cambric for a corset cover and two petti- coats. In agonies of indecision, her mind changing every day, she hovered over Hake's stock of Buttericks, all her longings on those creations which were most elaborately tucked, ruffled, chiffon-guimped and overskirted. But Miss Shatto's hints—"You'll find these plainer dresses make up better," and "Only a first-class dressmaker can turn out a good overskirt"—again made her compromise; she chose a style in which the basque waist came to three points, one below the other, in which the skirt had only the slightest of draping across the front, and in which the sleeve tops rose in the very newest points.

Now she also needed velvet ribbon for trimming; she had to have thread and buttons; time seemed to extend forever. Yet at last, in June, unable to wait for the cambric, she bore home the makings of her dress as surreptitiously as she had previously borne home her corset.

She herself had never learned to sew, but in spite of her father's dic- tum she did not question that she could get her mother to make the dress. For a few more days, however, she temporized, glutting herself with the thought, the sight, the touch, the draping against herself, of the corsets, fabric, ribbons, buttons and pattern in her bureau. Not until impatience outburst love for secrecy did she carry the materials downstairs, preparing herself defensively against those antagonisms and irritations which her mother was so sure to rouse.

"Where you get this goods?" As she had expected, her mother's first question was one of suspicion. The bleak blue eyes, fastening on the

gingham Frieda rolled out over the kitchen table, seemed almost to
recoil.

"I didn't steal it, if that's what you mean." Bluster was what was
needed, and bluster she produced. "Mr. Hake gave it to me, that's
where I got it. You could hardly expect him to think I look good
enough for his store the way I *am*."

"But such fine goods, Frieda." Painfully Ilse looked between daughter and fabric. "Such goods does not come for nothing——"

"I got it instead of a raise, that's what." This too was ready, and if
more was needed, then more was at hand. "*You* got that old sewing
machine from a lady you worked for," she added, pointing to the
decrepit castoff from which Ilse had risen. "Why is it so funny I
should get things?"

Uncertain still, but tempted, Ilse was moved to floundering acceptance and consent. Indeed, as Frieda saw but shut away, Ilse's yearning
over the fabric soon equaled her own. Again and again the pattern
was examined piece by piece, again and again the ribbon caressed,
again and again Ilse's dark work-rasped fingers trembled along the
smooth lengths.

Naturally all work would have to be done when Otto was out of
the house; that was tacit between them. At every home-coming of the
next week, however, Frieda found progress. One day the dress was
cut, the next its long seams were basted, the next showed a basque
ready for hand sewing. On a Tuesday, when Frieda came home to
guess, by her mother's lip-pursed nod, that the dress finally was
finished, she thought she could not live while her father ate his late
supper and sat endlessly retailing the day's doings at Pallini's. After
the kitchen was clear, and her mother at last brought out the pressed
and completed garment, the pressure of emotion was so great that,
against all precedent, she found herself rendering harsh thanks.

"It's—it looks all right." What she felt toward her mother, in that
moment, was an outpouring of gratitude. Ilse had produced a dress
exactly like the one pictured on the pattern envelope. The brown
velvet lay exquisitely on the plaid, the skirt draped in beautiful U folds
across its front, the sleeve tops rose piquantly from the shoulders. But
then stronger and more familiar urgencies swept up; snatching the
dress from Ilse's hands, she ran with it to her room, pausing only to
make sure that Lotte slept before taking out her hidden corset. Hands
shaking, body trembling as convulsively as on Shindy Day, she
ripped off her old dress and struggled pantingly into the undergar-
ment. More slowly then, trying to get herself calm—this, after all, was
an experience to savor—she turned herself before her little mirror,

caressing with her hands the firm rounding of her breasts, the incurve at her waist, the belling over her hips. No matter how many times she had thus secretly shaped herself, it still had to be a fierce satisfaction.

So far she had not managed the necessary back-ruffled petticoat, but no matter; another petticoat could be doubled and added behind. Cautiously, holding her new dress over her head and sliding herself up into it, she got the garment down, hooked and buttoned before she again allowed herself to look.

In the mirror, then, she saw her lit, expectant face; in the mirror she saw light dim, saw her head jerk backward as if her father had walked into the room to strike her violently. Numb from an intangible but real blow, she climbed on a chair, first crouching and then standing tall, to stare at catastrophe.

Beyond shoulder seams which drooped limply an inch or two down each arm, the sleeve points of her new dress stuck out ridiculously, one tipping forward, one backward; the basque protruded pigeonlike at the breast and hung limply at the waist, the skirt——

Slowly, as she pivoted sidewise, she saw the full calamity of the skirt, draped bulkily across her abdomen, pulled in beneath. She looked as if she were in what women whispered of as "the family way."

Attacked by vertigo and weakness, so that she had to cling to the chair to keep from falling, she got down. What she had just seen couldn't have happened to her. It couldn't. None of her mother's sewing had ever been anything but shapeless, but that, she had thought, had been because her mother never had had a *pattern;* with a pattern, she had thought—that was what other people used, wasn't it?—the finished product must be what it was supposed to be. What else was there she could have done? It was as if in trying to get what she wanted she was working against some outside power, some power of the Other People. She was ill; she couldn't, after all else that had happened, take defeat such as this, not when she had been so sure of immediate translation and success, not when she had believed so fully that things at last were coming her way.

But it wasn't she herself who had failed; it was her mother who had created this ruin—her mother, toward whom she had just been feeling so much unaccustomed warmth and softness. Under the backlash of a revulsion so heavy that she crouched beneath it, she ran downstairs to the woman who anxiously washed dishes as she waited.

"Look at me. This is what you did for me. Look at me." Inside the caricature of a dress she could not be still; she flailed about the table. "Look at me. You were really trying, I thought, but this is what you've done to me. On purpose, too, on purpose because you don't want I should look nice——"

It wasn't true, and she knew it. As the words lashed out she was, queerly and deep inside herself, wrung by some feeling of pity and guilt. But other emotions pushed more strongly; greater than pity was the need to strike out at the stricken face before her, the need to see pain bite deep, the need to plunge her tongue in bitterest vitriol to cleanse this defeat from herself and place it on other shoulders. Against her mother's broken and protesting sobs she produced only angrier vituperation, until, in quieter exhausted and desponding rage, she pulled the dress over her head, walked to the stove and lifted a stove lid.

No plea of Ilse's—"Frieda! No! It can be fixed! Someway it can be fixed!"—did anything to stay her hand from dropping the dress upon the rose-black charcoaled shapes of wood; what stopped her was something else.

Into the icy coldness that had succeeded the red blast of her rage, came—like the dripping of water—Junius Hake's careless voice. This time it was not saying, "Someday it might be yours," but "There's a word you'll learn. *Manipulate.*"

And with this came something from farther back and deeper down, something she would have said she had not heard.

CHAPTER VI

"Oh, Frieda, you do look funny," Rozzie had to giggle, before hastily sobering. "There's nothing *truly* wrong with the dress, though; it's beautiful cloth." Her hands, too, caressed the gingham. Then, head tipped, she stood back to consider. "I guess the only thing you could do," she admitted, "is rip the whole thing and start over."

Since the day Frieda had pushed at Rozzie and walked away, she had bothered over no resumption of friendship. Ten minutes after she had climbed to the photographer's shop above the hardware store, however, Rozzie had again been won.

"You're the only one could do it, Rozzie; I've got no one else." To be thus publicly in despair, to be a figure of fun, to be a suppliant, could only add to her injuries, but it was an addition which must be well concealed. Night after night, during the sessions which ensued— sessions in which Rozzie endlessly pinned, draped and arranged—she bit back on her hurts. Child's dressmaking such as this was something she had to endure because the person who should have helped her, her mother, was little more than a traitor (a reluctant, sullen "I guess you didn't really mean to spoil it" had bridged things over at home, but the sores still ran, underneath), because she had no money for a real dressmaker, because a whole world was against her.

After a long fortnight of labor, when Rozzie finally sat back on her heels with a sigh of completion—"There! I guess that's the best I can do, Frieda"—the most that could come forth in return was acceptance.

"At least it's better than it was."

Actually, as she saw with a shock of pleasure, the dress was almost everything she had previously hoped it would be. Rozzie's mirror was little larger than her own, so she could not be too sure, but certainly now the collar lay smoothly and roundly, the basque clung where it should, the sleeve tops were perfect. Perhaps the skirt still did not hang right on one side—Rozzie despaired over this—but even if the dress was a little askew, it no longer blasphemed what was in it; her bosom could now be seen as proudly rising, her shoulders stood back straight and narrow, the deeply pointed basque displayed her narrow waist, her legs were decently hidden. Let Other People see her as she now appeared——

One more hurdle, and only one, stood before her, and she need not wait long for that jump. Forthrightly, next morning, while the men of the house were still at breakfast, she walked downstairs caparisoned in her new person.

Knives clattered when she stepped into the kitchen; eyes and mouths grew fixed.

"Now it comes out." After the initial silence, the careful instant in which she stood poised, waiting, near the doorway, her father stood up from his place to walk toward her.

"Now it comes. In fine cloth and velvet our Fräulein is dressed." His voice became silkier. "Mama makes for you the dress, no?"

In all of her lifetime, impudence toward her father had been unthinkable, but now as she faced him the corset seemed to hold her in supporting arms.

"Mama makes for me the dress," she mimicked, and then in her own voice, defiant, "No! Rozzie Balik makes for me the dress."

Perceptibly he swayed backward. Obviously he had been about to strike, but now had lost the spot on which his blow was to fall.

Stepping nervously toward them from the stove, Ilse ventured timid explanation.

"Mr. Hake wants she should look nice in the store; Mr. Hake makes her a present——"

"Oh, a present! A present!" Obviously, again, Otto struggled, in his eyes a bafflement so complete that Frieda shrewdly saw his dilemma: he did not want Viktor and Gottfried to know of the Hake arrangement; it might give them ideas.

Upheld by this guess and his helplessness, she swished to her place at table, turning a bland face to the cannonade which ensued—it was nice for some people they got presents, nice for some people to make friends with Hungarians and cripples, nice for some people to be finer than their families. Having half expected he might rip her new clothes from her back, such a weak riposte could be but uplifting. And the draught to come was even headier. Purposely late to work, she knew the fruition of seeing her five fellow employees temporarily speechless.

"Miss Schlempke, you're *beautiful!*"—this, from a gasping Eddie Noble, was only the first of the golden shower that burst, from Miss Shatto's "Really, I can be *proud!*" to Miss Gibney's "Well, I must say I wouldn't have known you." Stepping demurely past this audience, she reached the customers' mirror, where, for a first time, she could see herself full length. There, pivoting easily, hands clasped at her waist, she looked long. This, from now on, would be what she would be, to the world. True, the skirt did hike up, but anyone could see only the dress was at fault. Beneath it she had the figure of a lady.

When Mr. Hake came in he passed her with no more than a twinkle. That afternoon, however, when she made an occasion to go to the balcony while he was at his desk alone, he stood up to put his arm around her, lifting one hand as he had once before, only more slowly, past the rounding of her bosom to her chin.

"Not bad," he said. "You'll get there. It's just lucky for you that clay feet don't show." Her chin took a second bump. "Now get the hell away from me, downstairs."

By late summer she almost had a wardrobe. Opera-toe boots of cordovan leather, which cost four dollars, but which, after what Mr. Hake had said, she couldn't wait to buy. Petticoats, plain in front but with a waterfall of seven starched ruffles from hip to hem in back. A black chip hat—Hake's didn't carry hats—given her by Miss Shatto. A stockinette jacket marked down from $5.97 to $2.97 because, high on one side seam (she could keep her arm down), raveling had started. A second dress of navy percale with a small rose and green sprig. Of this second dress she had been obliged to tell Rozzie, "It ought to be all right." Actually, as she well knew, the gown was almost flaw-less in its making; even the skirt was draped beautifully.

"By this pattern," modestly Rozzie disclaimed credit, "I would dare to make even a silk dress." Rozzie, by then, was spending half her daytime hours in the Schlempke kitchen, sewing for herself when she wasn't engaged on Frieda's clothes. Tacitly it was understood that use of the Schlempke sewing machine repaid her richly for anything she did.

Time, now, was for Frieda almost entirely a matter of next week, of next month, when she could have credit enough for twelve yards of cashmere, or perhaps a mantle. Toward her social ascent she equally was ebullient; now that she had made all these improvements in her-self, what was the matter with those Other People, that they weren't noticing? Such recognition as she did get was soon something to be tossed aside; it was not for Miss Shatto's gratification or Eddie Noble's awed admiration that she had aimed, nor for her employer's lurking titillation, either. What she did want remained formless; sometimes she dreamed now of walking into the store as a customer, sometimes of moving elegantly up the steps of First Congregational, sometimes of living, apart from her family, in one of the larger houses; she hadn't yet seen how she might attain any of these goals.

For a while she tried vying with Mr. Ives in serving the elite, but success here too she held cheaply. The women who came to greet her so pleasantly—"Oh, Miss Schlempke, would you recommend my old baking powder, or that new double-action?"—did so without abating their concentrated little frowns, their absorption in their own concerns. Even if she had been dressed in laces and brocades, she sometimes thought angrily, they still would have lifted their brows, insisting she remain a servitress.

West Haven, in that season, lay summer-dormant. June had scat-tered the college flocks like seeds, Cecilia Amiot had gone to Europe with her mother, Junius Hake had sent his son East to visit, other residents hibernated in a hiatus of heat. But even in this West Haven, she thought, there must somewhere be a step upward she could take.

And, as she asked, so she was given. Though what she got, again, was not what she had expected.

Ordinarily she still sold only groceries. But one July afternoon, in the absence of Miss Shatto, who was on vacation, and of Flora Gibney, who—a frequent occurrence—was in the back room with George Bibbensack, she approached two girls who came in on the dry-goods side.

"Yes, thank you, some blue lingerie ribbon." In accents of great gentility one of the girls had already made her wants known before business was thrust aside for surprise.

"Why, you're *Frieda Schlempke!*"

The speaker, Frieda saw then, was Schatz Klaumeister, the kitten-soft, kitten-pretty German belle whom she had so often and so enviously looked upon in church. In the mid-afternoon dusk of the store, darkened against sun and flies, she hadn't noticed.

"Yes," she answered distantly and stiffly—Schatz had been no friend of hers. "I work here."

The day after this brief encounter, Schatzi was back in Hake's.

"You know, you look so *different,* Frieda! That pink sprig, the way it *fits!* I've been going to late Mass, so I guess I haven't seen you for quite a while." Schatz at this second meeting had a hint to impart. "What time do you get out of here, nights?"

Frieda's "Seven o'clock, except Wednesdays and Saturdays, when it's ten" was again aloof; overtures such as this were so new she did not recognize them for what they were.

On the next Sunday, however, Schatz again sought her out.

"I got up early this morning," wheedled the butcher's pink daughter, "just so I'd catch you. Honestly, that dress and that jacket and your hair—you've got so much *style!* Why don't you come by us for dinner? There'll be chicken and noodles, and we could take a walk——"

Shrinking because of older slights, shrinking too, now it came to the point, from even such an unknown as the Klaumeister household, Frieda yet had few weapons against such persistence. Even then her answer might have been a short no if she had not glanced behind Schatzi to see Rozzie hopefully hovering.

"I could," she ungraciously acceded, "only I'd have to go home and ask Papa."

"I'll ask him. I guess he'd say yes to me." Schatzi had few doubts of her abilities with Otto. Nor, in this, was she wrong.

"Mr. Schlempke, you'll think I'm just awful, coming in this way on a Sunday morning——" The Schlempke kitchen was, indeed, in negligee, with the tub from which its master had just risen still scummed behind the stove, the wet towels still strewn on the floor. Otto, however, had had time to dress, and before a voice that coaxed and a small hand that playfully pressed his arm, before the wide worshipful stare of blue eyes under a flaxen fringe, he could afford to be paternal and benevolent.

"You want Frieda—our little Frieda—should come by you for the visit?" The answer was foregone.

In bed that evening, reviewing the day's experiences, Frieda could tell herself stirringly that never, even in her life as it was now, could she have expected such a day.

The handling of Otto Schlempke had not been the only instance Schatzi had shown of her ability to do what she called "twisting a man around my little finger." On entering the Klaumeister home, beckoning Frieda after her, Schatzi had tiptoed soundlessly into a dining room whose wallpaper, table cover, draperies and ball-fringed portieres had all been of one dark and engulfing bloody redness. On a button-tufted leather sofa, in that room, no one less than Karl Klaumeister, himself, had been stretched full length, hands clasped over abdomen, head covered by a newspaper, from under which emerged small snorts and explosions.

With a gleeful and irreverent giggle, Schatzi had nudged Frieda and pointed. "That's Papa. Isn't he awful? You'd just think he'd strangle." Becoming instantly demure, she had bounced forward to throw herself upon the couch beside her parent.

"Boo! Papa! Company!"

In deep food-drunken sleep her parent had started, legs threshing as if he did not at first know which end of him should rise, before his shoulders lifted, the sheets of paper falling away to frame a red, blowing, mustachioed but otherwise hairless head.

"Was ist's?" The hoarse roar had issued from puffed purple lips while the small eyes sought to focus. There was, about Mr. Klaumeister, something not too unreminiscent of one of his own hogs, well scalded. *"Du Lieber Gott, was——"*

"This is my papa." Sweetly ignoring the imminence of apoplexy, his daughter had spoken in tones of fondest beaming pride. "You know Frieda Schlempke, don't you, Papa?"

"Frieda, Frieda." Still shaking his head to clear it, Karl Klaumeister had stared across the table toward where Frieda had stood uncertainly, feeling, in spite of her adult dress, childish and alone. She had not considered that her entry would have to be approved.

Only too obviously Mr. Klaumeister had many more pretensions toward arrogance than Otto Schlempke. My butcher shop, his boiled eyes said, is the best in West Haven, such people as the Amiots buy from me their sirloins and their crown roasts, I am a man substantial, prosperous, this rich house is mine, this rich pampered daughter—who are you?

"Ooh, Papa, Papa——" Voice all trills and runs, arms encircling the thick torso, Schatzi had squeezed tightly. "Wouldn't it be nice if Frieda stayed for dinner? This would be the *first time* she's ever been here." The words managed to convey that the privilege of entering Karl Klaumeister's house, of humbly sharing in his rich provisioning, was one for which Frieda in her fifteen years had longed above all others.

At once expanding and subsiding, haughtiness rising as his irritation fell, Karl Klaumeister had been indifferent and affable.

"So you bring home a little friend, eh, Schatzi?" Before it made a waving gesture of dismissal, his hand raised to tousle Schatzi's fringe. "Dinner I guess we have in plenty. Now run away, play with your little friend. Papa needs his Sunday schnoozle."

Thus accepted, Frieda was made free of the house—of the big kitchen, so laved in heat that it shimmered and its walls seemed to be pushing outward, wherein a flushed panting Mrs. Klaumeister and the hired girl both bustled nimbly; of the room upstairs, as frilled and furbelowed as Schatzi's skirts, in which Schatzi showed Frieda all her "things"; of the gargantuan one o'clock meal at which, in addition to the chicken and noodles, Frieda had stared at a collection of *Kraut Salad, Mohn Strudel, Grummel Torte, Pflaumen Kuchen* and *Kaffee mit Schlagsahne,* and of which she had eaten until her corsets were agony.

Later, lying across Schatzi's bed with stays loosened, recovering, she had heard confidences to which, if she had had a mind to give them, she might have made not too dissimilar responses.

"Being German is just *awful,*" said Schatzi. "Don't you hate being German? Being German is so *coarse.* Sometimes when Mama and Papa laugh so loud and talk so broken I could just *die.* Whatever else I do, I'm never going to marry a German, like Gehsi did. You know Gisela—only we mostly call her Gehsi—had to go and marry that big stiff German out of Papa's shop. Whatever happens, *I* won't. You wouldn't either, would you, Frieda?"

Gisela and her recently acquired husband, a blond-stubbled young man with widely spaced teeth, whose admission of the Klaumeister victuals had been broken mainly by sudden blustering roars of apparently uninspired laughter, had also been present at the dinner. It had been easy for Frieda to agree she would not follow in Gisela's footsteps.

But it was when they had gone for the suggested walk that Frieda had really glimpsed what the future might hold for her if she allied herself with Schatzi.

For this walk Schatzi had prepared them both painstakingly, changing her own dress for a blue-banded India muslin, fussing with her hair, dashing at Frieda with the comb.

"I just lay down and died when I walked in the store and saw your hair." Schatzi was as profligate of admiration as of service. "I suppose you know you just absolutely have the handsomest hair in this town—it's such a *dark* brown, Frieda, and so curly! If you want to sit back and let me try, I know I could do it in ringlets."

Through an entire hour thereafter—Frieda promptly accepting—Schatzi had curled and recurled Frieda's hair over her fingers, achieving a waterfall of ringlets which she had looped high. The result, as Schatzi said, looked almost like on the cigar boxes, and it had been in the flush of this success that the two girls had gone out to parade, Frieda intensely conscious of the free yet well-balanced mass she carried on her head.

"Look. I know she was staring at your hair." Generously, in whispers, Schatzi applied to Frieda all glances coming their way. Undoubtedly it had been pleasant, pacing evenly with Schatzi down West Haven's better streets. By five o'clock the elms and maples cast long cooling shadows, sunlight lay in quiet horizontal bands, the town was soundless except for the calls of such ragamuffin children as were not restrained from Sunday play, and the occasional clop-clop and buggy creak of vehicles in the street. Older people remained somnolently indoors, but here and there on the unsteady yielding walks were other young people of both sexes, out to take the air, to meet, to whisper gossip, to exchange smiles and arch glances, perhaps to wander on in different permutations.

For Frieda it was a new scene. Unless she had been bound somewhere she had not walked much out of doors; her Sunday afternoons had been spent listless and companionless inside her home. Now, however, she looked on, almost was part of, a strangely moving promenade. True, other girls, as they passed, looked at them coolly, critically, with disdain. Who are you? those glances asked, and then replied, Oh, foreigners!

Yet Schatzi's interpretations were not entirely wrong; even in rejection the eyes judged at full value the dress, looks, hair, eyes, bearing of the two intruders; it was impossible, thus on judgment and display, not to hold one's head proudly high, not to pull in one's waist even from the confines of the corset, not to swish slightly as one walked, not to step elegantly with the toes turned out.

Since Shindy Day, Frieda had drawn back from boys, crossing streets or waiting around corners to avoid them, stricken, if one so much as passed her, by immediate fears that she might be again molested. On this Sunday, therefore, when two young men had become visible, approaching, she had stopped quickly, clasping Schatzi's arm.

"Look—those boys coming—let's go back."

"Go back? What for?" The astonishment Schatzi turned to her had been entirely blank. At sight of the two young men Schatzi's own features had rearranged themselves coquettishly. "Come on, Frieda!" She had been impatient. "You can't be afraid of *boys!*"

Still doubtful, Frieda had allowed herself to be drawn on. The two young men, as they came near, displayed almost as many signs as Schatzi of the close approach, turning to look significantly at each other, tipping their boaters to a more rakish angle, becoming elaborately casual, staring boldly at the two girls at the moment of passing, pausing to look back, whistling lightly.

Hot discomfort replaced by equally hot astonishment, Frieda too had jerked to look around.

"Oh, you *silly!*" Schatzi in time had restrained her. "You can't turn and *look!*" Schatzi's own gaze had been demurely cast down, but she raised it now gaily, giving her whole small form a gleeful shake. "That was *Harry Gurney* and *Bob Willis,*" she imparted. "You wouldn't catch Harry Gurney with Bob Willis if *Palmer Hake* was back in town."

After that they had not only several more times passed Harry Gurney and Bob Willis, always with an equal amount of notice, but also other pairs or groups of young men. If these were German or Norwegian, Schatzi was as disdainful as the "American" girls were of herself and Frieda, but of the others she knew the names, the friends, the girls each one beaued, whether he did or did not go to college, and his exact place in the social hierarchy.

Such was the world of magically opened knowledge and approach which Frieda saw Schatzi as richly holding. True, for all her fine clothes and her spending money, Schatzi was still German, foreign, Catholic, outside the sacred ranks of Those Others. True, Karl Klaumeister's arrogance puddled quickly into fawning at so much as the name "Amiot," and both Father and Mother Klaumeister spoke as brokenly as Ilse. But all these debits could, for the time being at least, be well outbalanced by the credits.

"Lise Hetweit—you know how I've always gone around with Lise—is away visiting, and this fall she's going to Sister School. It would be awfully nice, Frieda, if you'd want to be my special friend." So, at parting, Schatzi had coaxed. And Frieda, though she had not wanted to commit herself too extravagantly, had not said no.

Anyone could see how different this was, than going around with Rozzie. In some ways, actually, she could feel *superior* to Schatzi. And then, with all Schatzi had to offer—oh, no doubt about it, Schatzi had a friend.

CHAPTER VII

Fingers tapping the desk top, Junius Hake watched his son's swaggering back as it was swallowed feet first by the balcony stair. Palmer was a pup, he told himself again. Oh, Palmer had points, Palmer didn't get pushed much, Palmer had his code, Palmer could stick by a road once he'd taken it. But for the rest he had been born a pup, and unless something happened to wake him up all too likely he would die one.

"I fear, Mr. Hake, that we can afford no more of your son's influence on school attitudes or spirit. Undoubtedly he was the leader in last night's disgrace." Such had been the syllables which Dr. Watts, president of Amiot College, had incised that morning through his whisker-ambushed teeth. And this time not even a check for his museum of moth-eaten Indian relics had deflected the old walrus; politely he had pushed money back. An outhouse on the platform when the audience assembled for the Amiot October Concert—one cast one's pearls just so long before swine.

An outhouse. That was typical of Palmer; outhouses were what Palmer's humor reached to. If only he had ever managed something not so banal, not so thoroughly the yokel's trick, it would have been more bearable. This—all the years of seeing a son who seldom lifted from the peasant rut—this was what came of being saddled with what should have been a by-blow.

Sardonic humor levering the burden and disgust, his mind slipped neatly out from under. That had been retribution, sending Palmer East this summer. Was Martin Hake so certain still of wisdom and austerity? Martin Hake; he now was seventy; he had been fifty when he forced his son to marry the partner of a chance seduction, just because that partner promised there would be results. It was amusing to think of Palmer's bloody, juicy meatiness against that rigid taint-lessness, that loftiness of standard; amusing to imagine Palmer blundering bull-like through the quiet rooms where as a child he, Junius Hake, had spent the dark and pain-strung years that followed a rheumatic fever. Never, to his memory, had there been any woman in that house, except old Marthe, the one servant——

What a summer Palmer and his grandfather must have had. Yet Palmer, on his return, had said blithely that he liked the shipyard, and just now, faced with decision, Palmer had said the hell with college, and he wouldn't be caught dead in the store. What he wanted to go into was building.

Out of a long line of Hakes he, Junius, had been the only one without building in his blood, and now this boy, who was so little Hake, wanted to return to it.

Shrugging, he rose to stand, as he so often did, at the balcony rail, looking downward through the stiffened gilt serpents of his gas fixtures. Palmer would have to make his bed and then lie in it; he was, almost, out of his father's hands. Of all kinds of possession, Junius Hake thought, only the actual contact of money had held him; the others were slippery and slipped idly by, like the girls he had known since Lily and had not had to marry.

Not that he took them in revenge; he never wished them harm, he could not see that they suffered consequently. All he asked of them was long anticipation and complete—if momentary—conquest. Seeing them as satisfied young matrons later, catching their faint flush and tremble if he glanced their way, he knew only amusement at their deft concealments, wondered sometimes if they taught a boorish husband his finesse.

This present girl, this Frieda——

As her name came to mind, he saw her, moving down the center aisle toward a customer, her back to him. That was a dry-goods customer she took in tow, the little bitch; she had begun to see where her bread must be buttered. Someone had taught her a thing or two; she walked now with that exaggerated stiffness from the waist up, that exaggerated rolling movement of the rear, which women nowadays thought drove men mad. "Hussy" was the word; he'd soon be hearing it; let them come. Out of all girls he'd ever known, this one right now was giving him most fun for his money. The change she had made in six months was incredible. All her own doing, and yet his. She was entirely his creature.

Putting her in at the grocery side had brought another return, too. Objectively he moved his glance to the shoe section, where George Bibbensack, sweatily, was fitting a fat countryman with bluchers. He felt no anger toward George, but enough had to be enough. Well, killing a horse could be done in more than one way, especially when there was so little chance of getting one's own back.

"Miss Schlempke." He didn't raise his voice, but the girl at once turned, starting. "Come up when you're through."

It struck him, when she came, that she was flushed and flustered, but she took the drummers' chair, now, when he pointed at it, and sat waiting, one brow lifted not without impertinence, her dark head with its load of ringlets poised and lifted, her bosom, too, high, her figure straight in the damson cashmere that was new that month. Abruptly he felt the crosscurrent—dislike—which sometimes struck him with her, he never could tell when.

"You're happy with yourself, Miss Schlempke."

She grew warier, but her face remained bland.

"I wish I had some money," she said boldly, and so readily he knew she must long have had the request ready for just such an opportunity. "Money my father wouldn't know I got."

"Money? As your father would say, you, a young girl, only fifteen——"

"I'm closer sixteen."

"And what could you want money for?"

"Hake's doesn't carry hats."

"Damn expensive, too, aren't they?"

Since this was comment and not question, she did not answer; eagerness had replaced the wariness. Her eyes were gray-green, deepened by the rather overheavy fringe, but still small, still pale. He wondered idly what made them seem so pale; perhaps it was because her brows and lashes, in contrast to her hair, looked almost light. Her hand on the desk was large but—now he had taken her off the heavy work—not too puffed, not too red, not too badly formed. Scarcely touching, he ran the tip of his little finger along the inside of hers.

"I wouldn't be surprised," he indolently said, "if we had quite a few changes here. We will, that is, if you do a small job for me. Just tell George right away—whatever he's doing doesn't matter—that since he's gone into gents' furnishings and shoes the grocery sales have jumped at least ten dollars every week."

Faintly smiling, he watched her rise at his dismissing nod and run lightly downstairs, not even bothering to think through his command. That was one way of reaching toward a holster; a smart man chose the precise weapon.

Head full of the stupendous, the earth-quaking event which had happened earlier that afternoon, Frieda's mind had small space for her errand, or even for the fact that she at last had dared ask her employer for another raise, this one in money. George Bibbensack was still wrestling with the stout captious farmer; ordinarily she wouldn't have bothered him while so engaged, but Mr. Hake had said right away, and right away she made it.

"Oh, George." During her two months of alliance with Schatzi, she had lost most of her edginess with men; it had been weeks now since she had called George by anything but his first name, and there were times when she even fliply referred to Mr. Ives as Horace. Thoughtlessly she rattled off what Mr. Hake had said, while George lifted a face thickened by stooping and exasperation.

For what happened to George she was totally unprepared. George's gaze swept out wildly, as if for support or cover, his thin lips loosened, his cheeks took on the look of sour bread dough. Movements he made were equally out of reason; he looked down at the shoe in his hand, held it forward, moistened his lips, rose from his stool.

"You," he said thickly, "you, mister, you want a shoe——"

"Not today, I guess, young man, not today." The farmer, too, partook of strangeness, his eyes steadily on George, but his hands fumbling covertly about on the floor for his outworn footgear. In a moment, old boots on, the farmer was trundling rapidly up the aisle, glancing backward as if at something from which he fled.

"Thanks, Frieda, thanks," George mumbled. Lifting his right arm, which still held the shoe, he brushed over his face, then sank limply once more to the stool, to sit staring at the shelves of boxes.

Hastily, Frieda thought back over her message. Then, comprehension flooding, she too stared at George before backing away. All the rest of that afternoon, as she perforce moved about the store, she could hardly keep her mind on her own concerns. Although no further word was said, everyone knew; a pall, a sickness fell, a sickness to be seen in Miss Shatto's undirected gaze, in Flora Gibney's sudden flouncing redness, in Mr. Ives's averted busyness. What was it about what George had done? An act which, if you could get away with it, would be so easy and pleasant a way to what you wanted, but which was so awful——

At seven when, as usual, Schatzi came bounding into the store for that intimate and confidential walk which they now took every night except the Saturdays and Wednesdays, she looked at Schatzi almost as a stranger; Schatzi wasn't exposed to what was denied her, Schatzi couldn't know her sympathetic horror.

When she remembered what else she had to tell Schatzi, that other seemed almost old, its fine edge gone.

"Palmer Hake was in the store today." They had already walked for half an hour before she brought it forth.

"Frieda!" Schatzi, who had been frilling the interim with a report of the fashions in her new *Ladies' Home Journal,* stopped short. "Frieda! Did you say *Palmer Hake!*"

At this breathless reception, some of Frieda's earlier excitement re-kindled.

"Yes, I did. He came in to see his father. When he came down from the balcony, it—well, it just happened I was near the stairs. He bumped me."

"He *bumped* you? *He* did? *Palmer Hake?* Frieda! I suppose you know what he got the boys to do last night up at Amiot, don't you? Everyone in this town is simply screaming! I never was so——"

It wouldn't, Frieda heard, be necessary to tell any more; Schatzi, unleashed, could go on indefinitely, as so many of the customers had that day, about the outhouse at the concert. And as long as she didn't tell it, then the rest of that queerly moving incident would remain all hers—that clattering descent of the stairs, that impact as she was thrust sideward by the bulk of what, as she had been assured by Schatzi, was absolutely the most wonderful young man in West Haven, that quick clasp by which he had steadied her, the way his hands—their warmth striking through thin cashmere—had stayed above her elbows.

He had been there, right there, touching her almost all over. At first, remembering Shindy Day, she had wanted to break loose, but then she had felt how this was different, how both he and she were vastly different. His grin now was admiring, and his whole wide face, his tumbled hair, the hat on the side of his head, his blue eyes, his heavy-lipped mouth, his alive body, had seemed to pull her toward him.

"Where'd you come from?" he had asked. "I never saw *you* in this town before; where'd *you* come from?"

She had managed to gasp, "I just work here," at which he had taken pains to be incredulous.

"You work here? In this dump? Say, birdie, maybe you'll see me again." Squeezing her arms once more with his full hands, he had gone off with shoulders swinging.

"Maybe he'll see you again! Oh, Frieda!" Schatzi, when finally she had been told the whole, was so choked with rapture she could barely speak. "Oh, maybe he'll see me then too. And Harry Gurney. *He* might see us. Frieda, *think!"*

Frieda thought. She had, under Schatzi's tutelage, learned some things rapidly. Schatzi was possessed by ideas of romance and, as had happened before when a new insight made its entry, Frieda's conception of the world had fallen apart and then arranged itself in a new pattern.

It was by *marriage* that one could, at a bound, become one of Those Other People, and get money.

The solution was so obvious, so present, that she was filled by dismay at her previous immaturity, her ignorance, which had kept her from seeing it. Marriage would at once translate her to the name, place, family, money of the man she picked. It was so open, so dazzlingly broad a stairway upward, that at first she was almost confounded. To think that, once she was this far, the rest *would be so easy*.

For as week succeeded week, while the girls of West Haven kept well aloof, the town's young men had seemed to indicate that if Frieda and Schatzi were for any reason inacceptable they didn't know it. Two enterprising males one Sunday had added a German boy to their peregrinations; there was a meeting of surprise on both sides, introductions, and, after some confusion, an airy "See you sometime, Wechsler," after which Wechsler had found himself gawping alone on the walk, while Schatzi walked off affixed to Clint Mason's arm, and Frieda to Joe Ward's. After a few more Sundays and a few more introductions the two girls, as Schatzi said, "just couldn't tell *who* they'd meet!" Sometimes with this pair of young men, sometimes with that, they now were invited to Pratt's Drugs for ice cream, or even to go riding in a hired rig. Of these, the Pratt invitations pleased Frieda most. In the cool depths of the drugstore, with its spidery chairs, its small round tables, its long mirror that reflected gleam and darkness, its mysterious licorice and cough syrup smell, she wasn't just part of a pair or a quartet, she was right on the edge of being in with all the other couples who came there: Jessie Drake and Harry Gurney, Theora Watts and Bob Willis, Louise Leverett and Frank Kenneally. Within a short time she had at her finger tips those squeals, saucy phrases, slaps and glances which marked her as being in the swim. To any purpose behind the fumbling hands which went around her waist or brushed her knee, her immaturity kept her still unknowing, but she took on the bright, quick surface patina, the "I'm fly, don't tell *me*," which made her village partners feel that they were devils and that she—since after all she *was* a foreigner—might be no one knew how fast.

That there might be a difference between some of these approaches and those that ordinarily led toward an altar she had no way of knowing; not only at Pratt's but on street corners she and Schatzi saw girls from the best families doing pretty much as they did. Already, her dreams taking on form, Schatzi had confided to Frieda that—although he hadn't yet actually gotten himself introduced to her—the one boy

she wanted for a beau was Harry Gurney. Frieda, in return, had imparted intimacies of her own, but actually she was undecided. Each
time she met a new young blade she took occasion, afterward, to walk
past his family home or his father's business; if he had a mother or
sisters who came into the store she judged them with long measuring
looks. Once you were married, she knew, you couldn't get unmar-
ried and start over; you had to be sure your money was *there*. Frank
Kenneally, for instance, lived in a big, white, evergreen-hedged house,
but his mother and sisters dressed quite plainly. Wes Jenks spent
money like water, but it was whispered that his father (Jenks's Saloon)
drank of his own wares. It was hard, she could see, to be sure.

Walking with Schatzi on the evening after her collision with her
employer's son, however, she once more saw the stair before her as
wide, varnished, flower-strewn. *If she could marry Palmer Hake!* The
ambition was so audacious and the goal so high that at first she
scarcely dared face the vision. It was very possible to make a mash
with other boys, but *Palmer Hake!* Palmer Hake, who had walked
up a church entry with Cecilia Amiot! Not that she needed any assurance of what Palmer was. She knew about Hake money; she had
seen Hake money, so little considered that it could be thrown about
a floor.

"Someday it might be yours." Tonight those words could carry a
fateful ring. That actual money, those very bills, might be what she'd
get.

Hot and cold, when she was at home once more in her room, she
pressed hands to her cheeks. Cecilia Amiot was in Europe; people
said she was going to school there. No, it was impossible; almost
anyone else she might get, but not Palmer Hake. Yet his hands had
grabbed for her, he had been *open* to her, his eyes had been challeng-
ing, the way any really sporty fellow's eyes were now when he saw her.

At her mirror she reweighed herself. Dark ringlets and fringe, damson cashmere cut to the very latest pattern—wider, puffy sleeve tops,
green-braided revers and a skirt front absolutely plain, not draped at
all—no one could say she didn't have class. In just a few more weeks
she could have her mantle, and if Mr. Hake would let her get the
cash——

It didn't matter if she could or not. She had to have him. Palmer
Hake. There wasn't anything she wouldn't do to get him.

Hake's, that next morning, was still gripped by its own excitement.
George Bibbensack had been seen leaving town by an early train—

that much was to have been expected. What was more freshly titillating was that Flora Gibney had gone too.

"Got on the train right *with* him, bold as brass!" Miss Shatto was aquiver with indignation. "I never did like that girl; I can't say I ever felt she took an interest in finer things, like our American past. I might have known, too, from the way she used to let George——"

On the threshold of the indecorous word "pinch," Miss Shatto swallowed a first stuttered letter, choked, and lost the floor to Mr. Ives, who had been sure for a long time that George was not only a thief but a fool.

"Whatever he's got will be no good to him, you can be sure of that; even if he does get away now, he'll be in trouble, they'll both be in trouble, you just mark my words."

This agreed on, the next question was what changes there would now be in the store, and it was this agitating topic which occupied all conversation until Mr. Hake, toward ten o'clock, strolled urbanely in. Mr. Hake, disappointingly, looked much as ever, but he had not been twenty minutes on the balcony before he called for Frieda.

Flutteringly, followed by three pairs of charged eyes, Frieda flew. Since the encounter with Palmer (only yesterday!) she had been beset by tremors; suppose Mr. Hake should guess? He was sharp enough! Suppose he should cut off her ambitions—"You can just as well get one thing in mind, Miss Schlempke, you'll keep away from my son." But there was, now, also this other affair; she could not be blind to what Miss Gibney's departure might open. When she was pointed to the drummers' chair she could scarcely bend to it; inside the casing of her corset her internal organs seemed suddenly to have enlarged, so that her lungs labored painfully. Instead of speaking at once, Mr. Hake leaned back to look at his drumming fingers on the desk, and to give, shortly, his sad laugh.

"The light that lies in woman's eyes," he said. "I wonder if it's ever anything but the gleam of the carrion crow."

If she tried to puzzle out the meanings of such obscure comments as this, she knew, she would only grow confused, so she let the words slide by, waiting for what was to come.

Spreading his hands wide, he now lightly tapped the finger tips of one against those of the other.

"I hear Mr. Bibbensack has left us," he went on less raggedly. "Miss Gibney, I hear, has left us too. Eddie, of course, will go into gents' furnishings and shoes. Miss Schlempke, who has been only too solicitous at learning the work, will take Miss Gibney's place in dry goods. It is almost as if a pleasant fate looked out for Miss Schlempke, who wants another raise."

His language was too precious for her, but she felt the vitriol; she knew as well as he that sometimes he liked her, sometimes he didn't. She had had successes enough now, however, to stand her ground.

"I do my work," she said.

Immediately he liked her better; the knots smoothed from his face.

"You do your work damn well, as well as Gibney ever did, and you'll do better. Of course, you're still too young. I'll pay you four dollars this time—one in credit, two in cash for your father—after all, Papa should get some raise too——"

He let it hang there, but by now his smile was tantalizing rather than a taunt.

"The—the rest——" she could barely stammer.

"Miss Schlempke's own to have and hold, and I promise not to tell Papa."

This time it was inside her corsets that the knots broke, flooding her with ease.

"Oh, Mr. Hake," she whispered, "Mr. Hake!"

When she stood up, wanting to fly downstairs, to tell Miss Shatto, Schatzi, anyone, to release the steam pressure of her bubbling jubilation, he too rose, catching at her almost roughly, swinging her around, his hands holding her above the elbows almost in the same way his son's had. But any meaning in his eyes, his grasp, was as inexplicable to her as the phrases he had cast her way; she stood radiant in what he had done for her.

As abruptly as he had caught at her, he let her go, turning away. "No," he said, "I was right before; you're still much too young."

Her mind singing its paeans, she ran downstairs. What filled her horizon was a vast whirling pinwheel of plumes, veiling, flowers, lace, scarves, muffs and capes. Palmer Hake must be drawn to that pinwheel as surely as a June bug must be drawn to a porch light.

CHAPTER VIII

That very week she had an opportunity to see the worth of her contrivances.

With her father she was now on terms quite different from those of her childhood. Toward the rest of his family Otto Schlempke might remain as he had been, but toward Frieda he had grown so affable and courteous that she would have been stunned, a year before, if she could then have had a single sample of his present treatment.

Change, however, had been so gradual that she took much of it for granted. After the April night when Hake had told him of her credit account he had never again struck her. Visible wrath during the next weeks had sunk to glowering, glowering had turned to feigned indifference, indifference, during the summer, had bloomed slowly into pride.

This daughter, who swished fashionable skirts, this tall young woman with cool measuring eyes, a well-raised bosom and taut shoulders, was no slinking slavey. A man could walk proudly, smoking a big black cigar, beside this daughter; heads, especially men's heads, turned when they passed; customers in the shop commented, "Damn good-looking girl, that one of yours, Schlempke." By ignoring the fact of her withheld earnings he had managed almost to forget them. He could use her as an object lesson, now. A pity, he could say to Viktor, Gottfried and Ilse, that Frieda was the only one who took after her papa, the only one who took pains with her dress, who made friends with fine people like Klaumeisters, who undoubtedly was headed for big things at Hake's.

On this Saturday evening he especially felt gracious. Earlier that week Frieda had told him she was getting Flora Gibney's place and a fifty-cent raise. He had taken care to check with Hake; yes, Frieda was raised fifty cents. His opinion of the worth of feminine labor, even for such a daughter, was too low for him to think the increase impossibly small. On the way home from the store he affably discussed, pro and con, the advantages of that brand-new means of execution, the electric chair. And when the time came for his weekly reception of wages he reversed a familiar order.

"Tonight we hear first from Frieda." Opening his hands, he bent toward the girl an amiable nod. "This week Frieda does good—Frieda gets a raise. Maybe one week Viktor gets a raise, maybe one week Gottfried. From children who work hard, make the money, look well, from such children Mama and Papa can be proud. Now, Frieda——"

As she rustled forward (a taffeta ruffle now glorified her petticoat) to lay her two dollars on the cloth beside his hand, she had an almost uncontrollable desire to laugh. Her own one dollar was pinned neatly and securely to the inside of one stocking, where she could feel it against her other leg as she walked. Held by the necessity to conceal a gloating which pumped through her like her blood stream, she stood demurely with gaze lowered while he made his ceremony.

"One, two. Two dollars. I think for this week our Frieda should have spending money. For this week our Frieda should have fifty cents—so much she is raised. Frieda——"

The last was a benediction of bestowal. From his own pocket he took out the half dollar which he set with dignity upon her palm before dismissing her. Not until, followed by the consuming eyes of Ernst and Lotte, she was back in her chair at table did he turn toward his sons.

"So now, Viktor and Gottfried." It was said carelessly, with an inference: from you we have nothing novel to expect. Instead of rising, however, Viktor continued to stare stonily at the lamp in the center of the table.

"*We* know Frieda don't turn in all her pay."

At the words, the tone, what spurted in Frieda was a kind of imminence. Walled in her purpose, she had not bothered to look out much at any member of her family; each one was merely present as usual, moving past, around, beside her, too familiar to be seen. Now, however, she perforce looked at the two who were her elder brothers, and it came as a shock to realize that, on a Sunday, she and Schatzi would have walked past them with noses uplifted. In size, at eighteen and seventeen, Viktor and Gottfried were grown men; on the table their hands lay huge, cut, white-etched, the knuckles puffed and stiffened from heavy lifting. Hair which was flour-dusted fell low to their brows, eyes which had no near focus seemed to be set toward distant moving gleams, their necks stretched forward from thick shoulders. Everything about Viktor and Gottfried, as they sat there that evening, had a loose, forward bend; they seemed to be nuzzling, like great hungry dogs, for some out-of-reach bone. Otto glanced toward them only briefly.

"Frieda gets a little credit," he explained blandly. "To work in a store she has to dress well; her boss gives her credit." His right hand dismissed it. "At the mill, Viktor——"

"At the mill I could go naked." Viktor had always been so silent it was violating to hear him utter such mutinous sounds. "Gottfried and me," he went on with no pause for cover, "we talked it over. We don't want no more of this"—he mimicked—"'Viktor, Gottfried, pay the money, pay to Papa——'"

Breath now beginning to push angrily through flaring nostrils, Otto stood up to lean forward.

"Now comes the children will tell how Papa should do things?

Now we see how Viktor and Gottfried say should be at this house?"

"All we say is we just pay our board. Two dollars a week is good board. The rest we keep. We ain't kids. We——" The unaccustomed talking seemed to knot and tangle Viktor's vocal cords. "We both been working pretty near since we could walk. We made good money——"

"Maybe you don't know comes a time for being grown up? At twenty-one a boy keeps his money, maybe marries, maybe lives in another house. At twenty-one he votes. In three years you, Viktor, in four years you, Gottfried——"

Viktor said roughly, "I been grown up for years already."

He also, now, rose slowly, and slowly Gottfried rose to stand beside him, their two faces at once old and young. The bones were old, the bitten skins, the hard small eyes; only the mouths were young, tremulous and seeking. There was no belligerence as they stood together, but a sabled quiet of decision. In the pause which followed their arising the only sound was of Ernst and Lotte scrambling to cover. Ilse crouched low in her chair, her face in agony, and Frieda too felt the stirring seepage of an emotion so strange she could not have named it.

Instead of flying into the rage which was certainly now due, however, Otto assumed a winning and imperial benignity.

"Grown up for years, already?" he repeated as if they had joked with him. "You, Viktor, you, Gottfried, you are boys. In one house can be only one boss. What do you ask? Should Papa give to you the house, the stove, the beds, the lamps? Should you say what we in this house should eat? Should wear? So long as Papa lives, Papa is boss in this house. Papa pays out, Papa must take in. Come, give Papa now the money."

He had first straightened, then, as he talked, resumed his chair. Sitting back, he displayed a calm indulgence; all this foolishness was over; life would return to decency and order. Viktor and Gottfried, however, stood unmoving, their gaze fixed on nothing. From their pockets they had taken out cloth caps, which they moved in their fingers.

The pause this time was longer, much longer. In Otto Schlempke the anger which had been swallowed so tolerantly visibly pushed at the seams, but again it was suppressed.

"You, Viktor, give the money."

Viktor continued to stand silent.

As that silence continued, Otto once more got to his feet, and now his temples were swelling.

"So this is all, yes? So you tell Papa, yes? So Papa tells you——"
He was blustering now, threatening; with a quick sweep of his hand
he took up the cup and plate at Viktor's place and smashed them to
the floor. "So now we see what comes——"

Stepping lightly, he moved forward in the swing of an old rhythm.
This was the way he got people to obey him; this was the way that for
twenty years he had commanded Ilse and his children. Letting himself go, he bloomed like gunfire into the flower of rage. He was
surrounded by ingrates and imbeciles; he was a slave; he toiled, he
made a home, he gave everything; in return they worked only to
push him aside, he who had fathered them, he who had tended their
first stumbling steps, he who had fed, educated, found them work.
Everything they were they owed to him, yet at this hour they sought
to wrest from him his life, his place, his sacred rights.

Ilse was now at Viktor's arm.

"*Gieb ihm das Geld,*" she was crying, "*Gieb's ihm; Gieb's ihm
nur.*"

Above hers, Otto's hysteria swept higher.

"I am the boss this house; I should let know-nothing boys in my
place; if you cannot give to Papa, then for you I do not work, for
you I do not keep the bed, for you I do not buy the food, for you
I do not buy clothes. In this house is no room——"

As he shrilled he rounded upon Viktor, his body like his face
contorted by the spasm of his anger. Viktor, however, did not fall
back, he struck forward, and after the impact Viktor still stood,
while Otto staggered helplessly backward against the stove. Without
looking, then, without paying the least heed to the scream that arose,
Viktor moved up toward the door; when he reached it he stood
settling his worn cap to his head as if he could not hear the pandemonium behind him—his father's repeated scream, his mother's anguish——

"*Nein, Viktor, komm zurück; Gottfried, komm zurück; meine
Söhne——*"

Still without turning, Viktor moved his shoulder forward until it
opened the door, then stepped out. After him, Gottfried too paused
in the door.

"So long, Ma," Gottfried said. "You can tell Brink we won't be
at the mill."

Ilse rushed forward but he too was gone. Casting herself face down
on the floor, she kept up her insensate wail. "*Viktor, komm zurück;
Gottfried——*"

Crouched double, his face drawn into his arms, Otto ran shrieking in the room. Against their wall Lotte and Ernst clung to each other almost insensible with panic, and against the sink Frieda too crouched, for once shaken out of herself. Her father had been burned, she did not know how badly, but even if she could have moved forward she would not have dared. It was not until Ilse lurched to her feet, on her face the blank incomprehending stillness of death loss, that anything was done for Otto.

"Come. You will have to help." The order at last broke Frieda from inaction. Between them she and Ilse got Otto into a chair. He had struck the stove with his left cheek; the fire had been dying but the metal was still hot; from forehead to cheekbone the skin was puffed, fiery, glistening. To the accompaniment of his continued screams and those of Ernst and Lotte, which began as soon as Ilse moved, they laid unsalted butter on the wound, and bandaged it.

No one slept much in the house that night.

Even after the pain had driven him toward unconsciousness, Otto kept moaning, "What could I do? They were just boys. I had the right."

And, upstairs, Frieda was beset by a continuation of those strange emotions which had so shaken her. Viktor and Gottfried—they were strangers; even as children they had drawn off together, preoccupied by mysterious pursuits; they could have been little less known to her if she had seen them tonight for the first time, yet their shadows, in varying shapes and ages, hovered at the sidelines of her whole past. What would become of them now? Must they wander, hungry perhaps, forever roofless, forever cut off, forever alone, forever trudging in night down some endless road? Thick weight, at the visions she saw, seemed to oppress her body, a thick heavy aching filled her throat. She might never see them again; already, as shadows, as wanderers, they slipped swiftly from her.

By morning, however, the moral of all this had grown apparent. What had just happened could be a lesson to her; never, never again, would she go about getting anything she wanted in the too straight, too open way that Viktor and Gottfried had.

Mourning, to the elder Schlempkes, lasted long. For weeks, while his burn slowly healed, Otto kept his bed, his head turned to the wall, seeing no one, speaking little, eating almost nothing of the food Ilse brought him, leaving Frieda's money untouched on the bed for Ilse when it was laid beside his hand each Saturday. About the house, the animals, the garden, Ilse worked slavishly as she had always worked, but she too uttered only the most necessary words.

And as if it were not enough to be surrounded by this quiet and despair at home, Frieda found herself also aground in her new purpose. Her work at Hake's went profitably, her friendship with Schatzi flourished, their Sunday walks were still for a few weeks besieged, but none of the besieging was done by Palmer Hake. Three Sundays after Frieda's collision with him they heard the news: Palmer had gotten himself a job at a lumberyard in De Laittre.

De Laittre (pronounced "Delayt" by its own residents and West Haven's) had seven thousand inhabitants to West Haven's four, it had a granite works, a creamery and cheese factory, and, above all, it had the Habakanaw Hotel. The Benson House, in West Haven, was a mahogany-and-black-leather, whisky-smelling, drummer-infested hostelry which women were rarely seen entering, and if they were (slipping up the outside stairs to the gallery that led around to the second-floor rooms) the worst was at once known. The Habakanaw in De Laittre, however, was of a different color; going there was, for most West Haven girls, the highlight of a year, right next to a trip to Meridian. Being invited to a Habakanaw party meant taking the afternoon train a distance of full thirty miles, meant supping in surroundings of such elegance and dazzle that the participants found it hard, afterward, to relay their impressions, meant coming home—well chaperoned, of course—on the "Midnight." The Habakanaw's white, purple and gold dining room was lit by a prism-hung chandelier, and on its gilt and purple plush chairs sat the best people of De Laittre, some of the women going so far as to appear in low-neck gowns. It was the periphery of the dining room, however, its little palm-secluded boxes, that really made its fame and magic.

In these luxurious *boîtes,* unequalled even in Meridian, people could eat, drink, look on, part of and yet apart from all the glitter, in the very essence of romantic seclusion. When Schatzi's sister, Gisela, had come back from her runaway marriage, it was to the Habakanaw that Papa Klaumeister had conducted his family to set a seal of ponderous acceptance on the union. Schatzi had not failed to acquaint Frieda with the glories. Both girls, Schatzi with the correct material details, Frieda to an accompaniment of vague mirrors, music and *Kalbfleisch* à la Klaumeister, had dreamed of someday, as a climax of their careers, being invited there. When they heard that Palmer Hake was in De Laittre it was at once in the Habakanaw that they both visioned him: swaggering in through its portals with a girl clinging to his arm (for Frieda this girl cruelly had the outlines of Cecilia Amiot), swaggering to one of the little boxes, disposing himself elegantly yet with ease on the purple bench (probably with one foot on it and his back to the wall), masterfully ordering, waving away the waiter, leaning across the table to hold the girl with both hands just above the elbow, so that she felt, even through her dress, his warmth.

The picture had the effect of cutting him off from them at a blow; it was as if he dined there in that luxury while they, street urchins, pressed noses to the glass. Wordlessly leaving the two young men who had been their informants, they walked stiffly off together up the street.

After a block, Schatzi admitted tremulous disheartenment. "Oh, Frieda. We'll probably never see him again. Or Harry Gurney."

Frieda muttered, "He can't be at the Habakanaw *all* the time. You'd think he'd sometime come to see his father." She too felt slapped and routed, but this was not her first slap, nor her first rout. Palmer Hake might be absent, but—and this was grim—she would not give up until she knew him irretrievably gone.

After some weeks she imaged a venture so bold it shook even her. Why shouldn't she and Schatzi, some Sunday, take the train to De Laittre, and walk there? Schatzi promptly answered: she, Schatzi, could never go to De Laittre unchaperoned; the Midnight didn't get back to West Haven until almost two in the morning. Her father would kill her if she got in that late, with no excuse. Knowing that Otto Schlempke, by this time dragging himself about the house, would surely rouse enough to make life uncomfortable for her too if she came in at that hour, Frieda had no solution. Mulishly, just the same, she saved for a ticket.

As winter came on, social life for the two girls waned. Fewer and fewer young men strolled out on the increasingly chill Sundays. In snug parlors from which Frieda and Schatzi were excluded they met instead to pull taffy, to peer through stereopticans and pluck banjos; set parties, to which Frieda and Schatzi were likewise uninvited, took place at the colleges. Finally, on a sleet-driven afternoon when even Clint Mason and Joe Ward did not turn up, Frieda abandoned hope, and, flanked by Schatzi, stayed moodily indoors to hug the Klaumeister base burner.

Thereafter, in an orgy of knowing it was no use, she spent her ticket money, saved it again, spent it, saved it. Christmas went, it was 1891, her sixteenth birthday finally come around, Rozzie Balik bent nightly over more new dresses, more frilled petticoats, Rozzie developed an unexpected agility at retrimming bonnets, Otto Schlempke, his cheek drawn and shriveled, took up his old round at Pallini's and the Benson House, Frieda saw life, all life, including the Hake money, sliding past her. In March she talked the gospel of trying again. People should be getting around a little, she impatiently insisted; if they couldn't meet Palmer Hake they at least might meet Frank Kenneally or Wes Jenks; anything would be better than nothing. And on a Sunday in April—a day out of all season, with trees holding up new leaves like candles—they got under way.

That Sunday they met Palmer Hake and Harry Gurney.

They were, when the meeting occurred, already under tow. Emerging from the Klaumeister block, Schatzi abloom with fresh hope and ribbons, Frieda in serpent green with a tiny figure of crushed strawberry, they almost at once converged upon Clint Mason and Joey. The young men too, they found, were astir with spring, yeasty with the desire to look at faces other than those they'd seen all winter. Why hadn't Frieda and Schatzi been anywhere around? In whose garden had they stolen the flowers for their hats? Didn't they know that, without them, life was nothing but a desert waste?

For the first time in a long while, Frieda felt her spirits lifting; no one could say this wasn't more interesting than listening to Schatzi at the Klaumeister piano! Just reluctantly enough to be interesting, she allowed her hand to be tucked into Clint's arm.

"We really promised——" It was to hide the hideous secret of their unattended winter that she threw out the equivocal hint, knitting her brow and rising on tiptoe to look down the block past Schatzi's bonneted head. What she saw there pushed the breath back past her gullet. Not a hundred feet away, with Harry Gurney, approached the luminary who had occupied her thoughts all fall and winter. "Schatzi!" She could not suppress the prayer, the gasp, the clutch at her unconscious companion's arm. The two approaching males were out of hope; it could not be possible that right here on Front Street, on the damp-seeping boards her feet a hundred times had tramped, before the Nugent house, which was painted tan with pink trimmings, she could be seeing Palmer Hake with his wide swinging shoulders buttoned into one of the very newest short fawn topcoats, carrying a restless cane, and with a bowler on his unruly hair. The cane, alone, told her it must be real. Only Thomas Amiot, in West Haven, walked abroad with a cane, and his was a knobbed dark mahogany. She could not, ever, have imagined the blond finger-thin wand which Palmer carried against his right shoulder, then twirled to hold crosswise by both ends, then flicked negligently at the Nugent pickets.

Whirling, Schatzi also gasped.

After this, it could be no more than dream-come-true to find that Clint and Joey should *know* Palmer, that they should rush toward him yelling, "Hake, you old horse thief, whose backhouse you stealing this year? What you up to now, Hake? You meet any new queens in De Laittre?" and that when Palmer shoved them they should shove as heartily in return.

During the scuffle, by a convulsive effort, the two girls got back their breaths, their aplomb, their best aloofness. As if in disdain they turned to leave—but slowly.

"Hey, wait a minute!" The voice that called was one to coil around them in a tingling lariat of joy. "Don't you two young ladies run away! Say, fellows, didn't I see you talking to these two young ladies? Can't you introduce a man? I guess I ought to know who lives here in my own home town!"

Frieda and Schatzi were demure receptive vessels for the introductions.

"Mr. Hake, you said? I'm so pleased. And Mr. Gurney——"

"Say." Palmer was nothing if not forthright, moving his big shoulders in the loose coat, brandishing his cane. From the first, his eyes were for Frieda. "Didn't I see you around, sometime?"

"You just *might,* Mr. Hake. It so happens I work in your father's store."

"My fath—sure. Sure, I know. Didn't I almost knock you down there, one day? Say, I didn't mind, at that. Say, we're old friends. How about walking a block with an old friend?"

The elbow he held out to her was almost at the level of his shoulder and well forward; his air was devilish, knowing, entirely assured. Moving against a flying spume of bliss so intangible it stung and prickled, Frieda laid two fingers of her left hand delicately in the proffered angle, and fell into step.

"We know all about *you,* Mr. Hake." She had long learned not to let conversations languish. Behind her, as she was blindly aware, Schatzi and Harry Gurney followed; there was a flourish of hands on the part of the new escorts, a derisive "So long, fellows," for the two who were abandoned.

"The *things,*" she went on, "that people don't say!"

"Say I'm at De Laittre these days?" Palmer seemed well content with the turn talk had taken. "Lumber. You know. Building. Houses." The cane illustrated largely. "You won't catch me rotting in any kerosene and egg barn like my old man. Big money is what I go out for. Farmers, that's where you make dough. Country jakes. Why, they don't know pine from top oak—pay anything you tell 'em. I could tell you some stories——"

He did, to Frieda's breath-held listening. This, she thought exultantly, as she heard how this farmer and that had been "stung" while changing from log houses to frame buildings, was how money got made. She had no suspicion that, at twenty and after an affiliation of no more than six months, Palmer was not at least part owner of the yard in which he worked. Money was something she could really evoke, and as he described it, it was right there; her two fingers in his elbow touched not only cloth-covered flesh, but wealth.

Only her felicity existed; she had no idea where they walked, or to what conclusion that walk would come. When her escort stopped with one hand on a gate she had to come aware as if she'd been asleep.

"I guess this is where we leave you girls." In insolence so complete it did not know it was insolent, Palmer touched his hatbrim with the cane. "We've got a little appointment here."

In a rush, Frieda saw then across a lawn the white-porched house to which they had come. A house with a tower—Jessie Drake's house. Since Cecilia's absence, Jessie Drake was *the* girl in West Haven. To the horse blocks by the street three rigs were tied. Jessie was giving one of her parlor musicales.

"That's fine, because we really had to get along——" Her quickly stiff lips managed it. Already some steps up the walk, Palmer turned back for an afterthought.

"Say," he called blithely, "why don't you two come over to De Laittre some Sunday? I could take you to supper at the Habakanaw. It's an idea—I'll fix it with Harry. See you later."

Settling his tie, brandishing his cane, he once more resumed his approach to the Drake house, followed by Harry Gurney, who echoed the "See you then, girls," and the nod.

"Come away from here, come away fast, you fool," Frieda spat at Schatzi. Schatzi was showing a tendency to stand, bemused, her blue eyes turning moist and helpless, her undisciplined mouth drooping. It wasn't the first time that young men had left them, but always before there had been some face-saving grace. Frieda knew just how much they had been slighted; with an acuteness new to her she even guessed that they had been taken away from Clint Mason and Joe Ward merely as a proof of prowess, allowed to walk with the gods a few short blocks, and then cast off.

And yet, as she told herself with even more fierceness, she didn't care. This was nothing to slights she'd taken before; this was nothing to Shindy Day. Palmer Hake had been in on that too, but now, lightly as he held her, he still had allowed himself to be seen walking with her. He had invited her to the Habakanaw.

"Of course, I don't suppose Palmer Hake would even be *in* West Haven if he hadn't been invited somewhere." Schatzi too, as they swiftly fled, tried to decrease their hurts. "But oh, Frieda! Isn't he divine? And *Harry Gurney!*"

"They better ask us to the Habakanaw," returned Frieda. This was the balm to which her thoughts must be fastened.

Schatzi moaned slightly. "But, Frieda. The Habakanaw! You know what we said before——"

Setting her lips, Frieda looked once more at the difficulties of a trip to De Laittre, and this time she did so with iron purpose. There would be no fun and no use in going, if they had to be attended by Mrs. Klaumeister's rolling, heaving asthma. She could imagine Palmer face to face with Mrs. Klaumeister. Her own mother would be worse, even. Schatzi's sister——

Gehsi was going to have a baby.

She thought she had learned her lesson, hadn't she? Learned from Viktor, learned from Gottfried. Learned from Mr. Hake.

She said to Schatzi, "We'll go see your sister."

CHAPTER IX

During the long, shut-in winter Sabbaths, Gehsi had taken to joining the two girls during their long talks in Schatzi's room. All their activities, said Gehsi wistfully, were behind her now; never again could she walk out as she once had with Schatzi and Lise, not knowing whom she'd meet. Herman, she hinted dolefully, had been quite interesting in the first months of marriage, but sometimes now he got just awfully dull.

Gehsi was a big girl, ash-blond and protuberant wherever protuberances were possible—her heavy eyes blue-lidded, her bosom billowy, her rear reaching out for Lebensraum. Already her frills and flounces—of which she wore as many as Schatzi—showed the effects of having no real purpose. When, in December, she found she was pregnant, she lapsed entirely into despond. Only nineteen, and now how would she spend her lifetime? Changing diapers. Let Schatzi and Frieda be warned by her example, let them have fun while they could, it would end soon enough.

On this Sunday, when they turned up at her small gray cottage, Gehsi fell on them with tears. Since no decent woman ventured out of doors while visibly pregnant, she had not been able to get to Papa Klaumeister's for dinner, Herman had lumped off to a saloon for beer, she still was in her breakfast wrapper and without her corsets, her limp hair straggling down to two thin braids.

At the recital of their problem and its circumstances, Gehsi livened enough to drag her plump form upright on the short divan in her Japanese Art Corner; at a bald statement of the solution Frieda's busy mind had contrived she was aghast but trapped.

"I couldn't—oh, I couldn't, I just couldn't," she repetitively quavered. "Papa would kill me. Herman too. If Herman ever found out, he'd kill me, just like Papa. Even if he is young, he just never understands."

Her weakness, however, was perceptible. One by one, Schatzi joining her sister in the alternate quavers of trepidation and daring, the objections were disposed of. Yes, Gisela had a spare bed. Off the parlor. She and Herman slept off the kitchen. Of course they never locked doors; who in West Haven locked a house door? Herman drank beer every Sunday and never woke at night; he snored enough to drawn the sound of any entry. Papa and Mama Klaumeister could see nothing wrong in Schatzi's wanting to stay with her sister at a time like this—not just *one* Sunday night, but every Sunday night from now on, so there'd be no difference. Frieda's papa and mama would see nothing out of order either; Frieda had spent nights with Schatzi before this.

It all depended on Gehsi. Gehsi could decide whether her own sister—and Frieda—would have a chance to enter the heady delights of the Habakanaw, squired by the most enviable young men of West Haven, or whether they were to be abandoned to a fate similar to Gehsi's own: taking up with some German from the shop.

"Oh no, girls, take my word, don't do it." Gehsi grew drunken with responsibility and her own position as a sad and sore example. "Just *don't* do it. You've got to have something better."

Clasping and unclasping her hands, she held up her head while tears ran from the prominent blue-lidded eyes.

"Oh, promise me you'll never do anything you shouldn't, so I won't get into trouble."

If Palmer asked them, they were ready.

When Harry Gurney hesitated inside the door of Hake's, Frieda had no need to be told why he had come.

During six long weeks past, during Sundays which she and Schatzi had spent conscientiously with Gehsi, they had despaired and hoped. Palmer might so easily not have meant what he said; Palmer might not have known how flawlessly in style was the serpent-green India silk with the crushed strawberry figure; Palmer might have found newer girls in De Laittre. But now the liquid contents of her body could take a leap of pure joy.

Harry was a pale boy, not so blond as colorless; Harry at Hake's alone was a shadow without its substance. Actually he was tall, but he walked with his head ducked, propitiatingly, a smile coming and going on his uncertain mouth, color coming and going in his cheeks, his hands fingering the two books he carried—he was still a student at Amiot—as if they hunted the stops on a piccolo.

Swimming forward, Frieda flashed a keep-off glance at Eddie, whose job it was to pick up all males who didn't at once turn toward groceries.

"Why, Mr. Gurney," she said, "Mr. Gurney! Imagine seeing you at Hake's!"

"I might—I thought I might—might look at scarves." Harry's speech, too, came and went spasmodically, his chin jerking forward each time he got mired.

"But of course, Mr. Gurney! We have some that are *really!*" She led him to the rack of neckties. The actual words, muttered sidewise while he poked about the ties—"We thought—Palmer Hake thought—if you girls happened to be in De Laittre next Sunday—if we should happen to be going past the hotel, say"—were almost unnecessary.

Flying to Klaumeisters' when seven o'clock came, she initiated a furor. Preparations contributed deliciously to her sense of mastery. *Now* things were going as they should go! For a first time, boldly, she overstepped her credit, announcing to Mr. Hake that she was taking the expensive jacket—almost it was serpent green—on which she long had had an eye. Mr. Hake laughed, caught her hand, squeezed it, threw it back to her; Mr. Hake was always doing some such thing; ordinary things Mr. Hake did no longer snagged their hooks in her attention, not now when she had his son to think about.

Only when Sunday got them on the train, sitting well forward on the mounded green plush seats, did any lessening in her sense of mastery occur. Since the time, seven years before, when she had moved to West Haven with her family, she had not been on a train, and alone with Schatzi, she had to feel unguarded and beset. Only her consciousness of her appearance was supporting. She would have died rather than say so, but Rozzie had been right about everything. Her dress (she was wearing the serpent green, of course) was vivid, and the pearl-gray gloves and parasol Rozzie had suggested gave it tone. Her hat—gray for sobriety, color to hint sobriety was just a blind—was like a saucy dare, set pertly forward so it shaded half her right eye. It wasn't by accident that so many of the college boys in the party ahead kept glancing back.

Now that the moment had come and the step been taken, Schatzi had succumbed almost entirely to terrors. Suppose Papa and Mama *again* visited at Gehsi's? They'd done so, not too obviously suspicious, on a previous Sunday. Suppose Palmer was up to one of his tricks? Anyone played tricks on old people, but Palmer had been known to play them even on people his own age. Harry Gurney was a nice boy, but he'd do anything that Palmer said.

"They'll be there," Frieda promised staunchly, but she had her own infection. It wasn't so much the idea that Palmer might give her the slip that bothered her, as much as a sudden vision of him as an adversary, of someone she must subdue and conquer. So far when she'd met him she hadn't really tried to make him do anything but take notice. But if she were to get him to marry her—how would she go about that? None of the West Haven boys had got that far. She didn't know how any girl, really, got a boy to propose marriage.

For this nervousness there was, immediately after their arrival in De Laittre, some temporary balm. She and Schatzi were only a few minutes off the train when, up the main street, they glimpsed a pair of approaching strollers too casual to be anyone but their expected escorts.

Schatzi, who had passed into a later panic at realizing she hadn't seen Harry on the train, lapsed into a moist pink muteness; it was up to Frieda to meet adequately the gallant "As I live and breathe, Miss Schlempke and Miss Klaumeister—haven't we met you two cute birdies up some tree before?"

The relief came because she saw, at once, how much Palmer Hake was impressed.

"Whew!" he told her. "Where'd you get that hat, my cute doll, where'd you get that tile?" He whistled through a chorus as he offered his arm and started walking, but the hand that held the cane came up to let a finger run inside his collar and resettle his light plaid necktie.

Preening, mincing slightly, she could for the moment feel her oats. *Palmer Hake.* He was the best there was, and she had knocked him flat.

He almost said so, straight out. "You're a queen, you know that? Gosh, I wouldn't mind being seen almost anywhere with you."

At her coy, pouting "Mr. Hake! Don't you make fun of me!" he floundered deeper.

"Yessirree," he began, "class is what I like, and you've——" He got to that exact point when his attention was distracted by an object which, to Frieda's disdain—people didn't notice such things—was an approaching derelict, well in his cups.

The muscles in the arm that held two of her fingers tightened.

"Hey!" He was at once torn from her, in a sphere of mischief all his own. "This is where you'll see things." He half turned to include Schatzi and Harry in his project. "Here comes Pi Regan. Watch."

Loosing himself from Frieda with one gracious and exaggerated bow, he stepped forward to bend, with equal grace, before the shambling and furtive remnant of humanity he had spied.

"Mr. Regan?" he asked dulcetly. "Isn't this Pi Regan, the famed printer? I can't be mistaken—yes, it's Pi!"

Unfocused eyes peered out placatively. "Misther, I guess I——"

"Sure you know me!" Palmer grew heartier. "Jones. Your old friend, Jones. Many a glass, eh, Pi?"

Pi tentatively snickered.

"Here, have a pinch of Snus on me, old man—have a pinch of good old Copenhagen——" Thumb and forefinger fished from the fawn vest a small round box with a familiar label, flipped the lid aside.

"Don't care if I do, m'frien', don' care if I——" Waveringly the tramp took a good pinch, waving it twice for courtesy before holding it to his nose. Immediately, then, a convulsion shook him, his eyes and tongue protruded, his body was contorted by deep spasms before he began violently sneezing, one paroxysm so closely on the heels of the last that there was no close division.

Retiring into paroxysms of his own, Palmer bent double with laughter. Harry, although more weakly, joined him. Schatzi, shrinking against Frieda, giggled feebly.

"Of course it's funny—I guess it was red pepper. You don't think he'll die, do you, Frieda?"

Amused and fairly well untouched by compunction, but made wary, Frieda waited until the boys, recovering and tiring of the lesser writhings of their prey, were willing to go on. At once, she knew to what end the incident had served; Palmer, because of it, was recovered in his ascendency and his aplomb. It was of himself he now talked, as they walked on. Of course, his manner now said, being what I am, I also draw the top in queens. And later, during their supper at the

Habakanaw, he took pains to make his overlordship even more clear.

The Habakanaw, in some ways, began as a disappointment. Certainly the white clapboarded exterior with its colonnaded porch—patterned after a plantation house—lacked the immensity and flamboyance with which Frieda had endowed it. Only when, after passing through a dusky small lobby, they were suddenly exposed to the brilliance of the dining room, did she feel awe. Fully before her, then, hung the famous chandelier of seven graduated rings, each blazing circle dripping white fire from the turning facets of its prisms. Under this fire sat the diners at their little tables, chattering and gay, while threading in among them, like spidery agile figures in a dance, went the black-clad waiters. It was then, with Palmer displaying all the savoir-faire which she and Schatzi had conferred upon him, as he beckoned to a waiter, as he stood aside with a brief nod to let the girls go first, as he brought up, with detached insouciance, his little cavalcade, that she temporarily returned to her first stumbling, gaping wonder at the young man on whom her thoughts were set. Later he was equally lordly in the ordering of two whiskies (the girls were overcome at the thought of indulging and did not get urged). Their table was in one of the small boxes, and, sitting there hidden by palms from sight but not from seeing, Frieda began to regain her bearings. From here the other diners appeared as mortal—rich, of course, accustomed to places like this, but still human, just some more of Those Others to whom she now was nearer than she ever had been before.

Beside her on the purple bench Palmer disposed himself almost as she and Schatzi had visioned. Since she sat beside him, he didn't pull his foot up, but he did lean back against the wall, every angle of his body one of studied ease.

"You two girls know you don't want to get Harry really drinking," he said. "One whisky is all Harry gets. Get Harry drinking, and Harry will do anything."

This was a reference, apparently, to past happenings; color shot across Harry's cheeks, while Palmer laughed uproariously. The girls dutifully teased, to be answered with "What you'd say if you knew!" and "Shall I tell 'em, Harry?"

It wasn't so different, thought Frieda, from what other young men offered. Palmer knew his way around, all right, but so would she, if she went as his companion.

"I'll bet we'd hear things about Palmer Hake, too, if the daisies got telling," she put in with what she thought deftness; Palmer so far had never objected to having talk turn to himself.

This time, however, he turned to stare at her deliberately, his lower

lids rising almost to the middles of the pupils. When the drinks came
he took his from the waiter without turning, tossing it down and
setting the small glass on the table.

"Listen, dolly," he said coolly, "Daisies never get a thing on old
Hake. Neither do Gerties, Nellies or Maries. When Hake gets tied
up, he'll get something from it. Hake doesn't run in double harness
with just any filly, not that boy. He won't fix it so he can't take out
cute little chicks like you. Count on him, queenie, he'll be around to
give buggy rides."

His breath was loud and heavy in the little silence; with heat beginning at her belt and spreading fanwise up her breast, Frieda recognized what he had told her. She might have class and looks, but she
vas foreign and poor, she was second-class, she wasn't in the running
as a possible wife. Not for Palmer Hake. She had been right on the
train, thinking of him as an adversary.

He didn't know, though, that he had once said worse; he didn't
know he had called her a rhinoceros. Schatzi's eyes had widened and
her mouth again was soft and hurt; Schatzi was a fool and a baby; if
Schatzi had had some of Frieda's hurts behind her she could have
kept her face cooler; she would have known the necessity of striking
back.

"*Buggy* rides?" asked Frieda, with brows rising. "Oh, I guess. Little
bugs *must* want to go along with such a big bug, when they see one."

Harry Gurney, who had been stuttering, "Oh say, say, Palmer," and
the waiter who had been hovering for the supper order, both chose to
laugh. "Say, that's one on you, Palmer!" "The young lady is a wit—
I tell the cook!"

Palmer did not take a joke turned on himself with any grace; he
uttered a weak "So that's what you think of me, is it?"

Frieda, herself, was aghast at her small revolt. Riding later in the
moonlight down a country road, the rhythmic clop of horse's feet
before her and the whine and turn of buggy wheels beneath her, she
looked back with no understanding at her behavior.

Girls, she knew, didn't bristle, not at Palmer Hake. Wes Jenks and
Joe Ward had once or twice accused her, doubtfully, of being sharp,
but she had never felt as she had during that supper—pushed forward, ready, with the untaught words waiting at her tongue roots.
Immediately after the remark about the bugs, while Palmer was
asking them what they'd eat, she had let go again.

"Maybe we chicks should eat only what you roosters pick out,"
she had said.

Why had she? Why did she, even now, feel as if she would like to *fight* with the young man who, ever since they had gotten into the buggy, had sat greatly at ease, hat cocked, body lounging, feet upon the dashboard, reins light in his hands? His imperiousness was the hallmark of all she coveted; she didn't want to break his arrogance, only his superiority toward her. So many things about him were exactly right; any flamboyance in spending, she was sure, was all on the surface; underneath he was as thrifty as she was. His eyes in ordering had rested on the prices, it had been he who paid the whole bill with a lavish gesture and given a tip, but in the lobby later Harry had slipped him a full half. Harry had paid half at the livery stable, too, but Palmer got the fancier rig.

After her thrust over the ordering he had reddened, breaking into an unwilling laughter; during the meal he had talked only mildly, mostly to Harry about doings at Amiot, but toward her he had paid a puzzled, close attention. It was only her foreignness he had against her, she was sure of that; her lack of standing and of money. These she could do nothing about, but she exerted herself to overshine them. With Schatzi and the other boys she had developed a trick of mimicking customers and her fellow workers; when she got into her repertoire Palmer was at last reduced to helpless guffawing. If only, now they were riding and alone, he would say something, so that she could know where she was.

By the time they had ridden for an hour she had been reduced, almost, to meekness. She had tried, as they started, making sprightly comments; he did not reply. Her fingers tangling and untangling in her lap, she had had to retreat finally into a silence as complete as his own.

Yet his quiet wasn't murky; to himself he whistled softly, or hummed at the choruses of songs, as if he were having a reasonably good time. Not until she began to think it time they turn back did he break his quiet.

"Pretty spot here," he said equably. "You might like to see it. Here, step down."

He had halted the horse with his first words, skillfully cranking the buggy to the side, jumping down and holding up his hand for her to follow.

Taken up by the complexity of her emotions, she had scarcely seen where they went, had not noticed the moon-flooded high sky with its wispy drifting scraps of cloud, had not seen the dark passing tree shapes or the meandering pale ribbon of the road. Now as she obeyed she saw that they had come to a high, open hilltop, from which the terrain undulated downward. Taking his hand, she let herself be led to a zigzagging log fence where he tied the reins to a top rail and stood idly close beside her, looking at the moon-veiled country— gentle hills and hollows, clumps of thick trees, wide fields, windmilled farmsteads. From the tangled June grass at their feet came up the scent of lush growth, moist earth and wild roses, a light wind moved against their cheeks, small nearby rustlings and more distant swishings as of cows in pasture told of life around them. A mosquito stung her cheek; she slapped at it.

"You're a funny girl. More stickers than a cactus," Palmer said beside her ear.

She stood caught into a distant and expectant stillness, in which belligerence receded, but still throbbed pulsingly below the surface.

Taking her arms above the elbow, as he had that day in the store, he turned her deliberately until she faced him, and still deliberately he moved nearer until his lips were firmly against hers.

She had been kissed before this—awkwardly, experimentally, hopefully; she had before this felt almost nothing, been ready with her slap, her "Oh, you fresh thing!" her "Mr. Ward! The stars are twinkling down at you!" She had no preparation for what happened now inside her, for the rush of blood, the half-sick, aching sense of meeting, the need to cling. When he drew away he was more master of himself than she; in the moonlight his eyes had the gleam, his full wide mouth the set, of power.

There had been no softness in the kiss, there was no softness, no caress, in the tight grip he kept of her arms; they faced each other still as combatants.

Feeling the unbroken opposition in him, feeling the resistance in herself, she yet managed the shaky repetition of a password: "Mr. Hake, the moon's got his big eye on you."

Immediately he dropped his hands.

"What of it?" he asked. "I wasn't going to kiss you again. Here, we'd best get started or you'll miss your train."

CHAPTER X

From Schatzi she had heard much of *love*, a word applied by all better magazines to states of syrupy concordant bliss. But she did not connect the word with those confusions, doubts and tumults before which she now was blown.

On the train going home Schatzi was dreamy and transported, with no thought even for a Papa Klaumeister who might wait, like Jove with a hammer, at Gisela's. As soon as she and Harry got alone, whispered Schatzi, everything had been *all right;* it was too bad Frieda and Palmer hadn't hit it off.

Without arguing this, Frieda stared stiffly at her fog. Palmer, during the drive back to De Laittre, had whistled loudly all the way, while she dug at the dashboard with the ferrule of her parasol. At the station he had left her with an indifferent "You might see me again." But already there were needs she knew above all others: Palmer *had* to want to see her again, and alone; he had to hold her and kiss her; somehow the barriers that blocked him off must be torn and clawed away.

As days went by, these needs became a lash. There was no trouble at Gisela's; she and Schatzi could congratulate themselves that they had planned well and were free for future meetings. Taking her turn at optimism, Schatzi was sure, anyway almost sure, that Harry would want to see her again. Maybe Palmer and Frieda would get along better next time, or—this was more doubtful—maybe Harry would chum up with some other boy for Frieda.

To all this Frieda kept her counsel. She had no optimism; only her urgency. Every entry into the store jerked her head frontward, every careless footfall on a walk behind her had her listening. When Wednesday went, Thursday, Friday, her thoughts converged, with terrible intensity, on the coming Sunday. Even if he made no previous appointment, on Sunday Palmer must seek her out.

Schatzi had told Harry that on Sundays the two girls were always at Gisela's, and when that day came both girls sat ready with their hats on, Schatzi retelling for her sister's hungry ears the details of the Habakanaw supper. On Frieda the words fell like acid rain. When five o'clock came she could bear no more of sitting.

"Stay here if you want," she threw at Schatzi. "I'm getting out." But Schatzi too rose with alacrity.

"No, I'll go. I really need a walk. We'll be back, Gehsi——"

After another ten minutes, then, they knew why no knock had sounded on Gisela's door. Palmer Hake and Harry Gurney were in West Haven, all right. They were there with other girls.

Even a block away there was no mistaking who the boys were. Voices reached them, the cane was unmistakable, the width of shoulder, and the swagger. All Frieda knew of Schatzi was a clutch at her arm, an impediment she must drag. Her own legs were incapable of forward movement, yet bore her onward, in a progress to be forever after linked with wading in the chilly iron-brown current of West Haven's turbulent small river; she could feel water sucking at her knees, and rising. Yet as she neared that other group she knew in herself a terrible wild straining strength, as if, by directing her eyes upon the laughing and carefree quartet, she could have stricken it from the earth.

The girl on Palmer's arm was Jessie Drake, the pert black-eyed thing she had seen before—yes, twirling her parasol and twinkling up in this same way at another man—that Sunday long ago with Rozzie. Over Jessie's head Palmer's eyes met Frieda's as if he did not at first recognize her. Then, as if in half remembrance, the hand with the cane lifted toward the hat.

From the girl beside him drifted negligent amusement.

"Why, Palmer, you bad boy, you! Do you *know* those girls?"

The day had been warm, but now its air was icy against Frieda's flaming face. Tearing forward so rapidly that she could hear her own breath, hoarse and rasping, she ripped Schatzi from the meeting. What possessed her was no thought, but an emotion: I could kill them. She had sensations of slashing at Jessie's yellow dress, of clawing into skin and flesh, of seeing blood drip red in streaks down Palmer's face—Palmer's, and yes, that girl's, which had become Cecilia Amiot's.

"Frieda!" Schatzi moaned and panted. "I can't go so fast!"

"I could kill them," Frieda said aloud, beyond caring now that from this time on Schatzi must know at least something of what she felt.

On the succeeding Thursday a penny postal came to her at Hake's. Like all other Hake mail, it was brought in by Eddie Noble, who went to the post office after each train.

"Front Street and Ninth, 8 Sunday," ran the unsigned scrawl.

With blood and fury draining, Frieda stared at the incredible. *It was all right.* That was what the card said. He did like her, he wanted to see her again. Maybe he'd just accidentally met Jessie Drake last Sunday, or maybe it was a previous engagement. No one had to tell her what Ninth and Front Street meant, at eight o'clock. They'd ride, this time he'd talk, they'd stop again——

But again anticipation was only a respite from her seat of thorns. Immediately after midday on Sunday, too restless to stay in with Gehsi, she and Schatzi got out into a day made hazy by smoke from some distant forest fire. They might, as Schatzi said, see the boys earlier.

They did, again with Jessie Drake and Louise Leverett, again amicably strolling. Palmer's nod once more was negligent, Harry's more pleasant.

"They don't even mean to meet us tonight, Frieda; they were just fooling." Schatzi collapsed at once into a limp rag.

"Oh no," Frieda muttered, "no, they'll meet us." This time her face was a knife, fine-edged, cutting the red-dusted air. If she ever got Palmer where she wanted him she would make him sorry. *Someway she would make that boy sorry, someday!*

Yet that night at eight, with the heavier-than-usual dusk just fallen, when at the exact moment she paced nervously with Schatzi down Front Street toward Ninth, when for twenty agonizing minutes they waited, smiles sticky on their faces, under the indifferent elms, when finally the rigs drew up, stopping with a secretive whistle, when finally she once more sat on a buggy seat beside Palmer, she knew herself impotent. There was no nearness, no breached barrier, no apology in Palmer.

"Well, if it isn't my little chickadee," Palmer said. "Get in and we'll flip our wings out where there won't be so many gaslights."

As if he rested it there because it was comfortable for him, he let his left arm, pressureless, remain across her back.

"You and your small friend get a lot of exercise," he went on, speaking as if he had no interest in the words, but was making an effort to be pleasant. "Haven't I seen you do a bit of walking? We'll have a good dark night, tonight. The fire, I guess, must be up north. Too bad, when you think all this smoke is lumber. Enough to build maybe a hundred thousand houses."

From there he went on to speak, much less boastfully than before, about his job. She tried to keep her comments, questions and replies at his own level of detachment. The moon was now small, and under it hung the acrid smoke haze, heavy, murky and obscuring. Only once did her heart have its time to let go and her mind to think, Now! After they had ridden a short while he stopped the buggy, cranked it, jumped out and held up his hand, exactly as he had outside De Laittre.

"You can't see much tonight, but this place here is nice. Sometime I'll bring you when you can really see it."

The grove at which he nodded looked an impenetrable mass of trees.

"I've picknicked here, and picked wild strawberries. Belongs to a farmer half a mile away."

Then with no preamble, no altering of his detachment, he pulled her toward him. The contact broke the helpless impassivity in which she had taken what he had so far given: as if the mechanism of her furies had been set off by his touch, she began struggling, soundlessly, against him, slapping at him not coyly but with passion, straining against the arms that held her, grinding her heels into his feet, kicking, pushing, clawing. She was almost as tall as he, but while he did not move or seem to make much effort, his hold was inexorable; she felt as she had felt when she was a small child and her father had forced physical compliance. From frustration and from helplessness she started sobbing.

"I knew—that first time—that you had the stuff to be a—wildcat." In spite of his apparent inactivity he too was panting, but his voice carried a queer satisfaction. Little by little he pinioned her arms down, increasing the pressure and his nearness until she was powerless, then relentlessly bringing his face forward.

She had fought physically, but she could not fight back her own response. She felt as if he sank inside her; from the first light touch the kiss reached deeper until bones crunched against hers; when he broke away at last he was gasping, and she stood swaying, reaching to him for support.

Hair disheveled, exultance over, he looked as if he were drunk. At the touch of her hand he flung away.

"Come on, get back in that buggy," he said harshly.

This time on the way back he did not hum or whistle. Hunched into his corner of the buggy, as far away as he could get, he spoke only to urge his horse to greater speed.

After this she was sure she had lost him; it was a month before she heard from him again.

During the interval he went about with other girls, seemed blatantly, indeed, to parade them. Schatzi, who after the second date occasionally had meetings with Harry on week nights, reported pityingly that Harry had told her Palmer seemed to be quite gone on a new girl in De Laittre. Yet on the next Sunday they would see Palmer drive dashingly down Front Street in full daylight, with Jessie Drake.

To the torments she had suffered before, Frieda now had to add this icy certainty of loss. What had she done that was so wrong? Why did he dislike her? It had something to do with the kiss—by fighting him she had made him angry; no, he had seemed to like the fighting; it was the kiss itself he hadn't liked. Yet it was his own kiss; he had forced it. Turgidly, in the back of her mind, moved those things that, even after her acquaintance with Gisela, she both did and didn't know. Other subjects she and Schatzi talked over freely, but not *this* one.

When the second card came, "Front Street and Ninth, 8 Sunday," so like the first that she might have thought it the same if the postmark hadn't been different, she was stricken almost into torpor. Why should he tease her, toss her as a tomcat tossed a mouse? She couldn't undergo that experience a third time. Yet helplessly she did go, standing with Schatzi once more under the same elm until the whistles sounded, sitting once more in the place that was now more familiar to her than a kitchen chair at home, because it lived so interminably in her mind, studying Palmer furtively while again he talked inconsequentially—Amiot ought to have a better baseball team this year; Harry would be a junior, which made him eligible; Harry's father was a card that was a card; she knew Harry's father, of course, a prof up at Amiot; the boys called him Old Harry, or sometimes just the Deuce. What she tried to do was assess him with the same measuring objectivity which she applied to others, but she failed entirely.

All she could do toward him was feel: the warm vitality inside his hedged remoteness, the promise of his heavy mouth. Other activity suspending into expectation, she waited for what she was so sure must come—the halt, the buggy turned, the hand held up to her. Time went by that seemed hours; he began, with an effect of taunting, to ask questions of her—what did she do, really, in the store? In what part of West Haven did she live? Had a father and mother, did she? Brothers? Sisters? What did she do for amusement beside walk out with the little Klaumeister? Knew a lot of the fellows? he supposed. Come on, why not give him some more of those imitations she'd done so well at the Habakanaw? To all of these she had to force responses through her wooden lips.

When she knew for certain that tonight there would be no stop, when they were actually back in West Haven, she dug her fingernails into her palms until it seemed they must break through. This, she thought wildly, was the worst insult of all. By taking her riding he had obligated himself to one short truce of unison, and now he had withheld from her even that.

At Ninth and Front Street he let her out, with "Well, I guess this is where you leave me."

Stumbling as she got down, stumbling as she turned to run from him, she heard him call a final question as he whipped up his horse.

"You weren't disappointed, were you?"

Yet for the very next Sunday she had another card, and this time she did not see him with another girl beforehand. The date was for seven, he came on time, the fly-netted horse was one of the livery stable's finest pacers, the buggy gleamed like patent leather.

Until the card came she had again lapsed into despair; the thing was finished. When she got it she asked herself, face downward and sobbing on her bed, why she must go. She made no pretense now that she could stay away.

Made wary by experience of him, it now was she who pulled herself into a corner, bastioned and defensive, waiting for what he chose to fling at her. And as if by forcing her to this cover and retreat he could afford expansion, he was open in a way which two rides previously she would have misinterpreted.

"You're a dinger, but I guess you know that." His eyes rested on the small flat forward chip of straw, afloat with lilac daisies, which he had twice previously appeared not to see; his eyes moved downward to her widened shoulders in airy lilac muslin, dropped to her small waist.

"But you look lonesome, too, away off there. Here, keep me com pany." Cozily he put out his arm to draw her nearer. As if there had never been anything but sympathy between them, he talked of future plans he had. He wouldn't work forever for that outfit in De Laittre; those gents in De Laittre knew their job, but they were pushers now, they didn't need him. What he'd do was wait until he found a yard owned by some old gink with no children, then he'd get a bunch of capital together and buy in. There was no limit to the sky, the way he saw it. Take a smart young guy, a pusher—a fellow like that wouldn't have to stop with one yard. Get yourself set, save the profits up and buy another, get those two set, buy a third. By the time a man was forty there wasn't any reason why he couldn't cover half the state, maybe even have a big yard in Meridian.

She sat mummy-wrapped inside his arm, her sores tightly under the bandages of self-protection. But around her in the dark the dream that he unfolded fell like ointment.

Yes, she could not keep from thinking, yes, of course, that was the way. He was the one, the quintessence of Those Others; he knew his way ahead so surely. Her wrappings fallen away, she wanted to cry at him, "Me too; this would be a dream for me too! I know about trying, I know about working, I know about saving; it would be something we could do together. Forget I am foreign, forget I don't belong; I do belong, this dream of yours is mine."

But she did not dare say it. As if in punctuation to his words, after a while, he began kissing her lightly as they rode, leaning sideward to drop the little contacts anywhere about her face, leaning back to say recklessly and headily that there was no telling, maybe he might even someday do his own lumbering, own his own camps. Timber wasn't all gone yet, not by a long shot.

Stammeringly she interpolated small humble offerings. No one had to tell her that he was a comer. If anyone could do it, he could. Mr. Voorhees of the West Haven yard of course was a young man, with children, but somewhere there must be childless old men in the lumber business. And then, daringly, that it shouldn't be hard for him to get capital, with the father he had.

At this he fell, at once, into ugly silence, in which she felt him staring at her with shrewd, hard, cold eyes. Caught in an undertow, like drowning, she threshed back toward the surface. Anyone—a banker, even—would gamble on a young man so sure of success.

The hard gleam faded, some of the ugliness melted from his mouth. More boisterously he kissed her again, pausing to tie the reins to the whipsocket and then kissing her again, squeezing her shoulders in big hands.

"You've got the makings of a devil," he said thickly. "I guess you're young yet, but I've got an idea what you'll be." Placing his flat hand against her bosom, pressing her away from him, he at the same time pulled her toward him with the arm along her back.

"Ouch!" she objected childishly. "That hurts!"

"You'll have horns under that hat," he went on as if she hadn't interrupted. "And maybe, if I stop this buggy now——" The kiss that followed was long and slow, as reaching as the ones she remembered. "Look." His voice had become thin and distant, as he rocked his face against her mouth. "I don't suppose you'd want to—go farther?"

"Farther?" she repeated. "You mean ride farther? Of course, if you want to."

His head stopped rocking. "Don't even know what I'm talking about, do you?" he asked flatly. "That's what I've worried about—your being sixteen. Don't you forget, sometime, that I did this. We'll go back."

He took her to Gisela's, making no pretense that he didn't know where she'd be staying. Before the house he kissed her a last time.

"I'll see you again," he promised. "I'll see you as damn much and as damn little as I can stand. Maybe I'll even keep on seeing you till you're grown up." Taking off her hat, he ruffled her hair over her head, then stood up in the buggy, swung her out over the wheel and set her on the ground.

"Don't forget me," he mocked for a final gesture, and was gone.

She had little time to think about it then.

Running with head bent and throat and heart on fire, she made for Gisela's front door. Schatzi, from inside, jerked it open.

"Frieda!" Schatzi's face was bloodless, her mouth working, her eyes blank. "It's Gehsi! I didn't dare get Mama because then Mama'd know you weren't here, she'd know everything. I'll stay here—you run, Frieda; get the doctor, get Herman, quick!"

In the second in which it took her to orient herself, to hear from deeper in the house a horrible low racking moan, she got from Schatzi what had happened. Running pell-mell toward downtown West Haven, she reached her own hysteria; after this she never would forget Schatzi, never. Maybe up to this she hadn't really been a friend to Schatzi, not all the way down. But from now on she would be. She would do anything for Schatzi. Coming home an hour earlier and finding Gehsi in labor, Schatzi had persuaded Gehsi not to send out for anyone until Frieda got home, so Frieda wouldn't be found out.

Not until morning did she have time for any other thought.

The doctor had not been at home. With equal wildness she had had to run across town, to some house vaguely named as "Nelson's," where the doctor was said to be assisting at another labor. With no idea of what house might be Nelson's, she recklessly had banged at doors—it was then two in the morning—until she found out. The doctor had been washing his hands in a blue enamel basin on a reservoir while a naked baby screamed in an old woman's hands his protest at this entry into an alien and hurting world. At Frieda's face, more than at her spent words, the doctor had thrown instruments into a bag.

No, she couldn't ride with him, she had to find Herman. With no feeling that she might have saved herself she ran after the doctor's buggy down the road; in the main street of West Haven she burst into saloons, unseeing of the stares, unhearing of comments, until, at the one from which the boys had streamed out at her on Shindy Day, she had found Herman lounged somnolently on the bar.

That, even, had not been the end. At Gehsi's, when she got Herman there, she found the doctor frantically working at the stove, while Schatzi, wringing her hands, cowered in a corner.

"But I don't know how to make a fire," Schatzi was moaning. "I never had to."

"No fire!" The sweating small round man roared at Herman. "No hot water!" before he bounced back to the bedroom. It had seemed to Frieda that she was too tired when she got there, her lungs could draw in breath only for existence. But she still had debts to pay. Herman seemed as ague-struck as Schatzi. The range was unfamiliar, old and stubborn, but she lit a fire finally, it seemed, with heat from her own body, got water on. At sounds which came then from the little bedroom, Schatzi collapsed and Herman came out of paralysis to go crazy, forcing fuel into the firebox until the fire was almost choked out, running out for more wood, grinning at himself in the sink mirror, falling into a chair to drop his head into his arms.

The doctor dashed out.

"You!" He barked at Frieda, "You're alive, get in here and help!"

She assisted then at the savage needs of birth. Pinioned the spread arms of a screaming women on the bed, reddened the lilac dress with blood, held in her hands at last a bawling scrap that might have been just transformed from the house where she had found the doctor.

Only this one was a girl.

All that day at Hake's, with the thing done, Gehsi resting, Schatzi recovered, Mrs. Klaumeister puffing and beaming (*she* could beam, thought Frieda, but without rancor), after she had been given a coat of Herman's to put over her bloody dress so she could get home, Frieda moved about, tranced, but in no darkness. In, instead, a brutal, clear and blinding light.

No one had to tell her now. She knew. The warnings her mother had whispered. Screams from Gisela during the long night. Quarrels she had overheard, from her parents' room. All the words she had been taught, that were chalked on walks and walls.

Not something distant, vague, intangible, attached to other people. Not unreasonable, ridiculous, ununderstandable, but something close, attached to her.

Marriage itself had been her goal; she had not thought of what would follow it, except in terms of money, social standing and assurance. Now she knew that this other thing, too, was supposed to happen after marriage. *That*—at last she had the key—was (although this still was hard to understand) what made men marry.

But it could, as her mother had warned, take place outside marriage, too, if a girl wasn't careful. That had been what Palmer meant, last night, when he asked about going farther.

CHAPTER XI

Gehsi at one bound moved from despond to fervor. Gehsi lay with the sleeping infant on her arm, flooding it with maternal transports and with milk, Gehsi erased ravage from her mind. Schatzi, who hadn't been in the bedroom, also made haste to cover fright: "It can't be so *bad*," said Schatzi, "because Gehsi *did* come out all right, and if you think—well, that it might be for somebody like Harry——"

Mrs. Klaumeister, bustling authoritatively in the bedroom, dandling, mooning, in the fullness of her rapture even lending her own Hedda to the Feldt household and diapers, never seemed to have known. Herman Feldt and Karl Klaumeister, drowning in unison their gloom at the sex of the product, had no apparent afterthought for pain.

But for Frieda the birth initiated a panic in which she turned not only from Palmer but from living. If that was what there was in marriage, she wanted none of it. Women didn't usually have just one child, either; her own mother had five. Women like her mother must be fools. Any woman must be a fool to marry, to let herself in for that long distortion, for that final wrenching agony.

Her future now appeared as a thing of strict confines, with only two passages open, both of them hedged and walled, the one perhaps, if she could get Palmer, leading into the gold-chased valuables of security, leisure, assurance, the lovely envy of those less fortunate, but still concealing, under its silken coverings, that raw red crucifixion; the other always constricted, always plain and close to poverty, but still unmarred by nightmare—old-maidhood like Miss Shatto's.

It was a prospect before which she turned and twisted. Housewives she knew as childless came into the store; with down-drawn lips and hungry eyes on any infant, these women were apt to say that God had not seen fit to bless them, but to Frieda this sounded like hypocrisy; such women must, she thought, have some secret they kept in store. Since almost always it was the more comfortable rather than the poorer women who were childless, this was one of the many secrets, perhaps, held by affluence. *If she married Palmer he might know that secret*—but she did not feel she could depend upon it. Tacit in the air around her, an assumption so widespread that she held it long before she knew it, was the fact accepted by her generation as by her mother's—in the peculiar physical activities of marriage, men insisted, women gave in. If only, she thought with despair, she could marry and force Palmer not to insist. But she was practically certain Palmer was like other men; he would insist. He had asked, already.

That week when Eddie went to the post office she trembled all the while he was gone. When on Wednesday the card came her eyes cringed from the well-known words. Every ride, she knew now, was a trap which might be sprung. This time she really wouldn't go, she'd even write Palmer at his work to tell him. But day passed day until it was too late, and on Sunday she was underneath the elm.

In the buggy she quivered away each time Palmer's hand came near her, until he asked crossly, "What's the matter? You're as jumpy as a stung horse." But he himself had returned to more distance. Not too ardently he kissed her just twice, contacts against which she cried beseechingly, "No, don't! Don't, please!"

Instead of insisting, he lapsed into moodiness, which he broke, abruptly, only once.

"You wouldn't know Miss Amiot." His voice carried recklessness. "Cecilia Amiot. She's in Europe. With her mother. In Italy. They say she's got a beau, now. An Italian count. Jessie Drake gets letters, and— get up, there!"

The last, with no break or preamble, was to the horse. Snatching the whip from the socket, he lashed at the startled beast until it broke into long loping strides. For the rest of the evening he drove furiously, to Frieda's weak "No, I don't know her" making no response.

After this he did not see her until school had opened, in October. During the weeks of absence she alternately hugged the release, and despaired. She couldn't get him; he was still thinking of Cecilia Amiot. But why should she care? This was the safe way, just to go about her work at Hake's. Mr. Hake raised her to five dollars, half for her father, half for her. She saw before her Miss Shatto's circumscribed small life, a refuge.

For a day she glimpsed another refuge, too.

During the past two years of change her relation to the Church had remained much as it was; out of habit, out of lassitude, out of disinclination to increase trouble and suspicion at home, out of companionship—Schatzi was dutiful at her devotions—she had continued to appear at Mass each Sunday, and to make her unthought, impenitent confessions and communions.

To her annoyance, Father Doern had added to his whispered list of questions: "My child, have you not been touched by worldly ambition? Are you not addicted to the vanity of dress?" The first phrase had no relation, for her, to her desperate hungers, to her longings for money, place and superiority; she answered no without compunction. To the second she had, after a while, begun answering a sullen yes. Her liking for dress was too evident, even to her.

Why she performed the penances she could not have said. Before her first communion, when she was nine, she had had a brief period of religious interest. Unless you conformed to certain observances, she had gathered, you died and went to hell. Only it was not her body that would go, but some inner inhabitant of herself called a soul. With the fingers of her consciousness she had poked about in herself, but found neither the location nor the entity.

All this had quickly been submerged in her old dullness, but in her hunted new inquiet she now found—for what reason she again could not have said—some interest in the Church reviving. At Mass on Sundays she long had been a strange figure among the aliens. There they sat on the benches about her—evasive, uncouth, formless, cast into some inner concentration of devotion, of which the outward signs were the blank inturned eye, the mumbling lip, the humbled droop of shoulder; there she sat, shaped, clothed beautifully, open-sensed, alert, with nothing going on in her interior but the normal processes of a pumping blood stream and digestion.

On the Sunday two weeks after the birth of Gehsi's baby, however, something different did occur—the walls of her body enlarged, moved away from her; she for an instant had a sense of peace and spaciousness. As soon as she tried to grasp it, it was gone, but uncomfortably she wanted its return. That next Friday, although it wasn't a full month since her last confession, she knelt at the small familiar window, whispering her stock replies.

"Have you," Father Doern asked, as inexpectant of an honest answer as she was of giving one, "lent yourself to lusts of the flesh? To evil thoughts and companions?"

"No," she said. "No." Then, resting her cheek against the shelf, feeling the collapse of everything she had made herself, she whispered without thought or preparation, "I think I want to be a nun."

For once Father Doern paused. And when he next spoke he had dropped the rhythm of his questioning chant.

"Many girls at your age feel the desire to be brides of the Church. For most, this will is only temporary; for most the way of life is a more human marriage, the bringing of new souls into the world for Church and God." The words fall wearily, sadly, rationally. "Before you think of such a step you must prayerfully scrutinize your heart, your soul, your conscience; you must know what your life as a nun would be, you must be certain you have a true vocation for the Church. I admit I have not seen the signs in you, but you can come to talk with me in my study. Now for your confession——"

By the time she reached Hake's next morning, the idea was already lost and impossible; she didn't know why she had had it. This was the way the world was—selling, buying; it wasn't shut up behind thick walls in black whispering and concealing veils.

In revulsion against safety, too, in revulsion against a life of no struggle, she knew she could bear neither seclusion nor the narrowness of Miss Shatto's lot; she could not give up what she had visioned —Palmer and the money, and with them the necessities that came back in full strength. All she asked of him was his kiss, his touch. If this was enough for her, why not for him? At night she clasped her pillow, rolling her cheek against the casing, trying to elicit from the indifferent stuff some contact that was flesh.

Since she never went to Father Doern's study, the priest sought her out at home. She told him then, confusedly, that she had been mistaken. The only aftereffect of her aberrant impulse was a rather alarmed gravity in the attitudes of Otto and Ilse. The priest urged her not to lose what she had glimpsed; it would, he said, deepen her spirit, even in a secular life. To Frieda this meant nothing; she didn't realize that the sight of a way out, even if she didn't take it, had made her uncertainties more tolerable.

In October, with no explanation for neglect or renewal, Palmer one Sunday stopped her as she was hurrying home from Gisela's at suppertime, to ask if she would ride. Through the winter sometimes once a month, sometimes twice, he picked her up in buggy or sleigh, drove into the country for two hours or three, talked negligently, listened when she spoke, kissed or put his arms around her—caresses which she could not wait for him to give, yet which she always—the wings of fear fluttering at his touch—protested and fought off.

This was the way things were in April, when Cecilia Amiot came home.

Schatzi brought the news.

Spring was late that year, the days chill. Schatzi, blowing in through Hake's door on a gust of damp wind, still wore her seal-trimmed pelisse, her sealskin muff and hat with seal banding; against the black her flying hair was more than ever flaxen, her cheeks more than ever pink.

"Frieda! The most absolutely——" Such was the expansive power of Schatzi's information that her skin looked filled tight, like an over-extended balloon. "She's *here!* Nobody's seen her, but she's *here!*" In the seclusion of the jacket racks, further disclosures were let loose in a dire whisper. "Frieda, if you want Palmer you had better grab him; he did *go* with her and we know it. They say—anyway, Jessie Drake said so to Harry—that she'll bet the count has thrown Cecilia over, and her heart is broken. Frieda, whatever will you do?"

Schatzi, for some time, had been a bit petulant with Frieda; Schatzi's eyes now carried more than sympathy, they carried a healthy spark of "You'll find out!" She couldn't see, Schatzi had said, what did ail Frieda. What if you suffered a little in marriage? You had to expect to suffer anyway, and look what Gehsi got out of it. You could look over the whole state and never find a cuter, sweeter, more dimpled darling than Gehsi's baby. Either Frieda wanted to marry Palmer or she didn't. Anyway, she, Schatzi, knew her mind; she and Harry practically were engaged.

Frieda, meeting the look in the blue eyes, managed to lift her shoulders.

"Do?" she echoed. "Why should I do anything?" Yet the electricity from Schatzi spread and prickled in her own nerves. She had had no need to have the *she* of Schatzi's telling given an identity. "You wouldn't know Miss Amiot. You wouldn't know Cecilia Amiot." Just that once Palmer had spoken the other girl's name, but she had not had the illusion that Palmer had forgotten. Whatever there was between Palmer and Cecilia—it couldn't have been so much that Cecilia couldn't go off afterward and engage herself to an Italian count—had made marks on Palmer.

She, though, had made marks on him too. Alone behind the jacket racks, with Schatzi at last gone, she felt it, felt it with a power she hadn't had since—when was it, a year ago?—Palmer had invited her, that first time, to De Laittre and the never-repeated supper at the Habakanaw.

She had never before stood off to assess her meetings with him as a whole, but now as she did so she knew that he too had been pulled into these later meetings, helpless but resisting. If that was true, if the pull was as strong for him as it was for her, then foreign and poor as she was she might be able to hold him even against Cecilia Amiot.

She could remember when she had thought, If only Cecilia Amiot will stay away, maybe I'll have a chance. But now she greeted the return almost with welcome. People would see who got Palmer. Whatever awaited her with him—fire, flood or a dozen childbirths, she had to keep him from Cecilia Amiot.

Permanently breathless, Schatzi popped in with bulletins.

"It isn't true she isn't seeing anybody. Jessie Drake went to the house and Cecilia was just thrilled she came. Cecilia said it wasn't a word true about that count—oh, she had a beau, but she didn't care a bit; she said Italians were so *mercenary*——"

"Frieda, I *saw* her! She's in at Pratt's Drugs right this minute! She's got on simply the most divine dove-gray—Frieda, if you slipped out just one tweenchy-weenchy minute, no one would care——"

"She stopped Harry smack on the street, and shook hands with him. Anyway, she held up her right hand high, like this, and let him take two fingers. She asked how was everyone, and how was his friend, Palmer. Frieda, she uses French words and Italian *both,* mixed in!"

Frieda waved pennants of indifference. Run down the street like a child at a parade, to see Cecilia Amiot? Not she. Cecilia was asking about Palmer, was she? Let her. She, Frieda, had an appointment with Palmer for this next Sunday.

Palmer, on that ensuing ride, was a little noisy and a little boisterous, whipping the horse until the buggy careened and Frieda had hard work keeping her hat on and herself inside the buggy. But at last, when he let the spent beast stumble breathily as it would, he was unusually affectionate and unusually vocal.

"You know, Frieda, me and you get along all right. We do, don't we? With me, you're a queen, and nobody can say different."

He did not kiss her much; instead he rubbed his face against her cheek, holding her closely. That night he did something he had never before done; he asked her, when he let her out at Gehsi's, for another ride on the next Sunday. Flying up the path to Gehsi's door—no terror could be waiting, this time—Frieda's feet moved to a lilt. There was a *limit* to how awful it was to be foreign and poor. Palmer had just the same as told her she was his girl. Cecilia Amiot could go hang.

For all of April she was certain he did not see Cecilia. Then in May, although he made no break in his rides with her, she was as certain he did. Schatzi had it straight from Jessie Drake through Harry— Palmer had walked up to the Amiot house early one Sunday afternoon, dressed fit to kill; he'd knocked and bowed and taken his hat off.

"How do you do?" he had asked the maid. "Is Miss Amiot home? Miss Cecilia Amiot?" And then, to Cecilia, "Why didn't I know you were back? I've been out of town——"

All afternoon, Jessie said, he had sat in Cecilia's father's parlor, by

Cecilia's father's parlor fire, listening to what Cecilia had done in Europe, and he had stayed for tea.

Straight from there (this was Schatzi) he must have gone to pick up Frieda, because Frieda had ridden with him that evening, hadn't she? Frieda, who had, felt explanation striking with the news; that was why Palmer had been, again, so turbulent, why he had whipped up the horse, been rough and reckless with her.

With a queer, sick feeling of being gradually and visibly pushed back, she now had to see in Palmer the growing measure of the other girl's firm hold. No more was she glad Cecilia Amiot had come back. For two Sundays longer Palmer still made dates when he left her, but on the third Sunday he did not. She saw him, but it was late; he knocked at Gehsi's door at ten o'clock, when Schatzi was already back from being out with Harry, and the two girls were preparing for bed.

"Come on." What he threw at her was a brusque order. "I've got the horse and buggy outside."

He was wearing his best brown suit, but somehow—mostly it was his tumbled hair and lax mouth—he looked mussed; as soon as she was near him in the buggy she knew he had stopped for at least one drink. That night, again, he drove swiftly, almost viciously; it had been months since he had stopped, but now he went straight to the grove which he had long ago promised she would see in better light, stopped the horse, tied him to the log fence, swung her down.

"Frieda!" he said. "You're the girl I ought to marry. Why aren't you someone else?" She had no illusion he was proposing; the words were a groan, a cry against fate; this time he reached for her as if for comfort, resting himself against her, not so much pulling her toward him as pulling himself toward her. His kisses held the flavor of whisky and a bitter indecision.

"How did I ever get into this?" he asked. "How did I?"

As if he were compelled even out of his most inherent trait, secretiveness, he now almost openly let her see how he vacillated.

The late Sunday drives continued, and grew later; sometimes he did not bring her back to Gehsi's until three or four in the morning. As she slunk indoors she knew her reputation would be gone if by any mischance she were caught, but this danger was nothing against the real jeopardy.

Palmer one night had taken the lap robe from the rig and had lain a long time with his head in her lap; now he wanted her to lie beside him on the robe. She had only to think of Gehsi to keep herself well bastioned, but she could feel accumulating in him a hunger of such power that she was frightened.

No more than before, however, could she take herself away; she couldn't say, "No, I won't ride," when he came out of the dark to Gehsi's door; she had to go with him, had to have him want her. That was what she had.

Early in June he took a short vacation. That week he was in West Haven, staying at his father's, seeing Cecilia, she knew, every day, but seeing her too every evening, even if only for a short walk because—it not being Sunday—she had no excuse for getting home late. It did not occur to her that she had no reason for furtiveness; all approaches between young men and women, she thought, were secret.

This week again he was bitter, moody, going so far as to reproach her.

"Why d'you go out with me for? Why don't you say you won't go? You know now what I want——"

He had used the word "marry" to her, but she dared not say, "Marry me and you'll have me." All she dared do was infer it with a sullenness equal to his.

"There's a way out of that."

He did not mistake what she meant. Plunging at once into deeper glumness, he ended that night's walk.

"I'm going out and get drunk. I'll take you home."

The next day he walked into Hake's with Cecilia Amiot.

After he left her that night she had gone in with a small sense of assuagement and relief; at least she had made her position plain—he couldn't have her outside marriage. Foreign or not, what did he think she was? They weren't unknown in West Haven, girls like Kitty Heenan who let themselves go without marriage, who bore babies in unutterable shame, who were whispered at, giggled at, pointed at, denounced to their faces, and from whom respectable women turned away on the street. She, Frieda, with her looks and style, become a Kitty Heenan? Palmer must be—no, men didn't think, they thought only of what they wanted. All this had been implicit in her mother's warnings. A girl had to look out for herself. A man would take anything he could get.

She hadn't remembered George Bibbensack for months, but when Palmer and Cecilia came inside the door of Hake's, it was George, peculiarly, who immediately filled her mind with his emptied face, his random gestures; if she weren't careful she would drop the bolt of ribbon she was winding. Pale blue baby ribbon. It would lie around her feet in loops, and she would have to bend in terrible indignity to pick it up.

At once, to the finest hair, she knew all that was visible of the two who came in, Cecilia Amiot floating forward in a dress outside anything ever before seen in West Haven—pale heliotrope shot with green, over its shoulders a short jacket of black lace. Each sleeve of that jacket, rounded and ballooned between shoulder and elbow, was much larger than the part that could be called the jacket. That, unquestionably, was a Paris gown; Frieda had studied enough now, read enough in Schatzi's magazines, to know Frenchness when she saw it. On the head, held so imperiously high, sat a tiny, stiff-brimmed hat with accordion-pleated black lace spread to look like wings. Rozzie could never copy that hat, never, even if she had the starched black lace. And the hair beneath it—Cecilia's fringe was gone; the corn-silk stuff was fluffed from a center parting. The new Grecian hairdress. On Cecilia's cheekbones burned two high, bright circles. Paint. No, not paint. Disdain and anger.

Anger at Palmer, who, for some never-known reason, was trailing at her heels like a disgraced pup. Frieda knew of that anger, too, before Cecilia had had time to turn toward dry goods. Miss Shatto had a customer on the balcony. But even so Frieda did not move. She let Cecilia come to her.

"You *won't* have any jet." It came not as a question but as a petulant statement, with the opaque, unseeing eyes fixed on a point three feet from Frieda's face.

"Jet?" repeated Frieda stupidly. She knew well enough what jet was.

"Yes. Surely you know *jet.* In medallions, sewn on lace. Some of mine was torn. I must get some."

Slowly Frieda shook her head. If anyone else had asked, she would have laughed. "You'd have to go to Meridian for jet."

Lightly Cecilia stamped a small foot. "Isn't that typical? This town! I declare, anyone is *cursed* to live here! Palmer!"

Palmer, as she sailed out, kept his face, with its mixture of abjection and defiance, turned toward Frieda.

"Sunday." His lips formed the word, although he made no sound.

She stood a long time, that night, fingers gripping the cracked marble slab which topped the washstand under her mirror.

Inside the glass (a bigger one than her old one, bought with her own money) was held her intent figure, her eyes riveted to their thought, her mouth fined to a thin short line, her brown-black glossy hair, which she had parted in the middle and fluffed at the sides, then immediately brushed back again into a fringe. She wouldn't be caught dead imitating Cecilia Amiot.

In her mind was not herself, but Palmer's half-submerging face as she had seen it last. She had never before looked plainly at what Palmer wanted, but she did so now.

Cecilia had walked in advance of Palmer, superciliously. It was so apparent what Cecilia had: she was the best in West Haven, and Palmer always had to have the best, in clothes, in rigs, in food, in queens. For the first time, in spite of his highhanded bluster, she knew Palmer as uncertain, saw his efforts to maintain himself as a champion trickster, as a leading spirit. Yet—something inside her flew immediately to his defense—he had so *much;* he didn't have to make an effort; he really was the best. All the boys said so, all the girls, even Cecilia must know, or she wouldn't want him. It was only that he, himself, wanted continually to be reminded.

Behind Cecilia were all the other things Cecilia had. Family. Prestige. Clothes of mysterious loveliness such as no one else in West Haven had. A home of unimagined richness, where people did not even open their own doors, but moved serene, unlaboring, about nothing but their own adornment and pleasure. A father——

Gripping harder on the marble, so that the hard, frictionless and waxy surface seemed to grow into her hands, she saw Thomas Amiot, his personal lordliness, his bank, his mill. "I'll get some capital together"—it must be a lot Palmer wanted, more even than Junius Hake would allow him. The son-in-law of Thomas Amiot would not lack for capital. "By the time a man gets to be forty, there isn't any reason why he can't cover half the state, and maybe even have a big yard in Meridian." Palmer's ambitions ran high, and with Cecilia it must all look so easy.

She, Frieda, what had she to give him? She, who came of this cheap small loathly house, these cheap, small, foreign people? She, who had nothing but her style, her looks—and what he wanted?

Her looks, and his hunger. Hunger enough, maybe, to overcome even her foreignness. Well, she had learned a way. *Manipulate*——

With terror falling through her breast in warm, slow, liquid drops, she knew what she must do. She didn't have much time; that too she knew; Palmer had been driven and desperate; he perhaps was deciding. Palmer had wanted her before, but he must want her more; enough so everything Cecilia had would shrink beside it. This Sunday she would have to let him go so far that he would have to have her, so far that he would even marry her to get her.

Decision was around her like a shell, a casing, inside which the knowledge of her danger moved and lapped. She didn't dare tempt him, but she had to. She who had always been so careful, she who had kept his hands away——

Once in the terror moved a stir like laughter. Ever since Gehsi, Palmer had accused her of being a touch-me-not. This time he would be surprised.

CHAPTER XII

The surprise was hers.

Motionless and face downward beside Schatzi on the bed at Gehsi's, Monday morning found her numbed by what she had done.

It could not be possible. That *she*—not Palmer, but *she*—could have been driven so far from her purposes. Where had she been wrong in her planning? From what well had come the overwhelming impulse which had pushed her, helpless, toward catastrophe?

Over and over she relived the pulse in which they had started riding, the heat and dryness of the summer night which had lain like a light fever on her skin; as in the mirages of a fever she had known the night and the necessities of what she intended doing.

Palmer had been reckless again, hugging her against him, but keeping the whip in the hand that held the reins.

"You like me, don't you, Frieda? You think I'm all right, don't you, Frieda?" He had been smarting, she guessed, from the quarrel with Cecilia, released by drinks he again had taken.

"Oh no, of course, you've only got more flash than any other young fellow in West Haven; you're no good; I wouldn't want to get seen out with *you*——" She had been arch, while pains like cramps tore at her abdomen. *Careful. Careful.*

And then she had heard for sure how really little time she had.

"I haven't told you, Frieda. I guess I've found my lumberyard. Right here in West Haven. Voorhees is going West; he's got a cough. All this week I've been dickering. I'll want to get a lot of new stock; there's a big chance here. Farms ripe for building. Why——"

As he had gone on, talking of what he'd do in West Haven with his yard, she had seen with clarity what he was giving her; it was his explanation. "If I marry Cecilia," he could as well have said, "I get all this. Marry you, and I stick on at De Laittre, God knows how long."

All the time, while he was telling her, while he was saying half-heartedly, "Maybe we shouldn't stop tonight," while she was answering, "I don't care, if you want to," while she was sitting with his head in her lap, smoothing his hair back from his temples until he was almost quiet, while he was pulling her down to lie beside him, while his hand had cupped around her breast and with the queer small whimper he had buried his face in her neck—all that she still heard was the thundering whisper, *Careful,* with the twinges in her body which were its physical and fearful counterpart.

But then something happened to the night. Heat lightning tore across the sky; from far away a different air came fingering—moist, soft, gently scented like cut grass; that would go, the light dry heat surrounded her, but then the softness had returned. At some time the whisper *Careful* had gone, too, and the fear; instead she had been drowned in the other thing that swept her, the thing which had made her reach for Palmer as terribly as he reached for her.

"It can t be true! It can't!" she had sobbed, later. Impossibility—that had loomed above everything else there might have been—wonder, and release, and the shock of knowing. The impossibility of being so false to herself.

The idea that there could be a way out for her, even from this, had come from Palmer.

"It'll be all right," Palmer had said, as a promise. "It'll be all right, Frieda——"

In new spasms of anguish, suffering new wrenching lunges of the terror, she had faced then what she thought inevitable. "Palmer!" she had screamed. "You'll have to marry me! You'll have to! I can't be like Kitty Heenan; you wouldn't let me be like Kitty; Palmer, think about me, Palmer——"

"Of course I'll marry you," he had said. "What do you think? We'll run away to Meridian." All the way back to West Haven he had planned how it would be. Since his vacation was up, he would have to go back to De Laittre in the morning, to see about things there. It would take him a day or two, probably—he'd have to decide what to do about the Voorhees deal. He'd wind things up, though, as soon as he could. He'd come in on the Midnight from De Laittre, and they could go on to Meridian that same morning. Thursday, perhaps, or Friday; even if it was a week it made no difference. She'd better get her things packed, but she'd better keep it quiet, too. If it got to his father——

Over Junius Hake as she knew him was superimposed the image of a father, a martinet who would never assist any intended marriage of his children, but who, once the marriage was made, must meekly bless the young couple and "get them started."

"Your father will give you the money you want, Palmer, I know he will." She too made promises.

"Sure he will," Palmer had replied.

A gush of rain hit them, before they reached Gehsi's, with real lightning and real thunder; to Frieda it was in one piece with the night. After the first rushing spatter came a lighter, softer fall, like steady tears, which fell not only outside but inside her. At the last Palmer didn't want to let her get down from the buggy. Catching her back, he over and over gave her one more kiss, until a faint spark leavened her prostration. Maybe he was irrevocably tied, maybe he wouldn't let her go, maybe she wasn't ruined.

If that was so, then she had succeeded in what she set out to do. But lying beside Schatzi on a tumbled bed, with light drifting upward through the shadows in the room, she was possessed more by the holocaust than by the hope.

She must look ravaged, she thought, as ravaged as Gehsi after childbirth. She would have to rise before Schatzi woke, so she could go——

Where? Where could she hide what everyone must see? When, having slipped heavily from bed—her weight, she thought, had doubled in the night—she forced her eyes to the mirror, what she felt was a dull, slow incredulity. She seemed to look as usual on a Monday morning: hair disarranged, eyes half eclipsed behind crescent puffs from lack of sleep, small mouth lax and drooping. Even when, surreptitiously, she glanced down the neck of her nightgown (scrupulously she and Schatzi dressed under their gowns; any nice girl, Schatzi said, dressed that way, even when alone) the dull surprise only deepened. Her body, too, showed no apparent change.

With the easing of Schatzi's breath for warning, she had time to let the gown fall to her breast and to turn aside for her clothes before Schatzi sat up with a bound.

"Frieda! What time did you get in last night? Frieda, you can't let Palmer keep you out so late! If anyone saw you——" Scolding and sleep-fogged, Schatzi apparently saw no differences either.

It didn't show, Frieda herself at last accepted, with an interior relaxing which extended to much more than her muscles. It didn't show—so far. The unreality of not having it show made everything else unreal too—the clang of stove lids from the kitchen, the baby howling, Herman shouting—everything that was so normal for a Monday, when the Monday wasn't normal. Her clothes still fit, even her corsets; with Schatzi she slipped out quietly, not to bother Gehsi, and from habit she took the way home for breakfast. Rain lay in reminiscent pools in every hollow, rain filled the deep ruts in the street, but a bright sun shone; the same sun that had shone on her as a virgin. In the Schlempke kitchen her father lifted toward her only a half glance and a grunt, her mother rested on her the longer, troubled look which was her wont, but they too saw nothing.

For an instant, as she stood in the doorway, she felt the tug of wanting to cry at them what had happened; it could be wonderful, like falling into strong holding arms, to let herself go. She could lie in bed, then, doing nothing, letting the acid show where it bit her flesh— Palmer will never marry me; what can I do? That, she thought, with a swamping inflow of self-pity, was what any other girl could do; any other girl could at least say she wasn't feeling well and stay in bed; girls who moped about at home were always sick. But she couldn't; not she, Frieda: she had work to go to.

All that day, at the store, she strained at deception. *This* was the way I used to go up to customers, she told herself. I asked, "Could I show you this new silk, ma'am?" and then I held out the length of fabric, this way. But when she moved it was as if she were sleepwalking.

I've become blind, she thought. No, I'm not blind, it's just that light isn't what I see in, any more. It's better for me when it's dark. Palmer —maybe when he gets to De Laittre he can fix what he's got to fix right away. Maybe he had money enough in the bank for our trip. Maybe he'll be back on the train tonight and I'll only have this one day to wait; maybe tomorrow I'll be on my way to Meridian.

Maybe tomorrow is my wedding day.

With hands hot and cold, she cut cloth, made change, dropped change, fumbled for it with unguided fingers since she had no vision, feeling the raised brows on the faces she could not see. Again she relived the night. This was the way it had started—the evening had been hot and dry. The dryness and the cicadas had rasped against her skin—— It was impossible, not that Palmer had betrayed her, but that she had betrayed herself; impossible most of all that she couldn't turn the clock back as little as twelve hours so it would be undone. It could never happen the same way a second time.

Although there had been no time for Palmer to send a card, each of Eddie's trips for mail made her tremble. Get your things packed, Palmer had said; I'll come in on the Midnight and we'll leave for

Meridian that same day. There were deep holes in the planning—
where would he find her? How would she get her clothes from
home? He hadn't thought—*why should he, when he never intended*
—no, no, he had intended; he must know how she waited; he would
send some sign.

At night, when her mother went out to garden, she sneaked into
her room the telescope which had come with her father from Nuremberg, and which had accompanied the family wanderings ever since.
In it, with somnambulistic neatness, she packed her best clothes. If
I unpack this, it will be as Palmer's wife, she thought, but that like
everything else was unreal. She saw no vision of herself in a hotel
room, kneeling by the opened case, while Palmer lounged on a bed
near by. After the case was packed and strapped she stared at it, then
at the nails where her clothes had hung, the emptied drawers. When
Ilse straightened the room in the morning, Ilse would at once know
what was planned. Immediately she had this thought she began to
unpack, scattering the garments where they had been, hiding the
telescope under the bed. If Palmer came for her she would have to
take her chances with clothes.

She had thought she must lie awake all night, but slept the moment
her head touched the pillow. On Tuesday morning the mail brought
a card. "Everything fine," it said. Just the two words, but fireflies of
hope spotted the dense medium around her. It wasn't true he wouldn't
marry her. He had sent a sign.

From then on, although the sense of moving blindly in an opaque
tank persisted, she felt strong, uplifted. Not until Thursday did something like paralysis begin again. Thursday or Friday, Palmer had
said; this, then, was the first possible day. He might be waiting somewhere, lurking in a doorway between her home and Hake's; she lingered. By ten she knew that day was gone. It would have to be the
next day. Or Saturday or Monday. Even if it was a week, Palmer had
said, but he hadn't known what waiting was like.

Eddie, when he came back with the first mail that day, walked
straight toward her. He had no card for her, he just stood before
her, looking yet not looking at her, with a queer stiffness about his
too long, too thin nose, his too wide forehead, his too narrow, weak
jaw.

"Miss Schlempke," he said. "I——" That was as far as he got. Of her
fellow employees, Eddie was the only one who knew about the cards.
They weren't signed, but he might have guessed.

"What is it?" she had to ask.

"There was a crowd at the station today. A lot of people went up

to Meridian," he answered at last, but it was after he had appeared
to strangle on something else.

What might he have said? She couldn't ask him. There's a rumor
out—will you, too, be going to Meridian soon? Was that what he
might have asked? She had let nothing out, but had Palmer? Fear
beat its strong wings in her breast, beat again in her throat.

Just after noon Schatzi came into the store, and Schatzi too was
queer. Schatzi ran toward her, but stopped short, her face pale and
twisted, her breath rapid, her eyes big.

"Frieda, I—Frieda, I——" she gasped, and then, as with Eddie,
there was silence, only it was more filled.

Over her own face, her own figure, Frieda's mind flew, groping for
something that might have given her away. There in that bedroom,
on Monday morning, Schatzi might have seen something which she
had since remembered. Schatzi maybe had said something which
had made her mother pounce——

"Schatzi," she asked, shaking the plump arm, which seemed to
shrink from her. "What's wrong?"

"Oh, Frieda," Schatzi whispered, in a tone so low it was woeful.
At once her eyes were wet. Raising a hand to them, she turned and
ran, so blindly she caromed against the door.

Staring after her, Frieda was sure that her secret was out. *That must
be it.* Palmer had told.

At suppertime, however, she knew for sure that wasn't it.

"These little towns, gossip here, gossip there, all the time gossip."
Her father had a casual, indulgent grimace for the frailties of human
nature. "Today in the shop says everyone, Cecilia Amiot is run off
to be married. I wonder how old Thomas Amiot likes that, eh? He
goes to Congress, he is Honorable, he owns the mill, he owns the
bank, he sends the girl to travel, she learns fine languages, she buys
the best, like a queen on a throne she dresses. And then she runs off
like a farm girl to Meridian."

Philosophically he shook his head. "Hake's boy, she marries. Big
sport, drives fast, no good." He shrugged. "That's the kind gets the
girls. You know this Hake's boy, Frieda? By the store you see him,
maybe?"

Flat on her back, rigid, she lay motionless and barely living. So this
was the way it would be. Palmer was gone, now. He was completely
gone. When he hadn't wanted to let her go, that night, when he'd
kissed and caught her back, that had been good-by.

She'd tried to fool herself; she'd tried to believe what he'd promised, tried to believe the card, but she hadn't, really. She'd known this had to come.

For hours at a time she felt nothing. Then without transition, with no sense of waking or coming out of coma, across her consciousness memories or facts drifted, words said, sights seen. She sat with Palmer at supper at the Habakanaw; around her was the light and glitter; it hadn't been as much light or as much glitter as she had expected then, but now it was transcendent brilliance. "You won't catch me marrying—not unless I get something out of it." Palmer from the first had had his feet set on a path, just as she had. She had enticed, she had almost lured him from it, but what she had was not enough, and she had let him take what he wanted for nothing; no, she had given it to him, thrust it at him. She, Frieda, would have to be hideous, contorted and screaming like Gisela, but that too was far away. It didn't show yet; she still had a little time to do what she must do. "I guess I've found my lumberyard. Right here in West Haven." Maybe in all this there was something at which she ought to laugh. She, having nothing but what she gave away, wanting what Cecilia Amiot wanted.

She ought to hate Cecilia Amiot, ought to hate Palmer. But that was the way the world was, that was the way Palmer was. She hated no one. Not quite yet.

All she had was this night, this one night when she could lie here, like this, empty. She didn't know how she had got here, didn't know how she had managed to get here alone. She must have answered her father easily, so he wouldn't guess, "Yes, I've seen him once or twice, in the store." She must have said to her mother, "Schatzi and I talked so long last night, I guess I'll go to bed." Because it had been light when she got here, light when she got here and lay down. Now it was different; darkness had come for a thick cover, or else she had closed her eyes; she had no way of knowing if her eyes were closed or open, no sensation in her eyes or eyelids, just the covered feel of darkness. After a while when it was light again she'd have to walk out of this room and eat and speak. She'd have to go again to Hake's, where she would dust the shelves on her half of the dry-goods side, and when a customer came in——

Not now, though, not quite now. Now she could still lie here, empty.

She didn't know when she first knew what she must do; the pieces seemed to be there, ready. "Don't you girls get Harry drinking," Palmer said. "Get Harry drunk and he'll do anything." That was the big piece, telling her what she had to do. None of the other pieces had much meaning, not Schatzi saying, "If it were for somebody like Harry——"

It was too bad about what she would have to do to Schatzi; best not even to think of Schatzi. Maybe not right at first, but after a while she had grown fond of Schatzi; since that night when Gehsi's baby was born, especially, she had felt almost soft toward Schatzi. Sometimes, since then, Schatzi had been tiresome, but she never had quite forgotten about the other, and it was hard to forget now. Even an approach toward thinking of Schatzi made her twist and writhe upon the bed. If you do what you plan it will kill Schatzi, some echoing voice said, but it was drowned by the other voice. This is my life that's at stake; I've got to. Sometime, later, she could make up with Schatzi; sometime later she could do something nice for Schatzi, sometime later she could make Schatzi understand.

"Manipulate," Mr. Hake once said. "That's a word you'll learn. *Manipulate.*" Mr. Hake's money flew about the balcony; Mr. Hake grew until he touched the ceiling and his shadow filled all space. "Someday it might be yours," he said. He didn't know she had a way to save herself. She still could save herself, as soon as it was morning, when it would become important that she should be saved.

Now she had this night to lie in, broken.

His hand on the balcony railing, Junius Hake looked down. It was getting to be a habit, he thought, standing here at the rail, seeing below him his goods laid on his counters, his five employees and his customers. The act must satisfy him someway—yes, it made him feel that he controlled what he looked down upon, as if he were a puppet-master. Love, money, power—when you were young you wanted love, or what was called love. Then money, and then power. Was he old? Perhaps forty-three was old. If tiredness and detachment and occasional flashes of pain were the stigmata of age, then he was old, had been old for a long time.

He was the father of a married son. The wedding—Mrs. Amiot had gone along, to see that it got done with elegance, or such elegance as was compatible with Palmer's sudden haste—must be over by now, must be consummated, too. Palmer would get his fill of love —or would he, with that disdainful, spoiled young clothes rack? Palmer hadn't married for a body, you had to say that for Palmer. Palmer had kept his eye on the main chance: eight thousand from his father, eight from Thomas Amiot. Ten for the lumberyard, six for household goods. The young couple would start out in style.

Style must be what Palmer wanted. Style certainly would be what

Palmer got. Odd, this past week while Palmer was sweating this thing out, he'd had a queer pity for Palmer, as if Palmer were arranging his own cerements. Cecilia knew what she wanted in one way—he doubted if Palmer really filled the bill. What else did she possess besides assurance? Any judgment? She would need some. Palmer's head was too big for his hat, and, for all he talked so well, Palmer was credulous. What Palmer needed——

Without awareness of direction, his glance threaded through the counters and people like a bird dog hunting through tall waving grass.

Yes, he thought, his lips widening and his eyes deepening as he found what he sought, maybe what Palmer needed was a girl like Frieda. Palmer wouldn't stoop, of course, but maybe she was what he should have had. She had a body to meet his, she had the same fundamental if as yet leashed coarseness. She had something else, too—not mind, you couldn't call it mind. Some focused and ferocious drive. He wouldn't bet a penny on Palmer's business judgment; that money he had given Palmer was as good as gone. If it had been Frieda Palmer wanted, though—Gad, he might almost have put up the whole sixteen thousand himself. It would have been worth it to see the fun.

In that case, of course, he would have had to give up some of his own ideas. Which would have been a pity, after all these years.

Head nosing forward, he bent further over the rail. What was the girl up to? Sending out a customer she obviously meant should be her last—it was almost seven—she was sliding toward the back of the store. All this past week—longer than that, perhaps—she had been abstracted. He mustn't run her on too long a rope; she was old enough now, at seventeen, to fancy herself in love with some young sprout—some German farm boy, likely—who had met and dallied with her.

On the rail, his hands faintly tingled. If she was old enough to think herself in love, then she was old enough for him. He had made no approaches to her lately; it had become habit to think the time wasn't come.

The last customer out, she emerged at once, hat on. Evenly, coldly, as he always called any of his employees, he let his voice fall.

"Miss Schlempke, would you step up, please.

"No, don't sit," he told her when she came, directly. "Stand here by me. I want to watch the others out. You haven't done so well this past week. Anything wrong?"

Since he didn't have his light on, light came only from below. In it she looked faintly haggard, if such firm flesh could take on lines, could soften. She kept her face turned aside, looking down as he did, while Miss Shatto, Mr. Ives and Mr. Tow, the new man, left. Only Eddie remained, putting out lights.

"What's wrong?" he repeated, letting his voice grow quizzical. "Too much moonlight?"

The short pink underlip pushed forward. Curious, he'd always thought of a full mouth as sensual. This girl had as small a mouth as he'd ever seen, yet——

Below, Eddie looked up questioningly.

"No, leave that last light," Junius told him, matter-of-factly. "I'll be through with Miss Schlempke in a minute."

Eddie let the door sigh to behind him.

"Now, young lady."

She turned halfway toward him, but did not look up.

"I'm thinking I—you mustn't let my father know——" She stuck there as if something pushed her one way, something else another.

"I've stood by you."

She let out a long breath. "I'm thinking about getting married."

"Married?" he echoed her, and laughed. "It must be catching. First my son, then you. My son didn't hurt, but my best clerk!" Deep inside his body the pulse had begun to beat. This was the time.

"Frieda." Again he let his voice drop. "Frieda. Are you so sure you want to marry? Want to leave the store here? Want to leave me? No, of course you have to marry. Well——"

He took her shoulder in his right hand, turning her more nearly toward him, bringing his left hand slowly up to let it rest against her breasts. At the touch she lifted her gaze in a darting, wild flight, staring at him, while her comprehension flooded, deepening her color, quickening her body. Yes, she knew now, she'd learned somewhere. Moving forward, he bent until his lips, barely touching, brushed across hers, back again.

"Look," he said, "I hate to let you go with—nothing to remember. This is Friday. Suppose I got a room at the Benson House, on the gallery, for Sunday night. I'd let you know which one, tomorrow. Would you come?"

He smiled at the choked confusion in her eyes, and bent again.

"There'd be a hundred dollars in it," he said close against her mouth.

But then, still bent, he felt explosion underneath his hands. Her breath which had been held—tightly held—began coming in deep strangling gasps, her cheek quivered against his, her body shook. She jerked away from him, her face too convulsed, contorted.

"You don't know what's happened to me," she panted, crouched back and at bay. "You ought to know; I've got to tell somebody. It was Palmer, that's who it was; it was your son, Palmer—that's why I've got to get married."

He stood alone, rocking; he stood unsupported, rocking, taking the shock, taking the shearing away. Impossible, what she said, impossible——

Yet——

Reaching out, snatching out, he at last found laughter.

What under heaven, he asked, in the rise of that laughter, could she ever have given him at the Benson House, to equal the strike of this irony?

In a hotel room in Meridian, on the night of the Friday which was one week later, she lay feigning the deep, even breath of sleep. Stone-quiet and as far from her as he could get in the wide bed lay Harry Gurney.

Harry Gurney. She was Mrs. Harry Gurney. Out of everything that had come to her in these past days, this was what she had gotten.

Relaxing and then digging in again, her fingernails bit at her palms. Perhaps what she had managed wasn't what she had wanted, but it at least was something. Maybe what she should be doing right now was laugh as Mr. Hake had laughed there on the balcony, when she told him. She *might* not, Mr. Hake had told her, need to hurry, but she hadn't chanced it. This had been her time, now or never; there'd never be another Palmer. Mr. Hake couldn't have married her, naturally; Harry Gurney was second best, and she had known how she could get him.

"Oh, Mr. Gurney," she had whispered, when finally she had met him at night in the street alone. "I feel just awful. About Palmer. I don't know what I'll ever do."

She had let big tears fall, choking, and Harry had been as she'd known he would be, sorry for her, stuttering that he felt bad about Palmer too, things after this could never be the same. What Frieda must do was cheer up; all the boys were wondering if they'd have a chance. What she ought to do right now was walk along with him—they might meet Schatzi. No one could make her forget like Schatzi——

"No, she doesn't!" Frieda had sobbed. "Schatzi doesn't feel for me one bit!" And she had kept on babbling until it had seemed safe to burst out, "I just feel like getting *drunk!*"

And Harry, who hadn't thought she meant it, but who had been frightened by that time, she had wept so, holding to him, had said hurriedly, "Well, why not? I sometimes feel like that myself." Her whisper that she couldn't even do that, because she didn't have anything to drink, made him laugh. He had gone into a saloon, still laughing and indulgent, to buy whisky, disdaining the money she had tucked into his hand.

"Even now, I can't get drunk alone, can I? Can I, Harry?" she had asked, woebegone, when he came back. Manipulate. Maybe she had made a mistake, breaking down and telling Mr. Hake, but she had shown people about manipulating.

"No, of course you can't. Of course not, Frieda. I tell you what, I'll get a rig, we'll drive out and we'll both get tight. I guess Schatzi won't mind, not for her best friend."

She'd had him drive straight to the grove.

Over exultance, her lip curled. Harry wouldn't Ruin a Girl, and then Abandon her to Worse than Death. He had said he wouldn't, and she had known she could depend upon it. Harry wasn't like Palmer, looking out for himself.

Under her pillow her fingers touched a hard, square knob, like a square bullet, tied into her handkerchief. Mr. Hake had promised that he wouldn't tell; after all, he hardly could. And when she got her store money, on Saturday, it had come in an envelope, thicker than usual. "On my son's behalf," the note inside read, with one hundred dollars clipped to it. Tomorrow, before they went back to West Haven, she would have to get away from Harry for a few minutes so she could find a bank. No Meridian bank would ask her where she got a hundred dollars.

Beside her, Harry, who must think she was asleep as she pretended, started quietly crying. He was twenty years old, a grown man, married, but he cried against his pillow like a baby.

Part Two

SECOND SIGHT

Within their well-walled continent, in 1892, the people of the United States deep-busied themselves over stern concerns. Commodity prices, the newspapers said, had now reached bottom and must soon move upward. The Ladies' Auxiliary of the World's Fair Committee, those same papers also usually reported, had now raised additional funds for their State Exhibition Building. Germany, far away, seemed to be fighting Russia, but that was little matter. What of Blaine? Would Blaine really run? Thanks to pensions, that year, an uncomfortable treasury surplus was on its way out; cholera, that summer, crouched on its well-tensed haunches right in New York Harbor. "Give us Free Silver," cried the Populists, "and solve all money troubles for all time!" While Dr. Parkhurst wrote, "We are none of us so foolish as to think crime can be utterly stamped out, but we must have the right to expect and insist that the department which is employed and paid to make crime difficult should not be its chief reliance."

Marie Corelli, that year, wrote The Soul of Lilith; *Whittier died, so did a Mr. and Mrs. Andrew Borden, after soup for breakfast; "He licked me fair and square," John L. said in New Orleans, "but he's the only man in the world who could do it." Frick and the Pinkertons, that year (blood in the streets solidifying to bricks for libraries), were charged with murdering strikers; more blood fell in Coeur d'Alene, Buffalo; the Very Foundations of American Living, men of vision said, were being undermined by "that Scabrous Contagion of Organized Thuggery which is known as the Labor Union."*

Somehow, though, somehow in spite of all, living went on——

CHAPTER XIII

RETURNING to West Haven, she still moved in a
tight excitement. Her one day in Meridian, for all it
hadn't been what it should, had still been crowded and not too un-
gratifying. The telescope at which Harry strained (she'd managed, after
all, to smuggle it out) bulged not only with the best of her old wardrobe but with purchases; she herself bore a Meridian hatbox. Except
of course for her one hundred, now lodged secretly and safely in a big
Meridian bank, the shopping had taken her last penny, and some
beside that Harry had. That had been nice, that feeling of right to
Harry's money—her first taste of expansiveness ahead.

It was past eleven when they stepped down to the cinder path
beside the unlit iron-roofed station. At this hour Front Street was
almost deserted, almost dark; almost the only lights spilled into a
cloudy and rain-freshened night were those of saloons and the Benson
House; the only people still about were men on a prowl for pleasure.
Stepping daintily around puddles—think! Rain had fallen on West
Haven that she hadn't witnessed!—Frieda kept her hand on Harry's
arm, her profile clear and lifted from such passers as there were.
Harry's reason for choosing a late train had not escaped her, but she
had not objected. Now might not be the best time for a parading of
her new estate—not right now when she had the meeting with his
family to come.

So far, it had been possible to push aside anticipations of that
meeting; her thoughts could fasten themselves instead upon the
myriad seductions of Meridian: the meals in restaurants, the horse-
cars, the dazzling stores, the push and bustle of ambitious men, the
Opera House——

"No, we didn't get to Niagara," she could say to the fashionables
she would meet now—women, and men too—"but we did manage
the Pedestriennes. Oh, you haven't seen them? Imagine, six days and
six nights of walking——"

She could quite easily learn that lurching stagger; her take-offs
had been good enough for Palmer, and that meant they should go
over with others too.

Not until she recognized the shadowy night outline of Hake's—framing windows, lumpy covered tables, and, in a dim interior, the recessed glow which meant *he* might still be there, on his balcony, counting more of the money in which she now would never share, did she come quite suddenly to earth.

"Why, Harry!" she cried then, thinking, at first, that he just wasn't watching where he went. "Don't you live down Fourth? Here we are between Sixth and Seventh!"

Harry, in the half-light from Hake's, erratically slowed.

"But we—I mean, you—naturally, I thought you——" All day, in Meridian, he had been no more than decently responsive, tagging, for the most part, glum and wordless at her heels. She had tried—no one could say she hadn't tried. Even on the train she had chattered at him. But these were almost the first words he had spoken in reply for hours.

"Naturally," he went on in his silly stutter. "I mean we——"

Abruptly, even though he hadn't said it, she got from his floundering reluctance what he meant. *He thought they were going to her folks!*

Could anyone, anywhere, be such an idiot? This incredulity—even while the juices of alarm and battle squirted—stood out beyond other irritations. She had to be nice to him, too; after all, in addition to his being one of Those Others, he was still almost a stranger, and she didn't yet know what would happen if she talked out. There just might be some mulishness in Harry.

"But, Harry!" she cried, hurt. "You're taking me to *your* folks, aren't you? When I've so looked forward——"

Even in that murky lack of light, Harry's thin cheek and jaw could be seen as taking on a bony obduracy. He bent—this too was obdurate—to plank the telescope upon the walk.

"Frieda, you don't——"

She could have stamped her foot at him. "What don't I?"

"You don't want to go to my folks."

He too had reached something he felt to be decisive, that was what the bunching of his jaw muscles meant. Was he going to say—did he dare say—that she was too low, too alien, to go into his home? Was this to be open battle? If so, he'd find out who'd win.

"But why not?" her voice asked, still hurt. "They're my folks too, now, aren't they? I belong with you now, Harry, don't I? We're truly married, aren't we, Harry? From now on we——"

Face still tight, voice tight too with desperation, he broke in.

"I know—but in—I mean—it's *always* the girl's folks they go to, Frieda!"

Breath, the deep breath which she had just drawn in for another riposte, left her. Immediately she knew that what he said was true. In that moment she saw herself standing, solitary, more than life size, half lit by the glow from Hake's, the telescope at her feet and Harry facing her, while all around her spread a lifeless ghost town, in which such shapes as there were—the hitching posts, the store fronts, chimneys up above, and roofs—were nothing but worm-bored and vacated wood. When Louise Leverett had run off with Frank Kenneally two months ago, in May, it was to Leveretts' they had returned. Hattie Jenks had created a stir by marrying a Norsky, Al Stormoen. They had gone to Jenkses'. When Gehsi married Herman, even, it was to Klaumeisters' they had gone.

As always when reversal struck, she felt it as insufferable. This couldn't be the sort of thing that could be happening, not when she had lost everything, and then, by rising above even her own self-betrayal, recovered so much! So easily she could see what would happen. It was in Harry to sink. She could see him being polite to her father, polite to Ilse, coming to a subservience more abject than that of Ernst and Lotte. And she would be there too, forever.

"I don't care what others do!" Pushed, she gritted resistance even to the proprieties. "Don't you see? I want to be one of your people, Harry. I want——"

What could she tell him? Not that she wanted to have what he had! "Don't you see?" she repeated. "Your folks are what we've got to start from, Harry!"

When in return to this he merely turned his face aside, she for a first time saw what shrinking was under his stubbornness. It was fright that pushed and pulsed beneath his pale and straining skin. And with that glimpse some confidence returned to her.

"They don't have to know *all* about us, you know, Harry." She tried applying salve to his sensitivity. "We aren't the first to get married in a hurry."

"I can't face them," he replied despairingly, as if, once she had seen his weakness, he had no other cover.

She urged, "You'll have to see them sometime," but his return was that of a child.

"Will I? Maybe I—maybe I could just get a job. Any kind of job, anywhere. It wouldn't be so long we'd be with your folks, Frieda——"

"Oh, you're——" Again she had to call back what she would have answered. What kind of work did he think he could get, unaided? A job at the mill, perhaps, like Viktor's, or one at Hake's, like Eddie Noble's? That wasn't for what she had worked, that wasn't for what she had burst from ruin. She had to manage him, manipulate——

It took the old word, the key word, to make suffocation ease.

"I'll tell you one thing," she said clearly, coldly. "My father will slam the door in your face. And kick you senseless, too." At once she knew this was all she had needed—a different fright, a different repudiation, to oppose the one he carried in his mind.

"He couldn't," Harry said, but she felt him cringe.

"You don't know him." What picture could she build by her tone, her harshness? How make him see Otto as he had been when she was small, as he had been those months when she was trying for her first money, her first corsets? As if he saw the pictures with her, Harry faltered to another question.

"But what can we do then, Frieda?"

"Well, since your money's gone, we could sleep under a tree." She let the knife twist.

This time, impaled on the point, he writhed only briefly.

"All right then," he acceded, sagging. He took up the telescope.

She had short shrift, however, for her spate of triumph—for the head-tossed "There! That's like it!" which, she told herself, she surely had a right to utter. Harry, after his first few dragging steps back up Front Street, accelerated to a half lope, as if, having accepted the inevitable, he almost wildly rushed to meet it. With effort she forced her own step to keep even; there was no chance now for her to acknowledge her own trepidations, which raced on her like a footpad from behind. After this fuss there could be no way she could confide in or ask help of Harry.

Immediately, as she faced what now was so near, she was wrung, as she had been many times in the hours past, by the unfairness of her lot. This should have been Palmer beside whom she walked; Palmer would have had a few drinks by this time; Palmer would have thrust back his hat. "You and me, Frieda, we'll get on," Palmer would have said boldly, encouraging himself but encouraging her too. They'd have planned *together* what they must do; his purposes would have been identical with hers. It would have been Mr. Hake they neared—Mr. Hake who so well (only of course there'd have been *one* thing he didn't know then) knew her.

"Two more pigeons feathering a nest," Mr. Hake might have said. That was what he had said of George Bibbensack and Flora, though that, again, was different. Mr. Hake might, to begin with, have been contemptuous and hard, but in the end he would only have laughed as he always laughed. It was cruel it wasn't Mr. Hake she went to.

Instead, almost at Harry's heels, what did she face? Harry of course had parents—"You know Harry's father teaches up at Amiot," so Palmer had said. "The boys call him Old Harry, or sometimes just the Deuce." No parents ever liked a marriage; Harry's father naturally would rant about ingratitude and slyness—well, Harry might cower, but she wouldn't. A bride had to be demure, but she could stand up for herself too.

"I know this is a shock," she could say bravely. "But Harry and I —we're so fond of each other. We just had to."

Night, in the residence streets they now traversed, was an even gray, unpierced by house lights or by stars. Withdrawn, flitting, ghostly shapes of trees and houses were visible only as by some luminous quality within themselves. When, in the midst of her fore-shaping, Harry paused to fumble with a picket gate, this visibility grew more intense. As if they projected themselves deliberately and grayly to her sight, she saw a picket fence, a straight short walk, flower tubs at each side, scrollwork laced about a wide veranda, and a double door.

It was the scrollwork and the double door which forced her, finally, to know what might await her. If the Gurneys told her to get out, she could do little to make them take her in. Over Harry, a husband, she had legal holds, over his family she had none. When Harry pushed one of the doors inward, the step which carried her across the threshold was powered not so much by present strength as by the long unswerving impetus of all the way that she had come.

But then, once inside the door, inside the close strange darkness, some of her dread evaporated, leaving her with a quick, light tingle in tight muscles. She was here now; she had come. Lifting her nose, she sniffed out the odors of strangeness—dry old leather, like prayer books but stronger; furniture polish, wood lately wet, starch, varnish, soap, hot fruit, hot wax. Someone in that house, lately, had been cooking jam. This house was a far cry from Schlempkes', but in it went on a domestic routine. Managed through servants, of course, but still——

She was so far in her groping when palpation brushed aside for what was more immediate. Bare feet ran quickly on a floor above, and then a woman, carrying a lighted lamp, burst on them from the head of polished stairs.

"Oh, Harry!" A thin high voice came, muted. "Is that you? We've been so——"

She was a small woman, wispy, with thin braids upcurling from a head which thrust, peering, past the small hand-shaded lamp. Above the streaming light her face was caverned, white; the shadow of her nightgowned body lay out large and black upon the floor and wall behind it. Quietly that shadow lay, and then leaped wildly.

"Look out!" Frieda cried. "Look out for what you're holding!" That, she thought, as she ran swiftly upward, was the first thing she would say inside the Gurney house. As she snatched at the wobbling lamp she saw only with confusion—the light then in her own eyes—Harry too leaping the stairs to catch the woman (she must be his mother) in his arms. A second nightgown, also, was just visible in a doorway, and then, from the darkness of the nearest room, appeared a third white figure.

"Gracious! It's a good thing for us all I caught this thing in time!" Words poured from a source outside herself while, expectancy drawn to its tightest, she stared at the nearing man. This must be Harry's father; he had a presence before which she drew small. Yet when he came into full sight her first fear and her first impression fell like too rich cake. Could this be Mr. Gurney, this the devil—this tall, gaunt, bony, reddish-curled old man? Why, he caught at the doorframe as if he needed it to hold himself up! He looked almost sick!

After her own words limped to a halt, no other speech succeeded hers. Harry loosened himself part way from his mother, to stand with face averted and head hanging; his mother patted at his back. The girl who had hovered in another doorway (quite certainly it was a girl) had vanished inward; Mr. Gurney continued to stand holding his doorframe, he too looking aside. No one, as Frieda recognized with a crowding fullness in her throat, had so much as glanced at her, and yet she was conscious of nothing so much as their awareness of her. It was almost as if she had swelled, hugely, so that she brushed against the three who stood with her, pushing and displacing them. She would have been willing, soon, that they should say anything, no matter how insulting or how wrathful, just so there would be something tangible she could meet. Instead, they continued in their silence until, unable to bear the torment longer, she brought forth words she herself now scarcely remembered planning.

"I know this is a—a—a surprise. But we—I mean Harry and I—we're so fond of each other. We'll try—I know we'll both try, to do what you want."

Impossible as silence was, however, speech was even more impossible; words grew dry and large as balls of batting in her throat. After them Mrs. Gurney, audibly, drew in breath as if she too essayed speech, but afterward she let the chance pass, sighing. Instead, Mr. Gurney spoke.

"It's true then, Harry."

"Y—yes, sir." A miserable mumble.

Again, even more impossibly, silence, which Frieda this time knew she could not break, which she tried to endure by tightening her muscles, until her knuckles arched out white and rigid from the lamp. Yet when words finally did come—again quiet words from Mr. Gurney—they served only to bewilder her.

"It's late. We'd best get to our beds."

What was the matter with him? Wasn't he going to say *anything?* This couldn't be all—not just this silence, and dispersal. Still unoriented, she had to accept that it was; Mr. Gurney turned away, and Mrs. Gurney awoke to a fluttering activity, as stuttered of its kind as Harry's speech.

"Oh dear, I don't know—Harry, your room—but it's the only——" in the course of which Frieda was somehow wafted to an angle-ceiled small room hung with pennants, floored with drugget. Almost covertly, she was shut up in it with Harry.

"But that's—is that going to be *all?*" she put her baffled question, dropping to the Indian-blanketed bed.

Harry, back toward her at a walnut wardrobe as he groped within it for some garment, answered sharply, his voice cracking.

"Wasn't it enough?"

She had no time for such emotion as his reply carried. "Why," she went on with her astonishment, "they didn't kick up any row at all! There was just nothing to it!"

And later, "Whatever made you such a ninny about coming home to *them?*"

But afterward, trying to sleep, she tossed from one discomfort to another on her section of the narrow, cotlike bed. What was the matter with her now? She was here, wasn't she, inside the house, accepted? An hour ago this was all she would have asked—simply that she be where she was, in this bed, the meeting over.

But she could not be satisfied. What she had a right to be, really, was indignant. The Gurneys, every one, were just like Harry. No spirit. They'd put on no proper show at all! If they had, if they had walked up and down and yelled, denouncing, then that would all have been well over; she could have relaxed, knowing that everything ahead would be clear sailing.

Now she could hardly know where she was.

Annoyed as she was, however, by the Gurneys' failure to meet expectations, she yet had no idea but that, now she was ensconced, she must be entering the life of ease and glory.

Waking next morning to find Harry already up and dressed, yawning, stretching out sleep-heavy muscles, she looked forward with sensuous slow sureness to that fruition which must now be close. This day, Sunday, held the hour when, in panoply, she, Frieda Gurney, seventeen and a bride, could parade sedately with Those Others down the leafy length of South Front Street, her Louis Quinze heels could ascend the wide wood steps of First Congregational, her elegant back could be viewed by any ragamuffin child across the street.

"No, no, you go right on," she told Harry, who only too obviously was torn between manners and his wish to escape. "I'm sure I'll find the way down somehow." Clad in a Japanese wrapper which, the clerk in Meridian had assured her, was absolutely the newest in attire for a Bride at breakfast, she later stood hugging herself before the garments she had just unpacked and spread upon the bed—a glistening, almost crownless straw sailor, a black-and-silver striped silk waist, a black nun's-veiling skirt which, tantalizingly, could be lifted to show the scarlet ruffles of what usually was kept hidden—and this petticoat was *perfumed!* There was nothing of West Haven, nothing of Rozzie Balik, about this outfit; this was the latest out of Meridian, and if she didn't knock over everyone who came near her, then no one could.

Floating in this happy certainty down toward the breakfast table, critically noting that the stairs, though thoroughly varnished both on tread and banister, were not quite as wide as might be wished, she was prepared to shed abroad that graciousness which, she had decided, was suitable to her new estate. She had thought, before starting downward, that she might possibly get lost in tall dark chambers from which, romantically, she would have to be rescued, perhaps by an unbending Mr. Gurney. ("I just get *lost* in this big house!" "Well, we'll have to do something about *that!*") The reality, however, though strange and not too unimpressive, was almost prosaically unmystifying; what she descended into was a rectangle of hall which, in addition to the decent antlers, coat rack and brown glazed umbrella crock, was supplied only with bead-roped openings on either side, through one of which, on the right, it was possible to view, across the tidied chairs and brussels of a sitting room, another opening which framed the napery of a table.

Her first cognition, while she still stood among the wooden-bead portieres between sitting and dining room, was that the Gurneys were going to be no more help this morning than they had been last night. They sat (four of them) as stiff and hostile at their board as if she were an entering wedge of smallpox. Only Harry, blushing moistly, rising to pull out the unfilled chair beside his, gave any answer to her own gay greeting.

"Well, here I am, I guess! I hope I haven't made you wait!"

"Mmm-ster ZZbeth," Harry unintelligibly stammered, while, holding her head perkily (they needn't think their moping would cut any ice with *her!*), she advanced the four steps between portiere and table. Harry, she guessed, must be introducing her to the tall sallow girl (she had been right, then, that *had* been a girl in that other nightgown) who flashed a dark blue glance across the table before her lids discreetly lowered and her lips inaudibly murmured.

"Your sister? Elizabeth?" Frieda repeated as she sat down. "I'm so glad. I was hoping there'd be someone. It's so nice there is." In spite of all she could do, however, her voice was slacking; her mind, rocking, had been hit by too many swiftly piercing shocks. That man, that tall, chill, thin-lipped, rapid-glancing man at the head of the table, that man with long, flat, restless hands and a long, beaked, almost fleshless face, that man with tufts of satanic beard and horns of baldness pushing up grizzled orange screws of hair—could that be the sick old man she had seen last night? *This* Mr. Gurney could be called Old Harry, no doubt about that! Not just for look and color—his skin, like his hair, was almost orange—but for something intractable that seemed to leap about inside him, all the more threatening because it was so thoroughly pent.

And Mrs. Gurney, seen by daylight—could this woman be one of those worshiped Others? Sitting at the foot of her own board, pushing at milk pitcher and toast plate with incompetent hands, bleating out, "Harry, the sugar, did you get the sugar? There's more tea, if you——" Mrs. Gurney looked like nothing so much as a limp, vague, lopsided rabbit, with her side-tipping head, her side-twisting nose, her unevenly lidded eyes, her side-slipping hair. And as for the food, the table——

Where was rich elegance here? Where were iced melon, eggs Benedictine, *pâté de foie gras,* or even the heaped sausages, *Pfannkuchen* and applecake of a Klaumeister breakfast? This table was draped in white linen to the floor, but at each place was only a small gold-banded bowl of oatmeal, a napkin, spoon and saucered cup of tea; on the great central white expanse rode lonesomely a pitcher of blue milk, a sugar bowl, and a plate of buttered white toast with the slices cut diagonally in half. Why, this was as bad as a Schlempke breakfast! There at least Father had good food, of which sometimes there were leavings.

For a few seconds her unsettled psyche, steadying, supplied itself with explanations. A servant, entering, would bring in *courses;* she should have known that from her reading. Courses were much more elegant than everything on the table at once.

But as moments drained away, as Mrs. Gurney fluttered out to the kitchen for hot tea and *nothing else,* as the four people around her took in milk-drowned oatmeal, toast, and then set their spoons down with finality, the truth became inescapable—not only was there no other food, but the kitchen held *no servant!* This last she put off while she could—there *must* be someone out there; Mrs. Gurney just liked to do the serving. The girl would come in a minute to clear away—but when, breakfast obviously over, Mrs. Gurney matter-of-factly reached for Harry's dishes to stack with her own, the crushing fact had to be accepted.

Struggling, she essayed light prattle.

"I do hope we have a fine day; we should have one, after rain. This oatmeal is *so* good, and tea; I love tea." But as reality grew more stark, she could no longer keep it up. Had she fought up from catastrophe for *nothing?* Weren't the Gurneys *in,* at all? Elizabeth had no style whatsoever! Mrs. Gurney! This food, and no servant! But against these swamping facts were others to which she clung—Harry had *always* been accepted as West Haven's best, next to Palmer. And Mr. Gurney—you had only to look at him to recognize he, awesomely, *was* in. Antlers, too. Scrollwork. Double doors. Varnish——

After patting his lips a last time with a napkin, Mr. Gurney prepared to rise. Even before the flame-tipped tufts of eyebrow, leaping upward, gave signal of the utterance, she knew he was about to speak.

"Tomorrow we breakfast at a reasonable hour. Dressed." Neither voice nor strike of glance seemed aimed at her, but their passage crossed her like a burn.

Out of her welter of reversals, she gasped, "You mustn't wait for me. Whenever I have a chance I——"

"In this house," the well-iced answer came, "we preserve amenities."

To this he did not expect reply; already he had pushed his chair back; he rose to stalk stiff-legged toward the sitting room.

"But of course, I will try to get down," Frieda hurried, then, feeling the flatness, the inanity of that, she too arose.

"You must let me help," she offered Mrs. Gurney, who was halfway between table and kitchen door. "We'll all have to hurry, won't we, getting ready for church?"

This speech she reached for as safe haven; from it could be expected nothing but silence—more silence—or a murmur of compliance. Instead, the force of Mr. Gurney, unseen as he now was behind her, seemed to burst voiceless in the room. She was aware that Elizabeth's hand poised unmoving and untouching over a reached cup, that Mrs. Gurney stood fixed with her load of dishes, that Harry, half risen, sank back in his chair.

"This morning, madam," said Mr. Gurney in a tone of black frost, "we remain at home."

CHAPTER XIV

Upstairs, as she replaced her hat in its tissued box, as she hung away her new skirt and waist in Harry's wardrobe, she reviewed stormily what had occurred. Was *this* the way things were to go in her new life? It should have been perfectly possible, after what Mr. Gurney said, to laugh:

"On this fine day? Harry and I wouldn't think of staying home." Instead of that, why had she faltered, "Oh yes, we *do* need to get acquainted," and then jumbled her dishes together and fled with them to the kitchen?

Things won't go on this way, she promised herself. They'll find that out! As the day wore on, however, she found—with a kind of terror—that apparently things *could* go on this way. No one, that morning, left the Gurney house. Mr. Gurney (this was the one fact of which she could say, "Thank goodness!") kept himself in a room behind the parlor on the other side of the house—a room which Mrs. Gurney, hushed, called the "Study." For the rest, Mrs. Gurney and Elizabeth puttered about house and kitchen in a manner which just seemed absent and undirected until Frieda drew near, when it immediately grew smitten and barriered. Her certainty of servants came to be something about which she could have screamed and laughed. Servants? Why, *Mrs. Gurney* was the servant of this house, just as her mother was at home!

Always at Frieda's heels slunk Harry. "Could I get you a book?" asked Harry. "Would you like to look at our stereopticon views?" When she sat formally ensconced in the parlor, eying "Minnehaha Falls" and "Oh! That Slipper!" he vanished, to reappear nervously when she was done. "Could I get you anything? A drink of water?"

In late afternoon, after a dinner which could only be described as very light and commonplace, and long hours in a parlor which was half filled by a square Steinway, and in which no one, apparently, ever did anything but read, Mr. Gurney emerged distantly from the study. Fidgeting with *Robert Elsmere,* which Harry had assured her she must like, Frieda had thought she would welcome any activity, any outbreak. At Mr. Gurney's entrance, however, she refastened her eyes to her book; commerce with Harry's father was something for which she had no use whatsoever. Acting, though, stood her in no stead; after an interval which seemed shaped and timed exactly by the tall flat man in the straight-arm chair, he spoke, his tone uncadenced.

"Your father, I understand, madam, is a barber here in West Haven."

With the most careful and abrupt of starts, Frieda looked up. "Did you say—my father?" She had, she felt, known what was coming; this, not last night, was to be a time of judgment, and it was to be a time surrounded, not by the flurry of emotion and arrival, but by calm dispassionate questioning. Within her mind she felt her wits fly to their stations; the words she had so far uttered were merely to give herself time, but once this instant of preparedness was past, she knew herself ready, nimble and inventive. Harry had tightened in his chair, the faces of Mrs. Gurney and Elizabeth had dimly grown defensive. If they thought she was going to eat humble pie, they could think twice.

"Yes, my father *is* in the barbering profession at present," she admitted, but with gentility. "A pity, because he was brought up to be a gentleman, you know. Coming here as a stranger——"

Mr. Gurney inclined his head. "He is from Germany?"

"Bavaria."

"You yourself were born here in West Haven?"

"Oh no. In Chicago. My family traveled a great deal before settling here." She herself settled more firmly in her chair, as if resting from those travels.

"I understand you worked at Hake's, previous to"—for the first time the even spareness of the tone broke slightly—"to this marriage."

"Yes, I did. I *enjoyed* Hake's." There, let them take that.

"It is a pity," Mr. Gurney returned, "that you cannot continue a work you so much enjoy. You know, of course, that Harry's college work is unfinished. I have hoped—we have all hoped—that he might follow in my footsteps. He must have another year at Amiot, and after that——"

As if it could proceed no further, the voice stopped. In the ensuing silence he seemed to wait, Mrs. Gurney and Elizabeth seemed almost to beg, for some word from her; only Harry stayed inert. What was she expected to say?

"I'm sure if Harry wants to go to school, that's fine with *me*," she managed brightly.

"It is disastrous"—Mr. Gurney did not even seem to hear her reply— "for Harry to be married at this time. Disastrous."

So! Well, she could answer that one!

"Those things happen!" she tartly reminded.

"Yes, those things happen," went on Mr. Gurney heavily. "You, I suppose, underwent the usual West Haven schooling."

"Oh yes." She felt no need to amend this. Her father, often, had pointed out the superior education he was affording his children. Some girls, of course, like Rozzie Balik, stuck in school through the eighth grade, some even went to high school, but she had never been anything but glad she left school when she did.

"You and Harry have interests in common? Books? Music?"

Toward what was he moving? Did he expect her to say that she *liked* the kind of day she was having? He could just as well know the answer to that now as later; she could just as well strike now for what she wanted.

She broke into rippling laughter. "Books?" she repeated. "Horrors! You don't catch me often with a *book!* I'm too lively. Of course, once in a while——" She remembered about being gracious. "Today it did seem suitable to be quiet, but I'm sure that I'll soon be too busy for *books!*"

"Madam," began Mr. Gurney, but did not continue. As if all desire for knowledge of her had faded into tiredness and oppression, he once more, as he had begun, stared darkly forward. He had to say something, thought Frieda, but with slowly growing chill she realized he would not; he was initiating another of those silences which had so shaken her last night.

This silence, however, ended quickly. Mrs. Gurney broke it with a breathless flurry.

"We *are* quiet today," she acceded. "Perhaps Elizabeth will play."

"Oh yes," seconded Frieda, "do!" She would have grasped at anything, and music, besides, might be pleasant. Elizabeth, who wasn't without a thin, elastic vigor, might produce something with *go*. That, in a way, would be victory—the moment she complained of dullness they thought up something lively.

Almost immediately, however, she had to know that here too she was doomed to flatness. With no coaxing whatever (Schatzi had to be pushed, always, right up to the piano) Elizabeth rose.

"I'll do some Bach," she offered.

At the sounds which then rounded from the big dark Steinway,

Frieda sped quick glances at Elizabeth's parents. At Harry too. Weren't they going to ask Elizabeth to play something else than her *exercises?* Apparently they were not; Mr. Gurney, after sitting so long rigid, averted his face, resting temple against thumb, while a restless forefinger smoothed and resmoothed the high orange-tinted forehead; oppression faded from his eyes to be replaced by simple gloom. Mrs. Gurney lay back with eyes closed, mouth for once shaped and soft. Harry slumped more entirely in his chair, lifting one leg over its arm. At no time during the interrogation had his eyes met hers; now he seemed to collapse completely.

While Elizabeth played on and on, interminably, Frieda tried to assess how she had come out in this later interchange. She had come out all right, hadn't she? She had said where she stood, hadn't she? But she could not keep assurance high. For quite a while Elizabeth's playing remained what she first thought it. Then there came a time when the successions of tone began to have meaning, as if Elizabeth were speaking in a language which, though foreign, maddeningly contained known syllables. This, too, was not all; it was not just that Elizabeth's playing grew to be recognizable as language, it was that this language spoke, insufferably, of all that she found insufferable, was of a piece with everything she had met all day. No one spoke, no one sent her a glance; there was nothing going on in the room except that horrible persistent music from which she could neither twist nor turn. After some time her toes began to jump in her shoes, her legs and shoulders twitched, she could have cried for shutters on her ears to close herself away. Yet the thought, I could get away, was for a long time unaccompanied by courage; she had to stay where she was, had to hold herself against the music.

At last, however, too much was too much. Rising, she fled upstairs, to pace back and forth in her small cage of retreat, her body stiff, her fists clenched, her lips soundlessly whispering, "I could scream; I could scream."

This was what they gave her, was it? This was what they thought they'd make her take, instead of all the fun and luxury to which she had looked. "Are you fond of books and music?" Mr. Gurney asked her. *Books and music!*

She had to be nice to these hateful, hostile, thwarting people too. They were necessary to her. But they'd find out. She'd break through someway. They couldn't tie her to such deadly dullness.

Once having let Mr. Gurney keep her in on Sunday, however, she accepted that the whole ensuing week must be one not only of tedium but of postponement; she couldn't make it anything else without giving up too much of her dream. When Harry, on a Monday as glowing as the Sunday had been, suggested that she might like to go out somewhere, she returned haughtily, "Where?" and when he meekly answered, "We could walk, or there's Pratt's," she lifted scorning nose and shoulders. It wasn't thus commonly, strolling out alone with Harry, or imbibing an ice cream at Pratt's, that she would burst upon West Haven.

"Until we've gone to church," she made the fiat, "we go nowhere."

Bewildered by what to him was complete aberration—"I didn't know," Harry said, "that you cared so much about church"—he acceded and then tried again. Wouldn't she—this was Tuesday—at least like to see her mother?

More rasping than anything else in her new circumstances, she found this enforced juxtaposition to Harry. Whatever else his parents and sister might think of the marriage, they took it for granted that it had occurred because of a "fondness" to which both Harry and Frieda were liable. Frieda was expected to want to be with Harry. Harry was expected to want to be with Frieda. Mrs. Gurney, in her helpless vague detachment, washed clothes or dishes, she swept, cooked, ironed, sewed or sat embraced with a book. Elizabeth too—flitting about like an unobtrusive, slightly Puckish shadow—kept to her own pursuits, which included four excruciating hours of piano practice daily. Mr. Gurney appeared only at meals. Frieda's choice, in this vacuum, was Harry or no one.

Hours could be spent alone in dressing and redressing, in trying new coiffures, in reclining elegantly with a finger in a closed book, while one mentally laid out the social trumphs one would yet, in spite of everything, achieve. But Harry's presence kept recurring. He slid off to tinker, he said, in the woodshed; college boys on bicycles, with whom he held long conferences, called for him at the back door; each evening, since she wouldn't accompany him, he said nervously, "Well, I guess I need a little air," and went out. But from these disappearances he eternally returned, to stammer suggestions—all ridiculous—for her comfort or her entertainment.

As Palmer's satellite and Schatzi's beau, Harry had been someone about whom she knew comparatively little and cared less; now she was forced to look at him closely and in relation to herself. As he sat at dinner between the disparate poles of his parents, she had to see how he combined his father's long, flat, loosely coupled frame with his mother's hesitant apology. Harry was fair, he blushed pinkly, he turned always to others. He might have been a tall, soft baby.

Yet she was to learn that in spirit, too, as in speech and color, he could vacillate. When she woke on Wednesday it was to find that as usual he had roused before her, but this time he had not risen; he lay with both arms under his head, looking at her.

"I've been thinking, Frieda," he announced quite firmly, "we got off to a—to a bad start. But now, we're in it. We ought to—ought to get along as best we can. I be interested in you, I mean, and you—try, anyway—to be interested in me. Maybe we can make a go of it."

Spurred by such resolution, he whistled cheerfully as he dressed, he paused in tying his tie to slap mischievously at her as she swished past him in her petticoat toward the washstand, he peered out the window to say it was a bang-up day, he waited until she finished dressing, and then clattered boyishly before her down the stairs.

So yeasty were his spirits that even the chill gloom of the breakfast table lifted slightly. For a first time Mr. Gurney said, "Good morning," Mrs. Gurney smiled dimly, and when Harry cast at Elizabeth a teasing "Lizzy, Lizzy, makes me dizzy," the blue eyes flashed back an almost ardent glow.

After the meal he invited, "Come back to my woodshed, Frieda, and I'll show you what makes wheels go round."

Outwardly raptured—"Just promise me there won't be mice!"—but inwardly petulant (they'd cheer up for Harry, would they! That showed what attention they paid her!) she followed Harry's leading. His woodshed, it turned out, was no haunt of chopping block and kindling, but the receptacle, instead, for as dismal a litter as she had ever seen.

Unequivocal light from two big windows fell upon a dozen partially dismantled bicycles that leaned against weathered bare board walls, or lay as if flung upon a black and oil-gummed floor. Grease-blackened wheels, chains, tools and unrecognizable shapes of metal hung about on nails, or heaped black-crusted shelves and benches.

"Heaven is my home," Harry said, slipping out of his jacket and into overalls and an old shirt. He kicked with one foot at a wheel on the floor. "Alf Jensen's. Something gone wrong in the sprocket——" The last lapsed as he bent to probe at the central gears.

"I'm sure there must be mice here." Eying a tumble of unspeakable rags, twisted metal parts and paint cans in one corner, Frieda clutched her skirts tightly. She had not, yet, wanted to bicycle; she saw no vision of herself so crudely exercising limbs which certainly were more fascinating when hidden. Was this what Harry expected her to join him in? This filth, this mess, this *smell*? A livery stable she could understand; that produced the social grace of a horse and buggy. But this mixture of oil, paint, turpentine, rubber—by the minute, as she looked about her, it grew more repulsive.

"Mice?" repeated Harry, with no sympathy for her fears. "Oh, maybe, but not many. I guess you didn't know this is how I make my spending money, fixing wheels. I started when there weren't anything but high-wheelers, like those over there." He stood up to gesture toward one wall. "But I like the safeties better. They're the machine of the future. I never told you this, but"—shyness here attacked his voice —"I've been thinking a lot about bicycles. Suppose you could build in a little motor, say—just a little engine, so you wouldn't have to pedal——"

He kept on talking, but with inrushing and furious despair, Frieda quit listening. Was *this* cross, too, to be laid on her? Was Harry going to turn out to be one of those addlepated laughing stocks, an *inventor*? She should have known, when he said he had been tinkering!

"Wouldn't have to pedal," she repeated in cold furious mimicry. "Maybe if you built in an engine you could walk without legs too."

The lips that had spoken so nervously but eagerly drained of confidence; issued instead a short laugh.

"Oh sure, I—I know that's just a pipe dream," Harry assented. "I wouldn't expect anything to come of it. I just know, though"—this time a more uncertain gesture indicated the clutter—"I've got to find something in this, somewhere. That day when my father talked about what he wanted for me—I feel bad because he'll be disappointed. I've got to do something with machines."

After she had stood stonily wordless in reply to this, he awkwardly bent to pick up a chain, which he threaded through his fingers. "Right now"—this was pleading—"I sometimes make five, six dollars a week, Frieda; if I had a little capital so I could start a shop, say—put in a good line of new wheels—Rovers or Sterlings—if we worked together, Frieda——"

She had no ear for what pitifully and courageously was revelation of a dream as intense as her own, struggling as desperately as her own for life.

"It's too bad you didn't get Schatzi!" she snapped, hunting for what would hurt most. "Maybe Schatzi would like living on grease and crackers in a hole like this!"

Pain flaming into darkened eyes, the trembling of an unsure mouth, were adequate reply; she could turn, flouncing, for her exit. Later she could also congratulate herself that Harry stayed in his hole until noon, and that when he did emerge he was well sunk in his previous dejection. If she was to be throttled and confined in this marriage, then certainly Harry wasn't to enjoy himself. Yet she had to know the limits of her little victory; there wasn't too much use in letting Harry know where he stood—though of course that had to be done—as long as she gained nothing by it.

Hold to her determination not to go out until Sunday as she would, there yet came a time, and no later than Thursday, when she had to get away from Gurneys', at least for an hour.

The incident preceding this abandonment of plan was small. On Thursday midmorning when she ran down to the kitchen for hot water (early breakfast left no time for a good wash, and apparently the Gurney's habitually used cold water, because no one brought her any hot), Mrs. Gurney slid toward her one of those oblique, unaddressed remarks which so far had formed most of her converse.

"You mustn't let me keep you from the broom and dusters. I know you must be anxious to do up your room."

Returning upstairs, laden not with hot water but with broom and cleaning rags, thrust somehow into her hands, Frieda dropped to the bed in what began as stupor but ended nearer horror—was she going to have to do menial *servant's work* around this house? Not for a long time had she done drudgery at Hake's; if she flipped a duster over her counters that was condescension; she had graduated forever, as she planned it, from such labor. At home it had always been her mother who swept, scrubbed, dusted, brought hot water for the bedroom pitchers. In this house of These Others, wasn't she to get even as much service as she had had at home?

Staring now perforce at facts toward which she hitherto had been sightless—a gritty drugget, a washbowl so grimed its knot of faded thistles could barely be seen, a filled slop jar, she realized that probably the room had not been cleaned since she moved in. Yes, dust fluffs rolled on the lint-gray floor beneath the bed. The bed had been made, but no more than roughly; Harry must surreptitiously have smoothed it.

Somehow, even when she had known there was no servant, she had expected that such things must get done without her. It was impossible that she do them. Yet what could she say to Mrs. Gurney except the shameful, startled, inept "Oh yes" that she had uttered? Could she reply, "No! Certainly not! I couldn't do anything so demeaning"? Mrs. Gurney might then ask, in her blank way, "But who will?" You couldn't very well tell Mrs. Gurney, "That's for you to worry over." However much housework Mrs. Gurney did, it was all done as if she were really about something else; Mrs. Gurney always returned, the moment she was released from labor, to her book. "Have you seen my Emerson?" Mrs. Gurney asked, the moment dishes were done. If you *ordered* Mrs. Gurney it was uncertain what might happen.

Rising bleakly from the bed, she began a sweeping and a dusting which, she realized, she was condemning herself to as routine. It was then her plans changed. If she didn't get away she must burst.

CHAPTER XV

What she found away from Gurneys' was, indeed, healing. "Ach, Frieda! Frieda! First Viktor and Gottfried, then you!" From her mother's first cry, just inside the kitchen door, the world began swinging right. Against her shoulder she could receive the outburst of her mother's grief, with comfortable relief and an entire command of the situation.

"Now, now, Mama—I did leave you a note, you know that, Mama; you knew right where I was, the whole time. After all, a girl has to get married sometime—and you have to say I married *well*."

For here, once more inside her old home, even that last fact had to re-emerge. Had she ever, actually (and so short a time ago, too!) lived in a house as scrubby as this? While Ernst and Lotte, shouted in from play, were sent off to tell Papa she was home (Papa must know!) she stepped delicately about the confines of her former domicile, seeing it with the eyes of sophistication. Heavens! That kitchen! Everything from sewing machine to dining table in one room! That tiny cubbyhole under the stairs—one could hardly walk around the bed! The front hall, too, was so narrow one went sidewise, almost, past the unbalustered gray-painted stairs, while the parlor, which she had once thought too fine for sitting in—well, the scarlet velvet curtains were richer and brighter than anything at Gurneys', and the settee and lamp, too, were nice, but how *squeezed* they were! This parlor wasn't as big as Gurneys' hall! Her new life might not be all she wished it, but at least she had been delivered from *this!*

"Yes, it's different," she replied to question, after Otto Schlempke, breathless, beaming and preening, had got himself home. "Everything's so rich, you know. Work just"—she flicked a hand—"gets done. We eat always in the dining room. I spend much of the day up in my room—reading, sometimes. They've *such* good books. And then Elizabeth—that's Harry's sister—plays so well, it's quite like having a concert any time you ask."

As she embroidered, sitting on the parlor settee ("No, no, not the parlor, after all the years I've lived here," she had protested, but they had insisted), all her embroidery was almost real; at least it was real to the four pairs of envious, proud eyes that scarcely moved from her, real in her mother's aching "Ach, so it would be nice if we could make for Ernst and Lotte."

"Women, women, they're the ones have it easy. Marry a rich boy, live in fine houses, everything fine——" Whatever his first reaction had been to her marriage and the loss of her income, Otto Schlempke by this time was ready to succumb (aided no doubt by comments in the barbershop) to complete envy and more complete pride. He might never himself, now, be able to strike it rich and get on Easy Street, but his daughter had done so. Christmas wine must be produced, and last slices of the Christmas fruit cake.

"*Prosit!* Long life to our Frieda! Happiness!" When she left it was to more tears—"Do not forget us, do not forget you are our Frieda"— and to a hinting "Sometime your new husband, he will see us, no?"

Her replies—"I'll be here so often you'll shoo me out!" and "Harry? Oh yes, I will try, but—well, he has so many friends and interests of his own"—were, she could feel, superlatively right.

Her one other venture, too, was balm. On her way toward her parents' home she had allowed herself only a side glance at the summer muslins on display in Hake's window. On her return, however, she let temptation take her.

"Eddie! Mr. Ives! It's Frieda!" No sooner was she inside the door than Miss Shatto cried out shrilly, and from then on no one could have asked more. Miss Shatto said Frieda could have knocked her over with a feather. Mr. Ives, humorously, said, "Well, I knew she wasn't my girl when she quit scooping sugar." They hadn't anyone in her place yet; everything was at sixes and sevens. Mr. Hake had been shattered. Absolutely shattered.

"Oh yes, Mr. Hake!" trilled Frieda. "I must just run up to see my old boss." As she went she paused, critically, over a shipment of white muslin petticoats—quite the new style, gored, with machine-embroidered ruffles only at the bottom.

"Not bad," she commended. "Of course, after shopping in Meridian——"

On the balcony Mr. Hake, stretching his lips in soundless laughter as of old, pushed back his chair. Even knowing what he knew had made no difference in Mr. Hake; Mr. Hake, his eyes said, had heard and appreciated each word from downstairs.

"Mrs. Gurney" he congratulated, "you now manage consistently to astound me." It wasn't, of course, her first encounter with him since the night she had let him know; she had had to work as usual those days in between while she was waiting to catch Harry in the right place at the right time. Although he now stayed in his pushed-back chair, his eyes traveled over her, and she felt a slow, delicious shivering. The very idea of Mr. Hake——

"So you married a Gurney," he said. "And here, even after your small—revelation, I would have considered that a second string to your fiddle must be some young Dutchy; I should have known better. Disappointed as you no doubt have been, do you find yourself—satisfied?"

She lowered demure eyelids over warmth that must be a blush.

"Mr. Hake! You can't say such things to me! I can't stay here to listen!"

"Why not?" asked Mr. Hake, with a satyr's grin in wise eyes and lazy long mouth. "After all, in our present peculiar position, we must enjoy what we find. Can you think of any other father, Mrs. Gurney, who could have taken what I got with an equal urbanity? I still think it's a damn shame I was cheated. Tell me, Mrs. Gurney—no, I won't ask it—are you at all sorry that I proved—ineligible?"

She could only repeat from deeper warmth and a deeper confusion, "Mr. Hake!"

"I said I won't ask, and I won't. But I've nothing against you, Mrs. Gurney. I'm still satisfied by my—response. Would you like your job back?"

The last managed to catch her aside.

"Get my job back?" she echoed. "Why, I know my husband, Harry, could never think of such a thing!"

She herself had never thought of such a thing; no lady ever worked outside her home, for pay. Yet the suggestion, outrageous as it was—especially in the circumstances!—ballooned her self-confidence. At the stairhead, on her way down, she threw back, "I might—I just might—buy something on my way out. That's all right, isn't it?"

"Gurney's never chosen to trade here, but I guess his credit is all right." The tired eyes, their gleam perhaps intensifying, followed as she tripped on down.

Leaving the store half an hour later, laden with one of the petticoats, a silly new parasol of sequined black lace ruffles, a head scarf and two pairs of stockings, she felt completely returned to herself. How could the Gurneys have so shaken her out of mastery? Look at how she got on with Mr. Hake! If this next Sunday didn't see her at First Congregational, she would know the reason why.

Since their initial union in the grove, Harry had kept to himself, cringing, almost, to his side of the bed, a state of affairs she had been entirely willing to accept; he needn't think she wanted anything else! But that night at dinner, under the eyes of Mr. Gurney, and later in the parlor, her thoughts remained indetachably fixed to the moment ahead when she and Harry would shortly again be in a room alone. Somehow, after her meeting with Mr. Hake—all men were alike, weren't they? And sometime Harry would have to, wouldn't he?

Harry, however, had not reached necessity; after undressing with his back stiffly toward her, after bidding her a stiff good night, he took over with equal stiffness only a margin of their narrow bed. Pushed by more of the same impulses which had so overwhelmed her in the grove with Palmer, it was she who, to her astonishment, sobbed softly she was sorry, she knew she hadn't been nice to him, it was all right if he wanted to tinker with bicycles, it was just that everything was different, she was lonesome.

Next morning, beside a sheepish but dimly brightened Harry, she was a kitten filled with lapped cream. Let Mr. and Mrs. Gurney turn their glances aside. She'd manage them too. Perhaps she wouldn't tackle Mr. Gurney, not just yet. But she could handle Mrs. Gurney.

After supper on Saturday, having displaced Elizabeth with a "No, no, it's about time I helped," she followed Harry's mother to the kitchen. Mrs. Gurney, having surfaced long enough to point at a towel and emit a surprised "Are you wiping tonight?" immediately—hastily, in fact—resubmerged in her sea of vagueness. It was too bad, thought Frieda, that she had to stoop to dishes, but at least this way she got Mrs. Gurney alone.

"I'm so glad you let me do this, just for once," she outlined her position, although Mrs. Gurney, as she doused saucedishes in one dancing, sputtering tin pan on the stove top, and then transferred them to the clearer rinsing water of another, appeared too lost to hear.

"Harry's so shy," went on Frieda. Gurney suppers were too meager to make long dishwashings, and she had to hurry with her purpose. "But we've agreed that tomorrow we must go to church."

A fish jerked unmercifully from its element, Mrs. Gurney once more broke water, threshing.

"Oh, but do you think that's wise?" she gasped out. "Only a week—

Mr. Gurney feels—we both feel—if people could first get accustomed——"

Darting about as if for succor, Mrs. Gurney's eyes plainly told her panic at having to meet the question thus, alone and undefended, yet some strength, some dignity, kept her from running for support.

"We'll have to go out sometime," returned Frieda reasonably. "After all, we've done nothing of which we're ashamed; people every day get married——"

At such untoward assault, with the whole soreness of the marriage pushed into the open, Mrs. Gurney once more gasped, her wide-irised, taupe-gray eyes again seeking aid.

"But people know it is unfortunate, most unfortunate, for Harry to marry at this time," her mouth twitched out the words. "Everyone knows he wouldn't marry——"

Here the speaking of the unspeakable stopped her. With a slow heat over her body, Frieda knew it; this was not the first time that the Gurneys had expressed, by inflection or look, their certainty that in a few months, weeks perhaps, the reason for the marriage would be only too manifest. More galling was her own equal certainty; each day she looked for the first shaping of that shame to come; each day she thought that even the final torture which awaited was nothing to the present humiliation of having the Gurneys know they were right.

"He did get married, though," she struck out boldly, "and we're making the best of it. No one can keep us from our church."

"It isn't your church," denied Mrs. Gurney wildly. "You've always—you've never—you've had another church."

Yes, and wouldn't you like to push me back in that crowd? thought Frieda, while she countered, "When I married Harry, his church became mine."

To this, Mrs. Gurney found no answer, and she could go on. "Harry and I both know there will be stares and maybe whispers. We're ready to meet them alone."

Guessing that she need go no further, she stopped, imperturbable and adamant. Mrs. Gurney might twitter, but it was unlikely she would let her dear precious Harry face his ordeal unsupported.

At ten-thirty next morning, shoulders wide and billowing in striped silk against curved and varnished wood, she at last sat in that high place to which her own efforts had lifted her—a pew of the First Congregational Church.

True, it was a rear pew; she had not been able to evade that. Mr.

Gurney, entering first, had advanced only a few paces before he halted, hand to pew back, blocking any further progress. Harry too, Mrs. Gurney and Elizabeth—they had all stopped there, waiting for her to step first toward the seat the master of the house had chosen. She might have said, "Oh, do let's sit up farther," but Mr. Gurney's rigidity and the set of his mouth had not encouraged caviling.

She, after all, had won so much. From the moment when, swishing downstairs in her saved new outfit, she had found not only Harry but Mr. Gurney too, waiting at the stair foot, everything had been quite what she wanted.

"Oh, you're going too?" She had not been able to suppress this little pinch of triumph, since there had been no indicating word at breakfast.

"Yes, madam, you will be well surrounded." So Mr. Gurney had answered her, with acid in the words to say how clearly he saw he was used. Let him know; he'd find out she was no college girl to be struck dumb by a sneer.

Followed by Elizabeth, Mrs. Gurney also had come half tumbling down the stairs. Mrs. Gurney's belt wouldn't stay put; Elizabeth had had to pin it. Mrs. Gurney had been afraid the fire would get too hot for the roast; Mrs. Gurney had gotten soot on one hand and had had to wash it, Mrs. Gurney's gloves, which she had had just that moment, could be found nowhere. Patiently and in unbroken sweetness, humming a light tune as she swung a parasol from a tightly gloved forefinger, helping, even, to hunt for the lost gloves, Frieda had borne with these delays. It was all right with her if they were late—closed doors opening, heads turning, and then, in a deep hush, the Entrance. Mr. Gurney, however, had no idea of being late. Well in time they were out on the walk, Mr. and Mrs. Gurney first with Elizabeth between them, Frieda and Harry last. That too was all right; she had an advance guard.

Since all steps at that hour went in one direction, their progress might have been unseen, though eyes must have peered through lace curtains. As they neared Front Street, however, buggies began passing, buggies from which, as the occupants bowed, leaped question—"Is she?"—and then, as the glances shot back, *"Yes, she is!"* Family groups, too, stood assembled on porch steps or near yard gates, awaiting some tardy member; she had to fight to keep her brows well arched, her gaze unfocused; the covert glances she caught of start, of rustle, were too ambrosial to be passed unrelished.

This, she could tell herself, was *it;* she walked West Haven now a Gurney, held up for all to admire and accept. Let Harry (although she had allowed him to keep unbroken the amity resulting from the Thursday night) grow more and more abject, his cheeks rose-flushed, his eyes shrinking, his hands wandering ceaselessly to shirt collar, to tie; it was to her the eyes really looked. When, after a passage increasingly triumphal as the thickness of the onlookers increased, she put foot to the church step, she'd had to will no movement from her muscles. Mr. Gurney might be a devil against her, the staring groups might be thrusting out invisible hands to pull her down, but she was hard, bright, scorching fire that could meet and melt any indifference or resistance. As her right hand gracefully fell to the black nun's-veiling skirt, it took no volition to lift the fabric from any contamination of the steps; the sharply indrawn breaths that greeted the revelation of the scarlet ruffles—and the perfume—were what lofted her into the hushed decorous dimness up ahead.

That gleaming rich interior to which she came—how right it was! An arched nave, striped by the brown gold-throated reeds of organ pipes, banked tiers of choir at the side (no gowns, but good silks and broadcloths), a pulpit hung in gold-fringed red, thick red carpeting in the wide aisle, heavy varnish on the carved pews, banks of light—blue, red and orange—slanting downward from the high, gem-tinted windows. She had walked into it, permeated herself with it, given to it of her body as it gave to her of its richness, blood heat, haughtiness and compass.

But when, after the apogee of being, queenlike, the one for whom the other Gurneys waited, she had actually sat down, she could not thrust away increeping discontents. There was no movement forward, after she sat down, no impact. Busily her antennae picked up what there was—those people across were certainly staring, and this girl coming in now—Jessie Drake—she knew *she* wouldn't marry Palmer, or Harry, either one. One old woman, her rusty black hat bobbing with palsy, never would be done with turning round.

But so many walked in, eyes forward, without a single passing glance. If she could have sat up front, then everyone (eyes on a sailor's tilt, a faultless Psyche and a straight slim back) would have to know she was among them. Being at the end of the seat was bad too. Harry sat next, his shoulder close enough to brush, but his face remained stiffly forward. Even here the Gurneys were clipped in close union, leaving her outside. She moved, so close that Harry flushed even more darkly, whispering, but without turning, "It's quite hot." Spacing on the other side of him at once eased, so that he in turn moved over.

Waves of a different warmth now rising to her cheeks, she felt that this small action had been visible, even through the backs of necks, to the entire congregation. Not only that, but Harry had acted with impunity. What reproach was there? "Why didn't you sit close to me in church?" "But I did, Frieda, I was right there!" So he was, physically; it was in some other way that he, with all the Gurneys, drew apart.

Occupied by such dissatisfactions, she did not notice a hush, nor the ingress of a leonine tall man who strode briskly before the altar; she did not sing the opening hymn, although she stood with Harry, her right thumb and forefinger elegantly grasping the hymnal. When, some minutes later, the doors behind her once more opened, she did not turn; she was not there to stare at others.

She could not, however, keep from being pulled into the tremor which ensued—a tremor light, rippling, enough to turn sideward every worshiping head. Someone else, not Frieda, was making an Entrance.

Long before she looked, long before she allowed sight to exist, she knew who the Entrant was. Cecilia Amiot, Cecilia Amoit *Hake,* in a flutter of creamy bridelike silk, followed by both Palmer and her father, was floating up the central aisle.

She wanted to strike out for air, wanted to fight past the Gurneys, wanted people to impede her so that she ruthlessly could combat them, wanted to run until she could drop, exhausted, in some far outdoor place where she had never been.

Palmer had told her—how the words now rang!—that he had found a lumberyard right here in West Haven. Yet when she had given him up, when she had accepted that she could not have him, then he had passed into a limbo where he continued to exist, but as a shade. All week, as at the beginning, he had stayed constantly a partner of her marriage: Imagine Palmer sitting around with a book! Mr. Gurney wouldn't talk that way to Palmer! Oh, why couldn't things be lively, as they would have been with Palmer! But she had not actually expected to see him in the flesh again. To do so was to rip scar tissue from a still pulsing wound. There he was, Palmer, flourishing in a new tobacco-brown suit, hair in a devil-may-care tumble, eyes insouciant, heavy mouth smirking. Well, I guess you can all see I'm doing all right, that mouth said. Nothing about Palmer was hangdog or uncertain any more.

That was where she should have been; it should have been *she* who led in Palmer; they'd all have had to admit what she was then, these people. She had wanted the Gurneys along, as support, but now they were just something that hemmed and confined her. Although otherwise without sight or hearing (no slightest whisper of the service reached her), she had to see unforgettably each slightest movement of the three on whom her eyes were fixed: Cecilia cool, aloof, as if she had no idea of the titillation she was causing, fluttering sidewise into a forward pew, Palmer sliding in next, leaning possessively close to adjust a feather boa about Cecilia's neck, whispering as he did so something which necessitated a playfully reproving smile and nod in answer, Thomas Amiot, benign and lofty, standing back to audience while he parted his Prince Albert coattails before sitting down on the wide exposed expanse of finest broadcloth.

She herself must have sat down after the singing—perhaps Harry pulled her. She must later have risen again, sat again; behind the rack of her emotions she was aware of such movements. Nothing, however, had reality, except those three—the heads together over a song-book, the glances exchanged, the aura of assurance, satisfaction, lordship.

What Mr. Gurney saw or guessed she did not wonder over, but she had to know he saw enough to visit punishment and point a contrast. After the service, rounding his little group into an unspeaking, huddled knot, he forced it to stand, apart, while Cecilia, bulwarked by her two men, prettily flushed now, condescendingly held court and reception.

"Yes, a surprise," the light voice lilted. "We were so tired of traveling we just had to come home. Oh yes, with Papa and Mama, of course, until we find some small nook of our own—that's sweet, Mrs. Leverett, we'll be delighted. Oh, thank you, I know we will. Indeed, Niagara was marvelous, and Boston—oh, I do love Boston——"

Those individuals who so much as glanced toward Gurneys were driven off by nods so forbidding that no recipient came near. At one point Frieda knew that Palmer, engrossed as he was by his own responses to the hands that shook his and the voices that congratu-lated, saw that she was there, beside Harry with the Gurneys, and that after a blank moment his mind forced upon him what that juxta-position must mean. His cheeks, that had been so ruddy, turned the color of muddy water, vitality receded from his eyes, the hand which he had outstretched to the next comer hung limply in mid-air.

At a rallying "What's matter, Palmer? See a ghost?" he swallowed heavily, his head ducking down and sideward; when he returned to his responses and handshaking the heartiness had gone from both. But he did not look the Gurney way again.

This consolation of having knocked the breath from Palmer, of having shown him what she could do, was her only and inadequate ointment. Implacably Mr. Gurney held his family where it was until

Cecilia, having received the last well-wisher, said to her father that they really must go. Only then, in austere satiety, did Mr. Gurney let his band turn tail.

Prey to softer feelings, Mrs. Gurney, on the way home, proffered timid assuagements—Cecilia was such a popular girl, and of course, with the Amiots so prominent in West Haven, her marriage had caused an excitement. Palmer too, fixed as he was—the lumberyard was all paid for, people said, not a cent of debt—it was a *proper* marriage. Still, it did seem people made an unnecessary fuss.

By silence Mr. Gurney permitted the application of these rags of bandage, but they only exacerbated Frieda's lacerations. She heard too well what Mrs. Gurney's words implied—Palmer and Cecilia hadn't married *beneath* them; they hadn't *had* to marry. The pangs she suffered tore as much at body as at mind; gladly she would have crawled into her bed and stayed there, gladly forgone the Sunday lamb roast, mashed potatoes and sliced carrots to which she had so hungrily looked forward. From pride she remained erect and moving, from pride ate, but her stomach was a hard squeezed knot. This, that she had been forced to stand shunted and ignored while Cecilia played the part she had dreamed of playing—this was more galling than all other miseries of her marriage put together.

Yet worse was coming.

Apparently eased somewhat by Sunday, Mr. Gurney, that next week, expanded into a stately discursiveness which, it appeared, was his habit, but from which he had retired under the shock of Harry's marriage. When he came home at noon on Monday his manner carried an overlay of geniality.

"I believe I have discovered," he said as soon as he had unfolded his napkin, "some passages in the *Coriolanus* which go far to bolster my stand." The words rolled out shaped and rounded, as if he spoke from a platform, but the tone was pitched to the small room, his glance bent courteously, generously, upon Mrs. Gurney, Harry and Elizabeth, as if they must individually be delighted at what he had to confer. Mrs. Gurney, Harry and Elizabeth, in turn, relaxed into reception and relief, as if a household wrong were being righted.

Pricked out of her depths (somehow she must retaliate, somehow get even with Palmer and Cecilia, and all the Gurneys), Frieda tried to make sense of the rotund syllables which continued to roll—quotations, it seemed, from Shakespeare. These quotations Mr. Gurney later took apart at length and in detail, proving to himself—also to

Mrs. Gurney, Harry and Elizabeth—that they could never have been written by Shakespeare or, as Ignatius Donnelly was claiming, by Bacon, but only by someone called the Third Earl of Southampton.

"Oh, you're so right," Mrs. Gurney exclaimed, as a soft, uplifted and never-interrupting background. "I can see you're *so* right!"

To Frieda it was soon a matter of indifference whether he was right or not right; naturally she had heard of Shakespeare, but why all this fuss? At meal after meal, now, as the head of the house trolled out his words, plentifully interlarded with passages (which he quickly translated) from Latin, French, German, Greek and even Hebrew, she listened so little that on a later day, when he once more sat silent, she was slow to notice. Only when the meal ended, when he said, "I will see Harry and his wife in the study immediately, please," did she grow aware of difference, of Mr. Gurney's hard-pent devil straining behind his rusty eyes, of food remaining in the service dishes.

Wariness leaped then—could Mr. Hake, in spite of his promise, have talked? Could Palmer—— In the study when, after she had been motioned to stand beside Harry at the end of a roll-top desk, Mr. Gurney deliberately seated himself in the mahogany armchair before it, and then turned to fix her with a scrutiny cold and condemning, she gathered herself for what might have to be a supreme effort; only with audacity could she give the lie to what must now meet her.

Instead, however, of beginning with an ominous "Madam, it has come to my ears," Mr. Gurney in unbroken silence took from his pocket an envelope, removed from that container a single folded sheet, and then spread that sheet on the desk before him.

CHAPTER XVI

Even after she had taken in what was on the paper, she at first could know only bewilderment.

"Junius B. Hake in acct. with Harry Gurney, Esq., July 1, 1892," the message upon the sheet began, in the tight, black, even script of all Hake bills. What followed was simply a list of those small purchases she had made last week—petticoat, $3.89, parasol, $7.50, scarf $2.98, stockings, 2 prs., $1.44.

Swiveling between Mr. Gurney's anger and the bill, her glance sought reason. Somewhere on that sheet there must be some hieroglyphic, some symbol from Mr. Hake she could read that had given her away. When Mr. Gurney at last spoke she had not yet been able to form any understanding at all.

"These purchases," said Mr. Gurney. "Madam, were they made by you?"

"Why yes," managed Frieda. "They're just some little things I— one day last week when I was downtown——"

"Bought on June 23, after your marriage, and charged to me. Do you mean to tell me, madam, that you proceeded to a store with which I have no connection, opened an account in my name, and by this means acquired fripperies in the expectation I would pay for them?"

Words Frieda found were more jumbled than any of Harry's.

"But I—I mean I—after all, I——" What could be said? Could it actually be that what her mind jumped to was wrong and that Mr. Gurney out of all his plenty merely grudged her *clothes?* "After all, I have to get new clothes sometime!"

"Yes," responded Mr. Gurney in hair-whetted tones, "yes, madam, you will get clothes sometime. But you will not, in my name, buy anything you please, whenever you please. We do not, in this house, buy any but necessities."

While she stood, mouth open, mind spinning, under the unexpectedness of this assault, he rose to loom awesomely above her.

"It is not my wish to know"—the words flashed and glinted—"by what means you seduced my son Harry into marriage. It is plain, however, that in so doing you thought you married the son of a rich man."

Harry made himself audible, in broken syllables of protest.

She too began, "But I——" only to be cut off.

"So that you may be no more in error"—the tone here grew so thin and high it might have been a buzz saw singing through soft wood— "I will delineate for you, madam, the exact state of my finances. As head of the Classics Department at Amiot, my honorarium is eight hundred dollars per annum. This, madam, is my only source of income."

What he had said before might not make sense, but this, with merciless clarity, did. In a squeezing horror, which began at her abdomen and spread upward, she stood to hear what more must follow.

"For us, with our standards of plain living and high thinking, this sum in the past has been ample. You, madam, doubtless find it paltry. Eight hundred per annum amounts to sixty-six and two thirds dollars for each month. We are now five in family. Each one's share, if we be equal, is less than fourteen dollars in the month. From this the major portion must go for household expenses, and for food. Yet you, madam"

—the voice, which had seemed so thin it scarcely could be heard, grew thinner and yet remained mercilessly audible—"have in a few moments expended more than your month's share on worthless gewgaws."

She gasped, "But this house, this——"

"In my position, madam, it is necessary that we present a certain appearance. Doing so means we never expend an unnecessary penny."

She was fixed, frozen, overcome. From the first word, the first buffet, she had known that what he said was true; this was the key which explained too much—the scantiness of food, the homemade dowdiness of Elizabeth's and Mrs. Gurney's clothes, the entire meagerness of living. Any struggle she put up could only be the weak residual flopping of a fish flipped high and dry upon sun-heated and indurate rock.

Yet when she would have turned to slink off where she could, he yet detained her.

"There is still the matter of this bill. I take it you yourself have no funds"—this reached an apex of sarcasm—"with which to satisfy it. What should be done is that you return the articles to Hake's. Since it might seem harsh, however, to visit this public humiliation upon you, Mrs. Gurney agrees with me that we make such sacrifices as are necessary to pay it. I need hardly say, however, that this will be done no more than once. If at any other time you feel equally moved to acquisition, the goods will be returned, and by you."

Harry again was protesting, "I'll pay it back, a little as I can, sir. I never thought—I should have told her——"

This was the last she heard. No one impeded her then, no one stood in her way when she fled. Up in the room which once more must be her refuge, eyes shut, hands to cheeks, back beaten to a half arc, she dragged herself back and forth, her stiffened body almost refusing movement, yet refusing to be quiet.

"Twenty dollars in tips this week, more as many of these fine professors in the colleges"—how many times she had heard her father say it, how many times she had not believed him. Poor. The Gurneys were poor, as poverty-stricken as the Schlempkes, or, behind their hollow show, even poorer; she had jumped from one indigence to another. The fear in which she had walked to the study—the fear that the two men who knew her secret might have given her away—now appeared faded and paltry. Any disclosure concerning herself she could have brazened, but this—what could she do about this? This was the collapse of life's structure as she had seen it ever since that night on the balcony so long ago, when she had first known herself as an entity, capable of striving. Become one of Those Others, she had thought, and with that you got everything, including money, in profusion.

Her body bridged the years, coats pressed her back, Mr. Hake said, "Someday it might be yours," and the money fell—that crumpled, skin-soft money with its perfume of wealth and power, its melting, silky weight and delicacy to the hand. But immediately she stood once more in the study; she would have said that in her few trapped moments inside it she had not seen the study, but it was in her mind now, ready always to contain her—the sifted, dusky light, the windows draped in brown velours, the prisoning ranks of calf-bound books, the globes, the heaps of paper, the faintly dusty, faintly musty, citric smell of papery decay. "This, madam, is my only source of income."

Seeing Palmer and Cecilia at church had stirred her to storm, envy, jealousy, hatred, pain; now she could only be ice, feeling little. Whatever else she had missed in her marriage, it had not entered her head that she could have missed the money. If you didn't get money by becoming one of Those Others, then how did you get it? Frantically she reviewed a reasoning lost in time but still basic to her thinking— you couldn't get rich on six dollars a week, such as she had latterly gotten at Hake's; you couldn't get rich on twenty dollars in occasional tips. Such money vanished. How then did money get made?

Still bent, she kept pacing. One thing only she knew—she wasn't giving up, she couldn't give up; she still somehow must get money; what other goal was there?

Once Harry came inside the room, but without pausing to hear what he said she cried at him to go. *Men* got rich. Once all men had thought they could get rich by land, but that was exploded now; all you got from land was work and more work, the servile, dirty work of turning soil and tending beasts. No one, no one up-and-coming, any longer thought of land. Men made money now from people, and from business. Palmer would make money with his lumber. Mr. Hake made money, buying cheap and selling dear. Who else had money? Mr. Amiot, from the mill and the bank. Mr. Jenks, from his saloons. Sometimes, she'd heard, men made money in city real estate, or from mines or factories. But these activities not only produced riches, they presupposed riches. If you were a woman, and had none to begin with, how could you get it if you didn't marry it?

Oh, there had been nothing wrong with her idea—other girls married money; if she had managed to marry Palmer she would have had it. It was only because she had been unfortunate, because she had been forced and deluded into marrying Harry——

With a first slow return of feeling, the first slow geysering of emotion as thick and hot as lava, she considered how she had been defrauded. This was all Harry's fault—Harry, who had tagged about with Palmer as if he were as good as Palmer. It was Schatzi's fault—Schatzi with her eternal "Palmer Hake and Harry Gurney, everyone says they're the two swellest young men in town." If it hadn't been for that—oh, hurried as she was, she could have found someone else to marry! Wes Jenks and the saloon money—she could easily have got Wes, with what she knew by this time. It was all Harry's fault, all Harry's fault and Schatzi's, passing Harry off for what he wasn't. And now she was caught in it; she couldn't go back and begin over. It was too late now to marry someone else. She *was* married. To Harry. To boredom so terrible it made her very bones resist. To poverty.

In late afternoon, having come to a more dull acceptance, she took out, from the long wardrobe drawer where she had tumbled them unopened (none of them were things she especially had wanted), the articles she had bought that day at Hake's. With a held-in, deliberate strength that made even the muslin of the petticoat seem fragile, she tore each article—except the stockings, she might need those—into ribbons, and heaped the fragments in the wastebasket. While she was doing so her heart gave a queer lurch.

Her money in Meridian. When Mr. Gurney had sneered, "I take it you yourself have no funds with which to satisfy it," she could have tossed her head. "Certainly I have means to satisfy it—you didn't really think I expected *you* to pay?" That would have told him, that would have wiped the sarcasm from his face! But even while the retort and its humbling effect swelled so largely in her mind that the gratification almost was real, she could not wish she had made it. That money was her secret money, not to be thrown away on scarves and parasols, not to be gotten from her by any means. When she thought of it, as she did frequently, it was as something to be hugged, something certainly hers by right, something to be added to, but never, never subtracted from. More than ever, now, that hundred must be seed for all she would yet have, in spite of Harry, in spite of the Gurneys, in spite of the whole world.

When she went downstairs to averted glances and disconnected, covering-over talk at suppertime, she was able to do so in great dignity and as the injured party. You'd think they'd be ashamed to let her know they were such cheats. Probably right now, in cash, she was worth more than they were.

If she had been stricken by the interview in the study, so too had Harry. "I don't know by what means you seduced my son Harry into marriage"—this was the acid that hit Harry. Shadowing Frieda, his eyes asked, Did you deliberately get me drunk—and the rest too? Usually he supplied his own answer—No, you couldn't. Not knowing about me and Schatzi. It must have been accident, for you too.

To Frieda this distress was as open as her own, but knowing instinctively that to meet him openly would be to turn suspicion to certainty, she avoided the question. By maintaining her bitter dignity intact, by injured comments—"I wish I'd known what I had, home with my parents!" "I wish I'd known what I was giving up, when I left Hake's!"—she was in time able to break him first to more uncertainty and then to worried self-doubt. "I guess we aren't what you thought we were, Frieda, but then I never knew you thought we were."

From her father she had long accepted that any good manners, any courtesy of speech, any but the most practical ethics (you stole, you got found out) were all a show put on for strangers. After Mr. Gurney's disclosures, another section of this pattern fell in place. Most of those attributes which she had so long admired in Those Others—their lofty living in fine houses, their knowledgeableness, their airs of wisdom and assurance—these too, she decided, must be for the most part assumed. "In my position it is necessary to present a certain appearance," Mr. Gurney said, and so the Gurneys lived in a substantial house, within which they ate suppers whose main dish was applesauce. Elizabeth took piano lessons, Harry went to college—what reason could there be for such ridiculous activities, except to give the family tone? Among Those Others there must still be some, like Thomas Amiot and Mr. Hake, who truly did have money; for them the well-served ease, the arrogance, the good living, could be real; for the rest there must just be the pretext, illy or skillfully preserved according to the cleverness of the pretenders.

If that was it, then surely she, with her abilities, she who had made herself over from the vacant formless drudge she once had been into the quick, fashionable young woman she was now, should be able to pretend with the best. It wasn't that she wanted to be in this assuming group; it wasn't that she wasn't someday going to break into the circle of the true possessors; it was just that for the present, cast where she was, she would have to do what she could. Rebel as often as she did—I won't have things this way! They've got to be the way I used to think them—the Gurneys have *got* to have money—she yet came to temporary resignation; there was no other nearby road to take.

I'll go back home, she also told herself in the first black hours, but even when mutiny was newest she knew she wouldn't, not just because by doing so she would make herself a pariah (*"They say she's separated from her husband!"*) but because she could not again pare herself to her parents' squeezed and narrow house, she could not take up a discarded maidenhood, she could not see her father's envy replaced by malice—"So, our lady does not fly so high as she thinks!"

I'll stay on living here, but I'll go back to Hake's the way he asked me; let's see how they'll like that! she likewise teased herself, but this too sat queasily; it wasn't only on Harry and the Gurneys that such an action would redound; she too would be put by it forever from the pale.

Lost as so much else was, as she came slowly to believe, she still, while she remained at Gurneys', retained one thing: respectability, or at least as much of respectability as meant anything: the outward form. If she took up with the Gurneys their pretext of good living, then to the world would not their position—and hers—be little different than it had been? Of course her life could have none of that lavishness which had been the core of her dreams, but if she could manage the social elevation—the acceptance, admiration, parties, friends, gaieties—then surely she would at least have salvaged something—something which, besides being gratifying in itself, must still be the springboard to all she yet wanted.

To self-righteous dignity she was soon able to add, happily, a conscious virtue. By mid-July she knew she need have been in no hurry over marriage. The morning of deliverance she spent sitting on her bed in relief so great it was like shock, rocking herself, arms clasped to breast, whispering a repetitive "It isn't true! It isn't true!" This was replaced, when she had time to consider the release fully, by some reproach—Palmer should have told her—Mr. Hake *had* hinted a little, but he hadn't made her *believe* it. She could have gone right on working until some other fellow came along—someone so superior that she could just have laughed at ever wanting to marry Palmer.

That morning, though, she could not goad herself to anger against anyone. Arising toward noon to tiptoe delicately downstairs, she had the exquisite gratification of whispering to Mrs. Gurney, "I wonder if you could let me borrow—it seems I forgot to bring with me, from home——"

No more was needed. Mrs. Gurney's face shattered in all directions like a window against which a pebble has been accurately dashed. Later came the even greater pleasure of hearing, through the study door, Mrs. Gurney's sobs, "But then why? Then why?" Mr. Gurney's replies were inaudible, but he too, when he came out, was the color of dry mustard, and his gaze, at her and at Harry, was one of heavy, perplexed, miserable doubt.

Elizabeth, also, overheard or guessed enough. Only Harry, sunk in his complexities, remained for a long time unknowing. His parents must think she had told him, but she hadn't. Let him, she thought, stew in his juice; it wasn't by any care of his that she had been saved.

Spirits at once on the bounce, she now was restive for those social recognitions which so far had escaped her. Nothing much could be made to stick against her *character,* surely, after this! Some dregs of caution hung on from the churchgoing; Mrs. Gurney might have been right about that being a little early—anyway it would have been better not to choose that particular Sunday, though she could scarcely have known this.

To impatient questions—"Don't you think I should be going out more?" "Shouldn't Harry's friends be asking us around?"—Mrs. Gurney remained absent and evasive.

"But you are going out, dear," she would answer, or "When people get to see you are a quiet, nice girl, then in time I'm sure you will have friends."

Replies such as this were merely goads. Going out now—did Mrs. Gurney call what she did *going out?* Who wanted to be a quiet girl? Who wanted to wait for time?

True, as Mrs. Gurney said, she no longer spent all her days in the house. Every Sabbath, as a unit, the family now sat in its pew. But as with other things that had come to her through marriage, her attendance at First Congregational was proving peculiarly unnourishing.

"Ah, Gurney. A fine sermon this morning, or perhaps you do not agree." Invariably the men who paused for greetings were oldsters like Mr. Gurney, while the women who paused to yearn over Mrs. Gurney—"My dear, I simply had to stop to shake your hand"—were mostly stout old frumps. (Heavens! To think she had once considered those black satins fashionable!) When she, Frieda, was brought forward—"I believe you have not yet met Harry's wife"—the looks cast at her had that sad measuring espial more suitably reserved for corpses. No one could care what such moth-eaten old fossils thought, but what was the matter with the others? Everywhere she looked, in the shifting, Sunday-chattering groups outside, she saw quite dashing young men, sporting the latest in iridescent hose and in mustaches, but while their glances occasionally caught on hers as a roughened finger catches on a stocking, it was always on some other girl, who hadn't half her style, that they spent their quips and flourishes.

Each Sunday, too, she had to redrink the bitter tea of seeing Palmer and Cecilia in their varying (Cecilia did not have to repeat costumes) shades of glory, and no matter how often she tasted of that cup, the contrast between her lot and Cecilia's added new gall to the infusion. Gladly, after a few weeks, she would have given up churchgoing entirely, if only there could have been something else to take its place.

Why this something else eluded her she could not comprehend. Manipulate, she told herself. Manipulate. But there scarcely seemed to be anything she could even begin manipulating.

CHAPTER XVII

Willingly, now, she took those walks and made those calls at Pratt's which Harry first suggested. Obediently, at her direction— "Be sure you introduce me now, Harry; I've got to have friends"— Harry paused in the paths of half the passers-by.

On weekdays what ensued might be: "Mr. Kenneally—fine day—I —I guess you—guess you don't know my wife, Frieda. Frieda, this is Frank Kenneally's father." Or "I guess you heard I got married, Mr. Orcutt. This is my wife." Or, more to the point, "Hey, Bink, I—wait a minute, Bink and Fred. Meet my wife, Bink, meet my wife, Fred."

At Mr. Kenneally or Mr. Voorhees or Mr. Holborn or Mr. Orcutt she slid slow, bridling, upward glances. "Indeed, I *do* know Frank! I hope to be seeing a good deal of you too, Mr. Kenneally!" "Oh, Mr. Orcutt, why, then you're the one owns the furniture store! I hope you'll find me a customer, one of these days!" You never could tell about half-old men, she should know that from what had happened with Mr. Hake. Not that she wanted anything to *do* with them, but something soon would have to lead to *something*.

For Bink—or Fred or Deac or Cavender—she had a more glowing rapture. "You're Bink *Stevens*? And Fred *Pomeroy*? Harry's talked so much—I feel you've been my friends too, all my life!"

These encounters were not entirely bereft of satisfactions. The older men might be abstractly busy—"How do, Harry; how do, Mrs. Gurney. Stop in and see me at the business someday, Harry"—but they also occasionally had a glint—sometimes a startled glint—to show they noticed. "Got snagged, eh, boy?" they might ask, clapping Harry vigorously on the back. "And this is the new missus. How's it seem to be a missus, little lady? You're in luck, though. Fine boy, Harry."

As for Bink and Fred, or Deac and Cavender, these swains struck poses, they grew awe-struck. "Well, saw us old trees down and roll us through the rapids! Gurney and Mrs. Gurney! Harry, you old pie thief, Harry—where'd you find *her?*"

These same boys might later grow tedious about baseball or Amiot or their eternal bicycles, but always at leaving she once more got their full attention.

"Let's plan ourselves a party," she would suggest. "What do you say we get up a big bunch for the Habakanaw?"

"Say, why not?" they responded, always with enthusiasm. "We'll drop by the shed and fix it, Harry."

Sometimes on these weekdays she also had the fun of meeting young men who weren't known only to Harry.

"Why, Wes Jenks!" she could cry, tripping forward. "Wherever have you kept yourself? I haven't seen you since"—arch laughter here—"the stars used to look down. Remember that?"

"Well say, if it isn't an old friend of mine." Wes, taking her hand, would be temporarily stricken in the Adam's apple, which bobbed wildly. "Well say, Harry, I heard you were married—I mean, don't you believe her, Harry; she just——"

"I just!" she could take up, giving Wes a poke. No need to worry about Wes; he admired her, all right.

"Well, what've you folks got to say of marriage, now you've tried it?" Wes might come back. "Any tips for bachelors like me?"

This was badinage into which she could throw herself. And when, inspired, she added, "You must come to see us both now, Wes; we can't lose our old friends. Your sister Hattie too—the one who just got married—bring her along."

"You bet!" Once he got over his first nervousness, there was no holding back in Wes.

In the same way, on other days, they met Clint Mason and Joe Ward. The only trouble—the bewildering, wearisome trouble—was that nothing really ensued from these meetings. Mr. and Mrs. Kenneally, Mr. and Mrs. Orcutt, never requested the company of Mr. and Mrs. Gurney for dinner. Wes and his sister Hattie never turned up before the double doors. Neither did Clint or Joey. As for Bink and Deac and Fred and Cavender, ceaselessly as she prodded Harry—"Aren't you doing anything about that Habakanaw party?"—Harry always had excuses.

"I guess not right now, Frieda. The fellows seem to need their money. I mean, with school opening——"

If *she* got hold of them, she grimly promised herself, she'd fix it, but when she appeared in the woodshed at the ripe time she still got nowhere.

After her pause at the threshold, her surprised "Oh, you have company," Harry would rise hastily from some mess of wheels and sprockets.

"No, it's all right. Just Bink and Cavender. Fellows, you remember——"

"Us remember?" Bink would be dramatic. "Us remember *moonlight?* You aren't fooling, are you, Harry?" But scarce was this amenity begun before Cavender—or Fred or Deac—would interject, "Well, we just dropped—wouldn't want to get between wife and husband—we'll be seeing——" and the next thing she knew they would have slid sideward through the door.

As for Sundays, those days which with Schatzi had been so fertile, these were now less than nothing.

Each time she left the house with Harry, clad in go-to-meeting order (no Gurney dinner ever caused a disarranging of one's stays), she was determined that this time they would not prowl alone. If they emerged early, Bink or Fred or Deac or Cavender might soon be descried, but only in transit. "Little late—you know how that is, Harry." And if these same young men were later sighted, they were then busy as escorts—such absorbed escorts that they could hardly hear their own names.

"Oh, hello, Gurney, hello, Mrs. Gurney," they might finally have to reply, if their names were called very loudly. "I guess"—this latter, apologetically, would be to some young woman who might, the moment before, have been scandalously saucy, but who now stood with lips pursed and brows lifted—"I guess you know Harry. Mrs. Gurney, Miss Nettie Orcutt. Miss Cantrell, Mrs. Gurney. I guess neither of you girls know Mrs. Gurney——"

"I am *afraid* we do not have that pleasure," Miss Nettie Orcutt would drawl musically, while Miss Cantrell murmured.

In vain Frieda spread her graces. "This is *such* luck, just when we were on our way to Pratt's—I guess that must be where you're bound too. Shall we all go in a bunch?"

"Sure." Harry, in these encounters, always perspired, tongue-tied and anxious. "I'll set you all up to a——"

"Oh, we *couldn't!*" Miss Orcutt would deny, as if the suggestion shocked her. "Why, this *minute* we arose from dining. We're due at Nonnie's, too. Heavens, do you know the *time?*"

This last, as Miss Orcutt snapped open the enameled gold watch pendant on her left bosom, would in no wise be for Frieda or for

Harry. Struck by the breathlessness of time, Mr. Stevens, Mr. Pomeroy, Miss Orcutt and Miss Cantrell would sweep on, after only short nods for farewell, or a careless "See you later, Harry," from the boys.

"What's the matter with them?" she stormed, often. "Don't *you* have any *real* friends, Harry?"

But under this cover, which a silent Harry never tore aside, writhed a few maggots. She could not accept her fate as a bride, could not understand that if young men still pranced and preened and dragged their wings a bit before her, they did so only as the frankest kind of game, a duty to themselves, to keep their hands in. From one obtrusion, however, she could not twist aside. These young women of Harry's world who, the moment she appeared as one of them, should have clamored to become just such confidantes, ladies at arms, idolators, attendants and social aides as Schatzi had been, were doing nothing of the sort.

Week after week, as this fact was forced upon her, she moved from hard-breathing anger to something that had in it the fast-budding amoebae of panic. Since it couldn't be the young men who didn't want to know her, it had to be the girls who were holding them back. Naturally those girls would *want* to keep Frieda out; they knew what back seats they must take if she got in. But somehow, in spite of that, she still had to get around them.

The only question was, how?

Elizabeth and Mrs. Gurney she had at first dismissed as too negligible for any social good. As disregarded week vexatiously joined week, however, as it grew more and more apparent that Harry, as a social battering ram, was made of cotton batting, she had to turn, in a spirit of *try anything,* to the two feminine Gurneys.

"Heavens! Here it is two months we've been sisters and we're hardly acquainted!" she reproached Elizabeth, who, unless she were at the piano where her only vocable was an unhearing "M-m-m," was worse than spilled mercury to pin down.

"Perhaps it's because I'm quite busy." Even when secured in the upper hallway, Elizabeth retained an air of being loose and free. "I'm leaving now for a music lesson."

"Couldn't I go along?"

"I'm still playing Bach," returned Elizabeth, and managed to slip by.

Later urgings—"Come on into my room where we can chat all by ourselves"—took long in fruiting, but the day came, finally, when Elizabeth walked tentatively in.

"You'll have to tell me all about your beaux and parties," Frieda at once cozily invited. "I know you must have chances to go out a lot."

Elizabeth turned on her incandescent smile, which glowed dark blue and pervasive, but which, as usual, had doubtful meanings.

"Oh, I really have no beaux," she said before the light dimmed off. "Boys scarcely notice me at all."

This, thought Frieda, was all too likely; what boy would look at a girl in a bunchy white sailor dress—a girl who, as she saw at that moment with fascination, had hair on her face? Downstairs, in rooms genteelly darkened, she never had been aware of this growth, but now, as Elizabeth sat with hands folded in the sling chair just before the window, it was obvious that a silky fine down, like the feathering on a new chick, grew all along the edges of the sallow, bony cheeks.

It took effort to go on, assuringly, "Oh, you've got to have beaux. You go out with me, one of these first Sundays—I'll see you get some."

It was impossible not to wonder, with a shiver, if Elizabeth had that same hair all over.

Later, for Elizabeth's benefit, she took out all her clothes, asking Elizabeth's advice on improvements.

"Everything you have is *extremely* fashionable," Elizabeth repeated, over and over. "I don't see how you could add on more style."

Thinking how Schatzi would have pounced, abubble with ideas for a bow here and a flounce there, Frieda could not feel this lack of interest as anything but dulling and irritating. And by the time Elizabeth in turn made her proffer—"I'm afraid you don't find my music stimulating"—she was in no mood for finesse.

"You could do better though, couldn't you? Couldn't you sometime get some new pieces, like 'The Bowery' and 'My Sweetheart's the Man in the Moon'?"

"Sometime I must," Elizabeth replied while Frieda was hanging away a dress.

"Oh, do," implored Frieda. "Then we could get up a party——" But when she turned around again, Elizabeth was gone.

What, as she crossly asked herself, could you do with a girl like that? Just when they were getting to points of common interest!

Yet, for very lack of other fields to cultivate, she had to keep digging. Hard as it was, when the dark girl was present, to see Elizabeth as taking part in any gaieties at all, it equally was difficult, on those afternoons when Elizabeth was absent, not to picture her as stealing toward them.

"Couldn't you just *sometime* take me with you?" She pouted, until finally, one day, Elizabeth flashed compliance.

"Come this afternoon, if you like. Bach and Brahms, again, but only half an hour, so it should be bearable."

Ignoring mockery (Elizabeth too had inheritances from her father), Frieda instantly accepted. At least—she counted up these credits as she dressed—this meant that she, Frieda, could walk into Amiot College grounds, not a timorous onlooker, as before, but righteously, belonging there; she could step into one of the august buildings. And you could never tell (this would not down) just who might see her and be smitten.

Unhappily, it still was summer, unhappily the winding gravel paths were quite unpeopled. True, Amiot buildings, set amid spreading lawns and oaks, were inescapably impressive—gargantuan monuments of cut gray stone, with six-foot window embrasures and portals like caverns, but once you were inside! Almost with horror, she discovered that the building Elizabeth entered had quite the same narrow long corridors, the same smell of chalk and damp woolens, the same square classrooms, the same grayed blackboards, the same scuffed floors, that she had remembered from West Haven's public school.

Voice rising, she asked, "Is this what *all* these buildings are, inside?"

"Oh, more or less." Elizabeth was careless.

"Well." Words, right then, failed. If she had visioned the interiors at Amiot as anything, it was as a succession of parlors, well crowded with bric-a-brac, tables, brocade chairs, window drapes and statues, through which the luckier young people of West Haven idled sumptuously. What connection Mr. Gurney might have with such an institution she had not bothered to think out. Now, seeing one of these interiors at its barest, she had another falsity to chalk against the world. Like so much else, Amiot College too was just a sham. Outside, all that heavy spacious grandeur; inside, just a mess of miserable little schoolrooms.

By the time she had reached the eyrie to which, after three flights of stairs, Elizabeth led her, she was resigned to having the whole venture be dust in her mouth. Elizabeth's teacher proved to be a bearded old Santa Claus, sixty if he was a day, with eyes and ears for no one but his pupil. The playing went on for centuries, until Frieda was a rag.

"But that *can't* be *all* you do!" she insisted from despair on the way home. "There *must* be other things too. Things for *fun*."

"I'll be back in high school soon," replied Elizabeth, who, after her lesson, was spent and tranquil. "That's often fun."

"You know what I mean," persisted Frieda. "I mean friends of yours, girl friends——"

"I've got some friends, yes, of course." As with so much else Elizabeth said, this response too was barriered.

Rashly Frieda took the gage.

"Instead of taking me to anything like that music lesson, couldn't you take me to meet *them?*"

"Of course," came a ready answer, too simple to be simple. "If they ask you."

That was the slap, the wet cloth in Frieda's face. Useless for her to mutter as she did, "How can they ask me when they never even meet me?" To this Elizabeth let silence be answer—Frieda had met girls through Harry, and they hadn't asked her.

From Mrs. Gurney she had even less hope of social succor, but rigorously she set herself to getting what there was.

Daily, after the washing of noon dishes, Mrs. Gurney apostrophized herself, "Oh dear, I suppose I should spruce up a bit, in case someone calls."

Frieda's first experience of a call, however, did not come until her marriage was in its sixth week. Running downstairs on an afternoon when, out of petulance, she had elected to remain indoors, she found installed with Mrs. Gurney a woman whom she identified as the ague-shaken ancient peerer from the church.

"Oh! I thought you were alone!" Well inside the parlor, where Mrs. Gurney could scarcely send her off, she went through her formula for surprise entrances. Mrs. Twillett, for a change, was quite pleased to meet Frieda, quite pleased to have Frieda stay. Mrs. Twillett's almost buried eyes—the only fixed objects in a mask that twitched and jerked continuously—moved never a second's whip from Frieda's face.

"How awful," murmured Frieda sympathetically, to a recital of Mrs. Twillett's troubles with digestion. After Mrs. Twillett had had tea (spilling most of it) and gone, Frieda could not keep from taking off, before her mirror upstairs, some of the old crone's jerks and twitches. It was absolutely killing, how Mrs. Twillett came to life, and for once she felt elated and cheerful. Just let people—no matter how funny they were!—get accustomed to her, and they'd accept her, all right.

After a second call, however, she knew the shoals in even this inlet.

The second caller, welcomed by Elizabeth at the front door—"Oh, Mrs. Drake! Mama will be so delighted!"—was no Mrs. Twillett. Mrs. Mathew Drake, sailing into the parlor in a flutter of graciously puffed salmon silk, held conversational reins tight in her hands. Recognizing Mrs. Mathew Drake as the mother of Jessie Drake, Frieda once more did her best, but this time had harder going.

"Elizabeth, my dear!" Mrs. Drake greeted warmly. "And *dear* Mrs. Gurney!" When it came to Frieda, however, her "Oh yes, Harry's wife" was so perfunctory as to approach rudeness.

"You must forgive me," so Mrs. Drake rattled on, turning immediately from Frieda, "for not coming sooner. But I declare, that daughter of mine—nothing would do her, right in midsummer, but packing off to Meridian—that's where she is now, with her cousins. Never a thought in that girl's head but good times and beaux. I just look forward to the day—I declare I do—when she will settle. Though as I sometimes say——"

When Elizabeth went off to fix tea, Mrs. Gurney, once in a while, managed to squeeze in a few antiphonal remarks.

"Elizabeth, of course, is so different. I sometimes believe Elizabeth has never an idea but her music. Of course, Elizabeth has always been *spirituelle*——"

For the entire half hour of the call, even while the tea was being drunk, Mrs. Drake spoke Jessie, while Mrs. Gurney, sometimes politely waiting for a break, sometimes in unison, replied Elizabeth. Neither paid the least attention when Frieda tried to make herself heard.

"Will Jessie be back in West Haven this fall?" she asked, and "I think I'd rather know your daughter, Mrs. Drake, than almost anybody in West Haven!"

The words fell loudly, but apparently unheard. At the end of the exact half hour, Mrs. Drake stood, took both Mrs. Gurney's hands in hers.

"Don't imitate me, now, my dear; don't be so long." With a kiss for Elizabeth and a vague "Oh yes" in Frieda's direction, she was gone.

"Dear Mrs. Drake, always so interested in *everyone,*" said Mrs. Gurney in a glow, for epilogue.

At the time, Frieda retired with head high and heart hot—that woman would find out, that woman would be sorry. Afterward, however, she found herself moody, unable to disguise entirely the shortness of her rope. Harry, Elizabeth, Mrs. Gurney—what other resources had she? Certainly *Mr. Gurney* would do nothing for her.

From this state of beginning despond she was snatched abruptly, in late August, when after hesitation, palpitation and discussion Mrs. Gurney decided she would have some people—quite a few people —in for dinner.

"I'm sure I can manage." In considering the prospect, Mrs. Gurney wore a reckless air. "I'm sure I can manage somehow."

Twice burned as she was, Frieda's spirits, at this promise, could not be kept from lifting. Mr. and Mrs. Gurney, once or twice, had gone out for dinner, but so far, during her residence, no one had been asked in. Perhaps she was mistaken, but didn't it seem as if she were somehow concerned in this dinner? Wouldn't it—since she would have to be present—almost be a public avowal that the Gurneys had decided to make the best of things, at last?

Revigorated, she joined enthusiastically in preparty cleaning, scrubbing even the baseboards and the drugget in her room. Hours went for ironing her lilac muslin (old, but "wear something light and pretty," Mrs. Gurney said). Hours more went for burnishing heirloom silver, heirloom crystal, heirloom china and heirloom linen— "That piece, I believe my great-aunt Martha—no, it must have been Aunt Susan—oh dear, or was it Father's side?"—that Mrs. Gurney drew from cupboard, closet and chest. From Klaumeister's came a lamb leg, oysters and a turkey; Harry brought garden stuff in bushels; patty shells, jellies, rolls, shaped butter, shelled peas, bottled wines and cheeses heaped the buttery.

This dinner, as Frieda could see with exultance, really would be done in style; it was something to know the Gurneys were at least aware of good magazine practice. Continuously Mrs. Gurney ticked off names—"Dr. and Mrs. Watts, Mr. and Mrs. Drake, Dr. and Mrs. Simon, Mrs. Langesley—we can't leave her out now she's a widow, and anyway she'll make the table balance—Mr. and Mrs. Coburn, Dr. and Mrs. Thompson, Mr. and Mrs. Vincent. Let's see—with us, that's sixteen."

Not until the afternoon of the party, not until the table stood in day-shaded glitter, waiting to leap to brilliance at the touch of lamp and candle, did Frieda see the fateful omission of her mother-in-law's counting.

With Frieda and Elizabeth both hovering, Mrs. Gurney, in the last stages of lightheaded, driven frenzy, flitted around the table, laying down the menus on which the courses were set off by Emersonian quotations.

"Mr. Gurney's at the head, of course, mine at the foot. Mrs. Watts to *his* right, Dr. Watts to mine. Such a responsibility, the president of Amiot—oh, where will I put Harry? Mr. Drake by Mrs. Watts— or Dr. Simon—no, Mrs. Watts can't possibly speak loud enough; he's *so* deaf——"

All this to Frieda was just window dressing; impatiently she waited for the decision of consuming importance—where, between what two men, would she sit? When the folders remaining in Mrs. Gurney's hands dwindled to four, and then to two, and then, finally, to none, she stood staring at the table in a kind of stupor. This couldn't be

—in the whole preparation there had been an acceptance of her, an inclusion, more complete than at any time before.

Too taken by surprise for concealment, she blurted, "But me—where do I sit?"

The instant of taken-aback silence which received this, the succeeding gleam in Elizabeth's eyes, the dismay in Mrs. Gurney's, were things she scarcely saw; the fact emerging was too dwarfing.

"Oh dear," gasped Mrs. Gurney, "I thought you—it's *quite* customary—the young ladies of the household—Elizabeth could hardly do it alone——"

Elizabeth—and Frieda—were to serve.

She thought she could not hold herself back. One step forward, and all that white linen could jump toward her, the glasses and china could leap and crash; a few running steps and she could be in the kitchen where kettles could be thrust from the stove to spill and roll their steaming contents on the floor; meats could be slung from the oven, the contents of the buttery could be flung in one confused irreparable heap. Why she did not take these steps she herself could not have said; it was almost as if she had been robbed not of the physical but of the moral strength to take them. Before anything else could be said or done she turned to go up to her room.

After a period upstairs she came down in her lilac muslin to do obediently as Elizabeth directed, but she did so dully, as an automaton. She had no more expectations of the party. It could be no surprise, now, that the gentlemen and ladies who sat so formally and stiffly resplendent about the no less resplendent table (she saw them there for the first time) were a collection of oblivious Mrs. Drakes and Mr. Gurneys. Such fits and snatches of conversation as she caught— "Yes, both air and water on Mars, or at least so our spectroscope shows us." "No, no, that's his Achilles heel, I think." "At least you don't see Zola here in every hand, as you do in Paris"—should have had almost no meaning. Talking was done mostly by men; women confined themselves to brief, spurring interjections—"But how fascinating!" "I'd never have thought of that by myself!" "You must, you *must,* Dr. Watts, tell him your anecdote of Brittany!"

After the long tendering of food, after she and Elizabeth, in the kitchen, had snatched ashen bites (for once, she had thought, she would eat enough in that house!), after they had run upstairs for freshening and then, as if just arriving, tripped downstairs to be presented, she was prepared to have those smiles and greetings for Elizabeth be warm, while those for her were sharp and estimating, or at least reserved. There was nothing here but the old story, all over. When the last guest left she turned away under a load so heavy she could scarcely lift it with her body up the stairs.

CHAPTER XVIII

Stumping homeward from Gurneys', Father Doern knew himself, vexedly, as unsuccessful. He had not handled it well, that visit; why, in addition to all the other troubles that beset him, did he have to have another young person who proposed to leave the Church? Long ago he had given up dreaming of city benefices and cathedrals; the Church in America had but humble uses for immigrant priests. Still, within his sphere he had done his best; he had not faltered in the gathering of funds. Someday in this town, God willing, would rise a citadel of Catholic worship which should stand forever as a witness to his unrelenting labors.

It was no new problem, this problem of recusancy, but one he met all too often; they seemed beset, these children who were the first-born of another continent. Behind them, though, far beyond them, the problem was all part of another problem and another struggle— that battle in which his Church had engaged since the Renaissance, a battle to keep itself alive in an alien and secular world. This was the people's tragedy, their loss, that they could not see where any true fullness, and true richness, lay; all that had meaning to them was what they could sensually feel or hold—money and arrogance, wide farmlands, a lack of restraints—Lincoln and Bryan and democracy and a full dinner pail.

All the Church asked, in return for its benefits, was so little. Simply that its parishioners belong, believe, confess, attend, commune, contribute. This girl now, this Elfrieda, never had given more than lip service; she was one of that Schlempke lot, a family in which only the mother was devout. Once the girl had seemed to think she might have a vocation, but, painstakingly as he had received this possibility, he had believed little in it; even then, while still a child, she had had too much in her of the world, the flesh. As a young woman——

Undoubtedly she was handsome, or what some people would call handsome. Her pale small eyes, as she swished toward him in the parlor where he waited, were defiant under the elaborately dressed hair, her bosom in its frilled shirtwaist was high.

Taking her hand, keeping his tone kindly, he had at once said,

"You have been missed at Mass and at confession. I hope you are well."

"Oh yes," she had laughed shortly. "I'm quite well."

"Neglect of the Church, my child, is serious and must be repaired. Would you perhaps see me elsewhere?"

"I hadn't thought"—this had bold haughtiness—"of seeing you anywhere."

At impudence he could only be stern. "Sit down, my child. It is not thus easily that one forsakes one's father's church, one's faith."

"I'm married. From now on I go to my husband's church."

"Married. By what priest?"

A shrug. "It was in Meridian. A minister of some kind."

To let her feel the monstrousness of what she said, he did not at once answer. "Surely you were taught," he then reminded gravely, "that in the eyes of Holy Mother Church——"

She laughed fliply, preceding him with what he would have said. "Such marriage is no marriage. Well, don't worry! It's marriage to *them!*"

"For your soul's cleanliness on earth, its hope of heaven——"

Repudiation was in every angle of her body, turned contemptuously aside. Although he talked long and, he had thought, not too badly, he had known with each word the measure of its failure. When he warned, "Penitence needs always to be soon, before the heart is hardened," she replied, "I'd have to hurry."

Shaking his head as he trudged, he wondered if, indeed, she would not have to hurry. Even yesterday, when the young husband had come to him, saying that his new wife seemed lost and unhappy, he had not really had much hope; it was not in their youth that these changelings could be touched. The husband was a strange mate for that bold young creature—a pale boy, stumbling and uncertain; it must have taken courage for him, a Protestant, to ask help of a priest. That house, not one of wealth, but with books, a good piano—it was not often, with his parish, that he got into such places—reminded him of the Uberhofers', near Stuttgart.

Well, useless or not, he would have to see the girl again. Her father too, though he was a thin reed, and her mother. A pity, when he had this drive for funds.

Running back upstairs from her set-to with Father Doern—one of the things she did most often, it seemed, in the Gurney household, was run back upstairs—Frieda drank in to its last drop her little thimbleful of mastery and released defiance.

This was the way things should go—why was it that with people of her own world she could be so masterful and sure, while with people of the new she could be neither? Ever since Mrs. Gurney had said it was a pity she should break entirely with her old friends she had been expecting some such visit; she had known then they were up to something. Well, just let them go ahead. Just let them try. They'd find out how much they could force her.

Yet, after this cordial, she relapsed almost at once into the brooding misery which had held her since the party.

The Gurneys, she had found, could be solicitous. When, on the morning after her final straw, she had said only, "I'm not getting up," Harry had asked if he should get a doctor, Mrs. Gurney had arisen from her own prostration to quiver up- and downstairs with the best leftovers on a tray, Elizabeth had come near enough to banter, "It can't have been we ate too much," even Mr. Gurney, toward nightfall, had paused to pronounce, "Undoubtedly excitement." Three days later, too, after the doctor (called in with what hints she could imagine) had slammed his case shut—"Just vapors—get her out of bed—get her to doing something"—they had not followed the prescription.

With somewhat less than her usual vagueness, Mrs. Gurney, that afternoon, had sat by the bedside ripping an old coat that was to be a jacket for Elizabeth.

"We know it's hard for you too, dear," Mrs. Gurney had got out, with eyes tightly fixed on the ripping. "It would be different—I'm sure it would be different—if you had a place of your own. I want to say—I'm sure the others thought so too—that you did *well* at the dinner. You were *entirely* a daughter of the house, quiet and well behaved. They would have been quite displeased, you know, if you had sat at table and I waited. In time—I'm sure in time—when Harry's through school—when people have had a chance——" Aware, perhaps, that she was going around in circles, she had hastily, when Frieda did not answer, added a question:

"In the meantime, are you certain you should break so absolutely with your old life—with old friends?"

Over Frieda, lying iron-rigid in the bed, these words had fallen with no effect; she would have said she did not hear them. She had considered the Gurneys much too obtuse, herself too adroit, for them to be aware of her full purposes. She wished only that Mrs. Gurney would go out. When the Gurneys were safely away she could rise to lash about the room, to wear out that way some of her chaotic impulses. As she had that afternoon by the set table, she wanted to break out, to wreck the people and the things about her. Time and again she dreamed over scenes in which the Gurneys, Mrs. Drake, Dr. Watts, Nettie Orcutt, all Harry's boy friends, came humbly begging for her company, while she imperiously ordered them off. And then again she wanted only to be languid.

At home, at her father's, she had read few newspapers; there had been few to read. Perforce, however, during the long dull summer at Gurneys', she had come to know two—the Meridian *Journal* and the West Haven *Weekly Independent*. Of these, the second had become her spyglass.

Mrs. Farnsworth Watts and Miss Theora Watts, Mrs. J. P. Orcutt and Miss Nettie Orcutt, were among travelers to Meridian who enjoyed the concert given in that city Thursday evening by Mme. Augusta Oberstrom, the celebrated Swedish Prima Donna. The ladies returned to West Haven Friday.

Mr. and Mrs. Roy Page were the recipients of a surprise Saturday evening, when ten of their friends dropped in, the occasion being the eighth wedding anniversary of the popular young couple. After hours of discourse and jollity, a delicious collation, brought by the guests, was served, and the hosts presented with a handsome Greek vase. The *Independent* joins in congratulations.

Mr. Frederick Pomeroy of this city traveled to De Laittre by the 2:18, returning on the Midnight. Ah there, Fred. Could De Laittre hold some charm West Haven lacks?

At noon lunch Wednesday, Miss Beth Cantrell entertained nine of her young friends in honor of Mrs. Palmer Hake and Mrs. Frank Kenneally, two Brides of the season. The colors, pink and white, were carried out in sweet peas and roses, and also, to the admiration of the guests, in hand-painted place cards, ices, cakes and frostings. A gay time was reported.

The strains of Waltz, Schottische and Mazurka enlivened the confines of the Elks' Hall Saturday evening, as the alumni of West Haven High School joined hands in the Summer Dance. Amid the merry throng, which numbered well over fifty, were seen Mr. and Mrs. Palmer Hake, Mr. and Mrs. Frank Kenneally, Miss Nettie Orcutt, Mr. Walter (Bink) Stevens . . .

These events lived. That dance—why hadn't Harry taken her there? If only people weren't so hateful she could have been a queen there, seized from one partner by the next. She too was a season's bride; she should have sat with Cecilia Hake and Louise Kenneally at the luncheon, admired by all. Fred Pomeroy could just as well have let her and Harry—some other girl also, of course—go along to De Laittre. That any of these functions were dull she could not have been told. Never did she vision the Page party as an occasion when the wives gathered in the kitchen to talk recipes and babies, with the men in the dining room rumbling comfortably over politics and crops. She did not see the Oberstrom concert as another, somewhat more thickly attended, music lesson. All these events which took place outside her orbit were in a glitter; they, and her place in them, existed high, entrenched, resplendent, denied to her from nothing but malice.

One item, clipped from the *Independent's* filler section, she read until nothing remained but fuzzed ink on a fragile rag. This item was entitled "Women of the Day."

> Mme. Modjeska, it is said, could raise $75,000. Mrs. Mary Livermore is said to have $75,000 of the $120,000 made from her lectures. Mrs. Southworth's novels have brought her a fortune. Mrs. Harriet Hubbard Ayer is coining money. Mrs. Mary Ann Connolly, the well-known Dressmaker, is known to have a large income from her needle. Lydia van Finkestan, who talks on the Holy Land at $100 per lecture, often gives three such lectures in a day.

Even more than West Haven's social doings, this clipping fevered her dreams. What did lecturers do? They talked. Why couldn't she talk? If she found out what Harriet Hubbard Ayer did, she might be able to do that too. If she had one hundred thousand dollars——

That any change was occurring in her concept of herself and her universe she did not at the time discern. Two days after the doctor's visit she was up, fitfully resuming some kind of life about the house.

You've tried so hard, her mind said, these days. It's all right if you take a rest. Maybe a breathing spell is what you need. You might find some way really clever.

It was during this time that Harry made his ridiculous suggestion. She had known Harry had something on his mind; for days there had been a perverse pleasure in denying him a hearing. But at last one evening after they had come upstairs she wearied of holding him off.

"You know, Frieda, it might be—I've been thinking——" He was at the washstand, drying his hands, glancing toward her with those uncertain eyes which were so much paler a blue than Elizabeth's.

"All right, spit it out." Any graciousness toward Harry had long been thrown aside as superfluous.

"Father agrees—I mean it would be all right with everybody, and it would give you something to fix your mind on——"

"I *said* all right. What *is* it?"

He took a deep breath, and words rushed.

"Frieda, why don't you start school this fall too? No, wait—I know it would be high school. But you'd have Elizabeth to go with—Elizabeth is just your age. And you'd find, Frieda, that it would be *fun*. No one would think it queer; since I'm in school too they'd admire——"

The anger she was later to feel was slow in coming; she at first heard only humor.

"Me, go to school?" she laughed out. "Me, a married woman?"

"Lots of boys and girls who come in from the country are older than you are; my father would help with the——"

Once more she laughed, turning over, burying her face in the pillow, folding her arms above her head.

"That's the kind of crazy thing you would think up." She did not bother to tell him she was ineligible for high school; even if she had finished the grades the whole thing was impossible.

To his continued pleading—"It would be something we could do together, Frieda—I'd help with your lessons—you'd make friends"—she stayed unheeding.

"I'm grown up," she informed him. "I know everything I need to know now."

Not until next day did anger begin spurting. To think they could plan to humiliate her, a woman grown, to the position of *school child,* just to satisfy their supercilious disdain.

It was to exhaust emotions arising from this incident that she went out to walk, this time alone. And, somewhat to her surprise, such action actually was relieving. She met, for one thing, Mr. J. P. Orcutt. Mr. Orcutt was much more noticing than when Harry was along; he said he'd been looking for her to come in and pick that furniture for the bridal nest, and, playfully, he shook her elbow. High-and-mighty Miss Nettie Orcutt should have seen *that!* Except at church she never had happened to come upon either Cecilia or Palmer—Cecilia, probably, looked down her nose at plebeian strolling on Sunday afternoons. But after the pleasant small encounter with Mr. Orcutt, a slow delicious blooming woke—what would happen if, while she was thus out alone, she should meet Palmer, he too by himself? Whatever had gone on in Palmer's mind since his marriage, he couldn't have *forgotten*.

Neither that day nor the next brought Palmer, but the very possibility occupied her. Also she began thinking of Rozzie, and, a little, even of Schatzi. So far she had rather shirked the idea of Schatzi;

making up with Schatzi might take some doing. Now, however, she began to think of it as something that could as well be done sooner as later; after all, she had now been married a full three months, and Schatzi should be well over any pique she might have felt. Rozzie too—there wasn't any reason why she shouldn't take up with Rozzie immediately. Not that she was listening to Mrs. Gurney on the subject of old friends, but simply that she would soon have to do something about fall clothes, and since it didn't seem likely she would be able to employ a really good dressmaker—goodness knew she wouldn't wear a product of the *Gurney* needle—she could just as well let Rozzie have the work.

Harry had been meticulous in giving her of his woodshed proceeds, and on the basis of this asset—"I won't need it for a thing else" —she in course besieged him.

"I don't see why we don't have our wedding pictures taken. Everyone else does. I'm sure a great many people must think it's funny we haven't."

Harry's flinching response—"You needn't make *fun* of the way things are, Frieda"—changed, when he found out she meant it, to a rather numbed assent. Foggily he accompanied her to Balik's, where, before the momentous single eye of the camera, she spent a busy and almost contented afternoon, first posing and reposing Harry, then assuming a dozen attitudes herself, all to the excited radiance, the welcome, the running feet, the exclamations of Rozzie and her father. Harry also accompanied her for proofs, but when the finished pictures were to be picked up—fortunately school had opened by that time so she had no trouble—she saw to it that she went alone.

"Really, is that *us*?" she gasped, when swart, mustachioed Mr. Balik, with a breath-held, wordless gesture, placed his handiwork before her. "Really, Mr. Balik, I'm *overcome!*"

Actually, she thought, what she had gotten wasn't *too* bad; she had chosen the one in which Harry stood with his right hand on the chair back, left arm akimbo; if anything could give him an air, that did. She in the chair—of course the light made her eyes look not as large as they were, and Balik might have had the sense to have her tilt her head a bit—she'd done all the work. Still, no one could deny she had looks; no one could say she didn't hold herself well.

Mr. Balik's expectation burst at her enthusiasm.

"You like him? You think Balik makes good picture, eh?" Columnar arms flew wide. "I tell you—I *give* him to you!"

"Oh no, Mr. Balik, I couldn't. You have to let me pay."

Usually, on such occasions, Rozzie stood by with eyes anxious and head shaking a faint negative, but this time Rozzie too had only smiles and nods.

"Of course we give them to you," she acceded warmly. "It's our wedding present."

"Well, if you put it that way," wavered Frieda. Rozzie had almost improved in the past months; Rozzie's red-brown braids were now wound about her head instead of hanging, and she had grown taller. If it weren't for her form, Rozzie might almost have been presentable.

When, after the final "Of course if you insist, all I can do is thank you" Frieda went on to add a wistful "I just hate to leave here, it's so like old times," Rozzie was eager to retain her.

"Don't go—you've become so fine I hardly—but come back to my room; I've something to show you."

"Something" turned out to be a Singer, not new, but a much later model than Mrs. Schlempke's. Over this machine Rozzie hung with the ecstasy of a mother of forty for her first-born, and when she said that with this machine—well, just let her try, the offer was accepted graciously.

Leaving Hake's two hours later with a dress length of thin wool cashmere, rust-red and embroidered, as well as the pictures, she almost was in a glow. The cloth could easily be explained to Harry; she had dropped in at her mother's to leave one of the pictures, she could say, and her mother had made her a gift. Things still could come right for her, when she saw her way.

Since it was well to be substantiated, she made the trip down Water Street to her old home, and then, reluctant still to return where all too likely she would get her spirits dampened, she wandered a while longer about the lumberyard. But when again she did not see Palmer, she was visited by a rushing impulse.

Why shouldn't this be her time to see Schatzi?

It could not quite escape her, as she swiftly turned to go where that impulse led, that she might have reason still for trepidation. Schatzi had thought herself quite set with Harry, and Schatzi of course hadn't known how serious things were for Frieda—or at least how serious they had *seemed* to be. No doubt Schatzi for some time might be distant, but once she had seen the cashmere and the pictures —well, Schatzi had been cross before this, and got over it.

Before the Klaumeisters' porched and elled gray house she allowed herself only the briefest of hesitations. It might be dramatic to appear at the front door—that would set off her new position as a lady. But if she went in at the back, her first encounter would be with Hedda, likely, and that would take care of any awkwardness. Schatzi would never be anything more than stiff in front of Hedda.

In fact, she decided when the back door was reached, what she would do would be to rap lightly and then walk in without waiting for admission, just as she long had done. The moment when her knuckles beat their tattoo was a high point of anticipation; whatever happened now: welcome, pouts, even tears, must in its way be satisfying; Schatzi would hardly be able to hide her envy of what Frieda had.

"Surprise!" she called gaily, as, under her hand, the door swung inward. "Look who's turned up! It took all this time, but I got here!"

She could scarcely, as she saw in a rapid first glance, have asked for a better situation. Not only was Schatzi right there in the kitchen —at the sink—but both Hedda and Mrs. Klaumeister were there too, the girl dropping cut chicken into a steaming pot, Mrs. Klaumeister rolling noodles. Schatzi never on this earth would fuss before her mother.

For entire moments, however, Schatzi kept her back bent above the sink. Imagine, thought Frieda, catching Schatzi with *vegetables,* of all things—Schatzi, who said she scarcely ever went inside the kitchen! The wait lasted so long that, after this gleeful small perception, there didn't seem to be much more to think; all one could do, somehow, was look again, and more fully, at Mrs. Klaumeister, who stood with her rolling pin quiet above the board, her flesh-buried eyes fixed.

"Really," Frieda tried to bubble, "I'm no ghost! It's me—Frieda—come to visit! Schatzi, I've such *loads* to tell you——"

Two movements occurred at once. Schatzi turned, and Mrs. Klaumeister, heavily but swiftly, appeared at Schatzi's side—just how, Frieda did not quite see. She was too taken aback. It wasn't Schatzi at the sink after all, it was Gisela. No, it was Schatzi, but how *changed!* Schatzi had softened, she was flabby and colorless, her hair was any which way——

"Why, Schatzi," she said, more uncertainly. "I didn't know you'd been sick. I haven't heard one single word since——"

Schatzi was not moving again, Schatzi was not speaking. But Mrs. Klaumeister, rolling forward, was. Mrs. Klaumeister's eyes, lit, looked like tiny dark bulbs, Mrs. Klaumeister's bulk was ferocious, her advance that of a ponderous catapult.

"Yessss," she hissed. "She isss sssick. Not for that boy she is sick, but from you. Get from here."

"But you don't understand. I came only to——" Giving way back-

ward, Frieda traversed rather hastily those few feet of kitchen floor
which she had covered; she got over the doorsill, and the back porch.

In the kitchen doorway, Mrs. Klaumeister delivered a shout.

"You come here again, we set the dog!" The door slammed.

"Well!" Frieda brought forth from a deep vat. "Well!" Much as
she had expected—well! Could Schatzi actually have been *that* gone
over Harry? Over *Harry,* of all people?

But as she walked, stepping carefully, past the Klaumeister zinnias,
she reached another staggered guess. Could it be that Harry had gone
to Schatzi, sometime, and explained? That would be just like Harry—
but he couldn't. No one could give her away, not that far. "I suppose
you think *Schatzi* would like living here," she had said to him once
or twice—who could blame her, the way things were? "I suppose you
think your folks would have gotten on better with Schatzi." Harry,
at these assaults, had pinched shut, white and quiet. "Schatzi and I
would never have married until I was working," he had answered. "I
never intended to bring Schatzi here."

Now she had to consider that all too likely he had been guilty of a
climaxing treason. He had let Schatzi *know.* Schatzi would have been
certain Frieda acted deliberately—Schatzi had been so broken up she
hadn't even hidden what she was feeling from her mother. Schatzi,
who had held off getting a doctor for her own sister——

It took her all the way back to Gurneys' to get herself in any kind
of order.

CHAPTER XIX

That same week she learned of the splendor with which
Cecilia was to be set up.

PALMER HAKE BUYS LIGHTFOOT RESIDENCE—news of such import was
carried, not as an item, but on the *Independent's* front page. Ten
rooms, quarter-sawed oak everywhere, grounds covering two acres, a
carriage house, evergreens, a cistern holding five hundred barrels—no
slightest detail was skimped by the *Independent,* nor was any of the
succeeding flurry.

> During the extensive alterations on her recently purchased
> home, Mrs. Palmer Hake, together with her mother, Mrs. Thomas
> Amiot, is in Meridian for the selection of Household Furnishings.
> Two Antique Persian Rugs, gifts to Mrs. Hake from John M. and

Mark K. Amiot, her half brothers of Boston, are said to be the keynote for these furnishings.

Among incoming freight this week was an entire carload of furniture for Mr. and Mrs. Palmer Hake, the same being intended for the Hakes' new residence, now nearing completion.

Mr. Pierre Noval, Interior Decorator from Meridian, has taken up residence at the Benson House while he looks to the draping and arranging of the Palmer B. Hake domicile.

Mrs. Palmer Hake and mother, Mrs. Thomas Amiot, left this morning for New York City and the East, where, amid a round of social pleasures, Mrs. Hake intends to pick up those garnitures, ornaments and knickknacks which, together with those objets d'art which are the result of her European travels, will form the grace note of her new home. Mrs. Hake and Mrs. Amiot, it is expected, will be gone a month.

It did not strike Frieda that in these chronicles Palmer played a rather secondary role. All she could see was the dinginess and ever-increasing ulceration of her own sad lot, against the brilliance which but for a stroke, a single moment of misfortune, might have been hers. That there would then have been no Persian rugs, no sponsoring purse-heavy mother, no attendant father, that Mr. Pierre Noval would have been unlikely and the objets d'art certainly non-existent—these facts she did not for a moment entertain. This, all this, was for Palmer's wife, and she, if she had been Palmer's wife, would have attained it.

Under one of these bits of news appeared another which at first struck her indifferently. The *Independent* announced·

The Browning Society opens its Fall Season Friday, at the home of Mrs. Mathew Drake. Mrs. Farnsworth Watts will read from the Poet, Miss Elizabeth Gurney will oblige with music, and Miss Jessie Drake with a group of readings in the Lighter Vein. All members are cordially urged to come.

Long ago she had quit being moved by such notices; she was not among those urged to come. But this time her mind, sharpening, went back. Miss Elizabeth Gurney——

Once or twice, hadn't Mrs. Gurney mentioned the Brownings? "We would all, I feel, have gained so much more if it had been Emerson we studied——"

Mrs. Gurney, probably, belonged.

From apparently no source came another impulse—much stronger than the one that had sent her to Schatzi. With abruptness she accosted Mrs. Gurney.

"You're going to the Brownings, aren't you? Elizabeth is. I'll go along."

"Why really—I hadn't thought—I so often don't go——" Mrs. Gurney, obviously, was taken entirely unprepared; Mrs. Gurney, Frieda thought, had expected to wait until Frieda had gone out for a walk, and then sneak off alone.

She did not, however, voice this suspicion. Instead, she added glibly, "Then it's settled. Unless you decide not to. In that case I'll meet Elizabeth and go with her."

"Oh no, no," hurried Mrs. Gurney. "On second thought—I believe I will go." Here she once more struggled. "I'm afraid you'll find—it's all women, you know—I hope you won't feel slighted if——"

"No," returned Frieda. "I quite expect to be slighted."

In this expectation she was not, as she soon saw on Friday, to be at all disappointed. But now for some reason—some reason connected with Schatzi and Cecilia and the whole hatefulness of everything that had happened to her since her marriage—that fulfillment was a hair shirt to be hugged.

Mrs. Drake, a welcoming fond hostess in the glowing darkness of her front hallway ("Mrs. Gurney! How delightf——"), got no further before her voice squeaked upward, carrying her brows with it. "You've brought your—how—you'll find chairs, I think, in the sitting room; the parlor is *quite* crowded."

"I still see a *few* parlor places," contradicted Frieda. She was, she found, able and composed. When she steered Mrs. Gurney to the parlor, when a hush fell, to be succeeded by whispers, when she and Mrs. Gurney were met feebly, "So glad you came—oh yes, at church, wasn't it?" she didn't care. Cavalierly, head a bit tilted, she sat examining the Drakes' crimson looped overcurtains, their needlepoint chairs, their hand-crocheted tidies, their rose-pattern brussels, the shells on their whatnot; if she caught an eye before it fled she nodded happily, but no more. Not until she recognized a woman in a chair behind her did she speak.

"You're Mrs. Noble, aren't you?" she asked clearly. "Eddie Noble's mother? I know Eddie very well. From Hake's."

"Yes, of course." A mouse tail-caught by a cat, Mrs. Noble gulped and strained in Frieda's clutch. "Eddie is—I've sometimes thought I should make *every* sacrifice so he could go to college, but if anyone is to be our merchant princes of the future—the practical experience——"

"That's just the experience he gets, at Hake's," agreed Frieda warmly. "I'm sure Eddie will do well, Mrs. Noble."

Content with the small silence which went up after this, she settled herself for the program. To Mrs. Watts's reading of *Prospice* she listened with head even more tilted. No phrase intoned by Mrs. Watts made too much sense, but from the rather blank look on the faces around her she gathered that this was a state not confined to her. Elizabeth played. Miss Jessie Drake, just back from eight weeks in Meridian, saucy black eyes this time surmounting a violet summer wool with rows and rows of pale green satin baby-ribbon insertion, first pretended, in verse, that she was a child of four being held up to a cow, second, also in verse, that she was a young man torn between three young women, and third, likewise in verse, that she was a young lady on a picnic with a storm coming up.

In a slight way, Jessie did rather better than might have been expected, Frieda acceded, joining generously in the clapping. What, she wondered, would happen to the politely amused, gracious faces, if she, Frieda, were now to arise and give them Mrs. Twillett—or Mrs. Drake —or Mrs. Gurney? In pleased relish of this vision, she sailed through the tea drinking, and when Miss Jessie Drake, in person, came to take away her emptied cup and tea plate, she was not nervous, even though Miss Drake's immediate question had the same clear baiting tone that she had used to Mrs. Noble.

"Aren't you," asked Miss Drake, her black eyes not timid, "the girl who married Harry Gurney?"

"It's nice of you to notice," answered Frieda. "So few do."

"Really? But you're right here from West Haven, aren't you? Your father is a barber right here, isn't he? I should think you would know loads of people. Men, especially."

Frieda nodded, airy. "Oh, I do. I guess that's why I'm married, still so young."

Miss Drake pressed closer, with a playfulness not intended to be masking. "That's too bad of you, you know, marrying Harry. We can't have girls from outside marrying our young men—why, there might be no one left for us to marry!"

She was too bold for the women around her; gasps went up. But no gasp came from Frieda; this at last was open battle.

"That would be too bad, wouldn't it?"

"Oh, it wouldn't do at all. We'll just have to make things so uncomfortable for—for *intruders*—that no other young man will ever follow suit."

"That," said Frieda swiftly, "would be hard on the young man already married, wouldn't it—*if anybody cared?*"

Whatever Jessie Drake had meant to say next was held back. *You* went with Harry and Palmer both, a little, Frieda remembered again, that's why you're doing this, that's why you're open. But I've got you.

"Yes," Miss Jessie Drake at last said, quietly, "if anybody cared." After that she walked away with Frieda's discarded teacup, plate and napkin, quietly.

What had happened to her? Kicking fallen leaves as she went, Frieda walked strongly, rapidly away from Drakes' and all the Brownings. She had excused herself to Mrs. Gurney—"If you don't mind my going on ahead, I'd like a little walk." And Mrs. Gurney, dumb, had not demurred.

Not long ago she had reproached herself because with Those Others she was timid and submissive, accepting any slight, oversight or rebuff which they cared to tender. But right now she felt as bold and strong toward them as she did toward anyone. Was it because she now knew them more closely, saw through them, could measure and scorn them?

The answer did not come with this experience, but with two others.

Walking one day by the lumberyard, she finally glimpsed Palmer alone and on foot. Rushing forward, she keyed herself to be anything the meeting might demand—distant, reproachful, worldly, roguish, wistful—but she had no chance to display any of these virtuosities. When she was exactly three stores away, Palmer halted in mid-step, snapping his fingers and jerking his head back as if in sudden recollection. Then he dived into the nearest doorway, which was that of Kenneally's Hay, Feed and Grain.

Carried by impetus on past Kenneally's—after all, she could scarcely halt her rush to turn backward—she was forced to see, framed by the one big cobwebbed and dusty window, Palmer's back amid the grain sacks as he stood talking with Mr. Kenneally.

Numbed by the abruptness with which this long-desired meeting was dashed from her, she still was not deceived. Palmer had no business in Kenneally's. At church too he could have evaded Cecilia to drop her a word, if he had wanted to. She could just as well accept it now as later; Palmer didn't want to speak to her.

For the reasons she didn't yet know, she had been able lately to disregard other stings, but the barb of this one could not be torn out; in the soft flesh where it had struck it clung and festered.

The second and last incident came through Mrs. Gurney.

On a Tuesday evening—Tuesday was the *Independent's* day of

weekly issue—she came into the Gurney sitting room to pick up the
paper which, because of a long dress-fitting interlude with Rozzie, she
had not yet read. Mr. Gurney was in his study, Harry upstairs with his
books, Elizabeth at the piano. Only Mrs. Gurney—and Emerson—
were in the room she entered.

On the *Independent's* front page her eye caught that name to which
more than any other she was alert.

MRS. JUNIUS B. HAKE
SUCCUMBS MONDAY

Together with her grieving family, West Haven joins in
mourning the passing of Mrs. Lily Hake, wife of one of West
Haven's most prominent businessmen and citizens. Death,
ascribed to the heart, came after only a few hours of illness, and
was therefore a shock to all.

Born Lily Lensky, Mrs. Hake began life at Hartford, Connecti-
cut, residing there with her parents until, at the age of 18, she
was joined in marriage to Mr. Junius B. Hake, then of Boston. Coming West with her husband in 1872, Mrs. Hake has since been
domiciled in this City. A quiet lady of domestic habits, Mrs.
Hake seldom fared forth from the confines of her home, but
leaves there a sphere in which she will be sadly missed. In addition to her sorrowing husband, she is survived by a son, Palmer B.
Hake, also of this City. Funeral rites will take place Thursday
at the First Congregational Church of West Haven, 2 P.M.

Mr. Hake's wife, Palmer's mother—Frieda spoke astonishment
aloud.

"I didn't know there *was* a Mrs. Hake!"

Mrs. Gurney was immersed in Emerson; Mrs. Gurney, vague as
usual, perhaps forgot it was Frieda, not Elizabeth, in the room. Or
perhaps Mrs. Gurney had forgotten.

"Oh yes," came her absent answer. "But she was some kind of low
foreigner, you know. She never really was received."

For a long time, so long it seemed the whole evening might have
passed, Frieda knew the sensation of being a machine come to rest,
waiting for the jolt, the earthquake shock, which is to shake it to new
form and action. During that time Mrs. Gurney's body grew paralyzed
in its bent crouch over the book, Mrs. Gurney's head when it did
come up moved in slow jerks, until her appalled eyes reached Frieda's
face, until her stricken, flaccid lips could move.

"Oh," she began whispering, "what did I say?"

When voice at last reached Frieda's lips, she too whispered.

"That's what you meant by *time,* isn't it? 'Wait,' you kept saying.

'I'm sure *in time* you will have friends. *In time* people will become accustomed.' That's what you meant. Wait until I was dead, that's what you meant. You thought I'd wait until I was dead—*then* I could go to First Congregational—then you'd receive me for a *funeral!*" Storm that had begun as a whisper leaped in the last words to screaming fury.

She had been sitting in a rocker, the *Independent* between her hands; now she too leaped, through the paper, rending it, trampling it on her way to Mrs. Gurney; with first her right hand, then her left, she slapped with full strength at the cowering figure.

"That's what you thought when I came here, isn't it? She's a low foreigner—we'll see she never gets received. She's not good enough for Harry—make her do dirty work, make her go to school, ask people in and let them see her working like a servant, make her life so dull she's crazy——"

She was incapable of hearing Mrs. Gurney's terrified sobs, "No, no, it wasn't like that; we tried, we tried"; she was incapable of knowing when Elizabeth ran in, or when Mr. Gurney came, or Harry; she knew only that after a while her arms were caught, that she was being dragged back from Mrs. Gurney.

"But I don't care any more!" She kept up her scream. "I don't care any more, do you hear that? I can get on without them——"

How many times, since she had been at Gurneys', had she longed for this release; now she had it. From then on she no longer heard the words she uttered but she heard their sound and fury, healing, satisfying; she felt the force and push of battle in her muscles—yes, this was Harry, pink-and-white-faced, lily-livered Harry she was fighting; she could not have asked better. Mr. Gurney too—she at last had her hands on that devil; they had come to grips. She had the pleasure of sinking her teeth in the devil's flesh, of spending herself utterly.

When she awoke next morning she was fresh, restored.

Yawning, stretching arms above her head, she contemplated with complacence what had happened. Well! She had had a blowout that time! That was all right—with her father, she had a right to temper. "Some kind of low foreigner—she never was received." This wouldn't be forgotten.

The score with Mrs. Gurney, though, was small beside the larger beneficence which possessed her. She knew now why she no longer trembled before people named Watts, Drake or Orcutt. The whole explanation had been there, thunder-loud, in her explosion.

Just because as a child she had foolishly seen Those Others as the way to wealth and power, she had not for all this time—even after finding out the Gurneys had no money—seen her way clear of them. The Gurney dinner, though, had finally taught her different; They would always treat her as They, and not as she, desired.

What other way she could find toward her wealth she didn't as yet see, but that, at this moment, was almost a trifle. She had Modjeska, hadn't she? Lydia van Finkestan, Harriet Hubbard Ayer—those women had got money somehow, and not through any of Those Others, she would bet. All that was important now was the burden she had cast off. No longer need she be nice, in any way, to Gurneys. No longer need she truckle to supercilious housewives and their haughty daughters. She could flout them all as she had flouted Jessie Drake, with full knowledge that she lost nothing in so doing.

If the Gurneys had met her pyrotechnics with an equal display, she would not have been at all averse. The experience had been so pleasant she would have liked to repeat.

Repercussions, however, were of the quieting kind. Harry appeared even more white, more wilted, more silent than he had lately been. Elizabeth took to being home more, hovering watchfully. During the first morning (which Frieda spent tranquilly in bed) Mrs. Gurney trembled into her room to beg pardon for what had been said; she never would forgive herself. That, Frieda agreed magnanimously— though without forgiveness or return pleas of her own—was all right; they could just as well know where they stood. For the protestations which tumbled from Mrs. Gurney at this, she had deaf ears.

Mr. Gurney, his left hand bandaged, had Harry bring Frieda to the study.

"We will have no more such exhibitions, madam," he told her from between set teeth, "as we had last evening."

With her sense of power and restoration strong upon her (*he* hadn't been so much last night, for all his pinched nose and his devil) Frieda replied fliply, "If not, why not?"

"For people unable to control themselves," Mr. Gurney thrust past the same teeth, "there are both means—and places—of restraint."

"You wouldn't dare!" she told him, but found it unnecessary to return to temper.

The lid was off now, however, on her conduct about town. At church next Sunday it was she who, when eyes uncertainly met hers, turned coolly, scornfully away. Passing Nettie Orcutt with Bink

Stevens—Harry, himself, had suggested the walk—she asked loudly, "Heavens, did you see that getup?" And coming home one day from Rozzie's she again crossed Jessie Drake's path.

"If it isn't the young lady who's so worried over getting married!" This delivery she made swiftly, going on before Jessie had hope of reply, "I'm sure, though, there'll be *some* young man!"

Instead of seeing herself now in scenes of social grandeur, she saw herself on a platform (the Holy Land) while thousands listened. Or at some sort of machine coining money. Or traveling in exotic scenes— another much-fingered clipping had joined the first. "Female Globe Trotters," it was headed.

> Miss Bland, who is traveling around the world to see how quickly she can make the trip, left Colombo, Ceylon, Tuesday. Nellie Bly, who is circling the globe in the opposite direction, is due at Yokohama soon.

This was from an *Independent* of a couple of years back. Current issues exhausted, she had taken to old ones. But that made no difference. Miss Bland and Miss Bly would scarcely have made those trips unless it got them something.

So far she had agreed, unthinkingly, that Harry must finish college, but impatience with this course too grew big and unrestrained. If she wasn't to be one of Those Others, then what use was there in a husband who was college-taught? Harry had better be at something more important.

"I don't see why it should take all this studying to fix bicycles," she told him. "Your father can just as well find out now as later that you won't be what he wants.

"It must be nice for girls who have husbands who go to business," she threw in later. "At least they can have a roof to call their own. Even if some men don't *have* money they *make* money."

To these challenges Harry replied usually, and exasperatingly, with more of his white wilted quiet, though sometimes he could be pushed to answer.

"The folks would feel bad," he would say. Or "If I can finish, it might help me to make money, Frieda."

This was nonsense. What did it matter now how the Gurneys felt? However could studying make money? Look what Palmer was doing for Cecilia—that was what a man *owed* his wife. Palmer didn't keep a book before his nose; he rushed around, selling lumber for more than he paid—anyone could see the profit in that.

With Harry and Elizabeth both in school, she was more and more, as chill weather cut short her peregrinations about town, cast upon the company of Mrs. Gurney. But this last proved to have its uses.

Tired of old *Independents,* tired of inaction, tired of sitting with feet on the hard coal heater, tired of seeing Mrs. Gurney's lopsided and abstracted face (a twinge crossed it every time it turned toward Frieda), she one afternoon had an inspiration.

"It doesn't look as if we'll have a single caller this afternoon," she offered chummily. "How would it be if *I* called? I'll be Mrs. Twillett."

For Mrs. Gurney's repulsed but fascinated gaze, against Mrs. Gurney's "Oh no, that's unkind!" she presented Mrs. Twillett, Mrs. Twillett shaking herself to a chair, Mrs. Twillett peering at Frieda, Mrs. Twillett bumbling about her digestion, Mrs. Twillett spilling her tea, Mrs. Twillett leaving. She went on to produce Mrs. Drake—the sailing walk, the fond aplomb, the condescension and the self-concern—"My dear Mrs. Gurney, and *sweet* Elizabeth—but who is *that* creature? Horrors! The daughter-in-law! No matter, I won't notice the indecent thing. Mrs. Gurney, have you heard about my daughter Jessie? No matter, Mrs. Gurney, because anyway I'm going to cram Jessie down your throat. Jessie, Jessie, Jessie—don't mention sweet Elizabeth in the same breath—Elizabeth can't hold a candle to my Jessie—why, Jessie actually has beaux and parties!"

Then, even more inspired, carried away by the effect she was causing (Mrs. Gurney was now a rabbit with a snake before her) she went on to be Mrs. Gurney. Mrs. Gurney at the breakfast table, with her limp hands—"Harry, the sugar, do you have sugar, Harry? More toast— everyone must have a toast—there isn't a thing else here to eat so you can just as well make up your minds to toast." Mrs. Gurney with a caller—"Elizabeth, you must listen while I talk about Elizabeth— Elizabeth has hair on her face, but that's because she is so *spirituelle*— she *plays*." Mrs. Gurney after church—"I believe you have not yet met Harry's wife—oh dear, you mustn't *like* the nasty thing, you know, but there she is."

For a moment, when she at last stopped, when Mrs. Gurney continued to sit in her cringing, fearful silence, Frieda knew a liquid qualm. She might, just possibly, have gone too far. She knew by then, though, why she was doing what she did; it was to force an issue. Something had to happen sometime; she couldn't go on as she was, and by behavior as outrageous as this she would find out just where the Gurneys would go.

Whatever was to happen, however, wouldn't happen right then. Stumbling, Mrs. Gurney got to her feet, and stumbling she left the room.

For Harry's sake, that stumble said, I'll bear even this.

You won't though, Frieda vowed. And from then on, with increased, flaunting strength, she amplified her repertoire. Almost any afternoon, when the fit took her, she put on a show. Mrs. Twillett and Mrs. Drake ran out after a while, as did other people. But of variations to Mrs. Gurney there was almost no end. And these, obviously, were most effective, too.

She was right on knowing this must force an issue. One afternoon she looked up to see Harry and Mr. Gurney both, their faces ice-fast, in the sitting-room door. Amiot, for some reason, had dismissed early.

CHAPTER XX

Mr. Gurney said, "Go to your room."

She went, body trembling but mind tight, to wait, walk, listen. All right, this was the showdown, what would they do?

To her ears came, muffled, the sounds of speech, sobs. Once Mrs. Gurney's voice turned high, as if in pleading; Harry's voice sounded loudly in reply. Second by second, as time wore on, she waited for her bedroom door to open; second after second went by, and it did not do so. Instead, early darkness fell and still no one appeared; suppertime passed. *What* did they think they were doing? Unpredictable as they were, did they just think they could keep her up here starving?

The hour came when three pairs of feet (she separated them carefully) dragged heavily upstairs, but still no one came near her. When the house grew so quiet that she had to guess its inhabitants in bed (wasn't that like the Gurneys, too, to leave things any which way, and go off to bed!) she stole downstairs to the buttery. Since Harry hadn't come to their room he must, she thought, be on the sitting-room couch. In the dark lower hallway she paused for a moment, tempted to go in, to compel Harry to some kind of scene. "All right," she could say, "if you've got any piece to speak, speak it! Let's hear what you're going to do!" But she did not, finally, go in. All she would get, probably, would be more of that white-lipped silence. Right then it seemed better to get herself a sandwich, and some milk, and go back upstairs.

When she again emerged, next morning, Harry and Mr. Gurney were already gone, but Elizabeth had stayed home from school. Elizabeth, when Frieda walked into the kitchen, turned a face so fierce and so vindictive that it might have been a darker, sallower rendition of

Mrs. Klaumeister's. At the stove, more badgered, more distracted, more askew than ever, a tear-sodden Mrs. Gurney washed at dishes. Neither of them, as Frieda made her breakfast, spoke one word.

All morning that same silence kept. If they didn't want to talk, she determined, there was no reason why she should; she had made her point. At noon a place was set for her at table. Mr. Gurney came home, but Harry didn't. *Now,* she thought when Mr. Gurney's step first sounded in the hall, now, when he faces me, something has got to break; he'll have to talk. But Mr. Gurney, all too apparently, had himself reined; Mr. Gurney, mustard-yellow and rocklike, did not once glance toward her; Mr. Gurney ate his few mouthfuls and departed.

All afternoon the hush remained unbroken, and she was forced, by then, to recognize it for what it was—a lull of waiting, of anticipation, not only on their part, but on hers. When at suppertime again a place was set for her and one for Harry, but again Harry did not come, she had to see who was the focal point of this inertness. It was not upon her, but upon Harry, that the waiting depended.

Almost as soon as she had realized this, Harry came. Came as a door sighing inward, a slow step in the sitting room, before he parted the wooden bead portieres to enter the dining room and hold to the back of his chair.

The Harry for whom the faces about her flew to anguish was different than he had ever been. That Harry, the older Harry, had usually looked soft and blurred; it always had been difficult, when she was away from Harry, to remember at all what he looked like. This new Harry stood harsh and clear, older and somehow stripped of flesh, so that the hard ghostly lines of his skull could be seen. It was to his father he first spoke.

"I can't do it; I can't get out that way; I can't do what you said." As he stood on, after that, in the difficulty of what he had to say, it seemed almost as if, from his hardness, there came some kind of light. He glanced down, as if to hide what he felt and was thinking, but then his gaze relifted.

"I guess you know I'm not religious, but I can't seem to get away from it—a feeling I've sinned. Against myself and against—someone else. All this that's happening, this is my punishment. I've got to put up with it, as long as it's being visited on me—there's no way for me to run out."

Again he stood for a moment silent, and when he spoke again it was more matter-of-factly.

"There's no reason, though, why the rest of you should suffer. I've got a job, for nine dollars a week, driving the West Haven dray. I've

rented a house on East Willow; not too much of a house, but it will
be all right. If you're willing I should take some old things from the
attic, Frieda and I can be gone from here tomorrow."

So that's what they thought they could do, she thought viciously,
they thought they could get Harry to run off, to leave me; they
thought they'd get rid of me that way! Well! Well, Harry scotched
that! It's a good thing he did, too—they'd have found out!

Behind this, far below this, flowed other emotions too turgid to rise
to the surface. All the time Harry was talking, she had felt a kind of
panting. Harry was being queer, downright queer; what went on
here? All that talk of sin couldn't have any reality; what Harry really
meant—had to mean—was that he recognized Frieda's rights; he had
to do what she wanted. She was having a victory, that's what she was
having; everything was coming out just as it should.

Slippery as was this assurance, she found much—vindictively and
flauntingly much—with which to bolster it. Every line of Harry's body,
as he bonily, palely stood there that evening, told of his being burnt
out, ready to conform. The Gurneys too knew their defeat; a defeat
so great they didn't try concealment. For hours Mrs. Gurney begged,
wept, wildly pleaded—however hard things were, Mrs. Gurney said,
Harry mustn't leave home; she could bear anything, would bear anything; somehow they would get what Frieda wanted, somehow they
would make Frieda's life more gay, somehow they would get Frieda
money; they could manage anything if only Harry would finish college. Elizabeth, crouched over the table, cried soundlessly, her only
motion the down-squeezing of her shoulders. Mr. Gurney, refusing to
speak before Frieda (he had been found out!), took Harry off to his
study, where for hours his voice too could be heard in pleading and
argument.

"There isn't anything else," Harry kept doggedly answering. "There
never was anything else, from the first."

She herself spoke little; she didn't need to. What all the commotion
was over, either for Harry or his parents, she told herself righteously,
she didn't quite see. Of course, she had forced this conclusion, but she
had had to, hadn't she? Since Harry never intended to do anything
but tinker with bicycles anyway, no one was out much, though she
need hardly go into that. Let them *think* they were suffering a big
loss. She had lost plenty because of them. The idea of trying to tell
Harry he should leave her, indeed!

Unsettling as all this fuss was, she tried to keep her mind on the
main point, which was that she was getting her way, Harry would be

quitting school, she'd soon have a place of her own. This last satisfaction proved so corrosive that she was forced, sometimes, to thrust its contemplation aside; it ate too sharply at her stomach. Morning, too, proved a round of acid-sweet pleasure—the bustle of packing, the condescension of saying, "Oh, thank you, Mrs. Gurney, these will do *very* well until we can get better," in return for those quilts, pillows, sheets, cases, towels, table and kitchen linens which Mrs. Gurney wordlessly brought her, the disdain of poking for an hour in the Gurney attic—"Oh dear, these straight old chairs, isn't there a thing else we can sit on? That table must have been in the ark. I can't, I just can't see me and those faded old blue curtains in the same house!" And then the last-minute scurry, the arrival of Fred and Bink to help (Harry could use the dray only during his noon half hour), the staggering up- and downstairs, the helter-skelter piling of everything on the wagon, the hurried departure of the load, her own leave-taking.

"Though this needn't really be good-by," she forbearingly assured those she left behind her. Mr. Gurney (he should, trying to separate husband and wife!) had kept himself absent through the morning, but Mrs. Gurney and Elizabeth, pinched, dreary, quiet, stood side by side to take her farewell as she gave it. "Once you've become accustomed, you'll think this for the best, I'm sure. You must come to see us, once we're settled, but I'll take this opportunity to thank you kindly for the many *experiences* I've had here. It's been a time I never shall forget."

Each word of this, each nuance, she had thought out well beforehand; it had seemed a shame, the night before, to waste much time in sleeping. Neither Mrs. Gurney nor Elizabeth could miss her meaning, but both were too lack-spirited to reply in kind.

Mrs. Gurney quavered only, "He's such a boy——"

"Oh, Harry!" returned Frieda gaily. "Don't you worry about Harry, Mrs. Gurney, I'll look out for him!"

The December day into which she stepped was one to dazzle, with sunlight striking silver from new snow. When actually she had her back to Gurneys', when the cold pepper of the outside air was in her nose and her feet crackled on the crusty path, when she could think, I never need go *there* again! I have my *own* place! she tingled until she was almost dizzy. Look down as she did upon the furnishings she had just acquired, there yet had been something heady in the acquisition. Those things were hers now, not just to use, but to own, as she owned her secret beautiful one hundred dollars in the Meridian bank. Some of them, especially the cherry-pattern china and the furnishings from Harry's room, weren't *too* bad; she'd want new things, of course, for all the rooms that showed—hall, den, parlor and dining room—

but for kitchen and bedroom some of the Gurney hand-me-downs would do quite well.

Making no application of her knowledge that the east side was the poorer side of town, or that Willow was only two blocks over from Water, her old street, she made her way confidently toward that address—718 East Willow—which Harry had called out as he drove off. All the setbacks she had suffered had not been able to keep her, the moment Harry said, "I've rented a house," from soaring to what that house must be. Not as rich, perhaps, as Drakes'; possibly not as large as Cecilia's and Palmer's, but worthy of her. Harry, with his background, could scarcely pick a hovel. Seven rooms at least, fretwork, bays, a big two-side veranda, maybe a turret, and inside a wide staircase, perhaps of cherry, with high-gloss varnish wherever varnish could be laid. Nine dollars a week wasn't too much, but if they ran short Harry's father would have to help. West Haven would see who could set up as a lady. She wouldn't do without a servant, not she. Let company keep away—all of it; she'd need no one. Though as for that, it might not be long before the boys would be around, once they found life in her house was something *like*. Plenty of smoking stands, couches, heaps of cushions, cozy corners, shaded lights, no one around to be a spoilsport—those high-and-mighty young West Haven ladies might find out what it was to fight!

She had so far to fall that, before 718 East Willow, she had sensations of spinning dizzily downward. During those moments she actually stood foot-fast on the boardwalk, half her mind taking in evidence that she had indeed reached the right house, the other half as violently repudiating. This was East Willow, this the block, the persons of Fred and Bink bulked near an opened door, through which was visible a jumble like that from the dray. But this couldn't be her house, not this little streaked brown box with nothing but one step to its door, and only two windows in its one-story front—why, she'd seen *chicken houses* that were more imposing!

As on the night when she had returned to West Haven with Harry, her vision of the scene extended to include herself—there *it* was, that miserable shed, and there *she* was on the walk before it, in her forward-riding tilted toque, her snug-fitting and fur-banded coat, her elegant tight shoes, her small round muff—the very figure of fashion. She couldn't be expected to live in that house. The contrast was too great.

When Bink and Fred approached—"Mrs. Gurney—well—we waited around—no telling what these brats around here—but now you've come—unless you'd want some help inside"—they had to repeat their jerky utterances before she understood.

"Oh no," she supplied then, tonelessly. "You run along. I'll manage."

"We started a fire," added Fred, or Bink. "It seemed a little damp —that's why we've got the door open. It ought to be all right, though."

"I'm much obliged," she answered, but although she knew they went, she did not see their leaving; although she knew that ragamuffin children rocked like teeterboards on nearby fences, she did not see them either.

Once she turned to walk, almost to run, the way she had come. That was her reply; they couldn't do this to her. This was as bad as telling Harry to run off and leave her. Like it little as they would, they'd have to keep her.

But after a few steps she halted, this time panting, on the boardwalk. Harry's room, when she left, had been stripped bare. It didn't take prescience to know that if she appeared alone before those double doors it somehow would not be malleable Mrs. Gurney or Elizabeth who came, it would be Mr. Gurney. Without Harry she'd never be let in.

When, soon after six, Harry walked into the first room of the small house, she stood with hat and coat still on, her hands still cradled in the muff. Behind her in the kitchen the fire had gone out, the litter from the dray remained unchanged, and on the floor the dirt lay undisturbed, except for footprints.

"So you really dare come." The venom that shot from her had such force behind it that she could not wait to free it. "I'm not staying here, you can know that. Either you go out now and get me a decent house, or you take me back to your folks. One or the other."

Her mind, like her words, streamed white and hot. Although her body trembled for a leap and savage rending, this, she knew, was no time for the luxury of rage. This boy dragging his dreary footsteps inward in the last thin light of receding day, this blank negligible human in stained cloth cap, lumberjack and bagged shapeless trousers —the clothing of the most uncouth workman—was the person who had not only been advised to run off and leave her, but who had brought her to this trap. Beneath the flaming of more acid passions she again felt unbelief—how could it be *he* who brought her to such passes? But all question had to be pushed aside for purpose, in which she could not fail.

Across a face grayed, blurred and hollowed by exhaustion—his day of unfamiliar labor had begun at six—Harry drew a dark palm. His glance, when it moved, went not to her but to the furniture and boxes.

"You might have made a start," he said as if she hadn't spoken, and she knew that he too, in his peculiar unbearable fashion, was prepared to be immovable. Bending, he pulled at the footboard of his bed, to extricate it.

She snatched to wrench the wood he reached for from his hand.

"Didn't you hear what I said?" she asked. "I said I wouldn't live in this pig's house! You can't make me! Either you get me a decent——"

He looked as if he had no strength whatever, but the footboard came up.

"It's no use, Frieda. I've looked, and this is the best I can afford. It's not a bad house. Small, but tight, and the range was in it. We'll have to eat and buy clothes——"

The footboard rattled under his hand.

"I'll live as well as your folks do, or know the reason."

"Father earns more."

She shrilled, "What do you think you are, too proud for help? Oh, you're going to stay with me, yes—for *your* sake! Couldn't you think of me, once? What would my folks think, seeing me in this cowshed? What must your friends think—Bink and Fred? Don't you see what we are if we live here? We're just *scum!*"

He said, "If a house can make us scum, that's what we are."

The need to burst in violence grew so great that only necessity—the terrible position in which she was placed, since he might, after all, take his father's advice and leave her—could draw her proudly once more upright, with her hands back in her muff.

"Harry, just look at me," she begged then, her voice too controlled. "Couldn't you take the trouble, just this once, to *look?* Is this the sort of place I *belong* in?"

His gaze had been toward the footboard, but it rose, not to fasten on her, but to hover somewhere past her shoulder.

"Haven't you any idea, Frieda," he asked, low, "what I must think of you by this time?"

She had been bending forward, reaching forward with her body to exert more pressure on him, but as the meaning of his answer struck it snapped her backward.

"Why, Harry, who——" The staggered words fell, heart-hurt and incredulous. How, when she asked him for a judgment of her, could he set up other negligible, meretricious standards—standards different than her own? Unjust as it was, she had to veer from attack to defense. "You know I haven't done a thing that wasn't perfectly all right. Anyone—anyone with spirit—would have done as much, or more. Your mother had everything she got coming to her. And anyway, can't you see that hasn't anything to do with what I'm talking about, Harry? It isn't what people *do* that counts—you've got to know that, Harry; it's how they *look*. You've got to see me, Harry, you've got to see I don't belong in——"

He said with finality, "If you belong somewhere else, you're free to go there. This is what I've got to offer."

Huddled next morning under inadequate blankets on an ill-made bed, sunk in what almost was a coma of frustration, she stared out at another day. Fully dressed except for his shoes, Harry had spent beside her a night of collapsed sleep, and then risen at five-thirty to tiptoe blunderingly about in the dark, starting a fire in the kitchen range before he left. She had not slept at all.

Harry, not she, had had the final word. He had decided how they would live, and it was a way she couldn't tolerate.

Through endless restabbing that knife dulled, but kept on penetrating. She'd guessed early that Harry could be a mule, but she hadn't thought he could stand up against her, not when she called on her full forces. That she had done so last night there was no doubt —in the weeping, argument, excoriation and wild pleading into which she had thrown herself, there had been no holding back. Time and again she had wrenched apart the bed he steadily kept on assembling; nothing had deflected him. Worn out at last, she had had to throw herself upon the once more replaced mattress, abandoned to nothing but despair.

"If you want to go somewhere else, go right ahead." This, this blunt, spiked club, was what he had used to press her further into an enclosure from which she could not burst except through the one door so nakedly left open.

That she would find such egress even more intolerable than the trap, she scarcely had to ponder over. At Gurneys', where the idea of launching herself alone upon the big wide world had stayed a pleasant dream, only the vistas introduced by Lydia van Finkestan and Nellie Bly had occupied her, but now when such possibilities drew close, she could not keep from looking at the harsh unhappy aspects of reality. Where, actually, could she go? To her parents? She would meet there nothing but mortification. Soon, too, they would want her to begin paying, and with what? Would Hake, even, take her back as a *separated wife?* She might have to leave West Haven for some city like Meridian, where she might not find work, where her own one hundred dollars would soon be gone for food, and where, at no more than seventeen, she might get to be one of those ragged, homeless, unprotected females held up by all magazines to instructive horror.

At a picture of herself dying beside the cold hard wall of Frigman's (that Emporium where she had bought the scarlet petticoat) the emptied vials of her tears refilled and once more spilled. Strangers would take her, pitifully then when she was gone, pitifully they would find out who she was, and pitifully send her home. But at the ensuing scene—the one where she lay casketed in state at First Congregational —galvanic lightning shot her from the bed and to her feet.

That was what they wanted! *That* was what they were working for—West Haven, the Gurneys, Harry. Harry wouldn't leave her, oh no! His conscience wouldn't let him leave her. But his conscience didn't keep him from trying to fix things so she would leave *him!* Sin, he said. "As long as it's being visited on me, I've got to take it." If he could make it quit being visited on him, though—oh, he'd be free enough, then! Free to go back to his family, free to go back to Schatzi——

When next she took breath for looking about her she was once more in the tiny parlor, clothes on, hair up, lips tight, vigor beating at her bones. Harry would find out how his scheming worked.

Grimly, speculatively, her glance rested on the tumbled Gurney castoffs. There might still be ways to manage a little leveling of scores.

CHAPTER XXI

That evening when Harry came home she stood yet again in the front room, almost on the spot where she had stood the night before. But this time she stood with hands rolled in an apron, lips consciously and sweetly smiling. Harry, once inside, glanced at her, blinked, glanced beyond her, blinked once more, stood for some moments not seeming to see anything, and then walked slowly to the bedroom doorway to stare in at a bed smoothed and waiting under piece quilts, at clean windows frilled with muslin, at the thistle-pattern china glistening on the washstand; he turned to stare once more at the parlor, neatly if sparsely set out with drugget, chairs, harp-back sofa, old blue curtains; he moved on to the kitchen doorway to look in at a lamp shedding yellow light upon a white-naped table neatly set for two. He sniffed, drawing in strong fragrances of wood-warmth, frying roundsteak, steaming potatoes, dampness, strong yellow soap and order; he turned slowly back to Frieda, his mouth reaching for undiscoverable words.

"I expected—it would—be like last night," he managed. "I thought I'd have that—I'm so tired." The last sagged to nothing.

"You didn't think I *couldn't* do it, did you?" Frieda allowed herself just so much malice before once more taking on her role of housewife. "Do hurry, Harry, I'm quite starved. I went out this afternoon and got the steak." (He'd know tomorrow what else she had done this afternoon!) "It was most thoughtful of you to leave grocery money on the table."

While Harry, shaking his head, walked toward the soapstone dry-sink in the kitchen, while he washed, while he silently, almost wolfishly, ate—"Poor boy," said Frieda, "you must be weak from hunger" —she looked back, with no little gratification, upon her day. There the house had been, tiny bedroom, tinier parlor, big square kitchen where alone was warmth and space for living—all walls soot-streaked, windows grime-gray, floors caked. It had seemed impossible, at first, that she should clean it, but who else would? Leaving it to Harry would mean living in filth for days—his evenings were short. Calling in her mother meant voiced and unvoiced questions, and a tacit inclusion of herself as now one with her mother. Once she had seen herself as the only way, the work had gone forward in a steady, almost sensationless rhythm; it wasn't until the last pail of scrubbing water had joined the iced black runnel in the back yard that she had even stopped to notice her bleached crumpled finger tips, her forearms burning from soap, her kinked back. All that discomfort had been something to hold snugly between muff and body when at last, even the furniture in place, she had sallied forth, herself cleaned and burnished, for downtown West Haven.

Against these pleasant meditations, Harry blundered. "Last night I—I mean, after last night I don't—I guess I don't understand. All this —do you *mean* anything by it, Frieda?"

Although his plate was empty, he had not pushed it back, and before replying she reached archly across, to set his knife and fork neatly where they should be—across a plate corner.

"There!" she returned. "Mean anything? What do you mean—anything?"

"The house. The——" His gaze remained on the fork, his mouth screwed into a contortion of uncertainty and doubt.

"You mean, why did I clean up?" Her return was as puzzled as if it were her turn at perplexity. The rest of her answer wore dignity and reason. "Well, Harry, after all, if I'm to live here, I could scarcely leave things as they *were*. You may not think much of me, but I still can claim something; I can't live in filth and disorder."

His eyes gleamed in wild confusion and despair. "I can't——" he said. "I don't——" But quandary and indecision died limply in his throat. After a moment he stood up.

"If you don't mind, I think I'll just go to bed," he said.

But when, some hours later, she too lay down, he still was rigid and awake.

"I wouldn't want to be unfair." Woodenly he spoke outward at darkness. "If you—if you've made up your mind to be—decent, I wouldn't want to be unfair. Out of the nine dollars I make, it will take two each week for house rent, and three, I thought, for groceries. The other four—we could split those. Two for you, I mean, and two for me. If you——"

"I'm sure that would be a very workable arrangement," she accepted amicably.

The next night he knew what the truce was.

That night too she waited, once more aproned, once more smiling when he came in half wary, half expectant, to grow completely wary as he looked beyond her.

"Where," he asked, "did all those things come from?"

"Those things?" she echoed. "My furniture? Why, from Orcutt's, of course. That's the only place in town for anything half decent. You should know that, Harry. Orcutt's."

He went on with the same care, "Who's paying for it?"

"Oh, I didn't make that definite." Her reply was dulcet. "Someone will, though, I'm sure. Your folks, you know, Harry, haven't yet given us a real wedding present. I thought they might like to have me do the choosing. I picked only a hundred dollars' worth—just one even hundred. Isn't it all divine? Especially this, Harry——"

Sweeping forward, she moved to the pier glass which now filled a corner. As she came before it, it flung back her full face and figure in exultation and defiance. No wonder, she thought, seeing that reflection, that she had known she had to have this glass the moment she saw it; the moment she had set her expeditionary foot in Orcutt's. There it had stood, a six-foot oval, framed in gold leaf, hung between walnut standards, reaching itself toward her, giving her much more than she gave, because in the doorway she had been a little unsure, wondering if she could carry off what she had come to do, while in the mirror she had been superb and right.

When Mr. Orcutt, appearing from nowhere to give her one of his elbow squeezes, had said, "Well, I see you've found my handsomest piece, Mrs. Gurney; handsomer now than it ever was before, too," the small laugh she had managed had been breathless.

"It's something I just ought to have," she had told him without cover. "How much would it cost me?"

"That mirror? Say, I'd have to get six, seven hundred for that mirror," Mr. Orcutt had teased, but when he knew she was serious he had come down. "For you—well, I'd like to see that mirror as beautiful forever as it is right now, Mrs. Gurney—for you, twenty-eight fifty." Ecstasy, then, had lifted her like a balloon. Even if it had taken the whole hundred—that was the sum she had fixed, before, as being the most credit she was likely to get—she would have had to have the mirror. And after that, choosing had simply been a matter of flying about to find the mirror's accompaniments—the white bearskin to spread before it, the settee and chair in olive-green velveteen and spindled cherry, the yards of crimson velveteen for drapes, the crimson-and-black turkey carpet, the table topped in brown Carrara marble, with winged oak lions for its legs. One hundred and seven dollars, twenty-five cents, it had come to, but when she had pouted, "That would be an even hundred for an old friend, wouldn't it, Mr. Orcutt?" he had laughed. "That would be an even hundred," he had agreed, "and a good squeeze."

The rest had been easy. "Do get the other dray," she had said, "not Harry's—I want it to be a surprise. I'll see he comes in later, though, to take care of the money."

"Yes, knowing Harry, I guess I'll get my money," Mr. Orcutt had answered. Perhaps he had borne down a bit on the "Harry," but she had been in no mood to fuss over that. All the rest of yesterday, while she had so demurely bought beefsteak and cooked dinner, all yesterday evening, all day today, this had been her secret.

"At last," she said, "I've got a glass where I can see my figure." Every five minutes, ever since it had come, she had stood before that mirror, and now she could scarcely tear her gaze away.

"My folks have already given us everything they'll be asked to give." Harry's reply when it finally came was strained and bleak. "I'm sorry, Frieda."

"Sorry?" she threw back. "Why be sorry? These are *mine*."

"We can't afford them, Frieda. It's no use."

"Oh yes, it *is* use," she retaliated, and then, because she couldn't hold it longer, she let him have what else there was to know.

"They won't go back—I've taken care of that. Everything here is cut or scratched."

He jerked forward.

"You couldn't, Frieda."

"Oh yes, I could. Why don't you look and see?"

Going silently from piece to piece, he did, gazing first at the long cut she had made with the paring knife behind one standard of the mirror, then at the neat triangle she had sliced into a corner of the rug. When he stood up from the last—her little statuette of cupid on a snail—she'd long been ready, facing him, filled with laughter and triumph.

"They'll have to be kept now," he admitted, from what looked like a daze; the words he said were late and drifting, but they grew more clear. "It'll have to be your share, Frieda—the two dollars a week I thought you could have. I'll see Orcutt——"

She laughed. "*My* two dollars? Don't be silly. *I'm* not going to pay up. I'll need those two dollars for clothes. You don't think I'm going to go naked, do you? It won't be *my* two dollars."

He said, "I'm afraid it will be, Frieda. I'll turn them in myself, on paydays."

The room, that had been so bright in its new luxury, the walls that had been a box to hold her secret, darkened and drew in; the furnishings she had bought at Orcutt's swelled until they were almost ugly. This, she had thought, was a revenge she had made safe; it was impossible, *again* impossible, that he could so manage to fling back at her her own acts.

"But you can't do that!" Tug at receding triumph as she would, it still must ebb, leaving her to fight against another bleakness. "I can't get on without a *penny,* Harry. The grocery money can't stretch——"

He said, "You should have thought of that before."

"Let Orcutt whistle for his money. He's got plenty. I don't believe he'd ever do anything against me—he likes me."

"I've noticed. But we're paying."

"Take it out of yourself, then." Ever since he had said "your two dollars," she had had that money, had counted on it; money was something of which she couldn't be bereft. But even as she begged him, even when she beat her fists against him, he remained what he seemed able to remain in any conflict—weak, but immovable.

"You'll see if you can get away with this!" she promised at last.

"I'll be a punishment for your sins, all right; I'll make your life so damned and miserable you'll wish you never had been born!"

It was his turn for bitter laughter. "Is that new? I am already damned and miserable, and wish I never had been born."

The next morning at ten-thirty she turned in at Hake's. She didn't have to try it to know she couldn't exist penniless.

After she had faced Mr. Hake across his desk, after she had thrown out her challenge, "Here I am, back!" and Mr. Hake, with no lessening of repose, had coolly answered, "Then why've you got your hat on, at this hour?" going back to work brought mainly the release, the spreading ease, of taking off a too tight corset.

"Seven dollars—now I'm a Gurney you might do that well by me," she had said boldly, and Mr. Hake, with his low-lidded smile, did not say no. Seven dollars! No father to whom she need pay tribute, either! Running to throw exuberant arms around Miss Shatto, tossing her hat toward Eddie's open mouth, she cried her news.

"I'm back! For good! Don't talk society to me—let me be where there's hustle and bustle—give me Hake's!"

Right in the aisles about her, mouths as open as Eddie's, eyes squeezed small, stood customers. No one need tell her that any change in social level was behind her now—who cared? Cleaning her feet from their last contact with the cocoon of misvision, she soared. Had she been such a fool as to want to waste time in a *church?* Had she ever wanted to sit with stuffed owls of *callers?* Had she wanted to be one with fusty-whisker-sticks like Mr. Gurney? This was where life was, here at Hake's. She saw it now in every aisle, on every rack, on every goods-piled counter; she smelled it in the smells of shoes and sizing glue and cheese, of cardboard, varnish, wool lint, kerosene. This was where she had come up from nothing, this was where she had made her advances, this was where she had gotten everything she had ever really gotten, this was what made her. Mr. Hake, perhaps, knew a little more about her than was exactly comfortable, but since he seemed willing to put up with his knowledge, then so could she. Skimming along the dry-goods aisles, she laid welcoming, greeting, fondling hands upon the ribbons, spools and buttons, the stockings, corset covers, laces; she caressed the bolts of smooth unfashioned cloth, adored the racks of jackets—"Look at this one! Now, that's *style!*" This, not society, but *this* was where her goal must open; this was where the way must lie toward all she implacably would have— just such rich, disordered, solid, handleable plenty as was spread before her here.

Ecstasy had to lessen; in the everyday wear and tear that followed she had to descend to more rational emotions. No warning from Mr. Hake was needed to tell her that she would now have to make West Haven women—those same women who had refused her as a social equal—accept her as a rebel, as a clerking wife. But comfort did not leave her, nor assurance. The handling of goods and money, even someone else's goods and money, was at once a satisfaction and a spur. Hake's was home, and in it she was shrewdly able, so that she could find immediately, without groping, the highhanded manner— a blend of insouciance and assumed respect—which would carry her through.

"Mrs. Langesley, is there anything . . . ? Oh, you're waiting for Miss Shatto? Miss Shatto will be so *glad*.

"Aren't these lovely muslins? Why, it's Miss Orcutt! Of course, this line at fifty-seven cents is expensive—if you'd rather see the cheaper line——"

Against such impervious and bland good humor, the fluttered comers (there to convince their incredulous ears) in vain looked outraged, in vain haughty; their very coming she drank in as tribute. When, toward suppertime of the first day, even Jessie Drake arrived, sailing in to push home a pointed and more personal thrust—"Why, Mrs. Gurney, do I see you again behind a counter? How *at home* you look!"—Frieda had only to loose her honest jubilation.

"Thank heaven! I hope I'll never again be as dull as I was at Gurneys'!"

Miss Shatto, on the next day, brought news of more concerted action.

"They're saying if you keep on here, Hake's may find *out*." But this too Frieda turned aside contemptuously.

"Those women—do they think they'll stay away from Hake's? I'd like to see it."

As she had told herself long ago, so she retold herself now: of these women too, haughty as they were, Hake's was maker. Trade thinned in the next weeks; the crucial faces appeared only covertly at nightfall or early morning. "A spool of navy, please, Miss Shatto, and you needn't wrap it." "Miss Shatto, every last stay, I just haven't known what I could do——"

Miss Shatto, under these circumstances, was more flutter-fingered than ever, and the game soon dulled. Defiantly or shamefacedly, the customers began allowing Frieda's service. Within the month it grew to be assumed on their side, as on hers, that they had never met outside business. Only an occasional flare, a "Well, I see you're still here,

Mrs. Gurney," from Miss Orcutt or Miss Watts, or a "West Haven just can't seem the same, with you not walking!" from the implacable Miss Drake, was left as reminder.

In spite of financial panic, which that summer gripped the nation as it never had before, the night came finally (after all, as the women of West Haven said, if you were going to the Chicago Exposition you could scarcely go without clothes!) when she tripped lightly up the balcony stairs to bring Mr. Hake tills which were as heavy as she had ever known them.

"Look at the lovely stuff," she said, and dared to spill it out upon the desk. "But what a day! Miss Shatto—could she be older than she looks? She's got so *slow!*"

One vista, narrow though it might be, had not failed to open. Mr. Hake—why hadn't she seen this before?—was her person to manipulate; he always had been.

Against this flourishing life at work, her life with Harry, maneuver it as she would, continued to be nothing but exasperating—and worse.

A few weeks of doing housework with only Harry's bungling aid, of lugging foodstuffs home, of entering at night a cold house in which the bed stood still unmade, the floors unswept, the breakfast dishes unwashed as she'd left them, sufficed to let her know she wanted other arrangements.

"It's terrible, really; all this time you've never met my family," she told Harry, as if she spoke of something he had grieved her by opposing. "Now you've got to—they've asked us for dinner, Sunday."

Forewarned (it had been necessary, of course, to let her family know she had set up for herself), the Schlempke household spread itself for the visit. True, the period of parlor gentility had to be brief, since there was no space for dining outside the kitchen, but Otto, scrapingly genial, met them at the front door with an "Honored, honored!" an expansive handshake, and a fine Havana; Ilse, attached to her kitchen by constantly retracting springs, managed to get in for an anxious scrutiny and an appeal—"A new son I get, now"; Lotte and Ernst, flattened against the parlor wall on a leg apiece, uttered in chorus one shrill "Hello."

Harry, dressed in his best, naturally could not play up.

"I've wanted to come here for a long time," Harry said. "It's seemed all wrong not to know you."

As she had long ago guessed, although seeing herself right could be nothing but an annoyance, Harry merged naturally with her family. The transfer from parlor to kitchen he took as pleasure—

"No, don't apologize! This is comfortable! I like this!" For the pyro-technics of Otto's manner, wit and anecdote, brought out in full splendor for this new audience, he showed nothing but willing ap-preciation, and toward Ilse his response was even readier. When Ilse rose for her almost constant service of the table, he jumped to help; he filled coffee cups and glasses, he brought hot gravy from the stove. "I didn't know I'd be sitting next to a pretty blonde," Harry said, tugging at Lotte's long braids, and "Ernst, if we eat these apple dump-lings we'll have to work up a good fast ball game."

Otto, for this dinner, had not spared his money; juicy richness flowed as the knife sliced the tenderloin roast, the soured cabbage was not white but red, caraway thickly dusted the potatoes. After this meal, in the relaxed content of digestion, Frieda's opening gambit could be both simple and unalarming.

"I declare, I could sleep a week. Store ten or twelve hours every day, then home to get that dratted fire going——"

Harry, of course, immediately quickened. "I know that part's hard; if I could manage during the afternoon——" But Frieda quickly cut him short. Any recital of what Harry did or could do was entirely be-side the point.

"If only," she went on wanly, but drowning Harry, "I could just have a little help with some of that cleaning! If only we could go out for dinner, someplace where it wouldn't be more than we could pay!"

She had expected this to be sufficient, and it was. No sooner was the last phrase gone from her lips than Otto leaped to his feet, to pace and gesture.

"Why must you look? By us—why not by us? Mama is here, noth-ing to do——"

Harry, inevitably, rose to demur, and Frieda too, at this point, had to object.

"Oh, we couldn't allow that; I had nothing like *that* in mind. I should never have complained——" But she was, gradually, brought to hesitance.

"Well, I don't know—of course, you're right, it would solve every-thing, and of course we'd pay, but——"

Otto by this time was afire with his own inspiration. "Dinner—nothing. A lunch—nothing. Housework—nothing. Say three dollars a week, all to Mama——"

During the entire interchange, Harry had shown the nervousness of a cat at a mousehole, and at this, just the place where Frieda was ready to give in gracefully, he had to pounce.

"Oh no," he announced, with his terrible inflexibility. "Not three dollars. Not for dinners and lunches and housework. It should be five, and it'll have to be at least four."

Fury flowed so constantly from herself to Harry that Frieda scarcely felt the increase of the stream. Three dollars was the sum set in her own mind; three dollars was what they had for housekeeping money.

"Oh, but, Harry!" she cried her vexation. "Then we can't afford it! I just *can't* go on as things are——"

Harry was hasty, but adamant. "Oh no, I think it would be fine if Mrs. Schlempke—if your mother is willing to take us on. But we'll pay four dollars. That's the least. Four dollars."

"Four dollars! That's the least! Four dollars!" Frieda threw back on the way home. "Don't tell me you're going to your father for that dollar! Don't tell me you've been raised! Don't tell me you'll be cutting down on your dear precious Orcutt! And don't, *don't* tell me you'll be taking it out of yourself!"

These, during repressed hours (the Schlempkes, admiring and impressed, had protested, "It is too much, when we enjoy the company," but there had been no backtracking), were the only solutions she had been able to see.

"Why should it be any of those?" Harry now asked equably. Harry, in the intervening hours, had played yard ball with Ernst and Lotte, Harry had added a good supper to the dinner under his belt, Harry was showing a relaxed calm. "Your people are all right, Frieda; I liked them."

Frieda's right foot slapped down smartly. "If you can get any money that you——"

He went on as equably. "Why, we'll have plenty. I can pay in two dollars of our grocery money, which will leave me three for myself—more than I had before. And you can pay in two dollars of what you make."

She thought she was going to faint. She stood on the boardwalk and saw tree branches, raw and bare in a January thaw, bow and sway and circle; the whole plateau of space before her—street, walk, brown lawns, houses—tipped upward to meet her; she felt a draining from her face and hands, the sucking of skin close to bones, the harsh compression of lips left unfleshed.

She whispered, "Out of what I make? Harry, aren't you even going to support me? Oh, I don't expect much of you. I never expect you'll be anything, or make much money. But I at least thought *that!* I didn't think I'd have to go out working for the food I eat. I never thought you'd be so mean, that you'd——" She was herself unaware of what she said, or of how basic it came to be.

Against her Harry stood with eyes that had a queer deep gleam. "It won't work, Frieda. As long as you did the housework and cooking, I wanted to be generous; that was your share. But now your mother's taking over, you'll pay in your two dollars. I'm sticking by to see you do it."

CHAPTER XXII

He managed it. That was what seared and tore. He made it public.

"Since Frieda's working too," he told her family, as one telling what was only right and just, "we've decided she'll pay half our board and cleaning."

He made a ceremony of the payments, so that it was almost like Saturday nights before her marriage.

"Here's mine, Mrs. Schlempke, and no one ever got more for his money," he would say, laying his two dollars in Ilse's hand. Then gravely, expectantly, he waited, as they all waited, until Frieda did likewise.

"It seems to me a proper husband would at least see his wife didn't have to pay for her board." She tried carrying the fight to her family, but in this matter Otto and Ilse both solidly took sides—seemed indeed to enjoy taking sides—with Harry.

"Frieda, now, be right with the boy, be right!" her father urged. "You got nice work in the store, you make good money—should only Harry spend?"

"But for what I *eat!*" Frieda reiterated her colossal wrong. "I'm willing enough to buy my clothes, but the very food I eat——"

Her father laughed. "You think Mama should make, and not turn to the family?"

This on its face was so ridiculous that she had no reply. Mutinously she was forced to pay. Giving money to her father had been custom, galling but fixed; giving it to her mother was like tearing strips from her own flesh. She reneged as she could, she came late on Saturdays, she forgot to bring her pay from the store, she spent it before she came, she found it necessary to do midweek borrowing—"If you could just let me have a dollar back; I'm so short"—but Harry was relentless. "Is Frieda all paid up?" he asked, always. And as time went on Ilse too grew hard.

"I hear you make seven dollars by the store—what you do with so much?"

The only thing worse would have been going back to doing all that work herself.

She snatched customer after customer from Miss Shatto. She convinced Mr. Tow and Eddie that she was second in command—"I believe Mr. Hake would like these boxes piled more neatly, Mr. Tow. And, Eddie, I understand you're to help with this unpacking." After ambitious reading in a salesman's leaflet, she pushed Mr. Hake into a repainting and redecorating of the dry-goods side.

"Not brown again, Mr. Hake, but green, a good olive green, with window draperies—yes, even if this is a store, Mr. Hake—scarlet window draperies. And maybe scarlet curtains to shut off the back, too."

When this last activity was finished, customers walked in to stand stunned. "Is this old Hake's? Why, it's like Meridian!" But even tribute such as this last could not shake the gravel from Frieda's shoe, could not make her forget that out of her weekly seven dollars she kept but five to pay toward her new shoes, or toward the cheviot for a skirt, or toward the multiplicity of shirtwaists which, now she was always in the public eye, she had to have. So far her one hundred dollars had remained a sum complete and finished, but now when each Saturday she briefly held seven dollars in her hand, that money was so beautiful in itself that it was a wrench to let it go, even for clothes. Once in a while she hid a few bills, stuffing them deep into shoes, from which they had hastily to be transferred when she wore the shoes, tucking them inside clean stockings, inserting them within the slit she had cut under the settee. Harry and her mother, thank heaven, weren't snoopers. For months she kept herself from knowing how much she thus saved; it was such a warm satisfaction (I've got that little put by, just in case) to know she had it.

But one Sunday morning while Harry was with his family (Harry, it had come to be established, breakfasted with the Gurneys on Sundays, while she slept, then met her later at Schlempkes') she poked out all her caches, and sat with them tumbled in her lap, while sovereignly she smoothed and counted.

Six, thirteen, eighteen—as the sum mounted, her breath grew unsteady and her hands shook, while each bill she picked up seemed thicker, veinier, of more weight and worth. Forty-seven dollars! Unbelievingly, when she was done, she faced the total. Half as much, almost, as she had in Meridian! Enough to pay her bill at Hake's entirely, enough to buy a tailored suit, or a gold watch on a fleur-delis pin! But while she dallied with thoughts of these expenditures, what she really felt was that nothing, nothing in the world she could buy, was as worth while as what she held in her hands.

That day she went to dinner absently, and absent sat with her family in the afternoon. Seven dollars. Wages. She hadn't realized it could count up so fast. Suppose she saved, say, two dollars a week. That in a year would be a hundred. Suppose she got Mr. Hake to give her a raise, so she could double that——

Oh, it wasn't enough. Two hundred a year, even, wasn't anywhere near enough. Some opportunity would have to come, such opportunity as fell to those who saved a little capital. That was what she would do now—save capital.

Sometimes, in her maneuverings—after, especially, some more than daring coup—she came to temporary expectant lulls; Mr. Hake this time might think she had gone too far.

"I now do business in a boudoir," Mr. Hake said dryly. And "Revolutions, I've begun to suspect, are all started by women." But his attitude toward her seemed to remain as it had always been. Sometimes he liked her, sometimes he did not; he was amused by her; he kept her secrets. And that fall, financial panic or no, he raised her the two dollars she wanted.

"There's no sense piling fabric bolts like boards," she had told him. "I've set them on edge so all the patterns show at once. And why don't we move thread and buttons in back? Any woman has to buy those. Gloves and parasols are what should be up front—they're temptations."

Salesmen had been nuisances, wasters of time. "Mr. Hake's out. No, I can't be bothered." But in these days when her eyes never were quiet, she investigated them too as a source of advantage.

"Before you go up to Mr. Hake, just tell me—haven't you anything *new* I can sell? It's in the *Ladies' Home Journal,* this same featherboning? Then tell Mr. Hake I said we have to have it. A house gown, made up? You know I can't sell made-up gowns; they wouldn't fit."

Before too many months, with unquavering audacity, she had insinuated herself into the buying—"I'll just step up with you, and let Mr. Hake know what I think. I rather believe this petticoat would be better, Mr. Hake—the cambric *gives* more, and what women want now in petticoats is *give.*"

As she turned samples this way and that, as she crumpled and rubbed fabrics, as she gave her fiats, Mr. Hake merely sat back as if she were an entertainment for his tiredness.

"No, listen to Mrs. Gurney," he would tell salesmen who demurred. "She's the one meets the customers."

Not until toward Christmas did he show he knew what she was doing.

"I'm pretty sure," she told him that day, "that our last shipment of Levin's ladies' hose was short. Couldn't I take the bills, and check?"

All his dislike of her flared, to drown complaisance. "Why don't I just turn over everything to you?" he asked. "Why do I stay here at all?"

She had to back swiftly.

"I didn't mean——" she offered humbly. "It's only—I keep looking for places where I can be helpful——"

"Places, you mean, where you can improve my store, my buying and my business methods," he retorted, but then, as if tension were too much trouble to maintain, he let go, shrugging. "Well, I should know I'm lax. A proper businessman, undoubtedly, would check his invoices. Just tell me, though, Mrs. Gurney"—the voice still retained chill—"where do you expect to get by this devotion to my interests? I'm paying you men's wages now, Mrs. Gurney. Nine dollars. Valuable as you insist on being, I don't think I could pay more without being ridden out of town by my fellow merchants on a rail. Where beyond that do you think you can go?"

Chance, for which, win or lose, she must leap.

"If I can make your returns increase, I'm sure mine go along," she told him. "One thing you've always been is fair."

He snatched one of his gulps of laughter.

"You and I on certain occasions have achieved a fair degree of understanding," he said, grinning, "but you aren't by any means suggesting you might be a *partner* of mine, are you, Mrs. Gurney?"

She hadn't dared think the word, but once it was out she met it squarely, chin up, bosom up, only the taffeta whisper of her skirts against the chair confessing any inward tremor.

"I realize that would take capital," she returned composedly.

That same month, after a few days of ignored morning illness, she realized she must be pregnant.

She was alone in her small house—Harry was out somewhere with her father—on the night one small fact added to another, and she knew.

Pausing to beat her fists on the table, pausing to roll her head against walls and door casings, she walked what space the house afforded, bent, with face hidden in her hands, or straightening to stare through the pier glass at her figure—that figure which could still be upright, shapely, unrevealing in its fashionable skirt and shirtwaist, but inside which now lay hidden an incubus which, while it this time meant no shame, still meant ruin to her fortune and her plans.

After the first months of her marriage her mind had winged free of this possibility—if it hadn't come about *then,* it was scarcely likely that anything would come about because of Harry, scattered and unwilled as their meetings were, impelled on her side by nothing but immediate hunger and propinquity, and on his by what seemed like hopelessness. To have this happen now, after almost two years of marriage, now when Mr. Hake had spoken that word "partner" as if in half admission—the golden apple hung at the end of a long road (she wasn't yet twenty), it hung at the end of years, but still it was before her, and he hadn't said she couldn't race to reach it. To have a partnership in Hake's, to share that ownership, that spoil of profits; it was a paradise for which she would have given up all other possessions: her hair, her figure, her good looks; for which, oh, how gladly, if she had only known, she would have let Harry go back to his family, and even to Schatzi. Instead, just because she hadn't glimpsed the lurking hazard, because she slept in the same bed——

Once more she walked, once more crouched, in a repulsing terror. It couldn't be possible that within her body at this crucial time a treasonous growth could be imbedded, already swelling, already self-willed and impelling, waiting only for time before it burst into inevitable open living that would bind and enslave her.

At this time she had almost no thought of physical suffering; she already suffered. As she walked her body quivered with strength; she could have come victorious from any torture, if only destruction could be fled. Yet she had no hope actually of escape; no hope that again she might be mistaken.

The day came—and it was early—when Mr. Hake asked, "Aren't you walking double these days, Mrs. Gurney?"

She tried to reply out of his own disillusioned sang-froid, "I'm afraid so," but she could not keep the words level, tossed as they were by the tumult in her throat. As quickly as possible she got down-stairs to the small seclusion of the shoes, where she could beat out what now was despair.

Although Mr. Hake did not again openly refer to her condition, although he allowed her to take part in buying as before, still her authority slipped swiftly from her. Miss Shatto, who in the preceding months had receded to bewilderment ("I'm sure, all the changes around here, I hardly know——"), now revived like a sunstricken petunia under crisping dewfall. Almost at once, Miss Shatto bridled and resisted—"I've *always* kept my scissors here. And Mrs. Coburn was waiting for *me,* I think." Eddie and Mr. Tow too grew slow and recalcitrant, and as if this were not enough, she had to see Mr. Hake hire one Miss Wigness, a girl of twenty-two, small, brown, closed within herself, who went about the store so quietly that her capability might have gone long unguessed, except by Frieda.

Ilse too guessed early. Questions—"Something is happening by you, no?"—could for a time be tossed aside—"For heaven's sake, Mama, do you have to be so suspicious?"—but at last dissimilation could not be kept up longer. After that her father at once knew, and, from him, Harry.

Harry's fumbled and dazed query, "Is it true, Frieda? Your father says——" was nothing but a poisoned knife. She cried at him, "What's it to you? You don't have to see it ruining *your* looks! It won't stand in *your* way!"

Automatically he sat down on the bedside, bending to take off a shoe, although it wasn't nearly bedtime. "I can't believe it," he said. "I'd almost forgotten such a thing could happen."

"*You* forgot; you didn't let it bother *you!*"

Only one benefit could be wrung from Harry's knowing; she need conceal from him no longer the torrents of her bitterness, and she could get some relief at home for her body. For work she laced until her face was puffed and scarlet; that was better than customers' stares. When Harry protested, protested, in fact, at her working, when her mother added warning and Miss Shatto innuendo—"Miss Orcutt was mentioning just the other day, she said she'd never seen you quite so *plump*"—it did not dent determination. One week, even one more week, meant a few more dollars for her hoard; that hoard which must now stand to her for all she would have done and owned if circumstances had not been against her; that hoard which now was the only thing for which she worked.

In her seventh month, however, Mr. Hake called her to the balcony, and she knew her time was done.

"Harry spoke to me the other day," he said, "and since you can't go on forever, anyway—I'm afraid, Mrs. Gurney, you had best stay at home. A child as close to life as yours must be uncomfortable in that casing."

If desperation had held her before, it held her triply those last months. Nothing her thoughts touched—Miss Shatto and Miss Wigness, Harry, her parents, the never-seen Gurneys, her own figure—could be looked at without loathing. So far she had continued to think of the life within her as no more than the incubus it had been at first, but now when Mr. Hake spoke of it as a child, when her mother persisted, "Some sewing you will have to do now," when Rozzie came with tears in her eyes—"Frieda, for you I am so glad" —to bring a creamy coat and bonnet, "every stitch by hand," she had to begin enclosing the growth in skin and features. Harry's child. What could you expect of a child of Harry's? Some gnome, probably, with dark down covering its detestable and clinging frame, a shaming freak that she would have to keep on hiding as she had kept it hidden.

Nothing would have suited her better than to sink into torpor, and on some days she almost managed this. Except for her mother (Ernst and Lotte had been told they "wouldn't see Frieda for a while," in tones so freighted that they sneaked to peep at nightfall) her only visitors were Father Doern and Rozzie—Father Doern, who insisted on making just such tedious calls as he had made at Gurneys', and Rozzie, who was sewing the infant wardrobe. It was Rozzie who, hunting for anything Frieda might like, brought over a few *Independents,* and then, on demand, all the old copies she could find.

During the fulfilling months at Hake's, old obsessions had drained backward. Palmer, during those happier courses, had sometimes been visible in transit toward the balcony; but often she had been able to glance toward him with little more than malice; Mr. Palmer Hake, she had heard, had bought lumber a little too ambitiously before the panic, and undoubtedly his purpose in visiting his father was to ask more money. A time might come, she had thought, when both Palmer and Cecilia might wish they were on different terms with *her.*

With success swept away, however, with herself housebound, she once again had to see the young Hakes in heart-twisting limelight.

Forty of our fashionable maids and matrons assembled Thursday for a Chinese Tea at the spacious home of Mrs. Palmer Hake, where not only were minds regaled with facts of interest about China, but the senses also, since the Hake parlors had become a close-hung bower of apple blossoms. The finest Oolong tea, the daintiest of cakes and sandwiches, were enjoyed by the fortunate guests.

Foremost among those fortunates taking in the bedazzlements of the Chicago World's Fair are Mrs. Palmer Hake and husband, Mr. Palmer Hake.

At the time, she had scarcely been touched by that fever to get to Chicago which, in the summer of 1893, had taken off half the residents of West Haven, including Mr. Hake, her father, even Harry. What were Eskimo villages, or even Paris restaurants, against her advances at Hake's? But now as she pored over the accounts which every *Independent* for six months had afforded, she became afflicted with nostalgic need. This too had escaped her; she could never, now, in black-and-white striped taffeta, perhaps, with ruffles, bustle herself (envied by hundreds who stood by to watch) off on the train; she never could parade into the color, richness, light, sophistication of the great display.

Against all these afflictions, she had but one solace, that of her money—the three hundred and sixty-four dollars which, by pinching, she had managed to amass since her return to Hake's. Sometimes she sat for hours, money in lap, imagining the excitement if her ownership were known: Harry's "I can't believe it, Frieda!" Her father's respectful "You are rich!" Sometimes the packet with the stay lace around it seemed to have shrunk when she took it from its hiding place, so that she counted feverishly, her heart pounding. Suppose someone—Harry, Rozzie—had found it! But most often she hugged her secret, fiercely owned it. This was hers, and no one, under any circumstances, should wrest it from her.

Her first thought of her baby was that he was part of her money; surely he was as fiercely hers to own. Snug and contenting he lay in her arms, a being of silky weightlessness, in everything like money, except that he also was warm. Bemused, scarcely free, yet, of that unknown and unknowing wrack, that terror that had gone before, she looked up at the sweating balloon that was the doctor's face.

"Fine child!" boomed the doctor. "Missed nine pounds by two ounces. Now I'll leave you——"

"Leave you——" Yes. Leave you to Harry. That had been—how long ago?—a final wrong. At this time of all times West Haven had had to be beset with scarlet fever; Lotte and Ernst were sick of it, so that for days her mother had come no nearer than the window, Rozzie was sick of it, so was Elizabeth Gurney, so were uncounted others.

"I won't have anyone but *you!*" she had screamed at Harry when the torment began, but that was all gone now, with the torment.

"I'll get along—all right—with Harry," she assured the doctor. She was at once unneeding and sufficient; she wanted nothing more.

She *had* something, a fulfillment and an ownership which for the time being completed and sufficed her.

It turned out to be this. Wordlessly she communed with herself and the universe, pulling back a corner of blanket to marvel once more at the tiny face. Pink, rather a dark pink, but that would fade. Dark hair, like hers, over a head that exactly fitted, soft and padded, into her cupped palm. Eyelids over two eyes, a nubbin of a nose, a mouth and ears—when she felt them, there were curly beginnings of two hands, too. Two feet.

"He's—everything's there he ought to have," she once more said, at large. "He's a baby. I can go out to show him——"

Harry, hunched on his knees at the bedside after the doctor went, sobbed noisily and exhaustedly.

"You'll never have to go through this again. I *promise,* Frieda. I hope no one—I hope never in the world the same thing has to happen to anyone again."

She wondered what Harry could be so upset about.

"There won't be anyone in town," she said, "can show a finer baby."

Among those who died of scarlet fever while she lay abed were Thomas Amiot and her brother Ernst.

Her father and mother came at dusk one evening to stand outside her bedroom window with their faces wet and wrung. Where she lay with her son, Lloyd, the lamp was lit; a soft light shaded out, a nimbus; she saw her parents dark, hemmed by darkness, the faces swimming up from darkness and seeming to roll agonized and contorted for a moment against the glass; she held Lloyd toward them, but they only turned away as if the sight were fresh fuel to their grief, and soon vanished.

"It's awful, it's just awful," she too had wept when the news came. "Think, it might be Lloyd!"

But she could not actually touch with any thought of death the infant who so rapidly expanded and turned rosy, who breathed, slept, kicked and sucked so gustily. When she tried to remember Ernst, to push herself to deeper grief (after all, when your own brother——!) she found the pictures she evoked already turning vague and wooden; she hadn't seen Ernst for months, really; he'd had a stubble haircut last fall, which couldn't entirely have grown out; he was quite a thin boy, always out playing with Lotte. He and Lotte hadn't had to work as she, Viktor and Gottfried had.

In any direction her thoughts turned, they immediately came back

to herself and that extension of herself she had borne: Lloyd wouldn't
be out working while he was a child, either. She'd see to that.

Harry too was experiencing ambition.

"I guess I'd better get a hump on." Shyly, on one of the first mornings, Harry lingered at the bedside when he brought the boy to her
for nursing. "Nine dollars won't go far with a rascal like that in the
house."

"It couldn't hurt to have a little more income, that's sure," she replied from her distance. Harry was acting, these days while he was
perforce at home to tend them, as if Lloyd were as much his as hers;
Lloyd had had a hand curled around one of Harry's fingers when they
came in, and Harry didn't pull away; the look on his face was silly.
"Really, Harry!" she had to say, before she got the boy free. "If he's
to have his breakfast——"

When Harry stammered, "My folks can't come now, with Elizabeth sick, but they want to," she dealt with that summarily.

"They can just try coming around now. They certainly didn't do
a thing to help!"

But toward Harry's new ambition she was more uncertain. Even
before he was released from bedside duty, Harry was trying. "Sneaked
a minute while you and the boy slept—got out to see Kenneally. He
doesn't need anyone right now, but next fall when the grain comes
in——

"With old Amiot gone, I thought they might need a new man at
the bank, but it seems——

"Telegraphy can't be too hard to learn—I already know most of
the code. Smith at the station couldn't offer much to begin with—
five dollars——"

"Heavens!" she retorted to this last. "Let's not get stuck with less
than we had before!"

As long as she lay abed, these activities of Harry's could be viewed
with tolerance; she didn't really expect anything, but it was nice
to see Harry trying. When she was once more on her feet, however,
when the round of diaper washing, bathing, cleaning, cooking fell
to her, when Harry, not having found anything better, went back to his
draying, her discontents rose. Not that she was dissatisfied with Lloyd;
each stare of his unseeing eyes, each jerk of his fists, each pull of his
wet small lips was a torn and spilling agony of bliss. But for cooking
and cleaning, for the long hours when Lloyd slept, Harry had done
all right; why couldn't it have been *Harry* who was forced to stay
home, while she worked?

When Harry one night came home alight with hope—"Andreason

at the hardware store has lost his man who repairs farm machinery —that's a twelve-dollar job. He says he'll take me if he doesn't take a man he half promised from De Laittre"—she was two ways torn, wanting the extra three dollars, not wanting to reverse herself and expect anything of Harry. Harry was wild over machinery; if Harry got working with machinery it might just be that he could do all he said he could; maybe he could make machines run as machines had never run before, maybe he could think up new machines, maybe he could make money. But her mind stuck there, rebelling; it couldn't be *Harry* who owned, it couldn't be Harry to whom Lloyd would go for nickels when he was old enough to want nickels; Lloyd couldn't grow up to admire and depend on Harry. Every turn of Lloyd's face had to be toward her.

The next day, while Harry waited to hear, she took her money—it was the first time she had done so since Lloyd's birth—and sat with child and money in her lap.

"See," she told Lloyd, "this is Mama's. Mama could get Lloyd anything he wanted."

Face screwed to delight by this new toy, Lloyd kicked and hit at the packet she dangled by its stay lace, and when she pulled one bill free, he clutched and waved it.

"Mama's boy!" she laughed as she hugged him. "Mama's boy!"

And she was not to be fretted long. Harry, when he came home that night, was downcast—Andreason's job had gone to the other man.

"Well, you can't expect opportunity to *fall* on you, you know," she reminded tartly, now that uncertainty was past.

"I suppose I could have waylaid that other man and shot him." Feebly Harry tried to pass off disappointment with a joke.

"No, but you could have started a rumor he drank." She brandished her superior know-how. When *her* opportunity came around—say six years from now, when Lloyd began school—she wouldn't tamely lose.

A week later, the whole idea of her waiting any time at all suddenly grew laughable. No sooner were the Schlempkes free of illness than Ilse was in Frieda's kitchen, reaching with hungry arms for her grandson.

"Heavens!" Frieda told herself, the moment her son lay against Ilse's shoulder. "I haven't even seen my own nose!"

CHAPTER XXIII

This time her return to Hake's met what she considered no opposition. True, Miss Wigness was hostile and Miss Shatto took on the whispering airs of martyrdom; true, a few customers, to her face, spoke outrage—"It's always seemed to me that at least a *mother's* place should be in the home!" For a time, too, children could be heard chanting on the boardwalks, "Mrs. Gurney, me oh my, leaves her baby home to die!" Harry, on the eve of her return, came home so drunk he didn't know what he was saying, and had to be tumbled into bed by force, and Mr. Gurney, in person, poker-stiff as ever, actually turned up on the second day with an offer: "Madam, if you will return to your duties, I am prepared to supplement my son's income with five dollars weekly." But what were such acts of weak and undirected opposition? People this time kept right on buying, that was what was important; most of the women, as if helplessly, let her wait on them without caviling. A little ignoring was all most of them needed—that, and a glimpse of her baby.

Whenever her mother brought Lloyd in—which, by arrangement with Mr. Hake, was twice daily—she dropped whatever customer she had to run for him. No one could see her grab her son with hugs and kisses, no one could see her dance him on the counter, no one could view her pride as she ostentatiously bore him to the back room for nursing, no one could see the rich caparisoning of her baby, or his firm, fat, bounding, rosy self, and think him in any way neglected.

To Mr. Gurney she replied, "Oh no, it isn't only the money I make here, it's what I *do*," but to others, who naturally knew nothing of Mr. Gurney's offer, she need scarcely be so open.

"Well, you know, considering what Harry makes——"

Harry himself had given her these words, in the months while she waited for Lloyd to get old enough so she could leave him. Harry had pleaded, "But don't you see, Frieda? Your going back is such a shame for me. As if I couldn't provide for my own son. I'll make more money soon; I'll be in something else soon. If you'll just wait a little, and believe I can do it—I seem to need that, Frieda; if only you'd just *believe* I could do it——"

Not until the night he came home drunk did she find out what he had meant.

"Bink," he kept sorrowing that night while he was drunk. "Bink's got four hundred dollars, all for bicycles. If I had four hundred dollars I could buy bicycles too. Bink says there isn't a person he'd rather have with him in a shop than me. Everybody wants bicycles, and there isn't anybody Bink would rather have than me. All I need is four hundred dollars. But the bank won't let me have it, and Orcutt won't, and Kenneally won't, and Mathew Drake won't. They say I'd have to have a different wife. They say my father'd have to sign a note. And I won't ask Father to sign a note, the way Elizabeth's ears are after her fever——"

The worry he aroused (suppose, someway, he found out she almost *had* four hundred dollars, right in the house!) did not entirely leave her until, one morning, she walked past what had been an empty store, next to Kenneally's, to see it carrying a new sign: STEVENS AND CAVENDER, BICYCLES, above a windowful of shining new machines. Boys—girls too—hung about the place; you couldn't get downtown, these days, without being knocked from the walk by scorchers.

"Wouldn't Harry just *roll* if he were in there, though," she could remind herself, whenever she passed, but at the same time she could breathe a sigh of relief; such danger seemed well over. Harry, on the day of Bink's opening, once more came home drunk, and stayed half drunk for a week.

The day she brought her son for Mr. Hake to see, the day she let her little shell fall—"What would you think, Mr. Hake, of my working here again?"—she had momently been aware of difference in Mr. Hake; Mr. Hake, when she stood before him with her big squirming boy, had looked so spent, his eyes seemed to have receded so far into caverns, his skin to have drawn so close to tired and uncaring bones, that a quaver shook her. Mr. Hake couldn't, certainly he couldn't, be getting old! Why, he wasn't fifty! People lived years after fifty.

All he had needed, she told herself later, was someone to shake him up. As soon as she spoke he came alive.

"Come back now?" he asked. "With that?" His head went back for his gasp of laughter. "Oh, do come back," he said. "Do come, by all means!"

Afterward she noticed that he rather seldom climbed down from the balcony to move about the store, sometimes even waiting on a choice customer, as he once had, but why should he? He had her, now. Initiations she made were for a time small, but before she had been back half a year she had begun being infected with a tremendous project.

Time and again, when she helped in buying, she was exposed to made-up garments—not just jackets, shirtwaists, capes and loose cloaks which could fit around anything, but skirts too, entire suits, dresses. At first these were so obviously ill fitting and ill made that spurning them took no effort, but things now were changing. In a way, these made-up garments sometimes had more style than anything turned out by West Haven dressmakers.

Inevitably the hour came when, head tipped and hand to cheek, she stood examining a line of Ladies' Tailored Spring Suits being hawked by a passionately sweating salesman.

"You got to understand, Mrs. Gurney." The salesman was hoarse with his earnestness. "Ladies *like* these ready-mades. They're cut and sewed, already. The customer can see how they look——"

"Customers," Frieda reiterated the old argument, but absently, "still come in different sizes, not only sideways, but up and down. And if there is one thing in this world a suit has got to have, it's fit."

But she also knew that a moment of crisis had come. Turning to Mr. Hake, who as ever lay inertly in his chair, hands behind his neck, she brought out—a husk in her voice, too, since what she had to say could make or break her, as it could make or break Hake's— the end results of her being pulled forward and backward.

"Would you gamble? That's what it would have to be, Mr. Hake, a gamble. If we're going to do it, we'd have to do it the Hake way —full range of styles, full range of sizes. No, wait—we could hire a girl I know, a girl named Rozzie Balik, to do fitting—she's crippled, so she needn't cost much. She has a sewing machine, and we could charge a little—twenty-five cents, maybe fifty cents—for alterations, so we'd make a profit even there. It may be a terrible failure, Mr. Hake, but it's going in Meridian, and we'd be the only ones to try in West Haven."

The salesman's choked endorsement—"Now, Mrs. Gurney, now you talk! Listen to her, Mr. Hake; I tell you, she talks good"—was a gnat's buzzing; what she awaited, with no strength in her knees and only sloshing liquid in her stomach, was Mr. Hake's verdict.

"No one," Mr. Hake said, with hands still clasped and eyes no more than mocking, "needs urge me to a gamble, least of all Mrs. Gurney."

Half the balcony climb was behind him this time when the pains came. Not as bad as some pains had been lately—just a crack across his chest and then the flashes down his left arm. Gasping· a little, drenched immediately in dampness, mounting slowly, he got himself to level flooring where, if he fell, at least he needn't tumble humblingly on stairs. But the desk chair seemed far until the paroxysm should be gone; clenching and unclenching his hands on the balcony rail, swaying a little, he stood resting while he looked down at his store.

Even with the changes made by that minx, Mrs. Gurney, he knew so well every foot of it, groceries to the left, cheese rounds, salt, cracker barrels, Mr. Tow and Miss Wigness, now that old Horace was gone; dry goods to the right, silks, laces, ribbons, muslins, and the new forest of racks, Mrs. Gurney, Miss Shatto, Eddie and, for eight months now, Rozzie Balik, clumping from her cubby in an aura of busy adoration—adoration not of his racks and counters, but of Frieda Gurney. Odd, he had never thought of Frieda as a friend to anyone, and yet, in a way, although she pinched at it—if he hadn't insisted on the six, Rozzie Balik would have been paid four dollars, or even three—still Frieda seemed to be a friend to Rozzie Balik; at least she had gotten her the job, for which the Hungarian was almost cruelly grateful.

Odd how, whenever the pain came, it was usually to Mrs. Gurney his thoughts clung, as if in viewing her audacious hardihood there might be vigor, even for him. As the close clamp of stricture left his chest wall, she was the first person he saw, standing in the square below him.

"If you'll just step back with Miss Balik, Mrs. Page—oh yes, this street gown will fit, I assure you. Perhaps a pinch in here, Miss Balik—Mrs. Page has such a small waist—and then a little easing in the seam above. Mrs. Page has such a fine bosom." Oh, no question, she was adroit—had he, or hadn't he, given her that adroitness? Even in the spring, her ready-mades cut a swath; women who in the first weeks had poked about the garments as if snakes might be concealed in the pockets, had almost suddenly succumbed.

"Isn't it different?" they asked now of the clothes their bodies sported. "Oh no, ready-made. I bought it, you know, of that Mrs. Gurney."

Not "at Hake's," but "of that Mrs. Gurney." She had done that. Maybe it wouldn't last, but temporarily, at least, perhaps not among the best people, but at least among the second best and among the young, she had made it fashionable to buy clothes ready-made, from her. This, in a West Haven which almost solidly disliked and disapproved of her.

He knew his face had taken on that shape of silent laughter which it assumed these days almost for her alone; who or what else, under heaven, was amusing? That anyone should want anything—and especially what she wanted—with such desperation, that anyone should thrust forward with such driving and relentless need; that was the heart of the jest. She must be pushed by other forces too; since her marriage her body had increasingly become something that she flaunted; she had taken on that conscious, sly look of women who think constantly of what they hold for men. He might be mistaken —no one should know better than he how he *could* be mistaken— but he rather thought that since her initial divergence she had been confining herself to her husband.

Why was that? Was it because of respect for respectability, or because she feared her employer might not keep her if she took on too much notoriety, or because, so far, there had been too little to be gained by indiscretion? Dinner at the Benson House or the Habak-anaw, small gifts—she had too high an opinion of Mrs. Gurney to let herself go so cheaply.

Salesmen she bowled like tenpins. For his benefit, he had to admit, since the discounts were to his advantage. But for hers too; her peculiar ethics didn't reach to sampling. Still, no matter if it was the wholesalers who kept her a fashion plate. When she came back next time—and he'd bet his bottom dollar she wouldn't let this second infant keep her home six months—he'd raise her to twelve dollars, and maybe send her to do buying in Meridian.

Somehow girls didn't interest him so much any more; there hadn't really been anyone on whom he had been able to fasten his thoughts since that night—that peculiarly memorable night—when he found himself cheated of Frieda. Well, he had kept her secret; even to Palmer he hadn't spoken of it, though sometimes—no, Palmer must choose his own beds. As he had guessed almost at once, his loss in this case had been turned into gain; he still had his enjoyment; he still could watch her when she had her head. He intended to hold out for years yet; there was no reason he shouldn't, the doctor said, if he cut down on activity. But she wouldn't, through him, have forever——

For once, she looked forward to an absence from Hake's with at least some eagerness. It wasn't as if, this time, there could be any question of her leaving for good; Mr. Hake had agreed to the period —two months before the birth, two after. No one else in the store had any idea she would be gone long, either. Everything was snug and shipshape, stock well bought for the time ahead, Rozzie on hand to keep an eye out, her own sister Lotte to fill in. At fifteen, Lotte was a tall, blond, dimpled girl with fuzzy braids, much more docile than Frieda had ever been; Lotte could be made to quit any time Frieda wanted.

But it was not in plans well planned or duty done that she found her anticipation. Nor in the new child coming. It was in the fact that for a while she would be home all day, every day, with Lloyd.

Lloyd, at two, preferred Harry to her—that couldn't be hidden. "Papa come! Papa come!" was all he could cry, hurtling his chunky, red-cheeked self at Harry. "Papa b'ing!" he welcomed any toy or candy, even when Frieda gave it.

Anyone could see how this had come about; naturally it was Harry, free as he was with his dray, who could drop in any time at Schlempkes'. Even for Ilse—"Gowli," he called her—Lloyd had more affection than he had for his own mother.

"Just wait till he finds out what money is," Frieda could console herself stoutly, but that didn't take care of the present.

"Mama stay Lloyd." Trailing his pinned-on blankets to her bedside at six-thirty, Lloyd, for her first day at home, had the most radiant expectations. And for that day, too, everything was almost the honeymoon they both anticipated. Breakfast passed to prattle as indulgent on his side as hers, he afterward played house industriously with broom and dish towel, breaking a minimum of dishes, he lent himself good-humoredly to Frieda's lazing, and in the afternoon sunned himself on a trip downtown.

On the second day, however, his greeting was a question—"Go Gowli now?" Responses, during the morning, slowly grew more and more stubborn; he threw his blocks instead of building; at first hopefully, then with tears runneling the jam on his cheeks (usually if nothing else kept him quiet, eating would) he reiterated the same demand, "Go Gowli now." By midafternoon, napless and with his little skin-tight trousers soaked—if he couldn't have his way about forcing life to a normal pattern, he saw no reason why Frieda should have hers about naps or chamber pots—he had clawed on cap and jacket, kicked long furrows in the front door, and beaten out the parlor window with his fists. Before suppertime, exhausted, Frieda was taking him to Ilse for a short call.

It wasn't, she told herself, that she couldn't handle Lloyd; naturally, if anyone could do that, she could. But she felt very heavy with this second child and, in her condition, it might not be safe to do so much struggling. Next week, besides, she was having carpenters. They were getting a new small room, a bedroom off the kitchen. The rent would go up to ten dollars, but it would be worth it. Harry could sleep there.

"This propensity of yours for bearing," Mr. Hake had mocked, "isn't it rather an interference?"

"Oh, not really," she had answered. "After I had one baby, I decided I wanted two. But two will be enough."

She almost got more than she bargained for—twins. But the one twin was stillborn.

After the birth she again suffered shock—shock at finding she could stray so far from her purposes, shock at having death pass so close. After a few days, though, she was able to push back what had happened—the child she kept was so exactly what she wanted: a girl, Idelle. Idelle showed no signs of her near brush with death; Idelle was as lusty as Lloyd had been; Idelle at the scheduled two months took luxuriantly to an itinerant life between home, store and grandmother; Idelle at seven months let herself be weaned, so that Frieda could take off on her long-promised buying trip to Meridian.

As in most things connected with her life at Hake's this trip consumingly met expectations. At last, attended by great flurry, she got off on an early train, at last in her new hair-plaid green-on-brown tweed she sat enthroned on a green plush seat (not alone long, with all the drummers she knew!); at last, as a full-fledged businesswoman, spurred rather than held back by the newness of all she now did, she tripped smartly from the paid hack to the Merchants' Hotel, where she signed the register: "F. Gurney, Hake's, West Haven"; at last, within the precincts of a room alone, she shook out her extra shirtwaists, settled her plumed derby, nipped her belt in, powdered her face lightly (powder, here, could be left open!), and then, before banking hours could be over, hurried to add the seven hundred dollars of her savings to that original one hundred the bank held already.

At the moment of abandonment, the moment when she laid her money on the ledge and saw it taken up for counting by objective and too agile fingers, she could not fend away a temporary chilling; in one way the money was hers no longer; she could no longer hold and count it. But once she was out of the mammoth building (full three stories) with the figures in her little book, she drew in a satisfying breath; that had been purely careless, keeping her money all these years where it might burn up or be stolen; such carelessness was what should really freeze her. Now it was all safe, like her hundred. Eight hundred dollars, all together, and all hers.

In West Haven, she had eased so gradually into buying, in West Haven she was so ostensibly under the final say of Mr. Hake, that those buyer's appurtenances she had attained had been classifiable only as "nice." It had been nice to be told, "We have a new-style skirt with eight gores that we'd like to have you try out, Mrs. Gurney," nice to have heads shaken over her astuteness: "A few more like you, Mrs. Gurney, and we couldn't stay in business for a week." But the receptions she met at the wholesale centers opened her eyes.

"I'm Mrs. Gurney," was all she had to say, to bring men scurrying. "*Mrs. Gurney,* did you say, from *Hake's?* Come right with me. You'll want to meet our Mr. Johnson, here, and Mr. Frales. Mr. Johnson, we'll not bother Mrs. Gurney with the line that's out; bring what we're readying for next season."

Sometimes she felt herself almost drowning. The garments deferentially draped before her were so new, so varied—not samples picked as suitable for small towns, but full lines—that the pull to let go and cry simply, "Oh yes, I'll take this and this and this and this," became so strong she herself did not know how her voice, for the most part, continued to emerge cool and practiced.

"Still showing berthas? Gracious! But that shirred yoke might do. No, I like skirts with more flare—don't you use the umbrella design? Yes, hair stripes should be good again this year. Oh," slipping, "isn't that the mousquetaire sleeve? Oh, it's divine!" Recovering: "Yes, definitely I might try one of those. Oh no, I couldn't, not a gift for myself. This stem-green isn't bad—how silly, there's a muff. Gilt cords are out——"

The more versed and hard she showed herself, the more she was admired; that in itself helped her to be ruthless. Not until, headed toward West Haven, she once more sat embraced within the green plush of the day coach, not until she had mentally reviewed each garment bought—"Yes, I'm sure that one will sell"—did she allow caution to relax so she could look, with bliss melting out her very bones, at all she had enjoyed. Epicurean repasts at McCormick's, with herself as brisk and fashionable and well escorted as any woman there, Cleo de Mérode at the Opera House, a baseball game—"We can't miss stirring up a little diamond dust while you're here," Mr. Buss, that wholesaler, had invited. All this offered to her, as her right, because of what she was and could do, because she was a buyer.

Even a partner, naturally, would go on buying.

She had three years—three years in which she was Queen Bee (Miss Wigness's name for it) of Hake's; three years in which her visits to

Meridian were ineffably repeated every quarter; three years of change so slow it could not be visible until the years were gone.

Yet this too ended; ended on an April night in 1900 when she met Lil McCartney at the Benson House for dinner. Just going to the Benson House was still a fillip; it was so lately that West Haven's one hotel had suffered its sea change of management and morals, ripping off its outer stairway ("Terribly inconvenient that's going to be, too, for some people," Lil said, rolling her large handsome eyes), and adding—plate glass on two sides—the Corner Coffee Room.

The Corner Coffee Room, as Frieda critically saw above her oysters on that night, was getting to be quite the thing. Right there, two tables from her, sat Mrs. Fred Pomeroy, née Jessie Drake, in garnet cloth with a Medici collar of butter-color plaited lace.

"Among those present when Mrs. Fred Pomeroy entertained at the Benson House Coffee Room," Frieda recited stiltedly to Lil, "were Lil McCartney, of Faust's Shirtwaists, and Mrs. Frieda Gurney, Hake's."

"Yes, and aren't we glad we aren't stuck with those small-town stuck-ups," returned Lil in her thick smooth drawl. Strange as it had seemed at first to have Lil come around—a lady drummer!—there now was no one with whom Frieda felt as much at home.

"I'd still like to be told," Lil went back to what she had been saying, in that slow husk which was like the dripping of the very best and richest Hollandaise sauce, "what keeps you in West Haven anyway— some man? Women's styles are something I've been in for fifteen years, and I'm telling you right now you've got more knack in your little finger than half the buyers in Meridian who pull down their two, three thousand every year. Oh, I'm not saying you might not have to start small—six, seven dollars, maybe. But once you got in you'd travel, or my name's not Lil McCartney."

It was no new song to Frieda, nor one she heard only from Lil. Nevertheless, when she left Lil some hours later, her feet stepped lightly in a soft and rain-held night. In Meridian——

Sweet as the idea was, however, she knew it was an idea, and no more than that. She couldn't think seriously of leaving Hake's. Some-times now Mr. Hake didn't even come inside the store for half a week; he left almost everything to her. Oh, she had exasperations—why West Haven women wouldn't wear tunique overskirts she never would find out—but on the whole no one could say that what she bought didn't *go*. It wasn't eight hundred she had in Meridian any longer; it was fourteen hundred. Mr. Hake had never said what he'd ask from a partner—the subject had never been mentioned except that one time —but he couldn't be too unreasonable, seeing what else she'd be putting in, in knack. Let her get her share of Hake's, and all Meridian could go hang; even Lil might see then what could be done in small towns like West Haven.

Near Andreason's Hardware Store her mind was temporarily distracted from these gratifications by the sound of running footsteps on stairs—footsteps too light to be either Rozzie's or her father's. Looking up, she recognized the slight, down-running figure, and a different infection leaped.

"Why, Eddie!" she cried, at the half-caught, defiant face. "Eddie Noble! Don't tell me you've been calling on *Rozzie!*"

"What if I have?" Eddie tossed back, and as she went on she was wholly amused. Rozzie, of all people, to have snared a beau! Eddie and Rozzie! Not that it could come to anything; Eddie was never the boy to stand up to the teasing he'd get.

As a further break in what was usual, it was Harry, not Ilse, who waited her home-coming in the kitchen by the lamp.

"Saturday night," she asked, "and you're not drunk? How long have you been here?"

Harry fidgeted instead of answering, but so complete was her good humor that she went on to tell him, anyway, about Eddie and Rozzie.

"You—you haven't heard, then," Harry put in soberly when she was done. Harry, nowadays, stumbled over words only when he was someway moved, so her ears pricked. And then, with no other preparation, she got the news.

"Hake's had a stroke. That's what they say. Had it tonight on his way home from the store."

CHAPTER XXIV

"Paralyzed," a woman at his front door said, a woman of dark scalloped hair whose flat eyes only partially hid relish, a woman who rolled unction, with her arms, beneath her apron. "Maybe he'll live, Doctor says, if he don't have a second attack. But he'll be paralyzed."

"Oh no," Frieda whispered in reply, as she had whispered her one question.

The woman stepped aside. "Come in if you want. There's others."

"Oh no," Frieda replied again, and turned, pulling her gloved hand from the door casing where it had clung. She was not here to mourn;

she had fled here to find Mr. Hake corporeal and unchanged, his shoulders sagging and indifferent but his head going back for laughter.

"That's what they're saying, is it?" Mr. Hake should have asked. "Hope springs eternal——"

Staring at a high rectangle (the Amiot Flouring Mill, now three years closed), staring again at dull low parallels (the switchyard), she stumbled heedlessly in deepening rain, ingesting calamity, trying to recover, even from this blow, what must be recoverable. "Paralyzed," that woman said. "Maybe he'll live, but—paralyzed." Terror loomed, but quickly she cringed back to safety. Mr. Hake couldn't fail her— not Mr. Hake. Even if he were paralyzed, even if he lay stiffened on a dark bed in a dark room, he still was there and reachable, mockery could still light his eyes, he still could tell her with no words, "There the path lies, open; I'll be here watching while you walk it."

By morning she was able to stand alone before the numbed huddle of her fellow employees, speaking almost composedly.

"He can't see anyone, but I hear he's resting well. In a day or two"— how hope could soar—"he may be over it. Meantime we'll go on as if he were here——"

Under such firm authority, Rozzie must scuttle to her deep-piled workroom, and the others, too, perforce dispersed to their early duties. She herself stepped to the back room to check freight with Lotte; it was, she told herself, only her sleepless night that cast a pall of aimlessness over what she did. Again and again, through the morning, she had to break up the knot into which Miss Shatto and Eddie, Mr. Tow and Miss Wigness regathered as soon as she was out of sight; she herself found it hard not to linger in that same hushed huddle, repeating, "Terrible. I can't believe it." In order to keep herself aloof she had to retreat to the balcony where she, in Mr. Hake's own old way, stood to look down at those aisles where, today, the few who entered did so with eyes averted from all racks and counters, as if any desire for Hake goods at such a time must be indecent.

"Oh, he's *much* better." She herself hurried to answer the hushed inquiries. In the eyes of all these sympathizers, she began to see, just as in the eyes of her fellows, a queer light was discernible. And that light, after a while, carried its own message.

Maybe now, so ran the message, maybe now the *son* will take a hand.

From the minute her eyes (or was it her ears?) caught the whisper, the contents of her mind had to shift. Of course, Palmer. With Mr. Hake stricken, Palmer of course would have to come in. Palmer.

It was years since she had seen him in any way except casually, but at the prospect which now loomed close a lid seemed to dance on a fast-steaming kettle. They thought Palmer would be against her, did they? Why, if there was any one person who *owed* her something; if there was any one person in the world who could part way take Mr. Hake's place, it was Palmer; Palmer knew what she was; Palmer knew what she could do; her foreignness and her poverty need not enter into *this* conjunction.

Yet when Palmer did come, when there was, first, the dry rumble (tired, he sounded) of his voice at the door, and then the plod of his feet on the balcony stair, she did not rise to meet him; her knees would not have held her.

He's gotten fat. As his head and shoulders arose from the stairwell, this—in the midst of all else she was feeling—was what had to strike at her; Palmer was heavier and he looked old, his eyes dull, his red forehead seamed, his cheeks large and flabby.

"Your father. Do tell me he's better." Shaken as she was, this was the plea that must supersede all else.

Before answering, Palmer completed his ascent, and crossed the few feet to the drummers' chair, into which he sagged as if he were letting down a sack of wheat.

"He's—it looks as if the worst is over for this time." Even when he at last tonelessly spoke, he did not glance toward her; instead, pushing his hat back, he wiped a slow palm across his face, and then bent forward to fix his gaze on hands that dropped limply between his knees.

"Oh," she began, sinking back. "Oh. I'm so glad. I can't tell you what——"

Breaking in as if her voice were a mosquito's whine, he again tonelessly spoke.

"We'd best talk over, I guess, how things are." Sullenness and inimicality were so open that, automatically, her own forces rose in defense.

"Of course," she accepted. "There's no question, naturally, but that I can keep things going, until your father gets back. For a long time now I've——"

"Gets back?" he repeated, and this time his voice was hollowly loud. "I guess you haven't realized, Mrs. Gurney, just how bad he is. He can't—he can't even——"

He got no further, but in silence, a loud, choking silence, she heard much more than he could have uttered, felt the return of a terror greater than any he could have imparted. Last night she had been able to fend off that terror, but in its return it was a vise, inescapable.

She managed a whisper: "But that's just not possible. He can't——"

In the intolerance of torment Palmer twisted in his chair.

"He's done for, can't you understand that?" Brutally, the hatchet stroke fell, and this time he was looking at her. For a moment, as she sat incapable of moving, she had a queer sense of double living, as if the man in the chair had buried his head in his arms on the desk, while she bent over him, to comfort. Oh no, no, Palmer, it's all right, some part of her said, "we'll both of us come out all right." But at the same time—all the time Palmer convulsively shuddered and she crooned over him—he yet sat upright, keeping himself and his anguish aloof from her, while she, across oak, kept as distant from him.

"He can't talk much; I've got to decide what to do." Again it was Palmer who actually spoke. "You'll keep open—you'll sell what you can, for cash, especially. About buying, though—I guess you'd best not do much. There's only eleven hundred in the cash account, against over eight thousand in notes. I stopped in at the bank."

She sat struggling frantically for breath and voice.

"But that's impossible! That bank's lying—this is *Hake's!* You should see our profits! We——"

"All his life he's been a gambler, and he's had—expenses." The harshness against her did not ease. "He's got money around——"

Some breath came back. "Money around! Of course he's got money around! Thousands! All we need is to get in some of our accounts——"

The heavy head heavily shook. "They won't pay now. I know 'em."

Words rushed. "But all this is just nothing! I'll build up a reserve! Inside one month I can have us——"

"I've got one business and I don't like stores." No slightest inflection showed that he even heard what she said. "If I could get an offer——"

What was happening couldn't be happening.

"What are you talking about?" she shrilled. "Are you talking about selling *Hake's?* Why, you can't sell Hake's! Hake's is part of this town, it's——"

"I don't see why it should make so much difference to you." Reply to this, too, was brutal. "It's not your store." And before she had answer for this he had risen and lumbered away.

She begged of the doctor, in Hake's hall, "I've got to see Mr. Hake. I've got to."

The doctor had helped her bear her children, and she had helped him with Gisela; he bore her no ill will, only what seemed to be a kind of curiosity. He went off to a room under the stairs, but returned shaking his head.

"Not even you, I guess, Mrs. Gurney. Maybe in a few days from now, if he regains some strength."

In frenzy, a week later, after Palmer had again come to the store to sit glumly, silently counting over the week's small receipts, and after she had tried passionately again to convince him what a gold mine Hake's had been and would yet be, she plunged into a period of furious activity about the store. Profits must convince Palmer, if words couldn't. Maddeningly, however, sales stayed small; she would have run into the streets to snatch at people, if only it would have made them buy. Contrary to Palmer's edicts about spending, she ran a bold newspaper ad, HAKE'S IS OPEN FOR BUSINESS AS USUAL, above reckless adjectives about her suits and dresses. She had Rozzie offer to make up piece goods, she had Rozzie sew up sample gowns, she kept Lotte and Miss Shatto in a constant fuss of dusting and freshening. Before, she had ignored groceries, but now, since they were the only things that sold in anything like normal volume, she whipped at Mr. Tow and Miss Wigness to increase their sales.

Under this flailing, proceeds did increase, but not to a quarter of what they had been. Each time Palmer came in his brows dragged lower; against her repeated insistence that the drop was only temporary he continued unbelieving and sullen.

Added to this major fanning of the panic in her breast were other drafts. She had never had any illusions that Eddie, Miss Shatto, Mr. Tow or Miss Wigness felt any real subjection to her, but she had always taken it for granted they felt toward Mr. Hake much as she did. Now she was forced to see the error in this too. One day when she ordered Eddie to dust his shoes he flared defiance.

"I dust a shoe before I put it on a foot—that's the time."

"How does that look? Like carelessness, that's what."

"It's how I've done and how I'll keep on doing!"

She fell back to the appeal direct. "When Mr. Hake depends on us——"

Before, this had been enough to quell mutiny, but not now. Eddie continued to stand with lips blown outward.

"We may not all, you know, Mrs. Gurney," he said spitefully, "have quite the same reasons Mrs. Gurney has for loyalty to Mr. Hake. We haven't all been pushed as fast as Mrs. Gurney."

Her return was swift: "Mr. Hake apparently knows who's worth pushing." But although this had the desired effect, although Eddie then frigidly did as she had ordered, she felt how slippery was her hold. She could remember what had happened when Lloyd was about to be born.

What went on with the salesmen was equally unsettling. Palmer, every few days, carried home to his father the checks for bills due; she knew those checks were signed somehow and sent; she asked. But drummers who always before had been fawningly eager were now queerly reluctant. When Lil came around she put the case bluntly.

"A one-man business—you should know this, dearie—blows up when the man blows up. Do we want to see those of-course-you'll-settle-for-twenty-per-cent boys? Not if we know it. Of course, we'll take a *little* chance——"

Her constant sense of support gone, too, of no Mr. Hake behind her, ready to break in with his drawl, "Well, Mrs. Gurney, this isn't Boston," if she got reckless, left her bewildered and unsure. When she held up a heliotrope cloth jacket with gold galloon straps, a *dernier cri* of the ladies' journals, she could not make up her mind. Suppose they too should fail in West Haven? In Mr. Hake's day she could have said, "I'll take one or two and try; it won't make much difference in an order my size"; but now when between Palmer and the salesmen she was held to bare necessities, each purchase was a source of fever. "Was I right about that hair stripe? Maybe I should have taken the blue——"

Nor was this all. "Mice have gotten into two butter tubs, Mrs. Gurney." "That Mrs. Ward—young Mrs. Ward—is downstairs wanting a dress on credit." Had she ever thought Mr. Hake did nothing? She added the word "please" to all June bills; collections that month were smaller than in May. "Mrs. Langesley and Mrs. Willis went to Meridian on the ten-ten," Miss Shatto reported. "I never knew *them* to shop out of town before."

Lloyd got measles. Ilse cared for him by day, Harry by night, but his noisy fretting helped in keeping her sleepless; at home and abroad she felt herself beset as no human ever had been before.

Yet later she was to look back upon this time as a reprieve. More and more as she dealt with Palmer she had to feel she was giving ground, and the day came all too quickly when her back was against a last wall.

"Oh, all this is no use!" Slamming his hand on a sheet of her artful figures, Palmer on that day thrust aside her books. "There's only one thing to do with this business—sell it."

By reflex she kept on with argument: "I haven't had time yet to——" but she herself knew the uselessness of words.

"I can get twelve thousand, cash." What ensued from Palmer was, again, sullen. "It isn't good enough, but I'll take it."

Her hands, almost steady, gathered together a flutter of loose papers on the desk, her hands dropped them against the desk until their edges came out even on all four sides; her fingers, scarcely trembling, laid this small sheaf neatly on the desk, and on it piled the two account books. Sometimes, in the weeks past, she had wondered what she would do when this moment came—she'd had few doubts it must come. Now it was here she didn't wonder.

"I'll make you an offer to buy," she said, knowing in her very pelvis all the focus of this moment, all its possible loss, all she had learned in the past weeks of slips between cup and lip. "I've fourteen hundred of my own, in cash. In addition, I'll give you notes for twelve thousand against lock, stock and good will. That's fourteen hundred, clear, above your other offer. No, wait!"

Her hands moved when he moved, detaining him; words that had come chill, prefrozen, began to thaw and tumble. "You can't believe, Palmer, that this store, this business, isn't a good investment! As soon as it changes hands, as soon as it's known my money's in it, people will trade here again; they'll pay their bills. The interest, even, would be a good income; I'd pay ten per cent——"

She herself was only half hearing what she offered; she was seeing at last the real issue. Mr. Hake was out of this, now; she in a way had taken his place. She wanted money, but she also wanted to keep the store going, she was willing to give for it even the pound of her flesh, her savings. Palmer on his side wanted only money. What was behind his want she couldn't know; he had always wanted money, but besides that, now, his business might need money, Cecilia might be demanding money. After old Thomas Amiot died, it was whispered, there hadn't been as much left to divide as had been expected.

Palmer said, "Fourteen hundred won't even pay off the bank's notes."

"I can pay those off from accounts, little by little. You can have that fourteen hundred clear, right now——"

"I can have five thousand clear, right now." In an echo of an old gesture, his shoulders moved swaggeringly. "It takes five thousand to be money. Fourteen hundred to me is chicken feed."

She offered two thousand more, three thousand; soon she was standing, following him as he edged toward the stairs, her hands cupped at breast height; she could not open her hands because she felt they held something—life—and if she loosed her fingers, then life, like sand, would drain away. She held those cupped hands toward him, gathering herself to use a last weapon. Always before on the balcony they had met as strangers, but now she ripped that sham aside.

"You, of all people, Palmer, you must realize you have a debt to me——"

Lines at his mouth and eyes grew ugly.

"I was waiting for you to bring that up," he threw back, and flung away.

Still she could not let herself entirely despair. "I," Palmer said, and "me," as if his father were gone, but as long as Mr. Hake was alive, then she had a chance; he could turn defeat to triumph as he so often had before. Even if there was nothing of him but a husk on a bed, the name signed to a deed must still be Junius Hake.

After her final bout with Palmer she was again turned aside from the door to which she sped as soon as she had strength to get there, the next day she had the same answer, but on another morning the small mussed figure of the doctor appeared in the store, and almost before he had spoken she was on her way.

West Haven was a blur of gray and green through which she fled; the parlor and the hall at Hake's were antechambers; all she knew was that at last she was reaching to the coffer of her hope—a back room of drawn shades where bed and dresser loomed in darkness, where a light intermittent rasping sounded that was breath, and a half voice at once spoke.

"If it's Mrs. Gurney," that voice said from its distance, "let her come where I can see her."

The words were slurred, but that was what he said; she understood him. Air in the room was sticky with a sickroom dampness; unable, suddenly, to keep herself erect, she sank toward a chair shape by the bed. The shade which slipped up a few inches before the housekeeper left let her see him faintly as it let him see her; he lay long but scarcely mounded on the quilted bed, his dark face against the pillow sunken and askew, one eyelid drooping and mouth blurred. Only his nose had changed little; it was merely sharper and more beaked.

She had come trembling, filled with all she must in her small moment compass. At sight of him—of how little there was of him on the bed—her heart became a wet cloth wrung between inexorable hands.

The low croak continued. "At least you don't come to rejoice in my infirmities," it said, and when her mind had pieced the broken sounds together the twisting eased a little at her heart. The spirit in the shell on the bed might be tenuous, but in what there was of it, it still was Mr. Hake.

"Palmer," she burst, the name swelling large and painful in her throat, "wants to sell the store."

He didn't nod; he perhaps had neither the strength nor the ability to nod, but the twitching of muscles about his eyes was the rippling of knowledge—knowledge of Palmer and all Palmer wanted, knowledge of her and all she wanted. She sat once more pent above the press of all she had to say, the pleading; but as in those old encounters with him on the balcony, she could only lift her hands. He knew what she would have said; the best she could do was let silence plead for her.

"You or Palmer," he went on when she produced nothing, and a light flickered under his eyelids, as if he too remembered, as if he with pleasure remembered those other days when speech for her had been too crowded by emotion to be ready. "Who should the store go to— that's it, isn't it? You or Palmer."

She forced out two words. "I'd pay."

Actually, after that, his head did move, flopping sideward so that it faced toward her more directly. "Palmer says—you have—fourteen hundred dollars. Tell me, Mrs. Gurney, had you—saved much—when Harry wanted to buy in with Bink Stevens?"

His eyes were the burned-out coals of what they had been, but still they took her as she was, curious but unjudging; her clothes rustled faintly from her movement in them, but she managed to keep her gaze from dropping beneath his.

He said, "I thought so at the time. You're almost heartless, Mrs. Gurney." The shadow of a shrug went with the voice, even if there was no shrug to see. His eyes closed.

"You're so entirely what you are," the voice now drifted, "and Palmer so entirely what he is. If you got the store—it might last your lifetime; if Palmer gets it, I would expect it soon to be gone. But you'd manage somehow—you'd always make your money somehow, Mrs. Gurney, and Palmer needs this money now. Well——" The last word held so much removal and dismissal that she bent forward, her clothes once more rustling, her throat at last forming speech. But he was not done.

"So I'll do what I've always done," it drifted on, "I'll lay it in the usual lap. There's a deck of cards on that table by you, Mrs. Gurney. We Hakes owe you a queer debt, Mrs. Gurney, and the odds are yours. If the single card you draw at a single motion is a jack or better, the store goes to Palmer. If it's a ten or lower, then Hake's is yours, at your price."

As her hand lifted, hungry but shaking, she whispered, "Mr. Hake."

"What?" he asked, and this time there could be no question of mockery. "What, Mrs. Gurney, are you frightened of destiny? Frightened, Mrs. Gurney, of the gods? I might tell you how your chance is weighted, Mrs. Gurney—that's Drake money Palmer is offered; it's Fred Pomeroy—Jessie Drake's husband—who's on the deal. You see— one card, Mrs. Gurney."

Her breath was silken in the room, but the tear of silk can be louder than the rasp of metal; her limbs were powered and mobile, his inert, yet a freedom flowed in him of which she was bereft.

He said again, "Ten chances to three, and your play, Mrs. Gurney; you can't say I'm anything but fair," and still she could not reach farther. He lay long, watching her.

"As always," he said, "you give me the most exquisite pleasure, Mrs. Gurney."

The card she turned up was the queen of spades.

CHAPTER XXV

Afterward, after her last week in the store, after Fred Pomeroy, in person, with two weeks' pay in lieu of notice, had dismissed her—"The rest of the staff I can keep, Mrs. Gurney, but naturally I'll do my own buying"—after the days in which she lay more torpid on her bed than Mr. Hake had lain on his, the youth and vigor of her body forced her fitfully to some return.

At Orcutt's she told her story: "I wouldn't be caught dead working for Fred Pomeroy, but you, Mr. Orcutt——" Later this same story became "You, Mr. Pratt," at Pratt's Drugs, and "You, Mr. Cantrell," at the Bon Ton, but there was nothing from which the words could issue except complete negation and despair. When Mr. Orcutt was arch—"Well now, Mrs. Gurney, that's a proposition Mrs. Orcutt might object to," when Mr. Pratt was curt—"Nothing here, I'm afraid," when Mr. Cantrell, after hemming and hawing, offered her four dollars a week, it was all one; she had no desire to work in any of the places she solicited; West Haven had nothing more for her.

At home she lay again abed, her arms flung upward. This is the worst that could happen to me, she had told herself when she lost Palmer. This is the worst, she had said again when she found out the Gurneys had no money. But nothing could approach what now had stricken her.

"I never thought I'd see the day when you would fail me"—this, after she had turned the card, had been her farewell, at the door, to Mr. Hake.

"You might have guessed, Mrs. Gurney, that I couldn't last forever." That spent whisper had been his farewell to her. When in late summer she heard he was dead, the answer in her bosom was, He died for me long ago.

To replace what was lost she could find little; not even true commiseration. Her father could say, "You find out now is not so easy," and Harry, "Maybe it's for the best, though, Frieda; Lloyd's getting too much for your mother to handle."

Unpaid, Ilse for weeks continued her care of Lloyd and Idelle, but as time went on, as Frieda draggingly began to move about the house, Ilse began a partial shifting.

"Is good the children should be more by the mama," she hinted. "Maybe this afternoon I bring them early." And "Maybe tomorrow they stay by you awhile—I got the washing."

Ever since the one experience with Lloyd, Frieda had carefully limited herself, as a mother, to the dressing and undressing at night, to bedtime and holiday romps, to the giving of clothes, toys and nickels. Now, however, she had to know the relentlessness, the drag, of children left on hand for hours at a time.

"Mama! Mama! I want the hammer now! Mama, I want to hammer!" Lloyd, at six, was never quiet. "Mama, can't I have a great big box? A *big* box, Mama? Can't I go outdoors now, Mama? Mama, can't I get a cookie? Mama, why aren't I at Gowli's?"

Idelle was never more than a step behind. "Mama, I wawa ham'! Mama, I wawa bokth! Mama, I tookie!" Both children were pictures of darkly curled health; both were imperious and handsome; no children, she assured herself, were ever so loved by their mother. But the temper and vigor which had previously caused delight and congratulation—"There! It's from me they get those spirits!"—grew to be less winning when all day long she had to separate the two, when she had to console Idelle for a kitten smashed against a door, when she had to restrain Lloyd from smashing Idelle likewise because Idelle, in retaliation, had managed to bite him on a buttock. Children, she found out, tore and dirtied their clothes seven times a day; children, if they weren't watched, hung themselves on fences, drowned themselves in rain barrels, pitched headfirst into outside cellarways; children ate anything from green strawberries to potato bugs, producing stomachaches that kept a mother up half the night; children never ended, and for all the labor you put on them they returned not the least cash. On a Monday in September, with no word to Harry, she took the ten-ten to Meridian.

Bitterly this time—and cheaply, on a state-fair excursion ticket—she traveled on her own money. She had, as she told herself when she sat once more in the plush, familiar day coach, no illusions. "More knack than half the buyers in Meridian"—so Lil McCartney had said, and others too, but no one of them had come forward to say that, or anything like it, when she had been struggling to keep Hake's. "You'd start small—six, seven dollars, maybe"— this, at least, of what Lil said, would doubtless turn out to be true.

The prospect of being once more a beginner, of putting herself beneath direction and a thumb, was so insupportable that each time she faced it the flood of her miseries swept higher. That she, Frieda Gurney, she who but for the turn of a card would be sitting regal upon the balcony at Hake's—that she could be thus headed for some abject counter job! To think she must crawl from one store to another, humbly begging! It was intolerable, and yet, like so much that was intolerable, must be tolerated.

Under her haughty manner, when she climbed next morning toward the offices at Frigman's (naturally one began at the top), beat a pulse now strong, now fading; Frigman's was so thoroughly a big-city store; it might just be possible that she would be scorned. Once she was under way, however, once the woman at the office rail had drawn her aside from the line, her pulse steadied to a full, even coursing.

"You'll manage somehow—you'll make your money somehow." Why, all these weeks, had she forgotten that statement of Mr. Hake's? Of course she could make money somehow, just let her get going. When the woman at Frigman's dismissed her, with a pleasant "We'll put you on file, Mrs. Gurney; there might be something later on," she felt no depression; the woman had noticed her, all right. And Frigman's wasn't the only department store in Meridian. Walton's, Purley's, Westermarck's and the Hub—Mr. Leisling at the Hub, especially, showed himself impressed. Four mornings later, when for a fourth time (nothing like daily visits to let an employer know you meant business) she sat across from Mr. Leisling, it seemed only part of a pattern that Mr. Leisling should move toward an offer.

"Well, you look a healthy, strong young woman, Mrs. Gurney. Of course, to begin with——"

She could begin work on Monday morning, only a half week away. The pay, seven dollars.

Four days. Four days to uproot her household, to get settled again in Meridian. It was she who pushed the train, at thirty miles per hour, toward West Haven. Seven dollars of course wasn't much, but Harry should be able to find *something* in a city the size of Meridian. "I may say I expect you to advance," Mr. Leisling had said, although that wasn't to be counted on; any advance must go toward her capital. A one-room hovel would do to live in, if need be; only one thing in the world now meant anything—her chance.

When Harry got home that evening the face she lifted to him from a half-packed barrel of dishes was not only dust-streaked but radiant.

"Harry!" she caroled. Usually her greetings for Harry were less jubilant, but this was no time for old animosities. "What do you think? We're getting out of here! We're cleaning our feet of this mud-stuck old town! I've got myself a job in Meridian—do you hear that, Harry? In Meridian!"

She could have danced with Harry, could have hugged him. Shambling as Harry had gotten to be (no one knew better than she how he drank and slacked around!), still even he might pick up a little at this news; relief might flood his face too; he might at least mutter, "No one could be more glad to get out of here than I'll be."

Instead, forever and indissolubly Harry, he had to stand in the doorway as he always stood there, so loosely no one could see what held him up. His face took on its stern look, and she knew immediately that, impossible as it was, he in this too was going to offer obstruction.

"Where are Lloyd and Idelle?" This was what he asked—and answered. "I suppose still at your mother's."

"Of course they're still at Mama's! I can hardly be bothered with them around, all I've got to do! Didn't you hear me, Harry? I said——"

"I heard you." Harry remained unaltered. "You might think for yourself it won't do, Frieda." He walked toward the sink to begin washing, as if what she had just told him was nothing at all.

"But, Harry, this is something we've got to do, can't you see that, Harry?" For conflict on this subject she was entirely unprepared, but weapons were ready. "There isn't anything more for me in West Haven; you know that. This job I've gotten in Meridian is at a good big store—the Hub—two stories. If you want to *dray* you can surely dray anywhere; it doesn't have to be in West Haven——"

As he rolled his sleeves back he asked a quiet question. "Have you thought what you'd do with Lloyd and Idelle, Frieda?"

"Of course I've thought! We could live in a boardinghouse, couldn't we? Goodness knows I wouldn't have much time for cooking. There'd be somebody there—a landlady—I could pay to watch them——"

"That's not good enough, Frieda. Whatever else they get here, at least I can see they have good food, and decent company, and wide spaces to play in."

He bent to sluice water over his face, and as she stood behind his arched back, the founts of old poisons bubbled.

"You!" she spat. Until then she had remained slightly stooped over the barrel, but now she straightened, lifting a hand to push her hair back, pushing back with it something else. She could be quiet too.

"All right," she told him. "This is your time. You were frank enough once, telling me I could get out. All right, I will get out. Stay here and rot in West Haven, if that's what you want. Lloyd and Idelle and I can go to Meridian by ourselves."

What she expected in return she didn't quite know, but at least she expected he would immediately turn to face her. Instead, he sluiced more water over his face, soaped and rinsed his hands, before he took down the towel and let her see his face.

"You can always go, you know, Frieda." Stillness in him hadn't lessened. "But not Lloyd and Idelle. Judge Shotwell is a friend of Father's."

She had known when she spoke the momentousness of what she was saying, but not until he answered did she feel its shock. For moments, after that, she stood incapable of believing what she heard; the barrel approached as support; with knees and abdomen she reached for the hard curving surface; the rough tops of the barrel staves cut her hands.

She whispered, "You couldn't do that, Harry. You couldn't take my own children from me. You know you couldn't, Harry."

"That's up to you." Immobility remained immobility. "I'm only saying that Lloyd and Idelle stay here, not in some Meridian boarding-house."

Before, when he had held her in a vise of choices, she had had a way out. She had had Mr. Hake.

But in the shriveled silence which followed on Harry's departure to get Lloyd and Idelle home from Schlempkes', she knew herself as having no way out. If she stole off with her children to Meridian, Harry could get them back.

"My parents," Harry could say in court, "stand ready to undertake their upbringing and care." And no matter what she said or promised, no matter if she told at last about her fourteen hundred dollars, the judge would weigh what he knew of her against what he knew of Gurneys, and Harry would win.

Sometime in that shriveled silence she moved from the kitchen to the parlor where, in her pier glass, she could see herself strange and whitened, a ghost in the unlit dusk. Lloyd and Idelle had been at the pier glass as they had been at everything else the house held; their ungovernable fingers had splintered off the thin wood casing of the back, and scraped away patches of silvering; their kicks and scratches had defaced the walnut standards. Why, she asked herself then, in a despair-filled veering of desire, had she had children? In detail, as she could see the details of a custody suit, she could see her future in Meridian too—the tripping off to work each morning in new gowns (a fresh one at least every month), the quick garnering of customers from fellow workers, the rapid accretion of importance—"Well, Mrs. Gurney, I see by your book that you really sell!"—and from there the quick rise to assistant buyer, the reopening of the wholesale houses. No height could be beyond her, if she kept this chance.

By the time Harry brought in Lloyd and Idelle she was in a mood of dispassionate objectivity such as she had seldom attained. Idelle, as usual at a home-coming, threw herself down to lie frenziedly kicking and screaming, first because her wraps must be taken off, next because it was bedtime. Commonly such resistance produced cajolery and games, but on this night clothes were jerked off, the flailing feet were held rigidly by a knee while the nightgown was forced on, and then the animate small body—screaming now with fervor—was jolted into its bed. Lloyd, all this while, had busied himself peacefully by whittling at a window sill, but when she had Idelle in bed she whirled on him too.

"Now we'll see what happens to *you!*" The clamor ensuing was such as to support decision. Let Harry have his brats; let someone else struggle with them; let Mrs. Gurney and Elizabeth mop up their messes and their dirty faces. She would be as well rid of them as of Harry.

That night, however, unable to reach anything but wakefulness, forced to lie listening to the light, hiccoughing sobs which punctuated Idelle's breathing even in sleep, she got out of bed, and on bare feet moved to stand above Idelle's bed, to stoop until warm breath fanned her cheek, to run a hand lightly over a forearm that was more smoothly satiny than any satin. In complete soundlessness, so that Harry could not possibly wake and know, she stole to the back room, too, to lean above the small bed alongside the cot. No sob broke Lloyd's determined sleep; Idelle had started at her touch, but Lloyd wouldn't; she took him up into her arms, where he hung sleepy-heavy and inert, his head on her shoulder, his long legs dangling.

This, this weight, this fullness, this warmth, was her own weight and fullness and warmth; it was no separate child she held, but a segment of herself. He, her son, might still apparently put Harry and Ilse before her, but he was learning; he was finding out that what Harry and Ilse wouldn't let him do, she often would; he was finding out about money. No matter how little she had on hand of her own, no matter how Harry's earnings must be squeezed, Lloyd got his nickels, with the finger at lip that meant this was a secret between him and her. It couldn't be too long now before he would be hers entirely; others could tend and serve him, but she was the one to whom he belonged.

While she stood holding him the pendulum had to swing back. Maybe—with suffering not to be weighed or measured—she could give up Idelle. But not Lloyd. No matter what it cost, no matter what she must sacrifice for him, her son must be kept.

In the fervor of renunciation, she next day kept both children by her, dedicating her existence to them, patiently dressing them, spooning oatmeal, answering and reanswering questions (neither blithe child had any recollection of unpleasantness past), coaxing them into games, rescuing them from puddles, squabbles and more serious mayhem.

Toward nightfall, when they went in for an orgy of unruliness, the pendulum swung violently again. She couldn't stand this; all she asked was escape; she *must* escape. But by this time she knew her weakness.

Three days now; only three days left until Monday, when her chance would be gone. Saturday passed, as did Sunday. Sunday night she lay long awake, sweating through a cold night in a stare of terror; time was making her decision for her, and it soon would be irrevocable.

CHAPTER XXVI

In all her summer-long illness of loss she had not wept, but she wept on that Monday, dragging herself from one task to another about the house, blinded by unrelieving floods of tears, torn by pains like birth pains. This was the day that had held her chance, her chance which had been like a ruby to hold and finger in the hands, and that chance now was gone. Toward noon, almost in fear, she took Lloyd and Idelle to Ilse's; she could have hurt them.

For days afterward, too, her children could wring from her nothing but revulsion; they were what had cost her fortune and fame. After a week or two, however—after, in particular, a morning when Lloyd snipped off the tip of one forefinger with a neighbor's hedge shears and had to be rushed to the doctor—this hatred swung back into its normal channels, against Harry. Not Lloyd and Idelle, but Harry, kept her in West Haven.

Hating Harry was such long habit that her life at last reached

balance. Taking new stock of herself, and also of Mr. Cantrell's niggardly offer of four dollars a week at the Bon Ton, she quietly one day
took the job. The Bon Ton was fourth-rate; it had not changed since
1870. When she hinted that a small ready-to-wear department might
do wonders for the store, old Cantrell answered tightly, "We'll have
no foolishness here, Mrs. Gurney." Struggle as she would, she could
not advance from the place he fixed. As he admitted, she was a good
clerk; after eight months he raised her to six dollars. But that, he let
her know, was the limit; she had no further future with him.

And this, for three years more, was her existence. There were times,
when, curiously, she was almost satisfied; she had Lloyd and Idelle, this
way, with little of the labor; she paid three dollars to Ilse, each week,
and had three for herself. Her savings could increase scarcely at all, but
Lloyd and, as years went by, Idelle too began to show that they looked
upon her as a fountainhead of gratifications. Each had small secrets to
be kept from the other, from Ilse or from Harry. Lloyd and Idelle, she
could often tell herself, were worth all her sacrifices: upstanding, will-
ful children, who'd make themselves felt in the world.

But there were other times, and these more frequent, when she knew
desperately how her birthright had been sold, when she compared anew
what she was at the Bon Ton with all she could have been in Meridian,
when she plotted to get Lloyd and Idelle secretly away to some far city
where they could never be found, when she paced and wept, when she
felt she must burst from the pressure of all she wanted to do and
attain.

At these times there was just one whipping post for her bafflement
and despair—Harry. With years, Harry got so that, whatever was said
of himself or of his family, he remained unmoved, but toward mention
of Schatzi he never grew quite blunted. What his relationship actually
was with Schatzi—whether they sometimes met by chance or by design, whether they sometimes walked or rode in darkness—she neither
knew nor cared. It was enough that Schatzi's name could still make
Harry's flesh wince closer to its bones.

"I see Schatzi's going around town again." Usually she chose to
make her flailings light and casual. "With Lise Hetweit. They didn't
come into the Bon Ton, of course, but I saw them go by on their way
to Pomeroy's. I really believe Schatzi's perking up a little, after all this
time."

And again, "Do you remember Schatz Klaumeister at all? They say
she's taken up china painting and pyrography. Rozzie says Schatzi's
room is practically filled with burned dogs' heads. It must be fascinating."

Later, "Can you imagine? Schatz Klaumeister actually got herself a
store job in De Laittre. Lasted three days, Rozzie said, before she got
so tired and homesick she came back. Can you imagine that? Schatzi!"

Often, after one of these communications, Harry got drunk; Harry
got drunk often, anyway; he must, she sometimes thought, make extra
money, draying, because he never defaulted at his household payments. But it was pleasure to have him get drunk; she could know,
then, that she had cut deep; it was satisfying to be awakened at night
by cautious and subdued knocking at the door, to confront figures in
the dark outside—two upright, usually, with Harry a sagged weight
between them.

"Well, Mrs. Gurney—say, we're sorry, but Harry here—a drop too
much, I expect——"

"Oh, I'm used to it, you know that," she could reply. "Take him
on in."

The time when Harry's return was so different was, in its incep-
tion, quite like other times.

"What do you know?" she asked Harry on one summer evening in
1903, during their walk home from Schlempkes' with the children
after dinner. "I hear Schatz Klaumeister's got herself a beau at last.
She's started going with that new butcher in her father's shop. What's
his name? Zinzman? The one with no neck. Isn't that screaming?
If there was one thing Schatzi said and kept on saying, it was that
she'd never marry a German out of her father's shop."

Harry, that evening, turned on his heel, leaving her to walk on
with the children alone. Harry, that night, didn't come home at all.
But he must, on the next morning, have gone on with his draying.
That was what men told her when they came to get her at the Bon
Ton, just after noon.

Harry had been loading barrels at the brewery, they said, when his
load started slipping. Harry, trying to keep the filled barrels from
rolling, had been crushed beneath them.

She sat in the kitchen, away from the parlor where *it* was. They
had taken her up to the sofa where *it* lay, two men, one on each side
of her, holding her up and retaining her. "No, I can't look!" she had
cried, covering her face with her hands, twisting, when someone else
—not one of the two men, but someone else—had reached to pull the
quilt aside. Her house was full of people. People who stood in quiet
and whispering groups, but who seemed to jostle. For a moment,
until she got—how, she didn't quite know—to the chair in the
kitchen, she had a feeling she was reliving something, some past hor-

ror, some old nightmare; and then she knew: this was like Shindy Day. Why, she couldn't have told, but it was like Shindy Day. And then, after that sensation had passed, after she was sitting at last in the kitchen, there was the other sensation of emptiness, different from the emptiness after Mr. Hake had had his stroke. What was then missing was support; what was now missing was the steady force against her, the obstruction, the object against which she had had to spend all her strength. Harry was gone, Harry, who had begun as that tall, pink-and-white, gangling baby, and then progressively—all the stages of Harry could exist at once in her mind—had grown strained and silent, without any of that baby pinkness, and then desperate and stern, and then gaunt and haggard, but who, at every stage, had been as unfailing in his way as Mr. Hake had been in his.

Rozzie was with her in the kitchen; her father too; her mother. "Ac-ci-dent," Otto Schlempke said, separating the syllables as if each one were of tremendous import. "To us he was a son. An ac-ci-dent." Her father's voice was choked with tears.

"Accident," Ilse too repeated, and Rozzie; they seemed to say it almost with anxiety, to keep the word rolling and rerolling.

At her knees Lloyd and Idelle clung and clamored, their voices half hysterical. "Mama, where's Papa? What's the matter with Papa —is he sick, Mama? Can't I see him, Mama?" Her hands touched them, knew their presence. But her mind was occupied by death-shocked recognition. Her life with Harry was complete and whole now; no hands before her face could at this moment hide that life away; there was as yet no veil with which she could cover the direction of their life together. At heights of their quarreling she had often told him she wished he were dead, but usually afterward she had told herself she didn't mean it. Death was a consummation that one could not call down even upon an enemy such as Harry. Always she had pushed aside the death want, always kept it deeply buried; yet she had to see now how surely through the past years it had powered and moved her; what she had really been doing in the past three years was wait. The only way she had had to win over Harry had been to outlive Harry; that had been the only possible breaking of Harry's deadlock.

Not suddenly but gradually Harry had become that thing upon the couch. Ever since that night when she had taken Harry and the whisky to the grove, this had been what Harry moved toward; the seed Harry had sown that night in the grove had been no seed of life—how happy she had been when she found that out!—but the slow seed of this death.

So useless and so needless, when she need never have had a life with him at all. He could just as well have been left pink and white as he was; he could just as well have had his silly happiness with Schatzi. She herself could have waited until later to find the man who would be a fit husband for her, someone to father fitly the two children her hands stroked.

From this break of time she came back to the room she sat in only when new commotion roused her. She looked up then to recognize—could it be? Yes, it was—the figure of the man before her. She had not seen Mr. Gurney at close range since the day he had come to Hake's to offer her a subsidy, but he was here now, just before her, looking down. She would have remained seated if she could; her whole mind became focused on the necessity of remaining seated, but slowly her body rose until she was on her feet, until her hands were on the shoulders of her children as on crutches.

He, Mr. Gurney—maybe for years he had been as aged as this; she wouldn't know. Or maybe he had only become so this last hour. Beneath mustard-gray hanging folds of flesh his eyes had heat, but it was a last glow. Elsewhere there was nothing of him that was not charred and brittle, ready to break and scatter.

He said, "Madam, perhaps now my son may come home."

It took time for thought to arrange itself about the words. Come home? Why would they want Harry, now? And then, rather in scenes than in any progression of thought, she saw all that must succeed a death: the wreath on the door, the many who would come, the funeral.

"I hadn't thought," she said aloud. With a jolt, as of recovering balance, she saw the faces all around her, watching.

"Mr. Gurney," she said, "if you want—if it's better—I'm sure Harry might like to be with you."

But broken as the words were, broken to some extent as she still was, her world in other ways had righted beneath shock of a different order.

At the very least, if Mr. Gurney hadn't offered, a funeral would have cost two hundred dollars!

There was only one more moment that was really hard.

By keeping her mind busily on other things—the fit of Lloyd's Eton collar, which insisted on curling, and the sweatiness of Idelle's handclasp (if that child got sick, now, that would be a last straw!) —she managed, during most of the funeral, to keep herself from being too much affected by all that went on. The flower-banked casket stood now in plain sight before the altar, but, mercifully, it was closed. "No, I can't bear," she had kept on saying, and no one had forced her. So far, she could tell herself as the hushed mournful singing rose, everything had gone well. The Gurneys hadn't even tried excluding her; decently each day she had sat with them in the sitting room (Harry had been in the parlor), decently she had received condolence. "Oh no," she had returned, with fresh tears for every asker. "I've no plans. It was so sudden I can't seem to think."

Hourly those tears had grown easier; poor, poor Harry; it was too bad things had turned out for him as they had, and not much more his fault than hers. He could scarcely be blamed, either, if at twenty he had thought he had to marry. If things could only have been a little different for him—if he could have had a little success in business, say—he might not even have taken to drinking, although of course that weakness had been in him from the first.

Carefully she had made way for Gurneys; at a man's funeral the widow, naturally, took first place, but "No, no, you go first," she had said to Gurneys. "I insist. He was yours before he was ours." Behind the three shrouded and bent figures she sat with her children and parents, she too veiled, but upright; no one could say she hadn't done her best by Harry, or that she hadn't let bygones be gone; her black, and that of the children, had been bought and fitted at Pomeroy's.

The time came, however, when, after the minister had talked awhile, his voice rose to insistence. "Who knows," he asked, "the despairs and sorrows of a human soul? This man had parents and a sister, he married and he fathered children, but his life was in himself alone; as we all must, he died alone. Many would say he did not achieve much, many would say he arrived at little, but who can speak of the hopes that moved him, of the dreams that fed him; who knows what patience and what fortitudes he built to maintain him in his round of duty, who can decide the brightness of the soul that rose to God?"

It was because she hadn't wanted to be alone with Harry that she had had the Gurneys sit in front of her, and drawn her children and her parents close. But now, as before in that edifice, children, parents, even the eyes of those about her were torn off; hideously and starkly she sat there with Harry. Just as Harry had thwarted her, so she deliberately had thwarted him. Harry had wanted to marry Schatzi, Harry had wanted to work with bicycles; she couldn't say she didn't know. "If you'd only *believe* in me, Frieda—I seem to need that." So Harry had begged of her, once. That, more than anything else, was what she had denied him, and with it she had denied him life.

That night, children in bed and doors open, front and back (Harry had been gone from the house for three days, but there still was a clamminess), she moved from room to room, erasing. Harry's clothes she could hardly move out for a day or two, but they were in his room, and not many. Otherwise, looking at the house, you could hardly tell that he ever had lived there. Three pies and two cakes—funeral food and all partially eaten—stood on the kitchen table. Lloyd loved pie, and she hesitated, but need for erasure could be stronger than thrift; with a feeling of ruthlessness and decision she thrust pies and cake into paper, and bundled them outside for her mother's pig.

"I'll be glad to stay, you know that, Frieda," Rozzie had offered, and her mother too.

"No," she had bravely answered, "it's best I learn to be alone." There had been nothing terrifying about the word "alone" so spoken; there was nothing terrifying about aloneness as she swept and dusted, and as she paused, out of habit, before the pier glass. Perhaps she had thickened at the waist a little these past years; she'd have to take care of that. Twenty-eight, but she still had a figure; no one could say she hadn't; her hair was as thick and as glossy as ever too, and her color as good.

From the mirror she went to stand in the draft of fresh air sweeping through the opened door. Those few seconds at the funeral had been quite bad, but she was over that now; after all, Harry had said other things, too, to remember. "I sinned against myself and someone else—this is my punishment I've got to put up with as long as it's being visited on me." A wife who was made to know *that* was how her husband considered her could scarcely be expected to be too generous in return. Well, she wasn't being visited on him any longer. He was out from under, and she need carry no more regrets for him than for herself.

For she too was now out from under. Ever since she had left the cemetery—no, before that, ever since she had heard that clod falling with such finality—she had begun being buoyed and lifted. Good-bys had had to be said; there had been a scene with Mrs. Gurney kneeling any which way on the ground—"His children! They can't go too!" She had said the proper thing to Mrs. Gurney—"Of course not, Mrs. Gurney—why, you'll see them often!" But all the while she had been straining. They could be open enough now about wanting her children, but just let them try; a mother had claims over any grandparent. Harry was gone and *done with;* from now on no one held her in any clamp.

"I'm free," she said to the wind within and without her door. Her voice flew wide. Until now she hadn't had time to revel in her unshackled state; there had been too many things to do. Now, however, no task confronted; she was as free as the wind she stood in, as free as the openness which invaded and possessed her. Plans. She'd needed no plans; in one week she would be in Meridian. A small flat, maybe. The children were old enough now, nine and seven, to need no watching. Oh, Harry's money would no longer come in, but she'd make out; the Transfer Company had given her a hundred dollars; she'd make that stretch.

Ideas, like her life, lay arranged, in order. What was it she had first thought, long ago? That by getting to be one of Those Others—how ridiculous she had once been, thinking people like Gurneys were different from herself! Later she had thought her way must lie through Mr. Hake, and almost, there, she had been right; if Mr. Hake had lived she might, through him, have gotten her desire. But that, in the end, had proved an error too.

It was *yourself* you had to depend on. No one else. Oh, since everything was owned, it was from other people that you had to get, eventually, everything you got. But the only person to depend on in that getting was yourself.

Within her doorway she continued to stand, breathing deeply, arms crossed high on her bosom. Yourself—that was what it came to, and she asked nothing more. She was ready; she had long been ready. She, alone, would be enough.

Part Three
GETTING

Mrs. Astor died, that year, and Society from then on was never the same. Oh, any heiress of standing still married a duke, or at least a French count, but out in the audience reverence was fading. "New Shipment of Royalty in," one cartoon dared to jeer, "Bargain Prices." Beneath the jeer, too, lay a burn—think, only think, people said, of those good American dollars, being flushed down the Sewers of Europe!

The United States, in exchange for its money, got a few residents —around a million—mostly from Italy and Sicily. King Alfonso came too, for a visit; he had his picture taken, while here, beside Wilbur Wright in that New Improved Flying Machine which was being looked over by the United States Army, as a possible addition to its fighting forces. Women, in that year, were much in the news; they wore Merry Widows and got themselves stuck in doorways; they grew militant, too, and asked suffrage. One of their number, a Mrs. Belle Gunness, was discovered to have run a most profitable business in suitors, at about one thousand dollars per well-planted head.

"A wise choice!" Teddy Roosevelt cried happily, when told his friend Taft would most likely succeed him. The Illinois Circuit Court of Appeals, though, grew indignant. "Heavens, what is this?" asked the Illinois Circuit Court of Appeals. "Standard Oil of Indiana pay a fine for extorting rebates from railroads? Why, perish forever such an unfriendly thought!" Peary, that year, sailed again for his North Pole, front pages blazoned in detail a great Court Fight for Liberty (this one by Harry K. Thaw), while away on page six, if you read that far in, you learned that Germany was now occupied by a childish and gleeful new busy-work—warships; while Japan, through the Root-Takahira Agreement, was now irrevocably dedicated to respecting United States Territories in the Pacific, and to preserving the independence and integrity of China.

Altogether, as will be noted, this year of 1908 was one of great sobriety and straightforwardness; no silly extravagance existed, and no sensationalism; every word spoken meant exactly what it seemed to mean, and people owned no other devotion than that of God and the Common Good.

CHAPTER XXVII

Mr. Frigman's smile, that smile which spoke so brilliantly of intimate and almost fervid understanding, was already alight for her when, on a spring day in 1908, she knocked discreetly at his office door and slipped inside. ANY EMPLOYEE OF FRIGMAN'S CAN HAVE FRIGMAN'S EAR, the sign outside his door invited, with a convoluted ear, drawn larger than life size, to emphasize the readiness within.

Eighteen months earlier, when finally she had gotten her Frigman job, she had almost immediately availed herself of opportunity. "Fires at the drop of a hat, that's Frigman! Just let your sales book slump one little week, just look a little indisposed some morning, just let him think you don't add class to his stinking store——" Transmitted in tight undertones, such traditions had kept her fellows skulking at their little jobs, but no later than her second week she had stood with her hand on the fateful doorknob. *She* had no reason for seeking obscurity; her looks and her sales book met inspection, and there wouldn't be anything else she could get caught on, either, *not this time*. It had been in an exact and long-planned balance between hesitance and boldness (one was scarcely coy, after thirty, but one could still be arch!) that she poised in the doorway, head tipped, she too smiling.

"Do I dare? I'm Mrs. Gurney, new here."

"Ah, good morning, good morning, Mrs. Gurney," Mr. Frigman had responded in his breathless rushing whisper on that long-ago day, just as he greeted her now. Eighteen months before, of course, he hadn't had the many intervening visits which led him to go on so confidentially now.

"Miss Callahan is out at the garment centers again, I take it? Ah, that's fine. And how are things in ready-to-wear this week? That purchase of taffeta jumpers—the brown iridescents—how is that going? Only three—only *three* sold, out of two dozen? But that's frightful, Mrs. Gurney, that's appalling! Twenty-one gowns on which we may have to take a markdown! You were quite right—that was a poor buy on Miss Callahan's part, a very poor buy!"

As she stood beside his oak table (no roll-tops for him, Mr. Frigman said, he wanted to see people) Mr. Frigman's flattened, veined and purple-shining head, bald except for its inch-wide horseshoe of lusterless black hair, swung rhythmically in a quarter arc, the smile dulling on the downswing, flashing brightly once more as the dark small face swung toward her, tiny hot eyes glinting blackly, long nose hungering toward the teeth that likewise glinted.

"You can't know what this means, Mrs. Gurney, having you bring information in this way. Mrs. Blitt, now, is she doing a better job on stock, after you warned her? Hooks on, trimmings tacked? Still a bit careless? Dear me, we may need a change there—indeed, indeed, I quite agree, our major problem is in buying. A pity Miss Callahan can't seem to feel she needs an assistant. Two heads—oh, better, always better. With your knowledge of style, your experience—no, don't demur, Mrs. Gurney, you'd be the first person I'd consider. If only between us we could make Callahan see light——"

Leaving five minutes later, as unobtrusively as she had come (the girls got quite huffy, sometimes, if they thought you'd been seeing Frigman), Frieda told herself that this time she had made real progress; this time she had elicited what almost was a promise. But over and above satisfaction surged a stronger and older petulance— what *ailed* Frigman? Couldn't he see, by now, that what Frigman's needed wasn't Callahan with an assistant, but Callahan out, and Mrs. Gurney *in?* Hadn't she worked on him long enough? Hadn't she introduced enough improvements since she got to be head clerk of ready-to-wear? This way the problem of handling Callahan was left strictly up to her, and you couldn't just walk up to Callahan and say, "You need help, Callahan, you don't know your job." The only way to handle Callahan was to get her out quick, before she knew what was up.

This impasse still occupying the top of her mind, she reached that hushed, dimmed, plum-red, gold-pricked richness which was Frigman's ready-to-wear bay. Everything there, as she caught with such tendrils of attention as she had left over, was ostensibly in order; before customers seated on gilt settees her girls rippled out gowns as they'd been taught, hanger in right hand, left arm free for a caressive swirling of skirts. Other girls, garments quiet now across their arms, led other subdued customers toward fitting rooms. Any ordinary customer who said, "No, I don't think so," at Frigman's did so in accents of shame. "You've got to make them feel," so Frieda taught her girls, "that the only reason they don't take a dress is because they haven't the price."

Inside the stock room, for all her preoccupation, she had to take time out for a chummy pause.

"Better break it up now, girls," she advised the loiterers who gathered there whenever Callahan was off the floor. "Angel will be back here any minute." Friendliness such as this had been a lesson well learned during her first years in Meridian. "Heavens!" you could say to the girls. "Does Callahan expect us to sell these? Lunch-table buyers I've heard of, but sometimes I think Callahan must do her buying in bed!" Co-operation from the girls made it possible to control almost entirely what was sold and what wasn't.

"Ain't you awful, Mabel!" Miss Titcock told her now, in passing, with a playful pinch. Miss Titcock, in addition to being always a source of the snappiest new phrases, was also an admirer.

On this day, however, no pride in good governing, no awareness of competency, could hold down vexation. Just *what* could she do about Callahan? Most of her duties by now were supervisory—"Miss Vince, these ladies are waiting. Miss Titcock, I think a more expensive number"—but even these made concentration impossible. All too soon, too, she was forced to postpone even partial attention to her private concerns.

"Why, Mrs. McFee!" she had to cry, swimming forward. For a customer such as Mrs. McFee, only her own ministrations would do. "Don't let a whisper of this out, *please*"—this, naturally, in the lowest of murmurs—"but I've got a Paris copy put by for you—yes, the latest——"

Too many of Meridian's great ladies, the ones with real money, especially, still lifted their noses at store ready-mades.

"Oh, not for myself," they would answer, on those rare occasions when they floated in to rest perfunctorily upon the gilt settees. "But my cousin here thought she might pick up a little something——"

All too obviously, in these cases, the cousin would be a fluttered poor relation, for once being given something other than a hand-me-down. The great lady herself, staring through a lorgnette, never condescended to a fitting.

There were a few like Mrs. McFee, of course, who were different.

"You know what I want!" Young Mrs. McFee laughed as she breezed in. "The tightest sheath you've got. I don't want a thing, now, if it isn't tight——

"It's divine, all right," Mrs. McFee had to agree a bit later, as she posed before a Frigman mirror, swaying cased hips, swirling a skirt in the only place where that year's skirt had fullness—from the knees down. "Why, I can't—I hardly can—sit down! What else have you got that's simply wild?"

"Keep your eye on Mrs. Gurney, girls," Mr. Frigman said often at departmental meetings. "If you all showed as many double sales as Mrs. Gurney——" It took awhile, after such meetings, to channel resentment back toward Callahan. Anything like that, though, was nothing to think about now, when she had her Callahan problem to settle.

"You watch and see what turns up around here soon, girls; I think I've done quite a stroke of business today." Callahan, when she bounced in from the markets that day, was just as serenely top-of-the-world as ever; it was hard to dent Callahan. No one, watching Callahan, could see any slightest hint that Callahan had anything but friendliness for Frieda, but as Callahan spoke—and it wasn't the first time this had happened—Frieda's neck prickled. It wasn't from nowhere that packets of soap, hairpins and safety pins turned up in the pockets of girls who got careless. And you take anyone who could be that sly——

"Everything you do shows *such* experience." That afternoon Miss Callahan took occasion to speak almost fondly to Frieda, after Frieda had sold two gowns, each forty-nine fifty, to a mousy small woman who had crept in for "something inexpensive." "I just wonder what you'd be," Miss Callahan went on with one of her rolling laughs, "if you'd been brought up as I was—in Brooklyn."

Again, in Miss Callahan, there was nothing unfriendly—nothing at all suspicious—but once more Frieda's neck crawled.

Don't worry, I'm looking out for you, all right; don't think I'm not; it would be just like you—if you've noticed—to think you could get at me first. This, while her lips made some more suitable overt reply, was the answer Frieda's mind venomously supplied. What her mind still didn't seem able to do, though, was to solve her dilemma. It would be perfectly possible, of course, to persuade the girls that Callahan's buying was worse than ever. Customers could be sent off empty-handed. "I'm afraid we just haven't a thing for you—have you tried Westermarck's?" Frigman would notice, all right, if his sales really plummeted. The only trouble with an idea like that was that it would also hurt her; she couldn't let her own sales book slide. And as head clerk, responsible for order, she couldn't disarrange garments on racks, or see to it that invoices and bills got lost. Nothing in that line would be *final* enough, either.

And then, before she could reach anything at all acceptable, she had something quite different to face.

"It would be nice, once, to go home to waiting dinner and an ordered house." Wistfully, that night in the cloakroom, she made reference to her unfortunate personal circumstances. Few Frigman employees worked by choice, but not all were widows with two children. "I'll be up half the night, I suppose—ironing, cleaning, washing dishes——"

Sympathy which rose around her—"I just wish you could get in with my landlady, Mrs. Gurney." "You should have a hired girl, that's what you should have, Mrs. Gurney, a woman in your position!" —was not only warm but immediate; sympathy, at least, was something she could get. Turning, after she had slipped on her butterfly suit jacket, she moved to the mirror for a better balancing of the big Merry Widow, afroth with black tulle and white flowers, which was the glory of her street costume. It was then—right then in a sudden hush—that she found out what Callahan could be.

"Oh, Mrs. Gurney!" That was Miss Titcock, whispering. "Stand still a minute—there, I've got it tucked up under—it'll be all right, I think—here, I'll pin it. If you keep your jacket pulled tight, now——"

"But I haven't——" began Frieda in that terrible first instant, while the initial wave of heat was hitting her, the heat which so rapidly turned to chill. "I haven't anything under my jacket," was what she would have cried out, if reason hadn't arisen to prevent her. "There isn't anything beneath my jacket; I've been very, very careful not to have anything I had to keep hidden." That was what she would have gone on to say. But what she saw, in the stiff, arrested agitation on the face of Miss Titcock, so close to hers, and on the faces too of Miss Vince, Mrs. Blitt and Miss Forbush, was that denial would do her no good. "Walking out with the merchandise" was common practice at Frigman's—just look at the way they were treated! Look at the way they got paid! Only getting caught at it was fatal. If she ripped off her jacket, if she tore out what was hidden, she could only draw notice from other girls near by—girls from other departments who wouldn't be silent.

"Don't you worry, Mrs. Gurney, no one who's seen it would ever breathe a word," Miss Titcock was whispering, and yes, that was the fellow-conspirator look springing to the eyes of Miss Vince, Miss Forbush and Mrs. Blitt. *That Callahan,* Frieda's mind cursed to itself. No one had to tell her what her position was now.

Closely escorted by Miss Titcock, Miss Vince and Miss Forbush, she made her way out. As she did so she had to pass—almost to brush —past Callahan at the stairhead.

"Have a nice evening, now, girls." Miss Callahan was her jolly self. "Just don't stay up so late with your young men that you can't be on time in the morning!" The eyes that smiled so warmly missed no single one of Frieda's cohorts. If the time ever came when Miss Callahan wanted to strike, she would know just whom to call on for witness.

Crossing the small downstairs hallway of the wood-worn old house in which she had lodgings, shifting to both arms the groceries she carried, she was, as usual, accosted by Mrs. Purk, her landlady, who ran out at her from the small parlor near the front door.

"That boy of yours, that Lloyd—he's playing hooky again, you can take my word for that, clumping up- and downstairs with those big feet, trampling around up there so you can't think. Oh yes, he's been *in* again, Mrs. Gurney, you can know what to expect——"

"I expect it's all right for my own son to be in his own home," Frieda returned from weary old hostility. The emotions which she had just taken on were too pervasive to admit of any new entry. As Mrs. Purk had warned, the door to her two upstairs rooms was, indeed, ajar. Within the first room, where Lloyd slept on the couch and she and Idelle in the lightless bedroom alcove, covers had been stripped from couch and bed, chairs and pictures lay strewn on the floor; in the small kitchen beyond not so much as a cracker remained undevoured, and pieces of a shattered mixing bowl lay amid dirty dishes in the sink. Long ago she had given up hiding any money in the house, but Lloyd and Idelle, it seemed, never gave up hope.

Still without any new influx of feeling—all this, indeed, was too much a part of routine to arouse much feeling—she dumped her bread and bologna, her pickles, pie, coffee, milk and Egg-O-See, upon the kitchen table, and returned to the living room. Here, carefully and before she did anything else, she relocked the hall door—that way, at least, she'd get a little warning. Then, still near the hall door, she removed her jacket.

Once more hot, once more cold, she stood examining what her jacket had hid, and what, so far, she hadn't seen—a shirtwaist, of messaline and silk filet, pinned neatly, flatly, to the jacket lining—pinned so that one cuff, hanging down, would barely show itself.

Oh, Callahan had brains, you had to hand that to Callahan; Callahan could wriggle herself out of a spot. This waist—yes, now Frieda looked at it closely—was one she had paused to finger and admire during a recent lunch hour. Suppose she had chanced to look inside the jacket, even, before so carelessly slipping it on—what good could that have done her? The girls would still have thought——

Mechanically, jacket now under her arm, she picked a way toward the alcove, heaved the mattress back upon the bedsprings, and sat down. Innocence made no least difference, not at Frigman's, where suspicion was enough. Her upward progress at Frigman's was ended.

As she sat bitterly staring, assimilating this fact, what seemed to face her, from the unwindowed wall of the alcove, was not only what she had just met, but the whole of her five years in Meridian. That first job at Walton's, for instance—she had been doing so well there, she had moved with such smoothness into the buying, she could so well have kept on if it hadn't been for that Mrs. de Toven (who could have expected it of anyone so ladylike?) and her list of samples that Frieda had accepted from salesmen. After Walton's, her own shop, the Elite Variety Store—there too she had done well, in spite of a terrible mix-up. (She, of all people, getting married that way after a party, to a fat, no-good drummer—thank heaven few people had had to know about that!) The big trouble at the Elite had been that she had lived back of the store, and with Lloyd and Idelle—and those counters—well, it just hadn't worked out. Six months at the Hub, after that—she could stay at the Hub her whole life, she had decided, and never move forward one inch. Then again a business of her own, the Dujour Flower Shop. Nine hundred, cool, that had cost her, and again she could have made good—she *had* made good, in spite of what helpers were. That last one, especially, who had gotten a policeman and witnesses to prove it was Lloyd and Idelle who had been stealing her expensive blossoms to sell for nickels and dimes in the street. In the end it had seemed best to sell again. She had gotten her money out, just as she had out of the variety store, but not enough extra to make either venture what it should have been. Then this last job at Frigman's——

Knocks and kicks at the hall door, at this point, broke off her communings; all further assessment of her present circumstances must, she well knew, be put off until later. Hastily rising, hastily tumbling jacket and waist both into a ball which she thrust far to the rear of a shelf above the bed head, hastily unpinning her hat and throwing it to the mattress, she made for the door. There, snapping the door open, she surprised Lloyd with skeleton key in hand, in the very act of applying that key to the lock.

"Oh! So you've got another of those, have you! That's how you got in! I'll take that key, mister."

Lloyd's hand had started to streak toward his pocket, but she was quicker. He was as tall as she now; he was heavier, but she still was stronger; during a struggle panting and furious on her side, furious and loud on his, she managed to force open the hand she had grasped. Often as this struggle occurred, surrounded as it was by noise and anger, still there was satisfaction in it—Lloyd and Idelle found out who was boss!

"Leggo me, you ol' cat, leggo me!" Lloyd howled through the fracas, while Idelle, skipping out and in, kicked indiscriminately at both. When Lloyd abruptly gave up the key, however, he turned from the mountain to hurl himself at the gnat.

"Ma, he's after me! Ma, he'll kick me!" Idelle then shrieked, spinning off to get a table between herself and her pursuer.

"Quit that, you two! Quit that! If you want supper——" Frieda would have wrested them apart by force, but at her mention of supper they themselves separated, to leap past her toward the kitchen.

"What've you got, Ma? If there's meat, I'm going to cut it."

"No you're not either; I am, it's my turn——"

Once more Frieda rushed, this time kitchenward. Only temporarily, during the wolfing of food, did any lessening of din occur; as soon as the pie had disappeared it once more rose.

"We can go to the Nickelodeon tonight, can't we, Ma? You're going to let us, aren't you, Mama?"

"The Nickelodeon!" Frieda repeated. "Do you think I'm made of money? Didn't you each get a dime this morning? And what did you do? You played hooky, that's what you——"

"That wasn't me playing hooky, that was only Lloyd played hooky!" Idelle at once gave witness, while Lloyd grew sullen.

"Aw, let 'em go spit on their stinking school. Why should I stick around there for? *You* quit before you were fourteen——"

"Well, you won't, and you'll thank me, too, for it, one day——"

"Aw gee, Ma." Lloyd made an abrupt about-face. "I'll go to school tomorrow if I get a dime tonight, honest. All the other kids get dimes; can't we even get a *dime?*"

"You're not getting one penny." Usually, when Lloyd turned to wheedling, she gave in quickly, but tonight, as she told herself firmly, she would set an example of sternness. "No, I mean it. And you'll wash these dishes, too. That'll show you what playing hooky gets you."

Against geysers of protest, she got Idelle stationed at a dishpan, with Lloyd holding a dish towel, while she herself departed, with broom and dustpan, for the other room. She remained, however, expectant, and expectation was soon met. There was a resounding crash and splash, and, rushing once more kitchenward, she found Lloyd in a puddle of water and dishes, while Idelle, taunting, skipped sideward from his lunge.

"It was all her fault—she did it——"

"It wasn't! It wasn't! He grabbed me——"

"I don't care who did it!" shrieked Frieda. "This is all I can stand, do you hear that? Just shut up and get out!"

From the beginning, as they all three knew, this had been the inevitable end toward which the evening had moved; anything that had seemed to point in any other direction had merely been an upholding of the disciplinary decencies. Immediately amicable, Lloyd and Idelle clattered off, dissension at a minimum. "You can't sit by me, now, remember; the fellows don't want you around." "I am too; Mama said I should sit right where you sit." Leaning from a window, Frieda watched until their quick young backs were swallowed by the lavender-gray May dusk. As usual, once they were off her hands and out of earshot, she felt for them only fondness; no one could say that her children weren't handsome—the handsomest in the block, or, for that matter, in Meridian. Lloyd at fourteen was the very image of her—same upright strong carriage, walnut-brown curly hair, same gray eyes; it was impossible to look at Lloyd and not see herself. Idelle was a bit plump, more plump than Frieda could remember being at twelve, but Idelle too had the hair and the eyes and the color. One of these days she'd have to have a talk with Idelle. A girl as pretty as that, at twelve——

Sighing, she returned to the chaos behind her. It was a struggle, bringing up children by oneself, and for a moment, as she faced the litter, she had, horribly, a vision of Harry standing just inside the door as Harry so often had stood, strengthless, tired, but also stern and accusing.

Is this what you've made of them, Frieda? Harry's eyes seemed to ask. Is this what they've turned out to be?

With a shake, however, she threw off Harry; it wasn't the first time, and it might not be the last, that Harry had come around to haunt her, but she could always get rid of him. *She* was satisfied enough with what Lloyd and Idelle were; of course they had high spirits, but they had a *right* to high spirits. Right now, too, she had more important worries to keep her busy.

Not until both rooms, though, were cursorily righted and swept, did she allow herself to step upon the remade bed and lift down the roll of her jacket. Much more quietly than before, then, she unrolled the garments, looked again at the two of them so adroitly pinned together, and finally removed the pins. Fresh bitterness welled as she did so; crumpling the shirtwaist into a ball, she threw it at the opposite baseboard, but after a moment, thriftily, she moved to retrieve and smooth it. A shirtwaist was a shirtwaist—she could scarcely wear this one to work, but that still left Sundays——

Often, during the five years just past, she had formulated and re-formulated her vision of the world and herself in it; still, as when she had left West Haven, she believed in herself as a single means of rising. She had seen to it that that overnight wedding of hers got it-self undone quickly! By now, however, it had begun to be apparent —after this last brush with Callahan it more than ever was obvious —that something was at fault in her calculations. Oh, she could make money, all right—thirty a week, finally, in that job at Walton's, and twenty in her present job at Frigman's. Not too bad for a woman; she could hold up her head. But always, from somewhere, there appeared a wolf to shoulder her out—people like Mrs. de Toven and Callahan. Not that De Toven and Callahan were brainier than she, or that they had more business sense or knack—it was just that some-how, annoyingly, they managed to knock down what she built up.

If only—and how many times she had wished this!—she need work for no one; if only she could have a business of her own. Yet this too she had tried, and each time escaped back to employment. She wasn't going to be the one others cheated, from whom others stole.

Now that she had time to think things over, it didn't seem likely that Callahan was working to get her fired from Frigman's; what Callahan intended was to make her pull in her horns. I could pounce on you right now, you know, Gurney—that was what Callahan's smile had seemed to say, there at the stairhead. But I'm quite willing you should stay on, Gurney—you're very useful to me as head clerk. Just don't go trying any of your fast games on *me*.

Yet working at Frigman's, with no place to rise to, would, as she knew without trying it, be intolerable. "Callahan's buying has been rather better lately," she would have to tell Mr. Frigman. "Those French voiles are doing well." The Frigman nose, at this, could scarcely keep from stiffening, the Frigman head would swing a little faster in its quarter arc, the teeth gleam more whitely on the upswing. There's something behind this, Mr. Frigman would have to think, and once Mr. Frigman started thinking——

Oh, why couldn't it be possible to be an employer, and yet retain the privileges of an employee, still be the one who did the *manip-ulating?* Any money she made, any money Callahan made, even, was chicken feed to what Frigman took in. Why should a person like Frigman be able to rake in the coin, while she couldn't? Another store of some kind could be bought up, of course; she could be care-ful, this time, that Lloyd and Idelle were kept out of it. Not anything like the variety store—that was too small. Something else, more like the flower shop. If she had been able to get hold of anyone who really knew flowers——

At her birthday this year she had been thirty-three. Being thirty-three set a danger line; too soon, going on as she was going, she might each year earn less and less, while Lloyd and Idelle, each year, cost more and more. Her bank account, soon, might start emptying, and she couldn't just sit by to see that happen; something had to be done. If only she could get her hands on someone with the least bit of talent. For cooking, say. Gurney's Café. No, Ilse could cook, but what she turned out would always be too German. It would have to be something else. Hairdressing. Sewing——

Not pushing herself then, not thrusting herself toward anything, but just waiting, she sat with jacket and shirtwaist in her hands. Out of all the people in this world who sewed, you might think she could know one good one. "Mrs. Mary Something, the New York Dressmaker, is reaping a fortune from her needle." Had she ever been such a fool—*could* she ever have been such a fool—as to think it was by her one single needle that Mrs. Something reaped her fortune? By this time she knew better than that; no one by her own needle, no one owning any individual talent, ever *herself* made money; it was the person who knew how to *use* that talent, who built a business around it, who directed, managed, sold—that person was the one who made the money.

With the feeling that something was now eeling its way toward her mind, she slowly rose. Somewhere around was a letter she indifferently had skimmed. Shirtwaist and jacket still against her bosom, as if, for this search, they retained some meaning, she hunted the corners of her domicile until, behind a battered and cracked sea shell on a hanging rack, she found what she sought.

"By Rozzie is no more the papa, such pains he had in stomach," ran Ilse's awkward script, with a penciled addition in Otto's neater hand, "Appendicides."

The letter crumpled in her hand.

CHAPTER XXVIII

Rozzie was forever Rozzie. "Oh, Frieda!" she sobbed at the station, from a grief at least four months old. "My papa, if you'd seen him suffer—

"Oh, Frieda," she again breathed tremulously in Frieda's front room. (Come Sunday, Frieda had said, when they'd have a few hours to themselves.) "Are you sure you *meant* what you wrote? Now Papa's gone I have thought I should try somewhere—New York or Boston. But so much money. I can't let you——"

Frieda had scoffing ready. "New York or Boston? Why should you, when Meridian's right here? You're too old now—thirty-one, isn't it?—to be silly. I said we'd *both* make money."

Ever since the plan had sprung, full-armed, inside her mind, she had been filled by it. I'm being ridiculous, common sense had told her. How can that little small-town nobody, that Hungarian, a cripple who's never done anything in her life but sew up a few dresses and do fitting—how can she ever make a splash in Meridian? But at the same time another and nearer sense had beat insistent drums. This is your idea for which you've waited, this is your chance, this is the enterprise to which your life has tended, this is the undertaking in which it all can merge—that old (tiresome) friendship with Rozzie, your years at Hake's, your buying, your ventures into business, the job you've still got at Frigman's, everything.

"Don't breathe a word of this to Lloyd and Idelle, now, when they get back from the Nickelodeon." Masterfully she took care of this first. "As soon as school's out they'll be packed off to West Haven for the summer, as usual."

"But, Frieda," began Rozzie. "It seems a shame to——"

"No, we can't have them around underfoot, ever. We'll have our name done up in gold letters on the window, fancy script. 'Mme. Balik, Gowns.' We'll have cards, too, engraved. We'll——"

"Frieda, stop a minute!" Rozzie still was tremulous, although her eyes glowed. "It would at least have to be 'Gurney and Balik.' You can't just——"

"No, my part isn't to be known to anyone; I insist on that; you'll be everything. I'll come over evenings to take care of the finances, of course, but outside of that it will be in your hands entirely. You'll decide with me on furnishings, we'll get together on what fabrics, trimmings and machines you'll need for starting; you'll hire the sewing girls—we could run a classified, I thought, for apprentice dressmakers. They needn't get much, I should think, beyond their room and board. You'd choose the patterns——"

"Frieda! I'm bewildered! I——"

"I even know the place, exactly. It's an old house—a mansion once, but it's been a lodging house and it's still partly furnished—ten blocks south of downtown, right near the corner where Center Street meets the Parade. The Parade's where all the swells live, farther out. I've talked already to the man who owns it; Kober, his name is, Stillwell Kober—his mother was my landlady when I had that variety store. He wants fifty dollars, he says, but I know he can be squeezed to forty——"

"Frieda!" Rozzie by this time was entirely laughing. "You're *running away,* Frieda; if we're going into this thing it should be cautiously and *small;* don't forget, Frieda, you don't even know if dresses I sew will be liked. And customers—have you thought of them? It may take years before——"

Frieda's mouth tightened. "If I get you the best in fabrics and in patterns, I don't see why you can't turn out decent dresses—not if you don't spare yourself. And as to customers, don't worry. You'll get them, and it won't take years."

Impediments, when they arose, served only to prove how versed, how able, how ready to meet exigency she had grown.

"Oh no, Mrs. Gurney." Stillwell Kober, their new landlord, shook gloom over their plans. "You couldn't have kitchen fittings moved upstairs. That would be too expensive, Mrs. Gurney, much too expensive. I took up that same thought with Mother, once. 'If we put in an upstairs kitchen now,' I said to Mother, 'we could rent that house as a duplex,' 'That would be too expensive, Stillwell,' Mother told me, 'much too expensive.'"

Prepared to have this difficulty be insuperable not only then but for all time, the drooping gray man turned to Rozzie. "You wear black, Miss Balik. I too am in mourning. For my mother. I have had a little angina, Miss Balik, and I had sometimes thought I might go first. But it was Mother. 'The time will come, Stillwell,' Mother said to me often, 'when you will be alone.' And she was right, Miss Balik; she was right."

Forced to allow time out for communal grievings and commiserations (a little fellow feeling between Rozzie and Mr. Kober could scarcely hurt), Frieda waited only to sweep aside resistance. During her occupancy of the variety store there had been a moment or two when she had glanced at Mr. Kober with a speculative eye. Mr. Kober had been dejected even then, a big-nosed, big-eyed, dust-gray person well into his fifties, but as heir apparent to a string of shops, a redstone flat, this large house, and only heaven knew what other properties beside, he could scarcely be glossed over—especially not when he also had heart trouble! At the time, regretfully, she had had to forgo any such notion; in addition to the unfortune incident of the fat drummer, which had come up about the same time, there had also been Mr. Kober's mother, who obviously had had no intention of freeing her son from a maternal claw. Fleetingly, while Mr. Kober mourned with Rozzie, it occurred to her that, not only was the fat drummer long past and forgotten, but also that Mr. Kober must now be free and in possession of his own. Any such ideas, however, had again to be pushed aside; for such considerations there would be plenty of time later.

"We can't have cooking smells downstairs." Firmly, at the first lull in repining, she issued her fiat. "But still Miss Balik and the sewing girls will have to eat. I'll hire a plumber myself, Mr. Kober, and take it out of rent. That way the change won't cost you a penny, since if it isn't done you won't be getting any rent at all."

Blinking at this proposition—it seemed there must be some hitch, Mr. Kober said, but yes, he could see it would work out that way—the house owner not only consented to this alteration, but even to display lights in the front windows.

Wholesalers too (why should she pay retailers' profits?) balked but briefly.

"We have agreements, you know, Miss Balik"—for obvious reasons it was Rozzie who made these calls—"which prevent our selling yard goods and sundries direct. The stores, you know, offer discounts——"

"But I also"—when well coached, Rozzie could stand her own ground—"will be selling handkerchiefs, belts, reticules and lingerie from a counter. That, I think, establishes me as a retailer myself."

Many details of embarkation, in fact, took so little beyond common sense that Rozzie could handle them alone. Walking each night through the house they had taken, Frieda often could scarcely press down exultance. With its heavy brownstone exterior, its rounded-glass bays, its zinc-lined bathroom fittings, its water heater in the kitchen, its multiplicity of storerooms and closets, this house might have been abandoned as old-fashioned by the people of wealth who had built it; its neighborhood might have been taken over by stores, flats and rooming houses, but it still was a far cry from the shack to which Harry had led her. This house had double doors, all right —oak doors of such height and thickness as West Haven saw only in churches. It had woodwork, too—cherry panelings, balustrades and casings which, under the hands of Rozzie and a scrubbing woman, each day showed a more fiery and deep-toned splendor. She had never stepped foot into that house owned by Cecilia and Palmer, but it scarcely was likely that any West Haven home could boast an entrance hall of such depth and breadth, or a staircase of such winding and balustered majesty, or parlors and reception room so magnificently furnished with brown marble fireplaces.

Rozzie, coming up from West Haven, had brought a packet of news: Elizabeth Gurney, of course, was still teaching music at Amiot; her ears were much better. Father Doern, finally, had broken ground for his new church; it was expected that the edifice would take two years in building. Schatz Klaumeister Zinzman had had a second child, a girl, and this one lived. Cecilia Hake too, after all these years, was about to have a baby.

"Imagine!" was Frieda's response to this last. "Why, it's hardly decent! Whatever can have been the matter with her before?"

Rozzie had no answer for this, but it would be nice, Rozzie said, for Palmer and Cecilia to have a child, if Cecilia could come through it; Cecilia, of course, had always been frail.

"Oh, she'll manage, all right," grudged Frieda. "That kind does." During the long years past, Palmer and Cecilia had rather receded, but she had not forgotten that it was due to them, largely, that she had had to struggle.

As far as her new venture was concerned, however, she seldom allowed the thought of struggle to enter. Only at night did she sometimes face the chance she was taking—a chance which might well endanger everything she owned. To Rozzie she spoke as if capital was endless: "We've got to get value for our money, of course, that's just business. But we're not going to scrimp where it shows. We're doing this *right*."

Actually, and by no later than the second month, what she had was going fast. Twenty-two hundred, it had been, to begin with. Resolutely, however, she kept her mind from the dwindling figures in her bankbook.

"*Sumptuous*. That's the word we've got to keep our minds on, Rozzie. *Sumptuous*," she repeated more feverishly as time went on. Consumingly she pored over fashion and house-decorator journals; at noon she made visits (surreptitious) to Westermarck's; Westermarck's of course was a small store, but it had something that other stores lacked, even Frigman's. "Violet," she decided at last. "Violet will be our color, Rozzie. There's flattering light, good light, in violet, and it goes magnificently with gold. We could scarcely be sumptuous without gold."

Together with Rozzie she picked the stiff violet velveteens for draperies that must swing in profligate folds across window tops and to the floor; with Rozzie she chose the heaviest and widest of gold fringing. Some people were beginning to shrug a bit about carpets; some people were beginning to scatter small rugs about polished floors. Frieda allowed fashion to sway her to the extent of the hall, whose floor was left as a dark mirror, but for the reception room and front parlor, the two rooms which customers would see, nothing would do but the thickest of wall-hugging violet carpets. These carpets and the draperies alone, as Rozzie admitted, were almost overpowering, but recklessly Frieda added columnar tables for huge violet urns and vases; prodigally she added chairs and settees, soft damask and gilt armchairs.

"We'll have to have a mirror. One long mirror." In addition to her subdued list of sewing machines, cutting tables, scissors, pins and needles, Rozzie had but one furnishing request. And only here did Frieda allow sentiment to sway her; instead of buying a new pier glass, she took to a finisher the old mirror brought from West Haven.

"Ever since I got this glass it's been like my dearest friend." With Rozzie, on the night this last piece was delivered, Frieda chose the one place for it—a corner near the front parlor window where it would at once repeat the room and those who stood before it. She herself, in that room, was first to stand before it; throwing her head back, raising her bosom, drawing breath, she stood to see herself with all that depth and splendor extending richly, darkly—or at least as far as the closed sliding doors—behind her. This at last was a place where her pier glass belonged, this was where she belonged. No matter that behind her and upstairs the rooms were clattering and bare except for sticks and rags of boardinghouse leavings; all that would do well enough, always would do well enough, for the sewing girls and Rozzie. What mattered was this grand forefront, this show place for the public, this domain which was her, created out of her and by her.

"We're almost ready now for business," she said on that long breath. "First thing you do, now, Rozzie, is finish up those three dresses—the walking suit for me, and then the two gowns for display." Lavishly she had laid in her fabrics—(let the wholesalers risk a little)—and recklessly from that store she had chosen a green shantung, dull and heavy, and so clinging that it rose to meet the hand that passed above it. For it she had given Rozzie no pattern, but a picture covertly clipped from one of Callahan's magazines, a magazine named *Vogue*. The trotteur pictured was cut away like a man's Prince Albert, its lapels turned back to reveal braided underlapels; the high collar of its white lingerie front climbed to a sheer circle under the chin, and fell to a cascade of ruffles; its corsage skirt began just beneath the armpits, lay snugly upon the waist and hips, and then swung outward at the ankle in intricate folds and panels.

"It will be hard to make, I know that, Rozzie," she had frankly admitted, "but you've got to. You could say our whole future depends on this one suit."

Daytimes, between her other occupations, Rozzie had painstakingly cut and stitched; evenings, for as long as Frieda could spare, she had fitted. "You've got to remember," Frieda had reminded, "that I can do everything else, but the sewing will be up to you."

It was reassuring to see the care, almost the anguish, with which Rozzie labored; reassuring, too, to see the beauty at first inherent in and then so surely emerging in the dress. Two nights after the installation of the mirror, once more poised, Frieda stood while Rozzie tacked a bosom ruffle, and then knelt to rip a breadth of hem—the skirt must clear the floor by one inch, no more and no less.

"I can't do any more to it." After the skirt had been repinned, Rozzie sat back, looking up, humble, anxious and exhausted, but with eyes that carried lights. "It's—nice on you, Frieda."

"Yes," Frieda could say, turning before her mirror. "This, I think, should be it." Even she—yes, even she—could find few faults; the sureness inside her had been right. Rozzie could sew. Girls, under Rozzie, might sew only half as well as this, but that still wouldn't matter; as long as Rozzie did the fitting, people would have to be satisfied.

"As soon as you get those other two dresses done"—she spoke now from the height the dress gave her—"put them where I've told you: one at the back of the hall, where customers will have to see it as they come in, the other in the reception-room window, lighted, where they'll have to see it as they pass."

"You're so sure, Frieda," whispered Rozzie. Between sewing and worry, Rozzie, these days, scarcely slept. "No one's stopped in so far except that woman from the flats across who wanted a dress for ten dollars. The *prices* you want me to ask, Frieda, fifty dollars, sixty dollars—we'll never——"

Frieda's serenity was that of granite. "Wait and see."

For gasps, for hypnotic reaching of fingers, for reverence—"Mrs. Gurney, that *suit!*"—for these she was prepared.

"Nice, isn't it?" she asked, fluttering the cascade of white ruffles upon her bosom, before the girls and Miss Callahan. "It's a present —the whole suit—from a friend. I think it must have come from New York, or maybe even from Across. I'm not to ask."

Some man. Visibly that explanation leaped to close faces it did not make more envious. "Well, you might try to find out *where* in New York," Miss Callahan got out with a good deal more care—and a good deal less jollity—than Miss Callahan usually allowed herself.

"That skirt, Mrs. Gurney, hangs like nothing I've ever seen," Miss Callahan admitted later. "You *sure* you don't know where it comes from?"

"If I thought you could *buy* suits like that, I might go so far as to tell Mr. Frigman I could use you as an assistant." Actually, after several days, Miss Callahan let herself be pushed to this extremity; there was no hint now of stolen shirtwaists! Pleasant as was this victory, however, it was not for effect on Miss Callahan that Frieda was now working.

"That suit you've got on, Mrs. Gurney! The minute I laid eyes on that suit——" Even as the girls and Miss Callahan, so customers, too, noticed. And for customers, in the uneasy secrecy of fitting rooms, there was a different answer.

"Oh no, this isn't a *Frigman* model," she could impart in the most gossamer of whispers. "I hardly—yes, I know you're an old customer of mine, a most *valued* customer, but I scarcely like to——" Only by the most insistent cajolery could she be moved to the final whisper, "Promise that you won't let this get out then—*please*, for my *reputation!* But this was made for me by that new dressmaker who's moved in—yes, *Mme. Balik, Gowns,* at Center Street and the Parade. A very queer person, a cripple, Hungarian, I believe—no, I don't think so, although she did say something about her father—a photographer, and *quite* artistic—having been in Paris. A little expensive, of course, but I just don't like to let it get about, she's such a *find.*"

Strictly it was against rules for coats or jackets to be worn on duty, but during the weeks of its display, Frieda's jacket appeared whenever Callahan was off the floor. "I seem to have a slight cold," Frieda told the girls. "I feel chilly all the time, around my shoulders."

"I'd feel chilly too, if I owned that jacket," laughed Miss Titcock, who, envy or no envy, remained a friend.

After the suit came a black faille, with soutache and lace. Cards, engraved, were sent out to the right names and the right addresses, but it was the garments she herself wore—this Frieda knew with flaming triumph—which sent customers to Rozzie. Nights, during those first weeks after the opening (Lloyd and Idelle, for the first time, traveled by themselves to West Haven), she sat in one of the small barely furnished upstairs rooms at Balik's, adding her debts, figuring with hands that shook and a stomach that after a while seemed ice-packed. How long could she stave off Libman's? How many days' grace could she wring from Orpell's? This now was crisis; two orders the first week, two the second, four the third; Rozzie had two sewing girls hired, but what about money? You could send out bills but that was no guarantee of money; people who had never been squeezed for money were so careless. In the fourth week, stomach still more iced, she sat opposite a banker who for a long time kept his eyes on her figures: inventory, furnishings, so many gowns sold (but not paid for) at so much. When the banker looked up he was smiling, and she thought at first it was with contempt.

"You seem to be quite a businesswoman, Mrs. Gurney." His eyes had the same detail-finding scrutiny for her that they had for the figures. "New business, of course, but you've been a depositor here for some years. I don't see why we shouldn't risk three hundred dollars."

Again, with shaking hands, she apportioned that money. Forty dollars here, thirty there, a little, just a little, for reserve.

Only she didn't need the reserve. Other money began trickling in. Every night the apportioning continued, but it eased; the bank by late summer was repaid; her stomach, even at night, lay warm and snug. At first she fussed over Rozzie, pointing out trends in style and fabric; each night in a kind of agony she looked over Rozzie's choices of pattern and fabric for women she well knew; Rozzie in those days was almost distraught. But Rozzie too grew easier as time went on.

"They seem to *like* the dresses, really they do," she told Frieda with wonder. "Mrs. Houghtaling, today, said she had never been so pleased." While Frieda worked with money and books, Rozzie often sat by with bent head, stitching; Rozzie by the fourth month had four apprentices—one thing you could never stint on for a good dress, Rozzie said, was handwork. But planning and fitting were kept in her own hands, as well as the finer finishing. Names Rozzie mentioned by then were sometimes names Frieda knew only through social columns.

"There was a Mrs. Spurgeon in today," Rozzie would say. "Quite a young woman. She wanted a tussore, she thought, in faded pink, but I was looking at her, and it seemed to me——"

Rozzie, as she admitted, was departing from patterns. "They seem so willing, Frieda." In a quiet way Rozzie grew almost assured. "If you can just make the money come out, Frieda, I'm beginning to be pretty sure I can make a go of the clothes."

All fall and winter the enterprise rolled nicely—sixteen dresses a month, then eighteen. Gradually, even with the truly dreadful sums required by housekeeping for four girls and Rozzie, Frieda began paying off wholesalers.

"If this will just keep up!" she prayed in November. "Fabrics, trimmings, thread, buttons, rent, light, meat, groceries—oh, it's awful! Expenses of over four hundred! But even if I pay two-fifty on debts, that's still a hundred fifty for profit. When the debts are paid off——"

Superciliously these days she swished a chiffon panama about the ready-to-wear at Frigman's. The Callahan eyes had long ago slitted. Mr. Frigman, the visits to his office recklessly discontinued, popped up often, more unexpectedly, more smilingly than ever, at her elbow. They were both, she was sure, only looking for some means of retaliation before they pushed her out, but she did not worry. Let them accuse her of stealing now! During March Rozzie had thirty-two orders. In April they took on six new apprentices. In May——

In May she was finally let out, with a fair quantity of sound and fury, from Frigman's. But in May, also, the gross income of Mme. Balik, Gowns, rose above four thousand dollars.

CHAPTER XXIX

"Heavens," she could murmur to Mr. Frigman and Miss Callahan, on leaving, "was that all you could think up to do against me—blackball me with the other stores? I'm afraid, Mr. Frigman, you don't realize I no longer need to work at *any* store—you've served my turn so *very* well."

That last word could be hers, that exit. But later, saying good-by to the girls—"Yes, it's true, my own business. Send me any customers, now, who're too good for Frigman's"—she had feelings of queasiness—could it be possible that by leaving Frigman's she was breaking the spell? Would this somehow upset the balance and deprive her of it all—ownership, flooding money, flooding gratification, everything?

It just can't keep up this way, she already had told herself, that May, out of the fervid dazed delirium. It's just the Easter rush. We'll have to let those new girls go at once, before they get the idea they can stay. Next month we may hardly sell a dress.

But neither this nor being dismissed from Frigman's had any effect on the delirium. Money—money in quantity—poured on her in what she felt as an avalanche. Every evening checks waited, and new orders too—sixty-six in May, sixty-nine in June—it looked as if Mme. Balik, Gowns, had established itself at the new height. While she remained at Frigman's she grew almost exhausted by the nightwork; sitting at her little table, with Rozzie near by always stitching and chattering, her hands came to be not flesh but soft pink putty, her fingers had no feeling and the knuckles misbehaved; now her pen formed neat rows of figures, now it impishly spattered, staggered and trailed off in tails of ink.

Together with her almost swooning exultation, however, existed delirium of another kind. During their first summer, the summer of struggle, Rozzie naturally maintained herself—wasn't Frieda doing the same thing? Rozzie indeed made a timid offer: "I've a little money, too, you know, Frieda; I still have almost two hundred dollars if we should need it." It was rather than take this help from Rozzie that Frieda had borrowed from the bank; she couldn't have any question of ownership.

Implicit in Rozzie's attitude from the first had been a sunny expectation that if profits arose they would be shared equally. "Half for you, I thought, and half for me," Rozzie would have said; it took care, sometimes, to make sure the words were never spoken.

Fifteen dollars a week would be about right for Rozzie's share—this was Frieda's own unspoken decision. She can't have been getting a cent more than twelve at Pomeroy's, even with the way wages are up. When in November their business reached what seemed to be its level, she quickly broached (better for her to do so than to wait until Rozzie hinted) the results of her prudent figuring.

"Rozzie, I think it's safe we take a profit." Recklessly one evening (there could be no effect of care in the pronouncement) she pushed back her books. "We haven't talked of it before, but—well, I work here as treasurer, of course, I manage and sell and put up the money, but"—the next must come in a generous, bright burst—"how would you like it if you got one third—one third, I mean, of everything we make?"

Over the angular face which so eagerly had lifted at Frieda's first phrase, over the lips which had already cried, in happy disbelief, "Frieda! Do you think so? Already?" passed outward evidences of inward hurt: a flickering of eyelids, a trembling of lip corners, color flooding up over the wide cheekbones.

"Why, Frieda, that's fine," Rozzie said swiftly, and then, with an equally swift descent into humility, "It's more than I should get, I know."

Being Rozzie, however, she could stay humble no more than she could stay hurt; mercurially she brightened. "But I'll take it! Oh, I'm excited! How much, Frieda, will it *be?*"

If I'd said a quarter she'd have taken that. Frieda had to suffer the pang. It was annoying, it took dignity from what she was accomplishing, to have Rozzie put up no more fight. On the surface, however, she too glowed.

"Well, you can see for yourself, Rozzie, here where it's figured. Sixteen dresses—that's eight hundred and twenty dollars. Expenses— that's this long column here beginning with fabrics and trimmings." (One thumb covered an entry of two hundred fifty dollars against debts; not that that didn't rightfully belong there, but——) "Expenses, six five eight, sixty-two. That leaves us one hundred and sixty-one dollars, thirty-eight cents over—I don't see why we can't take that for a profit, do you? And one third of that is fifty-three dollars and eighty cents—I split the penny your way—here!"

With gay magician's laugh and gestures she brought forth bills and silver from the table drawer. But something somewhere had gone wrong; a mask of uncertainty, almost of bewilderment, again covered Rozzie's face. Rozzie mechanically accepted what Frieda handed her, but Rozzie was looking directly neither toward Frieda nor the cash. As Frieda saw swiftly, her ace in the hole must now be produced.

"What's more," this came with increased gaiety, "last month I didn't dare say a word, we were still so close. But actually we cleared expenses then too. A whole seventy-one dollars and eighteen cents, of which twenty-three dollars seventy-three cents goes to you. Here—you can count it—here!"

It swung the balance. Doubt left Rozzie. Casting aside her sewing, but keeping her money—or at least such of it as didn't spill—Rozzie sprang to her feet to tug Frieda up from her chair.

"Oh, Frieda, last month too, and you wouldn't tell me, when I've been so worried! Isn't it wonderful? Six months since we started, and we're doubling profits! We'll have to take one of the bathtubs— it'll get full of money and run over——"

It could be no fun waltzing with Rozzie, the wild way Rozzie bobbed, but, laughing too and in her own high spirits, Frieda allowed herself to be whirled. She had, after all, gotten away with a good deal.

For the next three months, then, few new monetary problems arose. Back debts swallowed their portion, Rozzie accepted her third, savoringly Frieda banked her greater allotment. But in March what almost was terror joined the awe and wonder; if Rozzie were to get a third of profits on March business, then what Rozzie got would be *frightful*. In that month, the business came to be hers, free and clear—every bolt of yard goods, every feather of trimming, every sewing machine, every fall of window drapery, every chair—and while in one five minutes she could walk through a now absolutely held domain, absorbing it, feeling it feed and fatten—hers, all hers, this richness, this activity, this fertility, this future—in the next five minutes she would stare at her figures upstairs in a panic. In this month of March, she had over nine hundred dollars left, after all bills were paid. How could she *possibly* let Rozzie take three hundred dollars?

In a frenzy-driven inspiration, she went to the public library to read up on cost accounting, and from there, much assuaged, returned to do over her books from the first. Interest on Investment, Capital Investment, Capital Reserve—entries which before she had been too unversed (could anyone have been such an innocent poor goose?) to use. With this new system, income channeled itself neatly (the surplus went into a second bank), but Rozzie's original fifty dollars could be no less than doubled. Even Rozzie, contorted skipping fool that she was, could scarcely be persuaded that there was no more income from thirty-two dresses than from sixteen. And then in May, when business again doubled, to remain henceforward only slightly underneath that figure, she again had to suffer torture.

"That seems a good deal of money for a little sewing." Curt expression of this torment could not be suppressed when, that May, she was forced to turn over nearly two hundred dollars.

"Think of you though, Frieda! With twice that!" In her flush of jubilant wonder, Rozzie appeared not to hear the agony in Frieda's voice. "Oh, I'm *glad* you get two thirds, Frieda; this is all your doing. You're the best friend a dressmaker ever had!"

"I've three people to support to your one, besides a lot of expenses I don't charge to the business." Frieda's reply could be no less than stiff and sharp.

Why was it, as she so often asked herself, that even now, when by her own Herculean efforts and by nothing else, her cup at last was filling, that it still must have in it this element of gall? For it was not only in the matter of joyfully accepting too much of Frieda's money that Rozzie turned out to be costly and a nuisance. Originally it had been simple to override Rozzie's notions—"I perhaps know a *little* more about how things are done here in Meridian," she could say, and "After all, if I and my children eat dry cereal and toast for breakfast, those sewing girls should find it good enough."

But as time went on, Rozzie every day grew harder to handle. Not that Rozzie quarreled—if Rozzie *would* quarrel, as Frieda wished often at frustrated heights of pique, things would be much easier. Rozzie's way was to be forever quiet and reasonable.

"Now we're making money," Rozzie cozily brought forth in December, "we really should pay the girls more than two dollars."

"More than two dollars?" Frieda at first scarcely looked up from her figuring, the idea was so inconsiderable. "Besides their room and board? Why should we?"

"They're doing good work, you know, Frieda; when I think what they've learned in these months——"

"Learned from us, they might remember that!" Frieda had a bitterness to roll between tongue and palate. "If they think they have so much coming——"

"Oh, it's not that so much," returned Rozzie gently, "as that as soon as they can say they're experienced they can get other jobs——"

"Well, let them go, then! *Girls* aren't scarce!"

"I could hardly do with *only* new girls, though, Frieda, the number of dresses we're turning out now."

"Oh, you could, too, Rozzie! What do those girls do? Sew up a few straight seams, tack on a few hooks and buttons——"

Again Rozzie's head shook. "They do a good deal more than that by this time. Of course you're right, though; we could start over with new girls, only then we'd have to do less business for a while, until I got the new girls trained."

Hung on this skewer, Frieda had to let Rozzie raise wages first to four dollars and then to five. But in April, when Rozzie wanted to pay her experienced girls eight, and start the six new girls at three, she once more struck.

"Don't you realize what you're doing, Rozzie? It's out of *your own pocket* you're taking that money, Rozzie; out of your pocket and mine. Every cent we pay those girls means less for us."

"But we're making plenty, Frieda." Rozzie understood nothing. "And with all this new business we'll be making more. After all, if you look at it one way, it's from those girls that we make *our* money. What I'd really like is a schedule: a raise each month, say, up to fifteen dollars. There'd be no uncertainty, then. The girls would appreciate that, I'm sure, Frieda——"

"Appreciate it!" spat Frieda. "Of course they'd appreciate it! Who wouldn't? What do they do for business? Do they carry any of the worry? Do they bring customers? Do they *manage*? Oh, it's just unreasonable, Rozzie; the whole thing's so unreasonable——"

"Maybe it is." Rozzie throughout was nothing but meek. "Grace Adams has been offered eight, though, and if she goes Theresa goes with her. I'll get on all right, of course; I can take no more orders the rest of this month——"

Always the issues were twisted around to this same conclusion— if Frieda didn't agree, then Rozzie would have to refuse *orders,* orders which, as Frieda well knew in an echoing subbasement of her mind, meant each one a profit of at least twenty dollars, almost no matter what the girls got paid.

"All right," she was eternally having to say to Rozzie. "Have it your own way—everything has to be your way. *All right!*" Sometimes a din of talk and laughter grew audible even in the fitting room, but "All right," she had to say to Rozzie, "you know and I know those girls could work faster if they kept their mouths shut, but if you think they're going to sulk, all right! Let them talk! Let them sing!

"This is the only dressmaker's in Meridian where the girls don't work twelve hours," she again had to submit, "but oh, you're right, of course you're right; ours do more work in their ten. They can't miss any of their evening appointments, no matter what our rush is!"

"But that's what they're so good about," was Rozzie's return to this one. "It's because they know they're free whenever possible that they've been working twelve and fourteen hours when we've needed it, *hard,* too, Frieda!"

All Frieda could do, under the circumstances, was see to it that the girls knew her—not Rozzie—as the source of benefactions.

"Beginning today, there'll be raises again, girls." It was she who, standing at the head of the long table, where so many young faces lifted from the multicolored froth, graciously made all announcements. The bright eyes met hers pleasantly, admiringly, following with affection on her figure the lines of a dress over which they had bent. They had better like her; if they didn't she would know where blame lay—though that was a game Rozzie was scarcely clever enough to play.

The other things that Rozzie managed, however, vexatiously continued to pile up. One girl came to be fixed at the reception-room counters, where accessories and fine hand-sewn undermuslins (no girl ever sat idle) displayed their seductions. In the beginning Rozzie and the girls had flown about at night and morning to help out on the cleaning, but among the girls hired in April was one May Fisko, who began with simple offers—"I'll run up and start dinner," or "You go on to the sewing; I'll finish this dusting"—and who from there grew so enmeshed she did no sewing at all.

"But that's impossible!" Over this too Frieda stormed. "What is this—a ladies' seminary? Those girls can do their own work!"

"Of course, if you think so, Frieda." Rozzie over this was as amiable as over anything else. "Only if all the girls cook and dust—they're terribly awkward at it, most of them—for an hour night and morning, that's twenty-two hours of time lost every day. When May does it alone, that's only ten hours spent."

"Living like millionaires, on my money!" For Frieda, the stiletto pierced and repierced. "Seventy-eight cents yesterday for new potatoes. Fresh milk by the gallon. Wholesalers' bills I don't mind—we've got to have the best of fabrics. But this——"

Beneath injury existed, partially, comparison—the disordered, dark and riotous rooms in which she still lived, the careless meals she shared with Lloyd and Idelle. So far she had not allowed discontent with her way of living to be more than a pinprick—"I can't *show* I'm making money!"—but after her dismissal from Frigman's, after Lloyd and Idelle, that second summer, had gone off again to West Haven, this pinprick rather suddenly swelled large and burst. Recklessly ridding herself of such sticks and tatters as remained of her household furnishings, she packed up her clothes and moved in with Rozzie.

What had been stinging acid grew to be, after that, the most soothing of unguents. It had been so long—six years—since she had hired her mother's service that she had forgotten how ease could sweep up and surround her. Not only the girls but she too, now, could sit down three times daily to meals deliciously cooked and well served; not only the girls but she too retired at night to a chamber neatly made up by hands other than her own. Since she now could be present all day long, it rapidly grew to be accepted that she was hostess of the house; it was she who affably came forward to open preliminary parleys, she who sent off for Rozzie, she who was Authority in those discussions of fabric and trimming, those applications of style knowledge, those fittings, which finally resulted in a Balik gown.

Living this life, so surrounded by amplitude and satisfaction, laved in creature comfort and importance, uplifted by a constant and unending reception of money, she could tell herself, often, that this was, indeed, the Good Life, this was the Possession toward which she had striven ever since that night—how clearly it could spring to life!—when Mr. Hake so soundlessly had turned upon her as she swept the balcony, and the money had fallen. Her hold wasn't secure yet; her residence at Balik's, for instance, could continue only until fall, when the children came back, and she had as yet only a beginning, the very beginning, of all the money she must have. But if she couldn't steam ahead now she was this far, her name was something else than Frieda Gurney!

Plans for other worlds to conquer—Mr. Kober, for instance, and the vistas he presented—had necessarily, during the long months of pressure, been shifted aside. With Balik's now running somewhat on its own, however, with herself freed from Frigman's, with her shoulders for a while delivered of their household burdens, such considerations could be taken out and dusted. Mr. Kober, with his dull large eyes, his dull large nose, his dull large person, and his angina, might appear the dreariest and least interesting of humans, but installed as she was in a house whose warm inner workings might be hers, but whose shell was still possessed by Mr. Kober, with her bedroom window offering daily views of the backs of Mr. Kober's six business buildings on one side, and his massive redstone flats across the street, she could hardly miss being reminded that Mr. Kober also had his charming side.

"The way Miss Balik and I work for our money!" she sighed in June when her landlord dropped by for what rent remained after deductions. "While all you do is walk around and pick it up!"

"It's not that easy, Mrs. Gurney, not that easy." Folding away what she had given him, Mr. Kober produced his dismal slow headshake, his harassed smile. "Owners have troubles too, Mrs. Gurney. If you saw my taxes——"

"Oh, you!" scoffed Frieda. "I know you. Was there ever a landlord who didn't talk poor?"

She herself, years ago, had paid the variety store rents to old Mrs. Kober, who incessantly and importantly had gabbled of "my properties"; Mr. Kober, she was sure, had been an only child; almost daily she saw him about his stores or his flats; it was almost impossible to question his ownership of what he appeared to own. Still, as she told herself with her astuteness warm around her, there was nothing like making sure. This wouldn't be any champagne wedding nor a *Harry* marriage either!

"Courthouse?" she inquired dulcetly, one day, from a pay phone. "I wonder if you could trouble to inform me who owns that business block at Center Street and the Parade. There's a bakery in there now. I'm thinking of locating——"

The next day, drawling heavily, she again phoned. "I've been trying to find out who owns the flat at 153 The Parade. . . . You could? Oh, thank you! Would you spell it?"

There! she could tell herself with busy triumph, these inquiries well consummated. That should cinch that! Once more at her desk, it was difficult not to dream out her dream on paper. Fourteen flats at twenty or twenty-five a month—besides the one he uses—they must pay that. Six stores at forty—a minimum. H'm—maybe five hundred fifty a month. Not too much, but still half what I make here at Balik's. There may be more, too—he's always out somewhere on streetcars.

Reply to this last question, also, was simply arrived at.

"You couldn't possibly have some little flat or house you could rent to me, could you?" That evening it was at the door of Mr. Kober's own first-floor-rear flat that she pursued her questing. "It's my dream to live in one of your apartments right here, but I can't do that because of the children; I'd have them around all the time. It would have to be something a few blocks away——"

Tribute to her own sagacity came to be made, during what followed, almost with awe. And to think, all the time, she didn't know—she had nothing to go on but a guess! True, as Mr. Kober in his melancholy never failed at pointing out, each modest workingman's cottage or duplex to which she was led showed the stigmata of long hard tenant wear and few repairs; porch steps gave beneath the foot, porch railings grinned with absent spindles, interior varnish lay only in patches, wallpapers had long departed from their first uncracked freshness, but this, as Frieda's kindling eye soon saw, meant little. Like the shops, like the flats, like Balik's itself, each was basically sound: foundations held, floors and woodwork were good oak, money had been spent on plate-glass mirrors in small reception halls, on colored windows above dining-room buffets, on well-shelved pantries, on furnaces and plumbing. Most of these places were occupied but, it was understood, for a tenant as good as Frieda, Mr. Kober would be willing to do some shifting around.

"I could make do with this one." Critically, at each house, she half succumbed, half didn't. "I don't know—did you say something of a six-room duplex?"

Not until Sunday, when Frieda had viewed twenty-two places, did Mr. Kober come to a particularly mournful halt. "Well, that's the lot, Mrs. Gurney. I didn't think I'd have anything you'd want to take."

"You just think you don't have anything I'd like to take!" bubbled Frieda. "Why, I liked them all! The particular one, though—yes, I'm almost sure, is that upper duplex, on Sixteenth, the one with three bedrooms and a front porch. Of course, it'll take decorating, but that shan't cost you a penny. I'll do it out of rent, just as at Balik's. It'll be a real home, Mr. Kober, a home such as my children and I never had. I'll get a maid——"

Enthusiasm for homemaking, however, was a dust mote in the larger landslide of excitement. Twenty-two houses, besides the stores, besides the flats, beside Balik's! Ownership could not be doubted, either; for vacant houses Mr. Kober had keys, and at the others most front doors had been opened by men or women who immediately stammered, "It's you, Mr. Kober—if you could make it next week ——" Oh, Mr. Kober might be the poorest businessman on earth; undoubtedly Mr. Kober *was* the poorest businessman on earth; maybe someday she'd show him about that! But he owned those houses, each one worth, at the very least, three thousand.

Back in her room, her body so aerated by opportunity that she could hardly anchor herself at her desk—a touch, and she could have soared free, like a balloon—she figured. Even at rock bottom, what Mr. Kober owned could scarcely come to less than one hundred thousand. And when you began to consider a single man like Mr. Kober, scarcely ever known to spend a cent, when you remembered old Mrs. Kober, too, and how tight she was, then it was almost impossible not to realize there must be other money somewhere too, saved up.

Forty thousand, maybe fifty thousand. All belonging to a man who—well, she had never *seen* Mr. Kober in an attack, actually, but with all the care he took of himself he must surely have *something*.

Her breast ached with the vision.

CHAPTER XXX

Kneeling behind Mrs. Rebedoux, swiftly stabbing up a hem with silver pins, Rozzie let thinking drift. This was the day's last fitting. Plenty ahead to be done, but nothing that was pressing. Perhaps she could slip to her room for a minute; maybe before supper she could write to Eddie. Each night for a week now she had meant to get that letter written, each night somehow she had been so tired she hadn't.

"Go on to New York or Boston"—that was what Eddie had said to her before she left West Haven—"but if you take up with Frieda Gurney, then you're saying good-by to me."

"But I'm saying good-by to you anyway, Eddie; do you think I'd be leaving if I wasn't?" This was the answer which had bled inside her, but she hadn't given it. Instead, awkwardly—when, ever, had she been anything but awkward?—she had wiped his hand across her face,

and laughed, and told him, "You're better off to have me going just
anywhere; within a week you'll have another girl, one of the pretty
ones in high school."

Burying his face in her breast, Eddie had whispered, "Don't go away
from me for any reason, Rozzie; don't let Frieda Gurney get you;
don't go to anyone else, either." But next night it had been the other
story; he had walked home with her from the store, insisted on it,
and at the door his face had been pinched.

"You're right, Rozzie. Go on, get out of West Haven, there'll never
be anything for you here."

Poor Eddie. "Look at Eddie." That was what Eddie thought other
people said when they saw him with Rozzie. "Look at Eddie, can't get
himself anything but that cripple, that Hungarian cripple."

Once there had been a time—how foolish she had been in those
days!—when she had let herself dream. This would be all she asked
of living: a little house like the one Harry Gurney got for Frieda,
where all day long she could sew for the ladies of West Haven (Eddie
needn't have bad worries over money) and where Eddie could come
every night to get strong. Because that was what Eddie needed of her
—strength. She'd known that from the first, and it had never hurt;
what he wanted was a mother, not one like his own, who herself
needed helping, but someone who could make him feel he was important and could do things.

"He won't have to be seen with me often," she had told herself in
those days. "I'll stay there in the little house, and go out mostly by
myself when I have to, and he can do the same." But it hadn't worked;
she had known all along that it couldn't work, really; people would
have had to know about it, if they married, and Eddie didn't have it
in him to stand ridicule or scorn. Even this summer when, after all
the months of being apart, he had come to Meridian because he said
he had to, still it had been right only for a few minutes. When she had
introduced him to the sewing girls he had shrunk back, and when
they walked out they had met Frieda.

Once she had thought her hurt could never lessen, but now all she
felt was the soft ache. Mostly she had broken herself from Eddie a
year ago, and he had broken himself from her. Only the last push of
old need had brought him to Meridian. Perhaps he had some other
woman, already, to whom he was beginning to cling.

"I realize we must make our separate lives," he had begun in his
last letter, stiffly, "so this is farewell." But then he had become entirely
Eddie. "I do wish you well though, Rozzie, and don't trust that Frieda

Gurney, she'll cheat you every way she can." Almost the same thing he had said before.

"But you're so wrong, Eddie," she had told him when she had him face to face. "Every month my share—well, it's almost two hundred dollars! More than I expected to make in this world, ever!" Why was it Eddie could never be persuaded? Always there was that old jealousy, from the time they had all been at Hake's.

"I must say it brings out my figure," Mrs. Rebedoux mused complacently from overhead, and, starting, Rozzie came back to black chiffon broadcloth which had fallen from her hands, all pinned. Clumpily—no matter how she practiced she still would clump—she got to her feet. Mrs. Rebedoux, smoothing down her straight front, patting at her backward-swinging hips, had only approval to bestow upon the figure in the mirror, which could look so stoutly fashionable; Mrs. Rebedoux had only gracious favor to bestow upon Mme. Balik, who had made her look so.

Oh dear, beseeched Rozzie's mind immediately, as it shunted Eddie aside, keep your eyes on your good points, Mrs. Rebedoux, because your figure's come out just a bit *too* much.

Why was it that so many women—*all* rich women, it seemed—had that awful cement block, that hard and flat plateau, above their stomachs? Someday—it never could happen, but she could imagine— she would say, "This year I sew only for tall, beautiful, full-breasted and slim-waisted girls, age seventeen to twenty-five; no others need apply." It just couldn't be fair that young girls usually had to wear cheap, overfussy, bundling ready-mades, while women like Mrs. Rebedoux got fitted.

But it's women like Mrs. Rebedoux who need to get fitted, her common sense could answer. Lucky for me, too, because that's my one talent, learned from my crippledness—I can hide bumps. Let's see now, I wonder——

"If I had one suggestion——" That was Frieda, coming in. "This underwaist, if we drew it in a trifle closer——"

Oh dear, thought Rozzie, wanting to giggle, now she's made the woman look at the very spot. But then, immediately penitent, she was humble—Frieda *had* helped, only it wasn't more tightness that was needed, but more fullness.

"Mrs. Gurney's right, as always," she said aloud. "I'll fix it. When you come next, Mrs. Rebedoux—Friday?—your dress will be done."

"I know I can depend on you." Having learned never to look toward that plateau, no matter what the provocation, Mrs. Rebedoux still was gracious, leaving.

Upstairs in her bedroom later, settling herself with pen and paper at her little table, Rozzie still felt warm and happy. Life was nice. Look, she had been able to think of the one thing to do. She must never forget what a miracle this was; never forget that it was because of Frieda she had nothing to do but the one most wonderful thing in the world: make dresses. This was a real world, so naturally there had to be flaws; the prices Frieda charged were frightening; some women, unlike Mrs. Rebedoux, saw nothing but their bad points, and maybe it had been nicer, just a little nicer, when Frieda had still worked at Frigman's. Frieda always wanted trimming: "I believe it could stand a bow," Frieda was always saying. Or artificial buttonholes, or plaits, or a shirred chiffon guimpe, or undersleeves.

"Sometime," Rozzie had once rebelliously told Frieda, "I am going to sew a dress without one snick of trimming."

"And I suppose you think you'll get paid for that?" Frieda had given the right answer.

No, Rozzie admitted to herself, as she wrote "Dear Eddie" at the top of her letter sheet, of course she could never get paid for anything so outlandish. And getting paid was nice; she'd never be the one to say it wasn't. Only getting paid seemed separate, somehow, from sewing the dresses. It always came as a surprise, each month when Frieda paid her. To think she could sew all those dresses—those dreams of dresses, of such wonderful fabrics—and get money too! Not that she could ever let Frieda know this was how she felt. Or Eddie either. They'd call her unworldly. But she'd hate, on the other hand, to think she might be cheated; once or twice, with what Eddie said, and that silly idea she had begun with, about dividing even, she had felt strange and uncertain. But Eddie was wrong; of course Eddie was wrong. Frieda was a businesswoman, Frieda in some ways was as hard as nails, but no one could say Frieda was dishonest, or that she wasn't a good *friend*. Two hundred dollars a month—you had only to think about it to know there couldn't possibly be more. No dressmaking business on this earth could ever make more than six hundred dollars a month. That would be one thing she could say to Eddie.

During the week of house inspection, during the long trolley rides, especially, when sometimes for as long as half an hour Frieda and Mr. Kober had sat side by side with not a thing to do but talk, opportunities for getting in a good word had not failed to knock.

"You should be thinking about getting married, that's what you should be doing, Mr. Kober, a gay young bachelor like you!" she had rallied, and "Don't tell *me* you haven't someone on the string! I know your kind, Mr. Kober; any day now I'll wake up to hear you've stepped off."

But while answers to these in one way were encouraging—at least she had no competition—in other ways they could be no less than dampening.

"No, I'm no marrying man, not me with my heart, Mrs. Gurney," Mr. Kober would deny with his unhappy headshake. "'You're not the man to marry, Stillwell,' Mother said often. 'Fortune hunters may seek you out, Stillwell,' Mother said; Mother was a great one to set store by property. 'But you mark my word, Stillwell,' Mother said, 'you're better off by yourself.'"

"Really!" Frieda at this had objected. "Why, what an idea your mother must have had of people! And your heart can't be *very* bad, Mr. Kober; to me you look *splendid*.

"It's a pleasure to be seen with you, Mr. Kober," she tried again. "I hope you realize you're a very *impressive* person, Mr. Kober."

"No, no, Mrs. Gurney, I assure you, nobody notices me at all. 'You're not the type to make a splash in the world, Stillwell,' Mother said to me often. 'If people make advances, you'll usually find they have some purpose.'"

That old scratch-eye! Frieda apostrophized the departed. Naturally the mother of a son in Mr. Kober's position would have done what she could to fortify him. But it was annoying to find the redoubt so invincible.

"These jaunts with you are something I'm going to miss, I'm afraid." On the night of their final journey, she allowed herself a more open thrust. "I'm lonely too, you know, Mr. Kober. I can't say what your— your gallantry is meaning to me."

It was on the dark stoop of Balik's that these words were spoken, and, finding his hand in the dark, she pressed it gently, drawing it up toward her bosom. Mr. Kober, however, jumped like a stung horse, jerking free.

"Nothing—nothing at all——" Tripping over his own feet and falling headlong—so that, in the moment before he picked himself up, she had a stricken instant of believing one of his heart attacks had come on all too finally—Mr. Kober fled as from something not only dangerous but shameful. Once or twice earlier—once on the street when she had made some jocose small remark and squeezed his arm, and once in a basement when a long gray rat had slid across the floor and she had screamed and clung to him—he had evinced the same embarrassment and furtive shame.

What's the matter with the old goat? she asked herself crossly, after her repulse at the door. He ought to be glad I'd bother with him! Well justified as indignation certainly was, however, it brought her no further forward.

I can just as well make up my mind, I guess, I'll never make any dents in him *that* way; he's too old. Grudgingly she met a fact which had to be vexing. *That* was the way she had gotten Palmer—not for keeps, maybe, but no one could say he hadn't *wanted*. That was the way—and how simply!—she had gotten Harry. That, certainly, had been what brought about that overnight alliance with that impossible drummer—could she ever forget? That was the way a whole lot of other men too—even Frigman took his pinches!—had drawn toward her; it was downright annoying that Mr. Kober had to be different. Still in the long run this too would make little difference; she'd get round him somehow!

Such cuts as she got in that autumn were, she well knew, only preliminaries, but that did not mean she was faltering. As soon as the pandemonium of getting Lloyd and Idelle housebroken to new quarters had somewhat subsided, her quarry was invited to a meal at the new flat.

"*Terribly* rich," she informed Lloyd and Idelle beforehand. "Just no end to what he owns. And there's one thing I've found out—he's crazy over a collection he's got, a collection of watch fobs. You do what I say, now, and you never can tell. I might even go as far as bicycles——"

Thus coached and buttered, Lloyd and Idelle, on the quarry's arrival, both soared to peaks of perfection.

"Say, aren't you the Mr. Kober who has those watch fobs?" Lloyd had no trouble whatever in moving into his opening gambit, Lloyd indeed was lordly, as he shook the visitor's hand.

"Why yes." Startled but dimly illumined, Mr. Kober relaxed from his usual guard. "Odd you should ask about that, my boy. As it happens, I have in my pocket——"

"You wouldn't have any of those new motorcar fobs though, would you, Mr. Kober? I'd sure like to see an Apperson Jackrabbit." Even half an hour later, on his way in to dinner, Lloyd was still carrying on. You could look awhile, thought Frieda fondly, before you'd find another fifteen-year-old who could put up a better front. Idelle, too, in blue plaid with a white mull guimpe (a nuisance, not being able to take Idelle right to Balik's, but Rozzie had been given the most careful measurements) was doing well—quiet, but interested.

"I regret I haven't with me my Negro on a gibbet. Bronze, most realistic, with flames——" Absorbed as he was with his prosing, even

Mr. Kober must notice with what style, manner and delicious food he was surrounded.

Later, with Lloyd and Idelle off on their own pursuits (no use pushing a miracle too far!), she took her landlord on a promised tour of the flat, and thought he must be blind, indeed, if he didn't see transfiguration.

"There! Remember that old kitchen? And I didn't use a thing but new linoleum, new paint. Bedrooms—well, even with my maid, Stella, right here, there's one bedroom I shan't let you peep at, Mr. Kober. But just look at Lloyd's—isn't that window seat comfy? All plaster-patched and newly papered, floors sanded and refinished light—just as in the front room. Oh, I know the furniture is plain—with a growing girl and boy it's better. We can have richer things later. But right now—with this nice fumed-oak set, and the brass, and the lace curtains —doesn't the place look—well, how does it look, Mr. Kober?"

"Miraculous, Mrs. Gurney, miraculous," tolled Mr. Kober. Somewhere his inner thoughts must have hinted that what he saw here was a sample; if Mrs. Gurney could cause this rejuvenescence in one domicile she could cause it in twenty-two. But such perception, if it existed, left him unmoved in his dolor.

"Of course"—Frieda produced a sigh of her own—"it's a woman's house; I can see that myself, Mr. Kober; it isn't as if I had a man to do for." But having inserted this side plaint, she returned to what, as things shaped up, must be her best bet. Mr. Kober through everything remained agnostic to the joys of marriage, Mr. Kober continued physically unstirred, but Mr. Kober, if he were truly as distressed by business harassments as he appeared to be, must pine for shoulders such as hers.

"Until I got working on this flat I just didn't know what you meant by an owner's troubles, Mr. Kober." This, spoken with grave fellow feeling, waited until they were ensconced in front-room chairs. "Workmen! The way they loaf, the way they charge, the time and worry everything takes—honestly, with all you have on your hands, Mr. Kober, I don't see how you do it!"

"Yes, now Mother's gone, I find what I must carry indeed heavy." Slumped, bleakly disconsolate, in the morris chair, Mr. Kober agreed to so much at least; agreed, in fact, rather too thoroughly. "Sometimes I doubt my life is worth it."

"Oh, Mr. Kober, what a thing to say!" Genuinely shocked, Frieda expressed electric horror, well bolstered with good sense. "*That's* no way to look at trouble! Even if you—it would be perfectly simple, you know, for you to get *help* with your problems; of course I can see why you might not want to let management out of the *family,* but surely that could be fixed someway. What you need to do is look around for someone you know well and can trust, get that person as a—well, a business *partner* would be better than nothing. You can't just give up!"

"Undoubtedly you are right," agreed Mr. Kober limply, but beyond that he never seemed to get.

Why, with all the cash he must have, didn't Mr. Kober improve his holdings? This was a problem she pondered often. With the state his health is in I suppose he just doesn't think it pays to bother. Or else he thinks the places are good enough for renters. Or else he's got his money tied up in other investments, stocks and bonds. I wonder how it might be if I offered to take one house at a time and fix it, securing what I did by a mortgage. The very sound of the word "mortgage" was tempting; she herself had never owned property, but naturally she had heard of mortgages; mortgages were one of the many means by which the rich kept their hold on the world. If any such plan could be worked out—it would take years, of course—but with an obviously poor manager like Mr. Kober——

"Just think of all the money you could get on mortgage, Mr. Kober," she tempted one day during a rent visit. "Money to spend right now! Doesn't that idea ever tease you?"

"No, no, Mrs. Gurney." That day, more than ever, he was gloom-fast. "My worries are bad enough as things are."

Unlike others, this reply could not be classified as annoying. "Never mortgage, Stillwell, never go in debt"—although, for once, unreported, she had no doubt that some such maternal admonition must have been given. It was just as well Mr. Kober didn't borrow; if he had, he would probably have lost everything by this time. Besides, she didn't really want to use her own money. By her original plan she could keep her cash and get what he had too.

"You ought to team up with me, Mr. Kober; between us we'd soon own half Meridian," she joked, but by that time she had no idea of getting anywhere with such tactics. On the other hand, even with fall rapidly advancing into winter, she did not worry. Just let her keep her mind open, and in the end she'd see her way clear, just as she had with Rozzie and the business. Morning and evening, on her way to Balik's, she lingered, with flooding ownership already strong, to gaze at the street frontages of the shops and the flats; the bakery needed its trim painted, and there was a crack in the coping over the hardware store; the redstone of the flats, too, was dingy; what was needed there was sandblasting.

"Why, Frieda, I believe that you've put on some weight!" During a dress fitting, one day that winter, Rozzie had an astonishment to blurt. Turning and preening before the mirror, at which she was being fitted, Frieda laughed at her own start of discovery; it had been years since she had been anything but thin—working at Frigman's wasn't conducive to weight! But it wasn't unbecoming, this little plumpness. "And don't you know," she could have asked, "what's making it? *It's Mr. Kober's property!*" At first uncertainly, but then more surely, she had experienced ingestion; her body had hurt, almost, with the influx of possession to her person, her arteries had felt crowded. All these years *getting* had been so slow, so hard, she had managed it only with such desperation and despair, and here of a sudden she had little more to do than stand, and all she asked came flooding to her, not only money (more than ten thousand in her two accounts, with another thousand added monthly!) but also Mr. Kober's buildings and houses, and everything else he owned, besides.

At this same fitting Rozzie had more chatter to impart. "I had a letter from Miss Shatto this morning—she says Cecilia Hake just died. Isn't that awful? A beautiful young woman like that, with everything to live for—but she hadn't been strong, Miss Shatto said, ever since the baby came. Poor Palmer, I wonder how he'll get along."

"Oh, old lady Amiot can take the baby; it shouldn't hurt her to stir her stumps once in a day." At first Frieda had scarcely listened; Rozzie always prattled. But then impact came. Cecilia Hake. Why, Cecilia Hake couldn't be dead—not the girl with the slender green back who had floated up church steps on Palmer's right arm, not the supercilious young woman who had cried, "Jet? Of course you won't have jet!" or the white bride who paraded a church aisle. Cecilia could never be dead, any more than Harry could really be dead, because Cecilia was one of Them, and people on your side could die—Rozzie, for instance, could die and you would still be here—but people on the other side couldn't die, because then you lost what made you live.

The whole of this thought was in her mind and then gone, so evanescently that as she shot upward through it she could not grasp her own response or that she had had it. Palmer, she was thinking, then. That makes Palmer a widower. He could marry again. Could anyone—this carried its gurgle of laughter—imagine *her* wanting to be Palmer's wife *now?* A little small-town owner of a little small-town lumberyard—failing, undoubtedly; it would be no surprise to hear, next, that he was bankrupt. While she had all of Balik's, and Mr. Kober on the string.

Inspiration proved slow, but still she did not worry; she might not entirely know Mr. Kober, but she knew herself. On a morning in February it was because of immediate circumstance and not at all because of Mr. Kober that she woke groggy and unwilling, tossing herself over, resubmerging in sleep. Let Stella get Lloyd and Idelle off, or Lloyd only, if Idelle still was sick; let Rozzie manage for a morning —what was the use of her money if she couldn't, for once in her life, sleep? Usually Idelle was in the big brass bed beside her, but last night she had put Idelle on the couch against the far wall; Idelle had been feverish, and if there was one thing Frieda could do without it was a cold. Even on the couch Idelle had been restless, wanting water, sobbing that her throat ached, sobbing that she couldn't rest.

"If you're still sick in the morning, I'll get the doctor out, but now for heaven's sake, *shut up!*" Frieda had had to be severe at last, or she would have had no sleep at all. It was the half memory of this promise which nagged at her now it was morning, dragging at her, tumbling her half conscious into slippers and kimono, pulling her across the room to let up a shade beside the couch where Idelle slept scowling, her lips moving in a mutter of unease, her head turning.

"Goodness, she's hot," murmured Frieda, hand to a flushed cheek. "Idelle," she went on, somewhat crossly—it was no end of trouble to have the children ill! "Are you still sick?"

Not waking, Idelle moved jerkily once more, the blanket falling from her neck and shoulder as she did so.

"Well, you might keep your covers on," grumbled Frieda. Then, as she bent, her body too jerked, one moment sleep-drugged as it had been, the next staggering forward, harshly awake. Red rash—that was red rash on Idelle's throat. Like Ernst, her mind whispered, sinking. Oh no, not like Ernst, that same mind supplied, re-emerging. What was around this year was hardly a true scarlet fever. Scarlatina, some people called it. Almost no deaths, except of infants. Get Lloyd away from here, get him out quick—the message was to her feet, and it was her feet that moved, carrying her toward the door. There was that friend of Lloyd's, that Jack Bucklin. Jack was always wanting Lloyd to come for overnight. Then the doctor. She, Frieda, was not apt to come down with it; few grown people did. But she'd be quarantined——

The doorknob was round and smooth in her palm, but the door didn't open, not that door. Instead she stood feeling the draft, the swift inrushing draft, of another opening. Get Lloyd out immediately —she couldn't risk Lloyd. But what danger could there be for a man well past fifty, even if that man did have some heart trouble?

Once more at the couch, she stooped intently low. Idelle's cheeks seemed even more red, her breathing more loud. Idelle was a strong child; Idelle always recovered from things quickly; nothing could happen to Idelle simply because a doctor was called a bit late; Idelle could stay here in bed the whole day, tended by Stella.

The head on the pillow moved once more, and from it came a moan. In Frieda the pendulum swung. "I can't," she whispered. "It's too big a chance. Why do I have to make these choices? Couldn't I have things a little easy, just this once?" She would have to wait for some other way.

But then, while she stood there, sunlight outside reached an obstruction, light dimmed, dulling as it did so the flush on Idelle's cheek; Idelle turned from her back to her left side, burying her face in the pillow. Idelle's breathing eased.

The pendulum again swung.

"Oh pooh," Frieda told herself, decision hardening. "Idelle stands to gain too."

CHAPTER XXXI

Leaning against the pillows in Lloyd's bed, Stillwell Kober closed his eyes. Four of his fobs lay on the bed beside him, and his Anna Held—the Anna Held that had come straight from the vest of Morton Mortenson, railroad magnate—smoothed the thumb and fingers of his right hand. That had been kind of Miss Balik, sending him some of his fobs. But somehow, they all, even the Anna Held, had lost Meaning.

Not that Mrs. Gurney, all along, had been anything but considerate. "Oh, Mr. Kober," she had kept repeating in those first days of quarantine, taking time even from her desperate anxieties, "if only you don't get it—maybe I can forgive myself then for letting you into this hardship."

"I know it wasn't your *intention,* Mrs. Gurney," he had assured her, but she had insisted on self-blame.

"If I'd even *dreamt* it was scarlet fever," she had kept on saying. "If I'd known——"

"You mustn't think of it," he had again assured her. "Now that the little girl is doing so nicely, I shall quite enjoy the respite from my burdens."

And for those few days, too, before he also grew ill, he almost had. He'd had none of his attacks at all. "About our business coming up," he had been able to say to Mr. Prenevost of Wells-West, by phone, "I'm afraid I've been caught in quarantine. If you could wait until——"

"Oh, think nothing of it, think nothing of it," Mr. Prenevost had said; Mr. Prenevost had quite hurried to say it. "Don't you try pushing that quarantine, Mr. Kober; you just wait until you're sure where you are." And so he had been almost easy; when he got out, he had thought, there'd be rents due, March rents, and surely this time some more tenants would pay. "Never give up, Stillwell." That had been his mother. "Like me, you'll always find the money somehow."

Sometimes he wondered if Mother knew what a nightmare "finding the money" had come to be for him. Mother had said she would know; Mother had said she would be with him always. "Promise me" —these had been Mother's last words—"that no matter what happens, you'll always hold on to the Properties."

He had tried; no one could say he hadn't tried; maybe (if only he could get over feeling his mother's outrage) he might get to thinking he had done what she said; he had secured the Properties forever. Odd, there had been times in the past six months when he had thought of Mrs. Gurney as almost unpleasant—oh, most admirable, of course, all that was confident, fashionable, handsome, a fine businesswoman. But her eyes were so queer, somehow—so light, so pale, like sword points. And she had sometimes come so *near*.

"I'll be lone and lorn tonight too, Mr. Kober," she had laughed on the afternoon that led to all this. "Lloyd's sleeping the night with a friend, and Idelle's in bed with a cold. You must come out to share my dinner." And he had gone, even if he had felt Mother pressing close and her disapproval deepening; with Mrs. Gurney it was always so much easier to say yes than no.

"Now we'll be comfortable," she had said when they got to the flat. "Make yourself cozy while I look in at Idelle." It had been a doctor who said brusquely, "Too bad I wasn't called earlier. Well, I'm afraid you'll be quarantined here too, Mr. Kober."

He'd had a chance, that night and the next, to see a Mrs. Gurney who dropped fashion and all airs, to be selfless, tireless, a nurse. Days later, when Idelle was almost well, but he had sickened, she had been that same selfless nurse for him.

"You aren't to think of a thing now, Mr. Kober. Just lie back and recover." In the next hours things had grown confusing; sometimes it had seemed that Mrs. Gurney turned into Mother, while Mother turned into Mrs. Gurney.

"Never let go of the Properties, Stillwell." That had been Mrs. Gurney speaking. "Never give up, Stillwell," Mrs. Gurney said, "I'll always find the money somehow," while Mother stood by with cold cloths for his forehead. "Just lie back now, Mr. Kober," Mother said, "just you lie back and recover; I'll be with you always." Even now, weeks after delirium and fever, muscles could jerk in his body whenever Mrs. Gurney spoke in tones capable and ordering, like Mother's.

"You're going to need care, Stillwell; you're going to need me." That had been the germ of Arrangement. "The doctor says at least six weeks in bed—not that your heart is any worse really, but that you need rest. I'll be getting out almost immediately, though—the quarantine should come off this week. And I've been thinking—well, there's one way I can make reparation. I feel so acquainted with you now, after the nursing, so intimate, I've learned how to care for you; it—well, I can't help seeing, Stillwell, how it would solve things for you if we should marry. I could take over things then—everything that's fallen so far behind—*no, lie quiet, Stillwell,* you're not to get bothered! It need never be anything but an Arrangement—a home and care for you, while I help with the properties. It's a—it's an opportunity for me to serve you, Stillwell, and I'll be very glad to do it."

She had smiled, with those light eyes. In the dead of night when he startled awake with that roaring in his ears, then through the roar and fright, through the tightness in his throat which was his mother's hand there, clutching, while his mother cried out, "No, no!" what he always saw, in the milky swirl, was the dew on Mrs. Gurney's pale eyelashes, and her eyes, and her smile.

"Thank you, Mrs. Gurney, thank you." Those were the words that had stumbled from his thickened tongue; he hadn't meant compliance, hadn't actually meant compliance, but when she said, "Oh, Mr. Kober, I'm so glad you see it that way," the difficulty of telling her she was wrong appeared insuperable. The bed had risen to hold his arms, his head, his legs that were so heavy, while she turned into a light, a dancing, vagrant light, a light cast from a moving mirror on a wall, now here, now there, now anywhere.

"So many things to do, Stillwell!" she had cried. "Thank heaven we have a phone!"

"You mustn't keep on calling me Mrs. Gurney," she another time had laughed. "You might try Frieda, or pretty soon it will be Mrs. Kober.

"Tomorrow now, Stillwell," she had said, "the doctor says the sign can come off tomorrow, and I've got everything fixed—minister, license, ring——"

Tomorrow had become this afternoon. "I do," he had said, this afternoon; that was all he had had to say. The nervous little hurried man, the minister, had hopped about. "Yes, yes, shall I stand here with you beside the bed, Mrs. Gurney, or would it be better if I stood at the foot?" Lloyd had come home mountainous in a new suit; Idelle too had walked in for a first time to stand with her brother near the bureau; Stella and Miss Rozzie Balik had been somewhere, and Mrs. Gurney, sitting by him on the bed, had held fast to his hand. The tears were on her lashes again, her eyes had been nothing but pinpricks of light, her whole person had been cloudy in pale blinking ruffles that whirled out to fill the room with motion.

"I do," Mrs. Gurney said, drowning Mother's cry of "No!" "I do," Mrs. Gurney insisted, so that the tones echoed over everything that followed, over Mrs. Gurney herself crying, "Goodness, is that all? Oh, Stillwell, I'm so happy," over people shaking his hand, over Mrs. Gurney later ordering, "There! Now, not another word! He'll have to rest."

After everyone had been out of the room for some minutes, Miss Balik had come tiptoeing back. "Here are a few of your fobs," Miss Balik had said. "I'll put them right by your hand." He hadn't opened his eyes, but his Anna Held had come toward him.

"My husband's fob—you'd like to buy my husband's watch fob?" Mrs. Mortenson had repeated after him, on the day, two years ago, when he had been ushered into the dark crowded room where she sat. "Why really—I haven't thought—I scarcely know—Anna, would you run up to that box of trinkets on the—now where did I leave it? It must be on the bureau in the grape room. Look there, Anna."

That was one thing he could never understand about the widows of great men; they never seemed to know about the fobs. Mortenson, Suetorious, Griggs, Rebedoux—the great men who had owned those names no longer walked the cities of the earth, but he had their fobs; he owned what they had owned, these symbols that had swung so kingly when they stepped. "Oh, I don't know, three dollars?" their wives asked when they were gone, or "Would five dollars be too much? I see there's a chip diamond." Wives didn't know the Meaning in the fobs, the Meaning in which he could forget the taxes and the interest and the payments and the court suits and the repairs and the tenants without money. The taxes and the interest and the payments and the court suits and the repairs and the tenants without money had been taken from him by Mrs. Gurney. "I do," he had said, and she had taken the nightmare. "There," the minister had told him, with that heartiness, that empty heartiness, that belonged to ministers, "you're in good hands, Mr. Kober."

But his mother sat upright in the chairless empty corner between wall and dresser, disapproving, and the watch fobs had no Power.

Within forty-eight hours after her marriage she had the truth.

At the beginning, during those hours when Idelle had been so limply ill, she had thought she could never recover from her fright. Later on, too, when Stillwell Kober had gotten so sick, it had seemed for a while as if the whole plan must blow up. She had gotten to see what his heart could do, all right; Stillwell Kober, in those days, had come very close to *going out*. Everything from then on, though, had been just as it should. No use putting the wedding off, she had determined; not with the way things were. And that part had gone without a hitch.

"I do hope this is going to make you happy, Frieda," Rozzie said at the wedding, accepting if doubtful. "You know I wish you everything that's best."

In the morning, too, when at last she had gotten to Balik's, things had been just as she wanted them—desk drawers still locked, stacks of mail still unopened, all according to the orders she had given by phone.

"You see, we did just as you said," Rozzie apologized. "It seemed a shame, when I'd have been so glad to do what I could. But since you insisted——"

"Of course I insisted!" Seating herself, setting about the stacking and rearranging which must be done first, Frieda had still been breathless from her reception. "No, no, now, girls!" she had had to cry. "Oh, girls, not *rice!* Yes, it's true—oh, thank you! I know it's surprising—I'm surprised myself. But really now, girls, I've work waiting——"

That sort of thing meant nothing, of course, but still it was exciting, and added its lift to her spirits, which already were soaring. Here, at last, she had *done it;* the last shoal seemed past. Idelle was all right, Lloyd hadn't gotten sick, Balik's was all right, and by virtue of wifehood she shared the ownership of flats, stores, houses—one hundred thousand dollars' worth. Even this house she sat in was now hers as it never had been before, not only in its thriving busyness, its profit, but also in its cherry-red and parquetry, its sweep, its staircase, its rich age. Any moment she chose, too, she could go about finding out what else she had gained—in money.

As she slit envelopes and stacked checks, her horizon for once seemed to lie clear of all clouds. "Pay to the order of Balik's, eighty dollars." "Pay to the order of Balik, Gowns, sixty-five dollars." There was nothing like having this money, this living money, in one's hands. "I'd have been so glad to do what I could," Rozzie said, and that was an offer to fill one's body with laughter—*wouldn't* Rozzie like to help with the books, though—wouldn't she, just! Oh, the world was funny, but by this time she had the key; this was how money got made, this was how clever people did things—they took chances and they got there.

"Isn't there something I could do for you this morning, Stillwell?" she had asked, early, at the foot of her new husband's bed, while she drew on her gloves.

"Oh no, nothing; nothing, I'm sure; nothing that can't wait." More gray than ever, from illness, Stillwell's long bony face had seemed to sink into the pillows, while one hand had fended outward, as if pushing something away.

Poor fool, business was just beyond him. There must be heaps of things to see to—rents to get in, especially. She could hardly wait. No doubt his accounts were in frightful order—what could you expect? What a pity he had changed clothes that first night, before he came to dinner! By this time she could have deciphered some of those dog-eared slips she so often had seen in his everyday suit.

Out on the corner that same afternoon, in a brisk March wind (banking was something that no one could do for her!) she kept her feet resolutely turned toward Balik's, but involuntarily her glance drew toward those buildings which were surely the crown of her new possessions—her stores. There they stood, hers to hold, to command, to derive profit from—Hobmark's Bakery, Stein's Meat Market, the Luxury Dry Cleaners, Sorge's Groceries, Nelson's Notions (that was the shop she once had had), and Vernick's Hardware. Once, not long ago, she would have been beatified by owing Hake's; now instead she owned these solid, brick, big-city shops.

Impulse growing strong, she broke step to go closer, to lay her hand almost tenderly upon the bricks beside the bakery window. Yours, that brick seemed to say, through its warmth. Yours to keep from now on. Yours to set you high among the true Possessors. And in addition to all this, she had twenty-two houses, Balik's, the flats——

Previously she had admonished herself that today must belong to Balik's; today, no matter how long it took, Balik business must be set in order, each debit and each credit posted, each due bill answered with its check, each room and each item of Rozzie's activities examined. But when, if ever, would she again have a day when temptation would be so blissful? Stillwell had his keys beneath his pillow with his wallet, and she hadn't liked to ask, not yet. But that was no real hindrance, not for her. With the flats so close, too——

"I've stopped for a few of Mr. Kober's things." This, aloofly spoken to small, monkey-wrinkled Reilly, the flat janitor, was all she needed for open sesame.

"Knock me over with a *feyther,* you could," Reilly said, rising from his rocker beside the furnace. "Mr. Kober sick, and then get married——" At the door which he so gallantly scrambled upward to unlock for her, Reilly showed tendencies toward staying around, but she was sure and casual, relieving him of mail which he bent to retrieve from the floor inside the door, pressing him backward to the hall.

"This is just fine—no, don't you bother. I'll bring the key to the basement when I'm done."

Ever since the day before, since the wedding, she had been full, pressed down, running over; this was the first time she had been alone. With mail in one hand and key in the other, she stood in a dim and dusty small living room rocking herself, hugging the mail and the key to her bosom with her handbag. Oh, this was life, this was living, this was what life should hold, just such moments as this. Platform rocker, horsehair, torn fringe, drab curtains (no, don't look at the desk, yet)— yes, the room was just as she had remembered from Mrs. Kober's day, when she had dragged herself down the long hall each month to pay rents. It was really a sin for people as well fixed as Kobers to keep themselves as dingy as this; Stillwell would find out that she wasn't *this* tight.

Stepping lightly, delicately, feeling the feverish flush of her cheeks and the rhythm of her blood, she moved forward to the center table, to lay upon it her purse and the mail. Regally, superciliously, she moved on from there—dining room, kitchen, and, beyond that, a stuffy dark bedroom that must have been Mrs. Kober's—dark high bed, dark high dresser, with a blue celluloid comb, brush and mirror upon it. Whew! The furniture in this place—the dust too—must date back fifty years!

First explorations thus swiftly accomplished, she moved back to the living room. There was another bedroom, off the living room, one that must be Stillwell's, but she would not go there just yet. Since this day was her day for temptation——

Slowly, stepping now in the significant, broken rhythm of a bride drawling her way up a church aisle, she let herself approach the high desk which stood between the two narrow windows of the living room's east wall. It was at that desk, years ago, that Mrs. Kober had sat while she wrote out her receipts. Of all places where Stillwell would most likely keep records, this desk would be it.

Thus lingeringly she reached her lodestone, and savoringly drew down the lid. As she had expected, the space inside was a hodgepodge; paper-back composition books, their leaves crumpled, were jammed in the cubbyholes, receipt books showed their thin black backs here, there, everywhere; envelopes, white, gray, brown—but all ragged and torn—lay heaped in the desk well, and over all drifted such slips as she had glimpsed in Stillwell's pockets—ragged small scraps that were dog-eared and scribbled. Putting out her hand by chance (no need to hurry this!), she retrieved one of the penciled scraps. "Bates," the note on it read in Stillwell's jagged hand, "Jan no—Dec, Nov? W fam way."

That took no brains to decipher. No January rent from Mr. Bates. Wife—or woman—in the family way. And Stillwell couldn't even remember whether the December and November rents had been paid! Had things been that bad? Heavens, to think of the way she had paid Balik rents, always up to the minute! Why, the old goofus might not even have noticed if she missed!

Indignation now coloring absorption, she took up other notes. "107 E. Bad r." That could mean anything—bad renter or bad roof. "Mon. See P. Ex ad?" It was irreverent, entirely irreverent, that business should be done in such a way. Burrowing deeper, coming up with one of the composition books—from Mrs. Kober's day—she riffled through that. Rents had been checked on then, all right! Casting aside envelopes, which could scarcely contain what she sought, she now began hunting in earnest. Somewhere in this disorder there must be some record of stocks and bonds bought, or perhaps a safe-deposit key, or a bankbook. Only more paper scraps, more old composition books, more old letters, more old receipt books appeared, however, and when the last cubbyhole had disgorged its contents she drew back with petulance pulling her eyebrows. Stillwell could hardly be so queer, could he, that he hid things from himself in his own house? Moving more rapidly now, she got herself to the one room she so far hadn't entered —a one-window cubicle off the living room, holding little except bed, dresser, rug and chair, but hung with velvet-covered boards upon whose black surfaces hundreds of fobs were pinned. Stillwell's room, unquestionably. Making sure, this time, that no scrap eluded her— how could it, in three suits and one dresser?—she hunted pockets and bureau drawers. Nothing, however, came up but more slips—"W— must call," and "See R—coal"—together with handkerchiefs, thread-tailed buttons, obituaries torn from newspapers, more fobs, a few clothes and pamphlets. Driven by this time to fury, she instituted a ransacking which would have done credit to Idelle and Lloyd: desk again, living room, dining room, Mrs. Kober's room. Curious things came to light, but not what she sought; it was not until she reached the kitchen—and the end of her rope—that she found anything even approaching what she loked for. There, in a half-emptied package of Blent's Coffee, her hand touched something that was flat, firm, small.

"So that's where he hid it!" she whispered fiercely; by this time she was in a frame of mind to be fierce. "Well, I beat him out!" But when she actually had the bag open and was looking within, she had a curious instant of pause. What she had found was a bankbook, all right, but, half submerged as it was in the brown ground grains, it some- how had a look of being not hidden but misplaced, as if, perhaps, Stillwell had been studying it while he ate, and then absently stuck it away in the measuring spoon's place. Her hand, however, shook as she plucked it forth; this, she thought, was a moment she might well remember, this moment of strong coffee scent stinging her nose, this moment when her hand closed on fortune.

A savings book. All I need's the last figure, her mind said while her fingers leafed through the book. This'll tell me how much he has now in money, her mind kept on saying, long after her eyes had snatched for the figure and found it.

For a while then, incredulous, her mind quit thinking anything whatsoever. Her body, too, with all its functions, seemed to halt in some kind of paralysis. One hundred and three dollars, sixty-four cents. *That* couldn't be what Stillwell Kober had in his bank; that couldn't be his cash. Even if he had other money—in investments— he could never keep himself this *close*.

Like moths at a screen, now, her eyes flew at earlier entries. De- posits in quite fair sums, sometimes—four hundred forty-eight, three hundred seventy-five, four hundred twenty. Withdrawals in sums even larger—one thousand sixty-two dollars and thirty-two cents. Eight hundred sixty-five. Right up to date, too. Seven deposits in early February, four withdrawals——

"This can't be it," her throat said, voiceless but repeating. "He's a miser, I'll bet. He's got money hidden right in this flat, in cash." But jubilance and exultance had slid from her; instead, a soreness like that of fright had begun to spread through her chest. She ran back to the living room, to the desk. Stillwell and his mother *couldn't* have spent all that income; where had they put it? Try wringing sense from me, the jumble in the desk seemed to jeer at her. Try, just try! Her hand went out to an old envelope—letters were the one thing she hadn't investigated. Then she remembered that if she wanted to read mail she had more recent letters at hand. Swinging around to the center table, she snatched up the top envelope and ripped it open.

"Dear Mr. Kober," the missive inside began, on a business sheet

imprinted with the name *Wells-West, Real Estate and Insurance.*
"Pursuant to our telephone conversation of February 17, I am happy
to inform you that after taking up the matter with Mrs. Archibald
D. Cummings, holder of the paper in question, we are able to extend
to you thirty days of grace in the matter of interest and payments——"

Words such as she was reading could have no real meaning. What
was it Stillwell once said? "No, no, Mrs. Gurney, I couldn't add more
to my worries." That had to mean—it *must* mean—that he didn't
believe in debt; it *couldn't* mean he was already so debt-ridden he
couldn't add more. But as, one after the other, she took up other envelopes and tore those open too, a great coldness gripped her.

"Dear Sir: We regret—payments on contract for deed——" "Dear
Sir: This is to remind you that interest in the sum of three hundred
and sixty-three dollars, forty-two cents——" "Dear Sir: Johnson and
Johnson, Fuel Dealers, having placed in our hands for collection a bill
in the sum of two hundred fifteen dollars, thirty-seven cents ($215.37)
we would very much appreciate——"

She could neither think nor feel, finally, but she could move, tucking letters and bankbook into her handbag, carefully locking the door
when she left.

CHAPTER XXXII

"Wake up." Again, as that morning, it was at the bed's
foot she stood; again, as that morning, the brass of the bedrail was
cold in her palms. Afternoon and evening had both gone while she
rummaged; when she got home it had been to a flat dark and quiet.
Gaunt, unconscious, shadowed on his bed, Stillwell Kober had slept
so deeply that when she jerked on the ceiling light he did not stir.
It was only when she had harshly repeated, "Wake up, I say!" that
the lids drew upward from his bemused dull eyes.

"What? What?" As he started he jerked covers closer, clutching
them tight to his ears—a gesture he usually used whenever she appeared in his room. "Oh, it's—you're here. I slept—I guess I slept.
The children—after they got home from school there was—it seemed
quite noisy. I intended——"

"Don't bother." What came from her was scarcely voice; words
had to be chipped from the ice block of her terrible discovery. "You
owe money. You owe lots of money."

"Money. Yes, yes. Money." He still was sleep-vague, casting out words helter-skelter, anxiously retreating, even if he didn't know from what. " 'You'll have to find money,' Mother said often; 'You'll have to find the money somewhere.' "

"Mortgaged. The stores are mortgaged, and the flats too. All the houses, even Balik's, I suppose." On her right hand above the bedrail something split; it might have been the skin of her hand, breaking, it might have been the leather of her glove. *Why didn't you tell me? Didn't you think I should know?*

"I don't—I don't——" He was more awake now, still bewildered, but trying to meet her with reply. "Surely my troubles, the troubles of which I've so often spoken——"

Fury could flow, it could have rhythm, it could pulse like her blood. This was what he thought he could do, was it; he thought he could throw it all back at her, he thought he could tell her it was all her own mistake. In that moment, looking at him, she knew what he from then on must be to her. He was *worse* than that drummer, of whom she had so quickly freed herself. He was Harry, dead. All that she had hated most in Gurneys, all Gurney helplessness, all Gurney fecklessness, their maddening soft-bellied lack of practicality, their inability to understand, to go along—all Gurney qualities from which she had with such writhing freed herself, she had with Stillwell Kober deliberately taken back.

"How much?" Once more she forced out sound. "For how much are you mortgaged?"

"How much? For how much, altogether? Why, that would take figuring." Actually brightening, as if her last question had put the whole matter upon an objective basis, he launched into more rapid speech. "For the exact amount I expect you'd have to see Prenevost —that's Mr. Prenevost of Wells-West. 'You can depend on Prenevost,' Mother said, often. 'One man you can depend on for the facts is Prenevost.' "

He didn't even know.

Detaching her hand with effort from the footrail, she got herself from the room.

Whew, Mr. Prenevost breathed, when his new client at last turned her back, to sweep off down the long aisle of desk. Whew and hell's blazes too. He had, almost, whistled when she walked in; old Kober married, and to a whiz-bang like this! Well, she had gotten what she came for, all right; he had handed it straight.

"All debts?" he had repeated after her, with care; in this case, he had seen, he had better use care. "Certainly, Mrs. Kober, it's right here at my finger tips. Yes, this second page, here. One hundred and two thousand four hundred and forty-eight dollars, sixty-two cents. That's the sum. Not paper held by Wells-West—you understand that, Mrs. Kober, but by clients. It's more than you could borrow on that property today, Mrs. Kober, I'll make no secret of that. I've advised Mr. Kober to let some of these properties go——"

"Suppose I—suppose we *did* sell," she had interrupted then, with eyes haggard—but no more than haggard—beneath the sweep of her fashionable hat. Oh, she had looked to make a good thing of Kober, no doubt of that, and she was taking what she heard hard, but she wasn't letting it show through her eyes. Rather curious eyes she had, too, when you came to notice—pale and narrow, set under light brows; they seemed to slide away from you, somehow. "Suppose we did sell," she had gone on to say, considering and businesslike, with her shoulders high in their fashionable furs, and her gloved hands steady on the fashionable handbag in her lap, "how much would we be apt to realize?"

"Well now, that's a different story," he had answered with the same care as before. "I'd have to figure that. The flats—well, income three-thirty per month, when you get it, that's thirty-nine hundred sixty dollars per year. You might get seventeen thousand for the flats—I'm not saying you *would,* mind, I'm saying you might. Then the stores and the houses——"

Ninety-six thousand. A little more, a little less. That had been the second figure he had given her, to stack against the first. He had known all along what it was, but there had been a kind of pleasure in making her sit while he figured.

"Yes, I'm afraid that's the story," he had concluded for her. "In debt for more than they're worth. If you and Mr. Kober would like to—ah—liquidate some of this, I'll be glad to handle the details. You could scarcely, I think, find a better buyer's list than ours. Or if you decide to hold on, well——" He had let humor in here, with a wave of his hand. "No one will try harder than we to get you accommodated. It must be a full twenty years now" (how much of this did she know?) "that I've handled the Kober accounts; a remarkable woman, your late mother-in-law. Buy at a bargain—and she had a shrewd eye for houses—mortgage heavily and buy again; that was her system; to start with I don't think she had a thousand dollars. She spread herself thin, no one told her that more often than I did, but she built up this whole list of holdings, and while she lived she carried it off."

Yes, and isn't it a pity she didn't carry it with her when she went; isn't it a pity she had to leave it behind her to trap and gull me— this was the bitterness behind the light eyes, but no tremor moved the mouth or the hands, or the crossed ankles cased in fine black silk.

"What I probably need most right now"—this was what she said aloud—"before I decide anything at all, is to know how much there's to pay off immediately."

Eleven thousand six hundred dollars, eighty-two cents. That was the final figure he gave her. Past due, he noted, but of course in a case like this there'd be grace. Odd, for most women he might have been sorry, but not for this one. She wasn't asking his sympathy. Almost you had to admire her, as she rose from her chair; anyone who had taken what she had taken, in the way she was taking it——

"I'll let you know," she said, head high. "You can expect to hear from me."

Catching her toe in the sill, hugging herself tight against the terrible attack, breathing, as soon as she was outside, in short pain-driven gasps, she got herself away from Wells-West.

Ninety-six thousand, against more than that owed. Oh, she hadn't made any least bid for pity, not from that crease-eyed and fat little ape she had left; the only attitude bearable from Mr. Prenevost would be that of entire respect. "You know and I know"—that was what those too well versed eyes had said. "You know and I know. But we'll both pretend, won't we?" Eleven thousand six hundred dollars to be paid off immediately. Almost the whole of what she took, in profit, from a whole profitable year at Balik's. There had been other times of her life that she had lived and relived; she had stood on the balcony, her back against coats, while Mr. Hake, turning, had streaked ceilingward in tall black fire. "Ever think how easy it is to throw this stuff around, Miss Schlempke?" he had asked. "Did you ever think it might someday be yours?" The money had fallen as she knelt, the money had yielded its soft crumpled power to her hands, but then it had gone; she had stood instead in a study, where brown velours wrapped her in soft palling folds. "Madam, I do not know by what means you seduced my son Harry into marriage, but I will delineate for you, madam, the exact state of my finances." Now, with those other times, there would have to be this one. Not yesterday, when she had found out, but today when she had sat on a chair in an echoing long room like a railroad station, and Mr. Prenevost (each oil drop of his fatness knowing) had told her.

"I'm just as well off as I was before I got married. I can divorce that old fraud like I did that drummer. I can kick him out. His whole pile of trouble can go with him." As she walked (stumbling onward by instinct) she knew this as her answer. No one with any common sense could act otherwise. When she reached the corner of Center Street and the Parade, she did not lift her eyes toward the stores, and a few feet farther on, in front of Balik's, she did not, at first, allow herself to glance toward the flats. But then, turning, she forced herself to look at them, full. More than anything else, the flats were debt-ridden; so smothered in debt, indeed, that they could be said to be already gone. Yet as her gaze touched the heavy red stones, as it once more took in the gables of the wide black roof, the dignified rows of tall windows, the huge cement pillars of the entrance, then each stone, each gable, each pillar was sensible as being somehow allied to her. For months now she had looked across at those flats with possession, and giving them up was like giving up a segment of her nerve-centered flesh.

She could turn away, to enter Balik's, but what remained most closely with her was that on which she turned her back. Balik's she could save, if it came to that; and the stores too—if she decided to hold onto old Kober. She had money enough for that. *But that isn't what I planned!* Denial came from the very scurry and laughter of the warmth she entered, denial came from the glide of her hand on the gleaming dark stair rail, from the welcome of her office door. What she still wanted was *it all*, the dream she had dreamed, the fulfillment, the possession of the cool hundred thousand.

At the mirror, to which she immediately walked, she stood to look on at her face—cool, handsome, assured, the light-catching eyes slightly tired but sure, the small mouth well controlled. *She* pay out a hundred and two thousand for something worth at best ninety-six? Not if she knew herself.

Since a little was always better than nothing, she began, that afternoon, making some efforts to get in rents. On the matter of back rents, she soon found, she was almost entirely helpless; Stillwell's scraps of record were so unintelligible as to mean nothing, and he himself was of little more use. "Millward?" he would answer, if she asked. "It seems—yes, I do seem to remember that they paid in February—or was that December? If you asked Mrs. Millward, I'm sure she would know." The tenants, naturally, were completely untrustworthy. "Receipts? Why, we never asked for a receipt from Mr. Kober; we knew we could *trust* Mr. Kober."

All she could do, as she came to accept with frustrated resignation, was to wring out the March rents, with only the most scattered additions. One thousand and seventy-three dollars—this was the sum that, during eight days, she was able to take in. A sum of exquisite cruelty, so small it was not a tenth, even, of what immediately was needed, so large it was heart-wrenching to think this was the one time she might garner it. Waiting for it were not only the hungry mortgagors, but also other bills that had cropped up by dozens. Instead of satisfying any of them, however, she kept the money for several days in a desk drawer, where it could be looked at and counted. Fruition, but not hers to keep.

Everything needn't go, she again reminded herself. I could always keep a part. But days dragged by, and she came to no decision.

If there was one satisfaction to be wrung from the wretched state of affairs in which she now found herself, it was that Stillwell Kober no longer need be handled with consideration or restraint.

"Rackets? Of course they make rackets," she could reply coldly if Stillwell complained. "Why shouldn't they play the victrola? Why shouldn't they tussle? This room you are in, I might remind you, is Lloyd's room, and if my children want to run in here, that should be all right."

Ready and waiting to spring out at a touch had been distaste for him so great it approached loathing. From as far as the doorsill the effluvium of his being Stillwell Kober could swell out to sicken her; when she was forced to be near him, when she handed him a dinner tray or helped Stella change the linen of his bed, her fingers curled back from the contacts, and the skin of her neck prickled as with the foot passage of a thousand fleas.

Against this loathing, however, much as she wished to, she also shrank from throwing him out; the marriage had been too public. If she rid herself of him, if she got an annulment or divorce, then she was not only cutting herself from the slight hold she still had over her buildings (for that, in spite of all, was what they remained) but she would also then betray before the world her hideous mistake. She was no longer an obscure clerk; she was a newsworthy figure, the owner of a business. DRESSMAKER ASKS UNSTITCHING, the newspapers might say. FINDS HUSBAND IS WITHOUT THE GOODS. Under orders from the doctor, too, a doctor who insisted on invalid's care, she had to take suggested courses—a visiting nurse daily, chicken, oranges, cream, fresh eggs, a good supply of his medicines always at hand. Nothing, however, stood in the way of flashing out her displeasures and contempts.

"I can't understand how any human being could get his affairs in a mess such as yours are in," she could tell him. "It must make your mother happy, knowing how you've wrecked everything she left."

As these whiplashings grew open, Stella, Lloyd and Idelle quickly caught on. "Oh, go fry your eggs!" Stella could cry from the kitchen when the invalid's bell rang. "What if I did lose one of your old fobs?" Lloyd could taunt. "You aren't so much around here."

To this change of treatment the man in the bed at first opposed only feeble irrecognitions and retreats. "Business—yes, business is something for which I never have been suited," he would reply miserably to Frieda. "Usually at this time of year, though, things pick up——"

Nothing she could say, no facts she could sling against him, could make him confront his financial ruin. "It can't be that bad, surely," he would deny. And at last, if pushed too far, he would come up with one of his attacks, or else with that inherited circumlocution which more than any other drove Frieda to frenzy: "I'm sure you'll find the money someway."

After some days, however, his tactics changed. "I can see I'm a burden to you here," he offered nervously one night to Frieda. "It would be better, much better, I think, if I got to a hospital——"

"And who do you think would cough up all *that* money?" Frieda ground out this crafty tendril with one stamp of her foot, but the reaching continued.

"It would be better for everyone concerned, I'm sure"—no later than the next night he was trying again—"if now that I'm better I returned to my flat. The nurse could come there once a day——"

"Oh, that would look beautiful, that would look fine!" Frieda was suffering, that day, some of her worst routs over back rents, and couldn't have let him get anything he wanted even if it had been something she also wanted. "*You* haven't any flat any more; I threw your junk out to make room for a renter."

"But I have to go somewhere!" he pleaded, sweating and trembling, his great eyes pushing out from his face in his effort. "I can't stay here to be a burden." This last he repeated so often that Frieda could do no less than snap it off.

"Burden—of course you're a burden. You're one now and as far as I can see you'll always be one."

Temporarily this shut him up, but it too wrote no finale. Next day, while she was at Balik's, she got an excited call from Stella— Stillwell Kober was out of bed, trying to get dressed.

"That——!" Fury had to be held to beneath-breath cursing while

she was being rushed home by expensive cab. "This——!" Impreca-
tion had again to be silent while, aided only by Stella and an in-
quisitive housewife from downstairs, she struggled to get the helpless man from the floor where he had fallen back to his bed before
the doctor got there. Stella—"There'll be an extra dollar for you
this week, Stella, you did exactly right in calling me before you did
anything else"—passed things off in the right light: "Just all of a
sudden he sat up and said he was going," so that there was nothing
to suffer from the doctor beyond a terse "You'll see this doesn't happen again, Mrs. Kober." But "That——!" she continued to breathe
voicelessly, while this reproof was being administered. The time
came at last, however, when disapproval could be vocal.

"Now are you satisfied?" she asked when the first flow was over.
"Getting me home from the office, upsetting the whole house, getting me charged up with another call from that damned doctor,
nearly killing yourself—can't you let well enough alone? Maybe now
you can do what you're told. Maybe now you've learned your lesson."

And for a while, at least, it seemed he had. Patently, after this
abortive effort, he labored instead at making a doleful best of things.

"It's not strange to me in the least that business should worry
you." At night he apologized to Frieda for her tempers. "I sometimes myself was so beset I didn't know where to turn." At Lloyd
and Idelle he attempted smiling—"So much youth, so much vigor.
I can see that when I get a bit stronger I'll quite look forward to the
hours after school."

Toward Stella his approaches were not, to begin with, so open.
Not until a week end did Frieda grow aware of the increased good
humor, or at least the decrease of rancor, in Stella's attendance.
"Just a pitcher of water, if you would, Miss Stella." Or "That window shade—if it could be pulled down——" One Saturday afternoon, however, when she came home to smell pipe tobacco in her
husband's room, and see three fresh newspapers on his bed, she told
herself she could be no longer hoodwinked.

"You've been getting tips from him, that's what's been going on,"
she accused Stella. "And this afternoon you've let that janitor,
Reilly, in here behind my back. Any little change he has in his wallet
can't last long, Stella; you might remember *I'm* the one who pays."

Even after the instant defection of Stella, however, the master of
the household struggled to maintain his mournful false good cheer.
"The doctor said today that I might be propped up a bit higher."
To Frieda he reported, as if she must be glad of it, any slight progress
he made. And one night she came home to find him quietly excited.

"I see here by tonight's paper that Hanson Bell has died—that's Hanson Bell who founded all the flour mills. I wonder if he wore a watch fob. One of the first things I must do when I can get around is go to see his widow. That would be an admirable piece for my collection, an admirable piece."

Toward evidences of returning strength Frieda was helpless to be anything but ungracious. "Well, that's something," or "It goes slow enough, I must say." But this last, this green shoot of return toward an old gratification, this was something she could scotch at once.

"Those watch fobs. That's one ridiculous expenditure I can put a stop to. There won't be any more money spent on anything as silly as watch fobs."

Idelle that night breathed evenly, lightly, in complete soft sleep. Idelle kept to her side of the bed in unusual quiet. But the scenes jerking across the lit screens of Frieda's inner eyelids were too emotion-fraught to let her be anything but restless. Those basement stairs in the flats, down which she had tripped to find Reilly— those stairs were hardwood, *varnished,* and the basement itself was back-plastered. That little yellow house on Euclid—she had gotten from a small boy there one slight slip about back rents owing, and now that house stood spruce in new paint and repairing, with not one cent spent by her. A tenant who was a carpenter could be made to yield more than one kind of return. Those more suburban houses out on Lakeway, too—it was hard to erase the picture of those houses from one's mind, garbed as they were now in a haze of April green. All the halls at the flats were in terrible need of replastering, and there was that crack in the façade of the hardware store——

So much that was too sweet for giving up, so much that needed doing. One hundred and two thousand dollars, every penny of which, if it was to come from anywhere, must come from herself. She could no more set her hand to it than she could give it up, and yet, as she well knew, the time for decision was almost gone. Fifteen days of grace was what Mr. Prenevost had given her; those fifteen days were now gone, and four more too. Lenience such as that couldn't go on forever.

Once before—years ago, in West Haven, when she had had to decide between her children and the big move to Meridian—she had let time give her answer. Then too she had felt her weakness; she had lain still, just as she was lying now, to let what she most wanted slide out of her hands.

Not only Idelle's breathing, but her own too could be heard—a breathing heavier than Idelle's, flowing through deeper channels. She and Idelle were two separate, different beings. Resolutely, since Harry's death, she had thrust aside any least feeling of loneliness, but on this night, bitterly, she felt her solitude. Idelle took no part in her struggles or problems. Idelle was a taker—just that, nothing more.

And then, beyond this other life beside hers in the bed, she had to remind herself of that other even more separate and disparate life in the house, that of the man she had married. The one really merciful fact of her existence was that he could give himself his own tablets; she needn't *sleep* near him. But again, as so often at night, he was inquiet, and again, as so often, she had to lie hearing and hating the creaks of his bed, the slide of his bedclothes, the turns of his body, the harsh rasps that were like stifled groans. Tonight, it seemed, these emanations were at once less and greater; the heavings of his weight upon the bed seemed to emerge as more covert but more purposed; his breathing, surely, was lighter—seemed at times, indeed, almost to vanish, until it broke forth again in sharp stabbing gasps.

He can't be trying anything *again,* she assured herself crossly. But the very wall she faced might have been in motion, advancing and withdrawing with the pulse of effort from the other room.

What if he *is* up—what if he is trying to make a break again— why should I care? she also asked herself, but at the same time she was sliding quietly out of bed, fumbling for her slippers and kimono. Then abruptly she was running, whirling in her husband's room to catch the light cord, once more running.

There had been one more means by which the man in the bed could escape her, and he was trying to take it. When light flooded the room he sat close against the bedhead, hands behind his neck and frantically working, huge eyes staring in disordered wild despair. Before she could reach him he slumped, head lolling sideward, hands falling open to the counterpane, neck caught in a strip of sheeting knotted to the headrail.

"Don't you ever try anything like that on me again. Don't you ever dare try, or I'll kill you."

This, senselessly yet with deep meaning, was what she rasped as she worked over him, wrenching the sheet strip from the headrail, loosening it, easing him flat, chafing his neck and his wrists, forcing tablets between his blue lips, lifting her own head to cry out for help, but then stifling outcry before it was made; no one, not Stella, not

the children, not the doctor—*more than anyone else, not the doctor!*
—could know of this attempt. She alone—with him—must bear the
knowledge.

Beneath her hands Stillwell Kober seemed, in spite of her, to be
succeeding in his final prodigality. No movements crossed the
sunken and inert gray face, the eyelids remained closed, the breast
neither raised nor lowered. I may *have* to get someone, it may *have*
to come out, she thought with panic, performing acts which by then
were compulsive. When his hands and feet, however, in spite of
other stigmata of lifelessness, continued damply temperate, when
her ear caught at last beneath his shirt the feebled beating of a torpid and unwilling heart, she relaxed. It was not death, not even one
of his attacks that held Stillwell Kober, but only a profound acceptance of defeat.

CHAPTER XXXIII

At the time, while she was stepping grimly back, while
she was saying, "So, you're not dead. Well, just don't try anything
like that any more," while vigorously she performed a few last acts of
succor and flounced back to her bed, she would have said that this
occurrence had no bearing on her other problems, that it could not
in any way affect her decisions.

I rather think that takes care of *that,* was her conclusion. I rather
think he won't be trying that—or anything else, either—any more.

But for the first time since her discovery of the financial quagmire
into which she had thrust herself, she for the rest of that night slept
deeply and in peace, and in the morning, try as she would to suppress it, she could not keep down a feeling of buoyancy. When I think
of what I'm up against, she reminded herself, but her spirits would
not down. At a downtown stop she stepped from the trolley and
tripped off to that public library which once before had proved such
a help, and from there, still more invigorated, she a few hours later
made for the offices of Wells-West.

"I notice your Mrs. Cummings isn't too quick about foreclosing her
mortgage on our flats," she told Mr. Prenevost flatly. No need for
concealment in this visit; no reason now why she could not be forthright! "I wonder—just suppose you went to that Mrs. Cummings
and told her you had a buyer who'd be willing to take that mortgage

off her hands—at a discount, of course. I wonder if she wouldn't take you up."

Prenevost's pigeon breast arose jerkily. "I could never do a thing like that, Mrs. Kober; this is an ethical firm." But the quirk of knowledge was erased from Mr. Prenevost's fat lips. "In the interest of Mrs. Cummings we could scarcely——"

"What's wrong? I don't own those flats, my husband does. *Tell* Mrs. Cummings, if it makes you feel better, that I'm the one wants to buy; maybe she'll understand a wife wanting to help her husband. Of course, if you'd rather I took it to some other agent——"

No need to supply, for Mr. Prenevost, what she left unsaid. Leaving Wells-West was a little different, this trip, than it had been the first time; she could laugh shortly, this time, walking away. Prenevost would know from now on with whom he was dealing. Fifteen thousand—maybe eighteen—was the lowest she could hope to get by with, for all three mortgages on the flats; she'd have to borrow, again, at the bank. But she wasn't worried, not actually. She'd come out.

Moving through sunny streets on feet which kept up an able and impatient rhythm, she walked all the way to her corner. Sight of the stores caused no injury this time; there could be no hurt in taking to one's eyes and nose those six façades with all their stigmata of profit —the tumbled dirty clothes visible through the dry cleaner's window, the moldy steam from his pressing room, the flies hungering about the butcher's door, the too sweet scent of fresh bread mingled with the scent of vegetable refuse from the grocer's. And when she went on from there, to stand before the flats, she knew a sudden need to draw them too even closer than they had been. Crossing the street, she first lingeringly stood within the tiled vestibule, and then in the hallway; carpets underfoot were heavy with tracked mire, walls and ceilings showed strata of grime, but even dirt, on this day, was something to hold lovingly. In an untenanted basement she laid fingers on the handle of the fire door and carefully drew it open; the furnace today held no more than a red inner heart of heat beneath cautious banking—not too much, just enough, for April chill. Warmth, the true close warmth of fire, reached out to fold her in, one with itself; she, like fire, was become this building's heart.

Taking herself shortly from this union, turning—and resolutely— toward Balik's (so *much* to be done!), she felt that what held her now was dedication. From the first, she had never *really* thought of letting her dream go; that was why she had collected rents, that was why she had maneuvered Mr. Finch into repainting and repairing. Her flats, her stores, her Balik's and her houses—there wasn't one she would give up, not one, even if this meant that, with them, she must keep Stillwell Kober too.

Oh, she knew what the next years must be—scrimped, harried, deprived of those little satisfactions she had been promising herself—a motorcar, a good-size diamond or two, a sealskin coat. She would have to worry, borrow, stave off, snatch from Peter to pay Paul. But she was the one to do it; already she had plans. Reilly and Hannagan, for instance, would both be fired; one able man could look after all the stores, the flats, and—why not?—Balik's too. In spite of what she had said to Stillwell, the Kober flat still stood as he had left it, but it wouldn't much longer. Repairs and redecoration couldn't be afforded, but she would afford them—she too would have a system. Improve, get better tenants——

At the bottom step of Balik's she turned to sweep a final glance over her buildings, and as she did so the swift backwash of repudiation hit her—*why* must she go through all this trouble? All she had asked of life, back there at the beginning, was so little; just enough for a few clothes. Just one man, Palmer. Instead, what had she gotten? Gurneys, and the misery of Harry, and the loss of Hake's. That was the way the world went, ever and forever. Yes, she had won to Balik's; she had that much secure. It was all Stillwell Kober's fault that she stood in her present position.

That, though, like so much else, was behind her. Until she had a firmer grip on what she wanted, no one and nothing should break in upon the concentration of her efforts.

And for the next three years, at those rare times when she came up for air, she could tell herself that she was holding singly to her purpose.

But on a morning in March 1913, sitting at her desk in Balik's, she rested her chin for a moment, smiling, upon the telephone whose receiver she had just hung up, and then, yawning, lay back to raise and lower her arms in long sweeping arcs, with the sensuous slow lift and fall of a moth unfolding just-born wings.

As she stretched, her mind too curled and uncurled. "Well, I got it for you," Mr. Prenevost had just let her know. "They were pretty sore about the price you offered, but they took it."

One more mortgage, then, had fallen to her, and at a bargain—she hadn't really thought that price of hers could stand. Not that she was in the clear yet—not by any means; she still had a good sixty thousand to go. But the heaviest woods were behind her; right now, if they had to, the Kober properties could pay their own way.

It wasn't alone achievement, however—not the restoration of security, not the happy consciousness of work well done, which was making her stretch and smile. Two weeks earlier, running her forefinger down a listing in the yellow section of a just-issued phone book, her eyes had slid to a sudden pause. There, in plain black type, had stood a name which had seemed to jump not from the page but from the past.

"Hake, Palmer, building and lumber, 4th and Exchange—6093."

After the moment of incredulous discovery, after her head had snapped forward and her fingernail dug into the page, she had actually heard words, long-forgotten words.

"You take a smart young man, a pusher—by the time he's forty there isn't any reason why he can't cover half the state—maybe even have a big yard in Meridian." Across more than twenty years the voice came, bringing not the Palmer who so bitterly had fought with her over the store, not the Palmer who so ruthlessly had thrown her aside for Cecilia, but the boy she terribly had wanted. Here he must be, this long time later, not bankrupt as she had half expected, but achieving at least a part of his ambition.

Well, good for Palmer. Under the many succeeding layers of struggle and success, old hurts, she found, no longer burned. Instead, fend them off as she would, came teasing thoughts of the possibilities there might be in this for mischief and excitement. It need be no concern of Palmer's that at home she had a dull invalid husband flapping about on slippered and blundering feet. What would be fun would be to have Palmer see *her,* to let him know all that she had become.

Rising in her fluid self-assurance, rising in her abundant strength, she stepped across to the pier glass which, now they had a newer and grander mirror downstairs, she had reclaimed as her own. During this past year, with pressure lessening, she had once more begun expanding.

"You keep on this way, Mrs. Kober, and I'm going to have to put you into stylish stouts," her corset clerk at Frigman's (whatever there was between herself and Frigman, naturally she hadn't quit shopping at the town's best store) had worried. Frieda too, seeing herself in an unflattering mirror, stockings falling and flesh bulging, had been a little disquieted.

"How do you expect to fit me in a cheap garment like this?" she had asked sharply. "If you haven't anything better say so—I can go to Westermarck's!" And sure enough, in another and more costly garment, stockings once more tautly gartered, she had been able to view herself with accustomed complacency.

I'd like to know who, over thirty-five, has a better figure, she assured herself now. Or more style. I'd like to see anyone doing the work I do, sitting all day at a desk as I sit——

No, she could certainly think, seeing the rich waves of hair pulled loose and drawn into a backward-pointing cone of coils and twists (none of it false, either!), seeing her new gown with its lace and chiffon bosom, its satin shackling at the knees, no, you'd look awhile, as far as Lillian Russell, maybe, before you found anyone to come up to her.

Out on the sidewalk, later, taking a route she many times during the past fortnight had taken, telling herself that this time things would be no different—actually she wouldn't, no, of course she *couldn't* go in at the yard and ask for Palmer—she yet knew from the bubbles bursting in her arteries that this was the day she would venture.

Trolleys, every few minutes, clanged hints of their swifter modes of progress, ice kept her teetering for balance, March wind plastered her dolman to her back and ruffled its thick swaddling bands of lynx, but she had no desire that her walk be less or faster; anticipation, she well knew, might be the high point of adventure. All too likely, when she actually saw Palmer, what she was chancing would fall flat; Palmer might by this time be as fat as Mr. Prenevost, or he might—worse yet —have shriveled; Palmer might be entirely bald; Palmer might someway—horrors!—have lost fingers or a hand; Palmer in all likelihood— oh, certainly, a man like Palmer would have married again. And anyway, what difference could that make? No use fooling herself that there was no such drag on her neck as Stillwell Kober! The most she'd get out of it, undoubtedly, was this tickle of not knowing.

When Palmer actually stepped out before her, however, when, after her genteel accosting of a passing workman who answered, "Mr. Hake? You'll find him around here somewheres, I guess," she had picked her way delicately amid stacked and unstacked lumber to be in turn accosted, and this time by Palmer, "Anything I can do for you, ma'am?" she knew that nothing she had anticipated could approach the shock of meeting.

"Oh." The exclamation wrung from her could be no more than a gasp. "I didn't see you come from *anywhere!*"

"Well, I came from right there behind that stack of lumber—didn't know anyone was around myself." The reply was genial. Palmer did not, as she at once saw, recognize her; he merely stood pleasant and ready, after a second and more appreciative glance pulling off his dark woolen cap to turn the ear flaps up and resettle the headgear at a smarter angle on his head, drawing off a mitten to find a handkerchief and blow his nose. "Fellow gets cold, out all day on a day like this," he went on conversationally. "Darn hard freeze we had last night."

"Why," Frieda said, "you've kept your hair."

Whatever she had meant to say, it wasn't this; whatever she had meant to feel, it wasn't this warm salty gush of tenderness and softness, which made her reach irresistibly forward to touch his arm. Palmer when she had seen him last had looked older and heavier than in his first youth; Palmer again was older, and certainly he had lost no weight, but curiously he looked not as old as she remembered, and flesh was hard and solid on his square-set bones. He had never been much taller than she; she remembered that now; the skin of his face was blue-red, toughened, leathered by exposure to all weathers, his rough clothing—mackinaw, thick black pants tucked into gum boots—was no better than that of his helper, his glance had the slow abeyant caution of a man who expects at any moment to start sparring, a man who has taken many beatings but always gotten back upon two stubborn feet. About him also, though, was more than a hint of the old Palmer. He swaggered when he changed his cap; he knew a woman when he saw one.

Immediately, at her feeling and familiar words, he drew back, covering himself, reserved. Geniality remained about a smiling mouth, but blue eyes buttonholed for sharper focus. And then as he looked more fully at her face, she saw in him too the impact of recognition.

"Frieda. Frieda Schlempke. Mrs. Gurney." Startled, impressed by her person, he could only flounder. "I didn't expect—naturally I heard you were here in Meridian, but I never thought—it's been so long since——"

"So long since you remembered I existed." Reproach might well have come in here, and rancor, but they didn't; behind her smile lay tears. Yet self-possession was returning, and with it quickness to seize an advantage; Palmer, all too obviously, couldn't be left to take matters in his own hands.

"I didn't come here, though, to bring up old times; I came because I've some carpentering I need doing, and when I saw your name in the phone book—well"—she laughed here, lightly, a little sadly, to indicate the maturing of years—"we're old enough by now, I guess, to know bygones are gone. If you'd be interested in the work——"

"I'm always interested in work." He couldn't entirely turn from her, but some such impulse struggled behind his reluctance. You didn't come here offering me gifts on a silver platter, his glance judged. Not after what's happened between us.

"What is it they call those things, now—a garage, isn't it? That's what I need, one of those. To hold a motorcar. Some people who rent a house of mine have bought one." Frank talkativeness of this kind, she had learned from Rozzie, could be most disarming. "I warn you, Mr. Hake, I'm a close dealer, but if you'd want to estimate——"

"I'd have to see the place——"

"Oh, naturally; I expected that; the address is 628 East Twenty-second. I'd want to know everything exactly—size of building, grade of lumber, grade of millwork, roofing, what paint—here's more warning, if you need it; I'm a good businesswoman."

"You needn't warn me." His tone remained dry and wary; only after an unfilled moment in which she stood poised, obviously in her turn waiting with brows lifted, did he in any way come round. "I've taken on a lot of work already, but I might see about it. I could call you on Friday."

"That'll be fine. Do that." After such partial and grudged compliance she could only draw off quickly, turning after no more than a brief, bright smile and nod, to hurry herself from his premises.

For once, as she minced at her best gait away, she felt constrained by the hobble of her skirt; it would have been good, for once, to step fast and freely. So much that might have been said had escaped her; of all the chords between herself and Palmer scarcely one had been touched. Magnanimously she had shown herself forgiving and forgetting, while he had kept himself in a position where, simply by saying, "I've got too much work already," he could set between them all the distance of the past. During an interchange which only emerged as more fumbling and unmanaged the farther she got from it, she hadn't even found out if he had remarried.

Yet in spite of all this, in spite of the ineptness of which she must accuse herself, she had to realize she was affected as she had never expected to be. Back at her office she took up the monthly balancing of the Balik books, but on this occasion not even the computation of profit could hold her. Figures which should have stood out clearly, hard blue against hard white, blurred off into a blank vague mist in which she sat dimly smiling. I saw him. He remembered. And he'll have to call.

To shake herself from such vaporing she reminded herself, sharply, that any goal she had with Palmer—if she had a goal there, which she hadn't—could never for a moment weigh against her real ambitions. If Palmer wouldn't put up her garage, someone else would; she didn't *need* him. Yet the instant she slacked work he again possessed her—his hair which, rougher, maybe, and perhaps a little dulled from its bright brown, was yet as thick as it had ever been, the settled, deliberate movements of his body, the expressions, genial or suspicious, of his covert, rather small blue eyes, the impression he gave of unused and contained vigor.

At night, when these obsessions clung even more closely, she grew impatient. I'm being ridiculous! All work and no play, that's my trouble. I need to get out with *men*.

"Say, Mrs. Kober, you and I ought to step out some evening." From wholesalers' salesmen such invitations were so routine that she scarcely any longer heard them. Next day, however, at an inexpectant proffer, she accepted promptly.

"Why not? How about tonight?"

"Why say, that's snappy of you, Mrs. Kober; we could—dinner, maybe, and a show. I hope I can show you a good time, Mrs. Kober; I hope you won't be sorry you spent the time."

An onset as stammering as this was a little unpromising and the man—a widely jowled young Swiss with froglike, hopeful eyes—was no one to whom she could ever be particularly drawn, but the café she selected was one mentioned often by her younger clients, and in it, as she saw with satisfaction when she reached it, appeared exactly those V-back trailing gowns, those floor-long tablecloths, those lilac-shaded lights, which proved the place really right. Through dinner she flirted gaily and with concentration, at the Essenay two-reeler (*Little Mary*) she let her knee stay within exploring distance, and on the way home, in a borrowed motorcar, and after a fair quantity of drinks, she lent herself graciously to being snuggled.

All in all, it was an evening from which she should have emerged relaxed and refreshed, aberrant impulses for the time being over. "You know, a woman like you, Mrs. Kober, you have no idea what a man might mean to you, Mrs. Kober." Breathily, in her downstairs front hallway, her companion had not failed to whisper that farewell need not mean conclusion. As she ran lightly upstairs afterward, still a bit dizzy, wrapped in enveloping scents of cigarette smoke, whisky, shaving lotion, and, under all, the merest hint of toothpaste, she told herself that this, indeed, was her cure. Palmer, after those assured, meticulously groomed men at the café, could hardly retain his hold on her musings, and that young man from whom she had just parted—well, she still couldn't say she cared for him, particularly, and undoubtedly he'd never get anywhere in business, but no one could say he didn't know his *way*.

After another day, however, even such efforts had to be recognized as ineffective. Let so much as one of her thoughts stray to the evening just past, and it came to be Palmer who dined at the white-naped table, Palmer whose strokes touched her knee, Palmer who, casting aside reserve, drank near her at another table, this one so small it scarcely separated bodies, Palmer who on the way home——

Rozzie, a dozen times that day, burst in for prattle and discussion; sewing girls knocked to announce important fittings; George Bibbensack—yes, George Bibbensack, ex-thief from West Haven, but for this past year her janitor, and the best she'd ever had, too—slid in obsequiously, cap in hand; she herself went out as usual—for rent collections, to oversee decorating and repairs, to spend a half hour with Prenevost. But activities which before had been as sharp as her bookkeeping figures—this exact thing to do now, that exact thing to do then—also ran into each other, merging.

Rozzie with three new orders, George with a bill—— "Who do you think I saw yesterday?" she could say to Rozzie or George, either of them. "Why, I saw Palmer Hake." "Property's taken a lift this past year, Mrs. Kober; you'll not get any more mortgages now at a discount." That was Mr. Prenevost speaking, but what Mr. Prenevost seemed to say was, "All those suspicions of Palmer's—you'll have all those to get rid of, little by little."

On Friday, the day Palmer had said he would phone, she arrived for work so early that Rozzie and the girls still sat at breakfast.

"Heavens, Frieda!" Rozzie laughed her surprise. "It's only a few minutes after seven! Whatever's going on today?"

"Important business, perhaps, if you must know." For Rozzie there could be a tart, dignified answer, but her own restlessness could not be dealt with so shortly. In her office it was hard even to remain at her desk. Palmer, a builder with a yard on his hands, would naturally be up and about early; Palmer, if he wanted to make an impression, would be prompt. Yet she couldn't really expect her telephone to ring. She took up a sheaf of grocery bills, but the entries on them seemed, this morning, to have little reality; her office too, the very desk at which she sat, seemed to partake of the same unreality. In a habitual and unconscious gesture she smoothed down her hips, and it was then, with her hands pausing midway, that she realized what what was so wrong: when she glanced down what her eyes had expected to see was not navy-blue chiffon and satin, but—yes, *serpent-green silk with a strawberry figure*. She knew then to what she owed the strangeness investing her; today, in spite of poise, in spite of all the hardness and sureness in which she had cased herself, in spite of all her possessions, she was almost back to being seventeen.

How, simply by seeing Palmer, by being reminded of him, could she have been so swept back to the past? Even if it were true—and in this startled moment she had to admit it was true—that for some ununderstandable reason Palmer remained more desirable to her than any other man, still there had to be something more. Was she hoping to *gain* anything from Palmer? What, after all these years, was there to be gained? Almost certainly not money; Hake money was long gone by now, and, if she had her guess, Amiot money too—those two older sons in Boston, she had heard, had gotten most of that inheritance. Already she had shown herself to Palmer, and he had been impressed; if she exposed him to the splendor of Balik's he might be impressed even more, but to what could that lead? He might, he just might, get to see something; he might see what a mistake he had made, not marrying her in the first place.

The answer was ready and alive in her mind, waiting, and as soon as she recognized it she burned with it; this was a fulfillment that she had to have.

Consumed as she immediately was by this new necessity, however, there came no early assuagement for it. By noon she had had to accept that Palmer was in no hurry to call; often as her phone rang it was only on ordinary business. "One of the furnace grates at the flats is half falling out, Mrs. Kober." "I'm afraid there'll be a slight delay on that last order of satins, Mrs. Kober." "Now, you remember you're buying me that mesh bag right this noon, Mama; if I don't have it for the party tonight I'll die."

By afternoon she could have wished the black toy of language would stay mute rather than rouse her to such expectation and disappointment; always it rang again, only to disclose still another voice than Palmer's. When five o'clock neared, her original necessity had long been transmuted by temper—he'd keep her on tenterhooks, would he! He'd treat her to some more of his high-and-mightiness! He might find out!

When, in the midst of these fulminations, the phone again rang, she had for it but one barking syllable.

"Yes?"

"Well, Mrs. Kober, I had quite a time finding you, Mrs. Kober." The voice reaching her ears, in addition to its caution, was almost entirely rallying, and for seconds she could scarcely accept it as Palmer's. Then, suddenly, she realized from what superior position he spoke, and what she had done to put him in that position. Relaxing, with anger flowing from her in a releasing stream, she sank into her desk chair.

"Oh, was I that *stupid?* Why, I didn't give you my name! Or where to call me! It's just incredible I could have been so thought-less——"

"For a while there I thought I'd seen a ghost." What came with this was a chuckle, and a tingle ran from Frieda's neck to her finger tips; Palmer, who loved jokes on people, had one on her. It wasn't a thing she would have chosen, but anyone could hear how it was working out.

"Oh goodness, I must have put you to no end of trouble; you must absolutely have been a detective to find me at all." Contrition could flow sweetly now, in many words. "I tell you—it's quite late, isn't it? Why don't you drop around with your estimate tomorrow, here at my place of business?" Oh, she might be fluttered, but she wasn't losing her head twice! This time, before she hung up, Palmer had directions. And when the connection broke, finally, she sat on, as she had once before that week, chin against the transmitter, smiling. As once before that week, too, she lay back to stretch widely. She might not be too sure, yet, of where it was going, but her ball was rolling.

CHAPTER XXXIV

Palmer had been married to an Amiot, Palmer had been around, but Balik's, for all that, bugged his eyes open.

"Say, this is some little outfit you've got here." Tribute, as might have been expected, was grudging, and accompanied by more of that wariness with which he had so hedged himself at his yard, but it had to be given. He had put on a better suit for his business call, a serge suit, but otherwise his gear was as before: thick plaid mackinaw, cap and gum boots, and when she skimmed down to him in the entrance hall (on purpose, that day, she had worn a dress in which she could skim) he had stood looking masculine and out of place. "You sure," he proceeded, trying to pass off his lack of ease with a joke, "that I'm safe here?"

"Don't worry, you'll see no ladies with clothes off." She too was graciously willing, here in her own domain, to ascribe any unease on his part to that rough masculinity which was even more palpable in this setting than it had been at the yard. With a good deal of flourish on her own part she drew him with her down the hall, pointing to aspects of her kingdom. "This on the right is our salesroom. Heavens, you needn't tiptoe, there won't be a customer in here for hours. That's our fitting room, across, and there at the back are our sewing rooms. We're a factory really, you know, with a fancy plush front for the trade. Up this way are our offices and living rooms —don't mind the girls; we get lots of men in here, naturally—salesmen and things. Any *undressing*, I promise, goes on behind doors. Then if you'll step this way——"

Palmer had been in well-furnished offices, too, before this; much finer offices than hers, undoubtedly, but that didn't mean that in spite of himself Palmer wasn't again impressed; Palmer for an instant didn't hide the shrewd glance with which he appraised her wide mahogany desk (secondhand, but not a scratch on it), her heavy green draperies, her thick green rug, her safe, her filing cabinets, her buttoned black leather armchairs and her pier glass which, for all its service, stayed incontestably handsome.

"You're doing all right by yourself, Mrs. Kober." More tribute, accompanied by an increase of caution, but it could add to the assurance with which she took her chair and waved him to another.

"Well, I hardly expect to start starving, not this week. You know how it is, though, in cities—you have to put up a front." This far she had come, she could think exultantly: she could belittle success. "Now if that estimate is ready——"

"Right here." He too, promptly, got down to cases, drawing two penciled sheets from a pocket and placing them before her. "That's your lot, Mrs. Kober—this sketch here. Only location for a garage is at the back line, but a few feet in—you'll need a few feet there for turning. Soft loam on that lot, so you'll want concrete for an approach, as well as for the floor." Apparently forgetful, now, of all else save caution and business, he proceeded from one item to another of a list he had tabulated, while a slow respect, as grudging on her part as his for her, grew within her. Palmer, obviously, had learned his trade. "I'll get to that," he made answer whenever she could think up a question, and sure enough, in its place that question would be answered.

"Well, that seems to be that!" she said briskly and brightly when, after a final flourish of his pencil, he sat solidly back. "How much?"

"Just about two hundred fifty, I figure it." This too was laid down with the matter-of-fact objectivity which had preceded it, and it took her awhile—her unwilling ears refusing what they heard—to swing from pleased acceptance to outrage.

"Two hundred fifty? For a *garage*? Why, that's just ridiculous! One year or two years, when this motorcar fad goes out, there I'll be with a shed, empty—wouldn't I look smart, though, spending two hundred and fifty dollars for a——"

"Motorcars won't be going out in any two years." What broke from Palmer, in return to her outburst, was only more of his stubbornness. "You're making a permanent investment in this, Mrs. Kober. I could put you up a shed for less, sure. No floor, say, no cement approach, all secondhand lumber—it wouldn't be what you want. That's a good small house you've got there; stucco it and it'll stand for fifty years."

"I'll never do it." She wasn't having trouble then in being affected by him. "You can just take up your little highway-robbery scheme and skedaddle, Mr. Hake. I'm not in business to get myself sold."

"Materials, labor and profit—what I've given you is the fair price." At once, stolidly, accepting her dismissal, he arose, sliding his pencil into a pocket, reaching for his papers to fold those away also. "Too bad we couldn't come to a deal——"

"Do you actually expect to get anywhere in Meridian—do you expect to get anywhere, any time, doing this kind of business?" What moved in Frieda was still the outrage.

"That why you came around, was it? Get your job done for nothing?" Humor, which had been absent during the business session, appeared in grim lines about Palmer's mouth.

"The *least* you could do is offer a concession; the *least* you could do is shave your profit——"

"That how you do business, Mrs. Kober?"

"Oh, you're impossible." Only impatience could answer. "Go on. Get out of here."

And if he had hesitated, if he had shown the least uncertainty, she could have sat stonily to see him go. Let him wish later that he had yielded a little, let him wish later that he had been less out for his own! But he went so promptly, stumping off with no single look back, no further word of regret, his very back signifying complete acquiescence, almost relief, in this turn of events. In that acquiescence was held the whole of their past; always he had been the one to go, while she willed him back.

"Oh, stop!" she had to command in exasperation. "You know I want that garage and you're putting it up."

Capitulation was so complete that for a moment after it confusion yawned; she sat stripped and helpless. "My trouble," she said crossly, "is that I'm so swamped with work it'll cost me less in the end to have you do it than to waste time looking up another man."

Whether he believed this or not, she did, immediately, and with rationalization came a return of aplomb. Palmer, on his side, merely half turned, shrugging, amusement draining from his mouth.

"That's as you want it, if you meet my price."

"When could I expect you'd begin?"

"Next week, probably."

"I'll be out to see how things are going."

"Most people do," he replied shortly, and on this conclusion went, offering her no chance to follow or be once more gracious, leaving her no opportunity to accompany him, as a hostess, to the door and down. Thumps of his feet on the stairway came back rug-muted and receding, and were cut off finally by the closing door.

Two hundred and fifty dollars. Before he was around the landing she was on her feet to walk it out. After taking over the Kober properties her first care had been to hunt out two superannuated decorators and two even more aged carpenters, men so old they couldn't get other work. It was only because, during the year just past, both old carpenters had insisted on dying, that she had had to go looking down that list of builders. If old Vatne and old Nelson had been living she'd have got her garage, as good as the one Palmer planned, for—well, maybe a hundred eighty. No more than Palmer did she believe that motorcars would soon go out; Lloyd teased continually for one, and she herself had been tempted. No, what she was making was a permanent investment, all right. Palmer hadn't in any way got round her. It was only that he hadn't let her get around *him*.

Struggle against it as she would, this view of their late encounter made her laugh aloud; it wasn't often, these days, that she was maneuvered into any such position. Besides, not all of this second meeting had gone amiss—Palmer had still been affected by Balik's. And in that clash over price, too, Palmer had cast off reserve just as much as she had. Now she looked back on it, the whole encounter had been more enjoyable than anything she'd experienced in a long time. Nor were accounts settled yet!

By her third call at the building site, the first one at which Palmer also was present, she was in trim to be not only appreciative but friendly.

"You're sure you've leveled this ground enough so the cement won't crack?" she had been able to ask sharply, in Palmer's absence, of the two workmen he had on the job. "How are you anchoring those corner posts?"

Stolid, slow-speaking and slow-moving, returning only the most costive answers—"Yup" or "Bedded in *see*-ment, lady"—it still had been apparent almost at once that Palmer's men were good men, knowing what they were up to. And when she learned—"You're new with Mr. Hake, I presume?"—that both men had followed their employer from West Haven, she had been able to be both charmed and charming—"Is that right? Why, originally I came from West Haven myself!"—in a way that could scarcely keep them from their best efforts.

Palmer, when he did appear, was visible as crawling along the outside of her framework, steel tape in hand. It was her turn to rally.

"Goodness, Mr. Hake! You in *that* position?"

Palmer had to be more sheepish than wary, as he arose to dust sand from his knees.

"Just making sure you're not being cheated," he told her. The sheepishness rather soon disappeared, to be replaced by the assurance he obviously felt at his job, just as she felt hers at Balik's. "You can look those joints over, Mrs. Kober. Look at the overlay on those shingles too. You won't get drips in this garage."

"Well, heavens! At the price I'm paying, the least I could hope for is good work!" Agreement could scarcely be given without rue, but it was a rue from which, as she had to concede by this time, a good deal of the sting had been drawn. "This doesn't mean I don't expect to get my money's worth out of every penny, just as I always have"—the adjuration was one for herself in private—"but maybe— well, it's nice, in a way, to be paying full price. After all, I guess I've got to the place where I can afford it."

Inspection over, it was from the full stately height of one who did, thus, pay in full that commendation could be spoken.

"I must say it's coming along as well as I could expect, Mr. Hake; I'll be around again before you finish."

But Palmer, this time, was not parting from her so shortly.

"Going along myself, so I could drop you somewhere, if it's not too far. A few blocks don't mean much in a motorcar."

It was stingily spoken, with a heavy resurge of that wariness which, in spite of everything else that had entered, still underlay his attitude toward her. But while the invitation was still being given blood rushed to her face in such hot and dizzying quantities that she felt top-heavy, and her fingers tingled, cold and drained. He continued to stand without looking at her, half turned toward the street as if it were he who had been arrested in leaving, while his hands finished the stowing away of tape spool and pencil, and then—the day was

another of March bluster—lifted to pull down the ear flaps of his
cap in a way that, definitely, was intended to produce not looks but
protection.

"You ready?"

"But, Mr. Hake! That's—how kind of you!" No words could have
been adequate. "I hadn't expected—why, I didn't even know you *had*
a motorcar!"

"That's my buggy out front." Swagger here was open. As he stalked
ahead of her, his shoulders moved in a flourish, and immediately
her eyes stung. *He was acting like Palmer.* She followed so meekly
at his behest that it might, indeed, have been old times. Ceremo-
niously he inserted her into the car, swaggered around the front to
seat himself under the wheel, and then stamped on the foot lever.
In every movement of his body, after that—the way he leaned forward against the wheel to help on upgrades, the way he drew back
on downgrades, the way he turned corners with great slow sweeps
of his left arm, the way he increased speed whenever another vehicle
appeared before him, and then swung out suddenly to pass and cut
in—more and more of his old boast and flourish was visible.

"There's a trick to these babies, but I can't say it took me long
to catch on. A little different these days, when all you've got to do
is step down on a lever, than it used to be when you had to get out
and crank." His conversation, as they drove, was entirely of himself
and his machine. "Kisselkar forty, that's what this baby is; set me back
two thousand simoleons but I guess it's worth it; first thing you
know they'll be turning out a woman's model. Look at the way she
takes this hill, now." Again he poised forward, pushing, to relax at
the hill crest and turn a grin of triumph. "In high. How's that for
power?"

Not only the car, but Palmer too had made the grade; behind his
last question was much more than pride in a possession.

You've got your Balik's, Palmer was saying, but I've got something
too.

What if you *do* have a machine; do you think one measly lumberyard can stack up against what I own? Her competitive spirit would
at once have struck back if polity had not risen to suppress retort.

"It's simply a marvelous machine." Gracefully upright, gracefully
swaying with the bounces, she in no way allowed carelessness to
relax her, or to lessen her rapt admiration. "And the way you drive
it—I'm sure I never could learn. Once in a while, of course, I've had
an idea—Lloyd wants an auto so badly. But I don't know—what do

you think, now—is a motorcar a *safe* plaything for a young man?"

Where she could with such nicety be feminine and appealing, she had to allow that role to be played to the hilt. At her door, before which Palmer drew up with such dash that he had to back almost half a block, she descended lingeringly.

"You're right, I'm sure. Lloyd should never" (this being Palmer's considered opinion) "ever have a car until he has learned the control of the Horse. I do wish—well——" A lighter substitute had to be inserted here, for what couldn't be said. "Couldn't you come in to meet my family? I have two children, you know—Lloyd, who's *such* a big boy, graduating this year—I hope—from high school, and Idelle, a junior. My husband, too"—she hadn't wanted to bring in Stillwell Kober, but under the circumstances he could scarcely be left out— "he's an invalid, poor soul, *quite* an invalid—heart. They'd all be so pleased——"

"Kind of you, Mrs. Kober." Palmer wasn't yet lending himself to family visits, but from his eminence in the driver's seat, with gloved hand on wheel, he made refusal amiable, with a plea of other business.

"Some other time, then."

Standing a moment after he had gone, breathing in as if it were perfume the gray mephitic cloud of exhaust by which she was surrounded, she watched him bounce from her presence in kangaroo leaps. *Showing her he had possessions too*—that might have been Palmer's one and only purpose in giving her a ride, but in spite of himself he had achieved something else also. He might remain on the defensive, but this ride had cemented another personal element into their relationship.

For some time she had been teased by a project, one alternately decided upon—There's no reason on earth why I shouldn't—and discarded—Oh, why should I? It would just cost money. In that moment, however, when she stood on the walk before her house, this project abruptly came to be inevitable. Balik's, this June, would have its fifth birthday. She must give a party in celebration of the date, a party to which not only the customers, sewing girls, wholesalers and salesmen would be invited (flowers, at least, needn't come from her pocket!) but also a few other people—Mr. Prenevost, bank officials who had handled her loans, Callahan and Mr. Frigman (wouldn't that be fun, though, if they came!) and Palmer.

As she went up her stairs she hugged more than her coat to her breast. Palmer could draw back again now, as he no doubt would, but she wasn't too worried.

As she so accurately foresaw, Palmer, at their next meeting, did try to retreat.

"Oh, you're here." His reception of her was at once indifferent and surly. "Well, your job's done. If you'll look it over I'll be going; you can send your check on to the yard."

It was impossible, however, for him to leave while she still fluttered praises—"Oh, it's quite perfect! And all that cement—it looks as if it would last forever!" When she produced a check on the spot, he could do no less than take it, and he could not actually say, "Thanks, but I want no more of your work," when she went on to indicate ruefully that what was finished was barely commencement.

"I suppose I can just as well make up my mind to it—two of my other renters are complaining because they haven't garages, too."

In laconic ill grace (the very most she got from him that day was a series of grunts) he took her to first one site, then another. Almost certainly, she judged, he had made earlier investigations into what she owned. When she hinted, "Heavens! I hope cars don't get common! Whatever would I do if I had to arrange car space for my flats?" he showed no least surprise. Instead, "You must own half Meridian," he told her coolly, echoing a phrase she had once used to Stillwell Kober.

He envies me; that's his trouble; he wishes he had half as much, she could tell herself, but his attitude wasn't as simple as that. Even in June when, by dint of postponements and remodelings, she managed to have him still in her employ, he had not departed from his stiff-necked reserve.

"A party? Well, I don't know." At her invitation his guard flew up so swiftly that she felt the wind of it. "What night did you say?"

"Saturday. Not a personal party at all, you know." The whole matter, fortunately, could be kept on a casual plane. "It might be fun for you, I thought, seeing how these trade parties go. If there's"—pretty hesitance, which must at all costs be kept from growing tight—"goodness, I don't know much about you, do I? If there's a Mrs. Hake, she's of course invited too."

"There isn't any." For this admission he stood with face averted, but her desperate need to know must have leaped, as her glance leaped, to his countenance. In all their months of dealings, this was the first time she had managed the question.

"Oh." She rocked, for a moment, on quite numb feet; it was so much more than she could have hoped. "A friend, then——"

"If I came, I'd come alone."

For the first time, then, as he turned toward her, there was a direct and close challenge in the strike of his eyes; they stood in a way which again was familiar. This, this defiant belligerence, was not unknown to them from their past.

Where do you think you are getting? might have been his eyes' query. Where is there to get?

She had to stand unsupported, while he thus probed, lipping her syllables—"It should be a nice party, really. All those fashionable women, and my friends. I even think I'll let Lloyd and Idelle come. They're so grown up now." She couldn't push him, any more than she cou eply to his unspoken queries. By this time she too had to sense that there must be more that she wanted from him than just an acknowledgment of his error in jilting her, but she no more than he could have said why she wanted that continued and deepened association; she only knew with what desperation she wanted it.

"I'll have to see when the time comes." Only this ungracious half acceptance could be wrung from him. As he returned to his work, however, it seemed that a thumb might have pressed, hard, against her heart. In his very questioning of her, hadn't there been a different interest, a compulsion? And if she got nothing else from her party, if he didn't come, if the whole affair turned out a failure from beginning to end, she had already gotten something which made that party worth all it could cost. It was something that couldn't possibly mean anything to her, but she had found out at last. There wasn't yet a second Mrs. Hake.

CHAPTER XXXV

To the beach of her position beside Rozzie just inside the fitting-room door, the sea of her party tossed its handclasps and its interjections and its smile-wreathed faces.

"Oh, Mrs. Kober, *who* had the idea of those lovely dolls in Balik gowns?"

"How I ever lived before Balik's, I don't know; I was a perfect fright, I know I was; a perfect fright."

"If you were a man, I'd sue you as co-respondent, Mrs. Kober." (That was a husband, laboriously jocular.)

"That suit over there on the figure—isn't it? Yes! That *divine* old green shantung I first noticed on you at Frigman's——"

Truly, as she could tell herself in the press, whenever there was time for private thinking, this was a court at which anyone on earth might be proud to be the central figure. How the Gurneys, how Jessie Drake, how Fred Pomeroy, how Schatzi Klaumeister and Nettie Orcutt and Beth Cantrell and Wes Jenks—people of whom she hadn't thought for years, but who, somehow, came alive tonight—would gape if they could see her now! How ridiculous then would be those little strivings by which they had kept her from their mean social life in West Haven, how they themselves must admit they had misjudged and slighted her!

Her buildings stood actual and solid on their plots of ground, but they could not voice, as this party voiced, the eminence to which she had risen. All about, beneath the twirling violet and gold canopies of her streamered ceilings, stood flowers, flowers in such profusion that they had had to be massed in banks and hillocks. Her own person, swathed in Carrickmacross lace and pale pink charmeuse, represented such a consummation of Balik art that she herself, seeing her image in her mirror, had felt dizzied by her own perfection—no one, possibly, could have looked more a figure of high life. At seven exactly a string of motorcars—the largest and costliest of Meridian—had begun pausing at the Balik doors, discharging perfumed, Balik-gowned, rich, gracious women, many of them, for a first time at that place, accompanied by men. Through all the ground floor of Balik's these women and their escorts now thronged, mincing, swaying, circling in enthusiastic, consciously mannered groups, pausing to exclaim over the dolls (Rozzie's surprise), pausing again to accept ribbon-tied small cakes or sandwiches from the sewing girls who threaded about as smiling anxious waitresses, with trays hung by wide ribbons from their shoulders, standing to gurgle over the two dummies, dressed for this evening in those twin seducers—the green shantung and the black faille with soutache and lace—through which their custom had first been enticed. In the sewing rooms, opened for a first time to public view, reposed a great bowl of tea punch, presided over by May Fisko, and flanked by lobster salad, chicken aspic, cheese balls, olives, stuffed celery, strawberries dusted in sugar. Interspersed with the personages milling about this table were other people as important in their way as the clients— heads of wholesale houses, an entire half dozen of bankers she had asked, several executives from Wells-West. Mr. Frigman and Miss Callahan, so far, had not come, but two enterprising young men from the Meridian *Journal* had.

"It isn't often, Mrs. Kober," one of these told her admiringly, "that we meet such a story of American success. You'll be an inspiration, Mrs. Kober, for our whole Northwest."

The incense was enough to float her, drugging her senses until she had trouble recognizing faces and connecting names. As usual, however, something impinged to bring back focus. Rozzie, for one thing, by those demure and slippery means of which she seemed to have such inexhaustible supplies, was keeping herself forward in a way not at all intended. Rozzie, in Frieda's view, might well have seen to the waiting, or taken May Fisko's place at the refreshment table. Certainly Rozzie might have made herself useful, instead of behaving as if she too were a hostess.

"Oh, Frieda, won't that be fun? You and I can stand together, as we *do* stand together, shaking hands with everyone who comes." Before Frieda had been able to edge in a word on arrangements, this, like fire from tinder, had been the picture to which Rozzie flamed. Neither then nor at any subsequent time had it seemed possible to point out how much better it must look for the Owner to receive alone.

Greetings given Rozzie by some clients, too, were so exaggerated that, hearing them in snatches between her own deserved plaudits, Frieda could scarcely believe her ears.

"My dear Mme. Balik, I do hope you know you're the most important person in my whole life."

"This very afternoon we were talking about whom we would hate to lose *most,* and *at once* I said, 'Mme. Balik.' If I ever lose you, Mme. Balik, I shall just be desolated."

"Heavens," she would have to tell Rozzie later, "how some of those women do gush over you!"

Then, too, there was Lloyd. Only after prolonged hesitation had she finally let Lloyd and Idelle make, at this party, their entry into what all these years had been held as a citadel. From Stillwell Kober, Idelle had already squeezed knowledge of Balik's; Idelle through a long campaign of espionage had pretty well established her mother's position. "Don't talk to *me* about being hard up," was one of Idelle's more permanent retaliations. "You don't just work there at Balik's, you're the boss."

Bad as it could be—this was the con—for Lloyd and Idelle to get the run of Balik's, it might be a good idea—this was what ultimately had decided her—for them to see her as she was, the respected head of an important business. Through the earlier part of the evening, while the press was greatest, the two who had come with her were lost sight of in the maelstrom. Idelle, later, was glimpsed as roving speculatively from one room to another, or as flirting innocently with salesmen. Lloyd, on the other hand, when first located (easily enough, since he was planted sovereignly before a fireplace, elbow on mantel and foot on fender, in an attitude to be at once recognized as that of the Young Master), was seen to be laughing with Doodie Bibbensack, as he accepted dainties from a tray. And the next time he appeared, too,—down a suddenly opened avenue of backs—he again was in converse with Doodie, and this time George and Flora were there also, the three Bibbensacks making a compact circle.

If the first glimpse hadn't set off alarms in Frieda's head, the second alone would have started them jangling. Seizing an opportunity when incomers thinned, she got down the avenue and to Lloyd's side.

"I can see you've met my boy," she proffered with dead pleasantness to George, Flora and Doodie. "Isn't he huge for nineteen? Still in school, of course, and that's where he'll be for years to come. Doodie, that lady and gentleman—I believe their plates——"

"Oh yes, Mrs. Kober." Doodie at once returned to duty, while George, scraping, edged Flora backward.

"Our greatest pleasure this evening, meeting young Mr. Gurney. Though it's a grand party, Mrs. Kober, a grand party."

As parents of a sewing girl (Doodie had now been with Balik's for almost two years) it had seemed difficult to discriminate against George and Flora simply because they were her janitors, when the parents of all the other girls (in a humble and unobtrusive way, of course, mostly hanging about near the kitchen) were to be allowed to come. As she took Lloyd's arm, however, to pilot him toward Mrs. Frelingheusen and Mrs. Frelingheusen's languid and ravishing debutante daughter, she thought coldly that letting George and Flora in had been a mistake. Ever since she had first found George in a group of shambling job hunters at an agency, she had known his usefulness for her would end if he didn't keep his place.

"No use in beating about the bush," she had told George at that first interview. "I handle all buying, so you'll make no shakedowns. If you get tips from tenants, of course, that's your business, provided I hear no complaints."

George, immediately, had indicated humbly that he understood. Three janitors previous to George had departed in lightning succession, but George stuck, hustling in winter from furnace to furnace, running, almost, as he mopped halls, developing agility at window washing and snow shoveling. Years of unsuccess on stolen fruits had lost George none of his pale flabby fatness, but to this later incarnation he added a good healthy sweat.

That in addition to Flora, grown gaunt and shadowlike, George also possessed a daughter, she had not found out until one day Rozzie made a hesitant suggestion.

"The janitor's daughter seems very anxious—I can't say I'm taken with her, exactly; she doesn't seem quite straightforward. But since she wants it so much, if it's all right with you——"

At the time, it had been all right with Frieda. But as she firmly affixed Lloyd to Miss Frelingheusen—"Do let this big boy of mine get you some supper"—she icily resurveyed the subject. The mother of an impressionable young boy could never be too careful.

As the evening wore on, however, it was another canker which swelled with real heat and soreness. Certain as she had been that Palmer must put in an appearance—out of curiosity if nothing else— no Palmer turned up. At first there could be reassurances—"Naturally he wouldn't come this soon, he's not likely to get here before—oh, say eight—any number of things could have happened to delay him; I *know* he was different that last time, I *know* he meant to come"—but when it got to be nine and later, when early comers began drifting up for farewells—"More businesses should do this, Mrs. Kober, it's been just delightful!"—she began to know frantically that soon it would be too late. From the first it had been understood that the elite guests, the customers, would never stay long; they would undulate in for a gracious obeisance, they would coo over each other, they would look about at what there was to see, they would stand awhile with plates held elegantly high, nibbling the luxuries she had provided, sipping her tea punch, and then almost at once go, leaving the party to those who during their presence were its servants and its hangers-on: the sewing girls, their friends, their parents and the salesmen. It wasn't that *later* party Palmer must view; it was this earlier part, this court of homage. Yet she was as powerless to make him view it as she was to make the homage last.

"Wait, wait, he hasn't seen you," she could have implored Mrs. Frelingheusen, Mrs. Rebedoux, Mrs Houghtaling, Mrs. Spurgeon and her bankers. "Unless he does, it's half a waste." Instead, she must stand smiling. "Oh no, the pleasure is entirely ours, we've been most honored." Hand after hand for a second time shook hers, face after face mouthed its phrases, the expression of her own face began to feel as if it had been put on with thick paint. Still the ebb continued, still Palmer was absent.

When she followed a late-goer out to the entrance hall, and there came upon him, talking easily with George Bibbensack as if he had been present for hours, she could have slapped him.

"What're you doing out here?" she blazed, before her controls took hold. "Why haven't you been in? Don't you realize the people who've been here are as important as any in Meridian? Can't you even have an eye out for your own business?"

"Oh, I've given up any idea of being a builder for swells." After a nod to George he stepped forward, feeling, as far as she could see, only good humor toward her anger and his answer to it. "Common people are more in my line."

"You're a fool." On this curt valediction she swept back to receive more farewells, but the incident smarted. Stay out there, would he, no one knew how long, not even bothering to let her know he had come. The interchange in the hall had not gone unnoticed, either; about her brows lifted, glances crossed meaningfully, bare shoulders telegraphed the lightest of shrugs.

Let them look cross-eyed. I don't care one fig, she could tell herself. This whole evening, ruined. Yet as she sped the last departing clients, this was not really what she felt. He had come after all, he was here, and she was right about a difference in him. Change was apparent in his shoulders tonight, in the ease and mastery of his bearing; he had cast off much of his wariness. What obscure course of masculine reasoning had moved him she might never know, but Palmer had decided he could hold his own against her; he had determined on taking action into his own hands.

She had an opportunity to view again, that night, the ancient ease with which Palmer, when he wanted to, could make conquests. Palmer, it seemed, remembered Rozzie; Palmer, in no time at all, had a nimbus of gigglers; Palmer, when the waltzing began, twirled first one sewing girl and then another in elaborate large circles, his highly colored face alight with pleasure.

Like a peasant! Frieda told herself scornfully as, in the supporting arms of more important salesmen, she too dipped and circled, left arm low for a graceful looping of her train. She could, she found, almost dislike Palmer, dislike the girls he so decorously held at arm's length, hate Rozzie when later on Rozzie bobbed beside him. In the interstices of dancing she already had on her hands more than she could well handle: Lloyd, every time she saw him, was again with Doodie, and all too apparently Lloyd was drowning rapidly under the spell of baby-blond hair and a baby-blue stare.

"Oh, Mr. Gurney!" Doodie was heard squealing, in her helpless, thin giggle. "You can't go on saying such things, you just can't!"

It wasn't the first time Lloyd had shown similar symptoms, and Frieda might have brushed them off this time—Lloyd usually could be made to listen to reason later—if George and Flora had not again been visible, sitting side by side against the wall, their fixed eyes never moving from the one couple. Something about that stare made Frieda nervous.

"This'll be just about enough of that!" she at last burst aloud, wresting herself from the arm about her. ("Stepping all over her, that's what I must have been doing," her abandoned partner moaned to a fellow later. "I can just as well quit trying for orders in this place.")

"Poor Doodie." Frieda was speaking to George and Flora from deepest sympathy. "That child looks so tired she could drop. She's worked too hard at this—why don't you take her home?"

"If that's all right with you, Mrs. Kober." Nothing but the meekest acquiescence exuded from George. "We'll do just what you say."

Ten minutes later Frieda herself was Palmer's partner.

"Well," he said, coming up behind her in the hall. "I see you got the kids off home. Dance?"

"Was that what you were waiting for, before you asked your hostess —that her children should be gone?" She had been aware of him, approaching, but still he startled her; she had still been so enmeshed in the scene with Lloyd.

"You're an old spoilsport, that's what you are," Lloyd had half shouted, with no care, apparently, for who heard him. "Don't think you're fooling me, it was you got Doodie's folks to take her home. I'll get even with you yet——"

"Oh, come on, Lloyd, let's go." Unexpectedly it had been Idelle who had slipped up from nowhere to pluck at Lloyd's sleeve. "It's a nutty party; let's beat it."

Usually Idelle was no ally of Frieda's; Idelle, in fact, usually made one with Lloyd, and it was only after several sullen, undecided glowers about the hall that Lloyd had grabbed up his cap and slammed it on. As the two of them left it didn't escape Frieda that Idelle, undoubtedly, had something up her chiffon sleeves; Idelle, these past years, had grown sly. When Palmer came up with his invitation and his innuendo it took effort to switch from one absorption to another; always, these days, she was having to go through these changes.

"No duty, Mrs. Kober." In reply to her charge, Palmer had a smile.

"Is there any reason *why* my children shouldn't see me dancing with you?"

"None they could know about."

There he was again, she thought pettishly; it was impossible, ever, to get Palmer in a corner where he couldn't answer. Then his arm came around her, her feet caught the music, and vexation faded.

"Do you realize, Mr. Hake," she asked, "that this is the first time in your whole life that you've danced with me?"

"Is it?" he in return asked, as if he were surprised. But he wasn't surprised. He remembered—she was certain of it—every incident of their past just as surely as she did; all evening while he had danced with others, and while she had been so fretted, there still had been a thread, friable but unbreaking, between them. Wherever she had been on the floor he had known it, his awareness of her presence showing in the very care with which he never glanced in her direction. She for her part had missed no slightest movement of his; she had known when he took out a handkerchief to dry his hands or his forehead, known when he took a sewing girl to the back room for lunch, known when he loitered behind her in the hall while she got Lloyd and Idelle started home.

The arm whose messages were so firm and certain grew tight at her back. Swing forward, swing backward, circle, dip, sway—there was no single reason in the world why she shouldn't yield, if she liked, to this pleasure; if Lloyd and Idelle cooked up anything she could take care of that later. As she yielded to rhythm and direction she could think pleasantly of her partner. Tonight he had appeared against other men of far more socially accepted trades and stations, men who sat all day in offices moving only to the half turn of a desk chair, exercising nothing but their brains. These men had much more true elegance than Palmer, these men could never be imagined in rough clothes such as Palmer wore about his yard. Even the salesmen belonged in their clothes in a way Palmer no longer did; Palmer, in tight blue serge, looked dressed up; for all his handy way of getting in with people, he was a bit out of his orbit. Just the same, not one other man who had been there could approach him; beside Palmer the husbands of her customers looked pale and lily-livered, the salesmen debauched and seedy. There was more blood in Palmer.

As they waltzed, he remained half busied by the business of dancing. But above the careful smile that determination which she had so surely sensed showed again in tight expectant eyes.

"Someone else taught you to dance, then," he said, "if I didn't."

"Lots of things happen to a widow in a big, big town," she began archly before, of necessity, she stopped. Body still in the flow of dancing, she turned to look back, finding herself in a cul-de-sac between flower bank and wall.

"Heavens!" she laughed. "We can't get much farther this way."

"No," he returned, and this time he was very deliberate, "we can't."
The hand that had pressed so closely to the small of her back moved

but affixed itself again, this time to her right arm above the elbow; his other hand caught her left arm, forcing her to drop her train.

"It's sometimes handy for a man to know," he said, "just how far he is going, and where." The tightness was spreading, now, over all of his face; he stood holding her as a combatant, and once again, as she swiftly sobered from her laughter, it struck her how old this was; this was the way that they always had met.

He himself did no yielding; it was she who was pulled toward him until, hard, asking, his mouth pressed hers.

"In some ways you're a damn fine woman, Frieda," he said thickly. "No matter what else you are—and don't think I don't know—you're a damn fine woman." This time his hands curved in past the backs of her arms until she was thrust violently against his body.

"You couldn't forget, could you, Frieda?" he asked, whispering and boasting. "That's why you looked me up, isn't it? You couldn't forget." He held her, taunting and triumphing, making sport of the hunger which, in his hands, leaped to such strength she could only tremble, trying to contain it.

"You're insulting!" she fiercely whispered. "People will see, too! Let me go!"

He laughed, not letting her go, though she struggled.

"Is that what you really want, Frieda?" he asked, and repeated, "Is that what you really want, keeping me at this little dab of job and that little dab of job—is that what you really want—to be let go?"

"Oh, you're insufferable!" she once more whispered, violently. But she knew, and he knew, that it was no answer.

CHAPTER XXXVI

By late summer her position had to be intolerable.

Palmer's approach at the party had no possibility of being anything but brief: after her last protest he himself cut it short by whirling her roughly back among the waltzers. And when that dance was done, as if nothing whatever had been said to violate accord, he left her with a buoyant nod.

"Let's dance again, sometime."

Twice more during the evening she became his partner; each time, with great outward haughtiness but inward trembling, she waited for him to advance further along the road he had taken. But each time he merely danced the number through as if he had no idea in his head but that of a rousing good time. When the festivities ended he would apparently have walked out alone if she hadn't stopped him.

"Are you taking me home?"

"That's a privilege I'd have thought I couldn't get."

Acceptance was quick if mocking, his glance impish. On the way home he applied himself breezily—again as if nothing new had occurred—to small talk. "Say, those are some little peaches you've got working for you, Frieda; makes me wish I could use girls at the yard. That Rozzie Balik, except she's crippled, is a handsome woman—ever notice? Darn good party all around; those two accordion players should make a try at vaudeville."

Long before his car drew up in front of her house, her fingernails had dug through their pink silk glove tips.

"I hope you understand by this time, Palmer, how mistaken you were in what you said tonight." Chokingly, humiliatingly, it was she who at last was goaded into reference. What she had expected in return was at least "Oh, so I was mistaken, was I?" and a sudden hard arm at her back; instead he returned, "That? Oh, forget it," and swashbucklingly descended, to swing around the car and let her out, with great manner but scarcely a touch, on her side.

"I guess you were right that day in the yard." Speciously he now took another tack. "We've got far enough, all right, to let bygones be gone. Thanks for a fine evening, Mrs. Kober; if that husband of yours ever lets you out, I'll take you to dinner and a show. Pay my debts."

"My husband doesn't let me out."

"You're just saying that; I'm sure you can handle a *husband,* all right." His squeeze of her arm was as taunting—and flaunting—as his words had been at the party, but when she swept in hauteur from him, he merely once more waved, and got back in his car.

A month later, when he revived his invitation—"I've got tickets for Maurice Costello tomorrow night, if your husband could trust you"— she had been reduced to the despair of believing he had taken her at her word, and wouldn't make any more advances. During the interval she had seen him at least every week, only to find him nothing but the efficient and indifferent workman.

"Maurice Costello? Oh, that's a frightful temptation. Actually, my husband *likes* to have me go out, since he can't take me himself. I don't know though——" Her scene of dignity and hesitation had to be played. "The question is, can I trust *you?*"

"Trustworthy Hake, that's my nickname. Don't you worry about me."

He *couldn't,* she thought, mean dinner and a play alone; he too, by this time, must feel driven. But the evening was proof he wasn't.

"Didn't I hear you had a small daughter?" Just once, during an intermission, did she manage so much as a personal reference. "Is she up here with you in Meridian?"

To this charmingly spoken query Palmer's reply was curt.

"She's with old Mrs. Amiot in West Haven. I expect her to stay there."

From here he went on, as before, discussing Clara Kimball, old times, Kodaking, suffragettes, and the high cost of living. He did not even sit close to her.

After this demonstration of control and restraint, he desultorily from time to time again asked her out—another dinner and show, a headline baseball game, a dance—always with the same covert hints as to her married state, always with the challenge that was close to insult. With Rozzie as chaperone, he took her on an overnight motor trip. Then in August he discontinued even such courtesies; she had to call him.

"I'm eating alone tonight, and I wondered——"

"This heat is simply exhausting; I've been thinking all day how nice a drive would be——"

Always, when she asked, he responded with vigor and the highest good humor, just as he responded the two or three times Rozzie invited him to have dinner with the girls; this was what was so intolerable. Like a smiling and well-fed mountain lion, he now crouched, muscle-flexed and ready, beneath his treed hunter.

Why should I do any climbing? purred Palmer's attitude. She's certainly going to climb down! Whatever changes Cecilia had made in him—and there were such changes—she hadn't eradicated his arrogance as a male. Palmer thought he now knew what made up her interest in him, and for the mastery it would give him he was determined she should beg.

This wasn't any position she had wanted. Against him she lived in a chaos of contrary hungers so desperate she could scarcely have said, by this time, what she hoped. *She* couldn't break, first and most fiercely because it would be unbearably humbling, but also because, in her circumstances, it might not be safe. From her night out with the Swiss salesman there had been a repercussion, different but just as annoying as the results of an earlier night out with another drummer; the young Swiss had not welcomed dismissal.

"There might be people who'd be interested in parts of that evening," he had reminded ominously. "Your husband, for instance. And customers. I might open up *their* ears."

She had been able to laugh at him.

"Oh, please *do* tell my husband. I'd just love to see it. And the customers too—maybe you could get a piece in the papers. There's no ad for a dressmaker like having it said she's fast."

But the incident snapped open her eyes. After her marriage to Stillwell Kober she had realized, glancingly, that in her position private affairs were no longer private; now she had to be more sharply reminded. For days the young Swiss had lurked about near Balik's and her home; only after weeks did he submerge.

Palmer, probably, would not go in for blackmail, but if he got her where he wanted her he might ask something—a loan, or continuous employment of his workmen at high wages. Besides, it wasn't—it never had been—Palmer's light-o'-love she desired to be; what she wanted was to be Palmer's openly acknowledged *choice;* the only way she could yield to him was in marriage.

More and more, as summer wore on, the impasse was torment. To think that when she married Stillwell Kober, Palmer had already been a widower, and she had known it! If only she had taken a little more thought then, made a few more investigations! For always and forever, too, she had to feel on her flank the bite of that other rowel. Stillwell Kober, in the years since his scarlet fever, had managed to crawl from his invalid's bed, but up or down he was still an ulcer. All day long, dismally placating, mournfully anxious, he shambled about at the duties of Stella, dismissed; in the morning it was he who got together their jumbled similitude of breakfast. "Eggs, now—yes, this morning I remembered eggs. Toast, yes, toast in the oven, hot. Jam—let's see, now, there must be jam—where could I have put it?" In the afternoon it was he who greeted Lloyd and Idelle as they came from school. "Bread and butter on the table, jam and peanut butter, but no pickles. Your mother says we're buying entirely too many pickles. No, now, please——"

At night when Frieda got home it was he who had dinner, or stabs at dinner, waiting. He did such bedmaking, dusting, carpet sweeping as got done; he bought groceries, answered the doorbell, tended fires. That he could never be anything but hopeless at these activities he as well as they had long ago accepted. If he forgot butter at the store it was usually on a Saturday when they could get none until Monday; night after winter night, when Frieda or the children got home, it was to find the flat freezing.

"I can't think why it's so cold in here." He himself would be blue and chattering in the deep chill. "The fire's going nicely; I've been down time and again—oh dear, did I leave that window open again? It must have been when I shook the dust mop." No matter how many times the same mistake was made, he could never trace down his errors. Whenever Lloyd's dresser was dusted, Lloyd had to hunt collar buttons and cuff links on hands and knees; if the ice card stood in the window the door remained locked.

"I can't imagine why we didn't get ice today," he would say. "I hung the card." And then in the next breath, "Someone made a great racket this morning, pounding at the back door. But I wasn't expecting anyone, and I was resting, so I didn't go. I wonder who it could have been."

Long ago, for his personal living, he had been shunted to an enclosed portion of the front porch—three hundred dollars, that had cost her, but she had had to get him out from underfoot. Ridding herself of him by the easy route of divorce, unfortunately, was still not to be thought of; too many of the properties were still in his name. He might, beside, ask for a settlement! Many times in the years past, maddened by his incurable incompetence, by all the repellence of his physical being, she had asked herself why, on that night when he had tried to remove his blight from her life, she had rushed to stop him; certainly it had not been because of any softness, but because she hadn't been able to stand by and see life thrown away, when it more than anything else was what one owned.

Since then they had neither one made any references to that night. But like that other night in the grove with Palmer, it too retained a strong life of its own. Almost never did she have any private speech with the man who legally was her husband, almost never did she look at him directly, but sometimes when the two of them stood by chance alone in the kitchen or dining room, he in his bent and yet straining dejection, hastily mumbling—"The coal's out; I thought you might like to know," or "A bread man's started coming around; I thought I might take from him"—she had a feeling as if behind the given words some other statement or some other query lay hiding, one waiting for a far different answer than any she gave.

Once before, in West Haven with Harry, she had lived through a situation equally insufferable; then too there had been nothing she could do but—wait. During all those years with Harry, she had never once let herself think of her one way out; she had not—and how grateful she had been for this later—actually ever wished him dead. With Stillwell Kober, though, the situation was so different. A few months, the doctor said. A year at best. He might go *any time*. Yet day by day, week by week, month after month, there was no change in him; his very dimness, his frailty, began to seem like something concocted to tease her, to strain her nerves beyond what they could bear.

If he tried again I'd never stop him. Struggle to dislodge it as she would, this thought was a worm that ate deep of her mind, never ceasing. I don't really mean that, she told herself whenever the worm worked too close to the surface; I'm sure I wish no harm to anyone. Why, from that day to this, I've never allowed rope in the house. If he were really determined, though, I suppose he could twist string together——

From this uncleanness within herself, she again snatched herself horrified away. Wait—that was all she could decently do. Wait for a little while more——

No resolution, however, no amount of virtue, could inject comfort into what wasn't comfortable. On a morning in late September Palmer broke all later precedents to call her.

"I'm running up to Lakota this afternoon—business. Might be a nice drive."

For several days she had been feeling especially determined—in a matter such as this she couldn't put a single foot forward. But at Palmer's voice so much that was temptation beckoned—Meridian for a week past had been an oven, the day at Balik's was proving unusually dull, ahead she had nothing but an equally dull dinner and duller evening.

"Why not?" she returned recklessly. "I could do with some air!"

As she at once anticipated, the afternoon fruited into almost perfect pleasure. Palmer called for her before noon and they lunched together —chow mein, the first time she'd had it—at one of those Chinese places springing up; the car functioned beautifully, they rolled from the dust and deadness of city streets to the airier shades of country roads. She could not hold off a feeling of lightness and escape, and Palmer too was in high fettle, elated over two jobs he'd gotten.

"Bungalows, that's what people want these days. Front room, diningroom, kitchen in a row on one side, two bedrooms and bath on the other. No reason I can't build that same house over and over. Everything neat and compact, attic upstairs to finish off if the family gets big or the old folks move in, laundry tubs in the basement, a good hot-air furnace, mission woodwork——"

His enthusiasm was one to which she easily warmed—a bungalow like that, attic finished, was just what she dreamed of for herself. With hired girls asking five dollars a week, no one wanted a big house any more. Once again, as before in West Haven, she wistfully felt herself touching an ambition that could be owned in common, and surely this time there was less to separate them. Cecilia was dead now, the social strictures of West Haven long broken; nothing really remained to part them but the one obstruction, and that of the slenderest.

While Palmer busied himself at the Lakota lumber mill, she wandered about the little town, abandoning herself to an unusual confidence. Eventually, this time, things must turn out for her. Palmer wasn't actually pressing her, after all, and surely, at thirty-eight, she could wait! *Four* marriages, actually, a *fourth* husband—it sounded terrible. None of those others had been *real* marriages, though, or *real* husbands—not one of them. Marrying Palmer—that would be her true marriage, the one that counted. Just let her go on as she was going. Just let her keep Palmer where he was——

When Palmer reappeared, after an hour, his exuberance was heightened.

"Best lumber buy I ever made. Went through quick, too. Say, here's an idea—how about celebrating? We could pick up some stuff here, have a picnic——"

She had no reason to oppose him; suddenly both as silly and carefree as adolescents, they bought steaks, buns and fruit; hilariously, in the car, they explored for picnic sites.

"That hill's too much like a cemetery—those stumps around like gravestones."

"How about this pasture? No, I guess not. It's had cows."

"By that pond? Oh good gracious, no. It reminds me of one where I once lost a shoe."

When they stopped at last, in a little clear hollow near a patch of woods, twilight was nearing. Laughing because packages slipped from Palmer's arms, laughing because Frieda in her tight skirt was forced, finally, to roll under the fence, laughing because this spot too had recently been well visited by cattle, laughing because their fire wouldn't start and then because it riotously did, they got their steaks on cut sticks, shared the ravenous redolence-teased hunger of the roasting and the equally savage satisfaction of sinking teeth into deliciously seared flesh, shared the arrival of repletion and comatose satiety.

Satiety, however, could not be complete. Although Palmer remained lounging on his side of the fire, arms under head, and she with stiff discretion kept to hers, although for months now no intimate words had been spoken between them, still as soon as quiet settled a strain settled with it, perceptible first in the short pauses that broke up their banter, sensibly growing into longer and more straining pauses, gaining substance like a dusk-gathered ghost, smothering even the fire that separated them, so that across the broken shapes of spent wood, red, gray and black in the late light, through the thinner lazing trails of smoke, they had to be nearer to each other than they had been while the fire blazed.

"There's no place like outdoors, is there, Frieda?" Palmer asked after one of the longer pauses. The remark was one which on its surface could cause no exception, yet from his tone and the presence around them she had to hear another meaning; across the fire his eyes reflected smoke and burning, his mouth carried the hard waiting set of stubbornness and his desire.

At once blood was in her face and her hips squeezed inward.

"Palmer," she whispered, "how can you say a thing like that?"

"Why not?" His mockery didn't whisper. "Wasn't it what you were thinking?"

"No." She must again make denial. "No, of course not."

"Why fight so? There doesn't—any longer—seem to be much point."

"Doesn't there?" The words on her lips scarcely carried sound. She could see what he thought he could do; he thought he could add this much to her humiliation; he thought he could make her move to him, around the fire.

And for one hung moment, while his eyes held hers through the smoke, while the stirred compulsions of her body writhed in their terrible necessity, while swelling desire crushed her lungs against her throat until she had no breath, it seemed that, against any command she could give herself, she must crawl through the fire, if that proved to be the only way in which she could move, to reach him.

"Palmer," she whispered again.

But then, from somewhere, self-command came back.

"What do you think I am?" she flared. "What makes you think you can treat me this way?"

"Not yet?" Acceptance was both lazy and mocking. "Well, there'll be other nights. If we want to get back to Meridian by midnight, we'd better be on our way."

There was no plan and no determination that a mind could face. But when she arose next day just before noon, after a night which through most of its length had been nerve-taut and sleepless, she knew something had come to an end, something been broken.

The flat, as she found when she got out into it, was empty except for herself. The children by this time were of course in school, and Stillwell Kober, leaving scraps of breakfast on the table and scraps of broken Victrola record in the sink, had apparently gone out on one of those errands which drew him at such haphazard from the house.

The surrender, the relinquishment which now possessed her were states that called from her no overt activity; in the bathroom she washed slowly, pausing to stand with the wet cloth against her face in a kind of numbness. In the kitchen, staring straight before her, she picked up a slice of cold toast and ate it; huddled in her kimono, she walked from one end of the flat to the other, everything about her off focus, as in a dream—walls looming up large, much too large, furnishings faded away into littleness, so that she stopped, taken by surprise, when they bumped her.

In her bedroom she tried, with her clothes, to put on a workaday naturalness; nothing of any moment was happening today, she reminded herself; this was just one more day, like any day. But when the back door downstairs was heard opening, and slack steps shambled upward, her whole body seemed to draw up. "Nothing is happening today, especially," her dry lips repeated. "Nothing at all important." It took her, after that, almost an hour to complete her toilette; every slightest movement of her hands required an infinitude of time. When she walked out at last it was with the same slowness, the same inevitability; she could have stopped no more than she could have hurried.

During the latter part of her dressing she had had to be aware—excruciatingly she had had to be aware—of her husband's presence. Erratic rattlings and cracklings had sounded from the kitchen; she had heard the slide of his feet as he snailed past her door toward the living room. That, she knew now, was where he still was, in the living room. Fumbling about in there, forever fumbling——

When her heels clicked on the polished wood floor at the edge of the dining-room rug, he turned precipitately, tie flying askew, blotches of color appearing in his cheeks, his right hand almost dropping the square centerless brown paper envelope it held.

"Oh," he began stammeringly, "I didn't know you—I supposed you'd gone. I mean—I thought you——"

"Naturally, you took it for granted I'd gone." She could, she found, speak quite crisply, though it was a shock, almost, to hear her brisk voice. "I didn't know," she went on with chill sarcasm, "that you too had become a friend of the phonograph. Were you about to *play?*"

For it was at the phonograph that, when she came in, he had been standing, hat still on, furtiveness over him like a half-concealing blanket.

"A most unfortunate accident." Once she had him, he immediately gave up, surrendering to his own ineptitude with a kind of harassed despair. "A record broke. One of Lloyd's. The front doorbell rang, and when I got back up the teakettle was sitting on the broken record, though I couldn't at all remember bringing the teakettle in with me. I went out at once, though, right at once, to replace it. I couldn't find quite the record I broke—'Oh, You Beautiful Doll' was the name of that one. But I found something else that should please him." Nervous hope here rose over the nervous despair. "I wish you'd listen to it. Much more agreeable, I think, than what broke. If you'd wait till I start it——"

Feverishly now he rebent to those activities she had interrupted, jerking at the hand crank, fumbling his record from its envelope, dropping it to the turntable.

"Lloyd, as I hope you know, is going to be furious," Frieda was able to assure him as he worked. "I hope you can guess what Lloyd is going to think of anything you pick." When her ears actually accepted, however, what soon assaulted them, when into the otherwise silent room beat the knelling slow low muffled thunder of a funeral roll, what broke in her suddenly had nothing to do with the record, but only with that imminence which all night and this morning had been so inexorably gathering.

"Like it?" She drowned the music. "Do you expect anyone to like a thing like that? Can you expect anyone to like *anything* you bring in here?" No sense of motion touched her, but she was at the machine, her hands had the record while the needle still slid screechingly across its ridges. " 'Funeral March from Saul'!" She read aloud. "Could anything ever have been more typical of just how impossible you are?"

From far off came a crash as the record hit the wall, but she was not turning to look. *"You* trying to pick a record for Lloyd!" she told Stillwell Kober. "You! You couldn't pick a record anyone would like. You can't do anything else right either."

That was what had to be said; that was what had waited, all night and this morning, to roll from her tongue. No holding back, now; this was too late, much too late, for holding back.

"Even when you tried to make away with yourself, you couldn't do that. Just hold off taking your nitroglycerin sometime and you'd go out like a light, but you had to fiddle with strips from a sheet. You had to fail even at that."

In her mind, in the place from which the words had been emptied, there now seemed to be a huge space, resounding; she couldn't have vacated all that large space with just those few words; there still must be other things, too, she must say—a great many other things, which someway escaped her. She stood reaching within herself for those words to say, and not finding anything. Within her, also, was a curious sense that something starkly terrible had just taken place, although nowhere was there any exact shaping of what that terrible thing was.

Against the wall near the phonograph, when she began speaking, Stillwell Kober had leaned in his usual helpless disconsolateness, almost cringing, but as she spoke he straightened, until as the last of those too few words spurted forth he stood quite upright, looming with a look of dignity and sad remoteness, of alleviation from hope or apology, such as hadn't been seen in him for a long time.

"You might try, just try, acting like someone with a brain, for once." Just those brief words she found to add, and with them turned to go.

Her feet tapped on the stairs. Her feet sped her down sidewalks, at a pace which almost tripped her. Think of it—here she had been gone from her work all yesterday afternoon, and this morning too. Rozzie would be wondering what happened to her. She must hurry. Hurry to get to Balik's, to her work, to life. Yet she was oppressed and strength was robbed from her, because it was backward that some part of her seemed to hurry.

"Nothing of what I said was true." Somewhere there were different words that still might be said to Stillwell Kober. "You can't pay attention to what I said. Not taking your tablets—that's something you can't do; you've got to take your tablets when your attacks come on; of course you've got to take your tablets. Everything is just the same as before."

But her feet waited on the corner for a trolley, and when one came, mounted its steps. You said nothing, her feet told her. Actually, you said nothing.

Part Four

KEEPING

"Oh, all right, criticize," people said in that year, just as in many years past. "But anyway there's one thing you've got to own up to: we're too civilized to allow wars, any more."

CHAPTER XXXVII

RETURNING from her honeymoon in July 1914, she rode on a full swelling tide of vigor and well-being. "I came straight from the train, I simply flew!" she sang to Rozzie on the morning of a reunion with her workaday affairs. "Everything's all right, I hope? I've got hundreds—literally *hundreds*—of improvements to suggest for Balik's; the first thing we've got to do is raise prices. Those Eastern places are charging at least a hundred for gowns not nearly as fine as ours."

So much to tell, so much to ask, so much to do. As, after a month's absence, she once more sat slitting envelopes—"Do just as you did when Idelle had scarlet fever, leave all mail for me," she had again ordered Rozzie, and Rozzie again had obeyed—it seemed as if this too, like her wedding night and her travels, was a crest of marriage.

"Oh, it was marvelous, the whole trip, marvelous," she told Rozzie. "But nothing is as good as getting back. You're sure now, everything *is* all right, isn't it?"

This was the second time she had put that last question. Already, in reply, she had Rozzie's reassurances: "Why no, Frieda, everything's fine. Nothing unusual came up at all." But suitable radiance was wanting. Once or twice, especially while Stillwell Kober was still alive, there had been hints that Rozzie, in her peculiar way, rather liked Palmer too, but that could have nothing to do with her attitude now. Rozzie had been entirely pleasant about the wedding.

"For heaven's sake!" Frieda had to press. "Spit it out! Don't make me worry!"

"There's nothing about Balik's, Frieda, really." This return, too, was halting. "If there's anything, it's—well, Lloyd. Isn't he supposed to be in West Haven?"

"Of course he is. Both he and Idelle. Isn't he?"

"I don't know, but last week—one evening last week—I thought I saw him near the corner." This was as faltering as the rest, but what followed was more swift. "I may have been entirely mistaken, you know, Frieda. I may so very easily——"

"Oh no, you weren't mistaken." Even through good humor such as

hers was on that day, grimness could raise a cold and coiling neck.
"You can be quite sure that you weren't mistaken."

From the very beginning, when she and Palmer had first begun
plans for their wedding trip, Idelle and Lloyd had protruded as the
rocks that must somehow be bypassed. Both children, since the party,
had been more than ever out of hand, sneaking at night to appointments one could only guess at, demanding those allowances—twenty-
five dollars a month for Lloyd, fifteen for Idelle—against which she
had fought such a protracted battle, but to which in the end she had
had to give way.

"When you saw Lloyd," she asked Rozzie through tight lips, "he
wasn't by any chance walking in the direction of the *flats,* was he?"

"Oh no," Rozzie answered at once, though she still, obviously, held
something back. "No, he wasn't."

"Well, what else is there?"

"That's—that's all, I guess, Frieda." Rozzie got out the door very
quickly, and Frieda had to remain nagged by the certainty of something impending—something to do with Lloyd and, all too probably,
Doodie Bibbensack.

"You're not to see anything more of that Bibbensack girl—is that
agreed, now?" This had been the basis on which, finally, Lloyd had
gotten his allowance. And Doodie too had been called up for warning. "I know you've been seeing my son Lloyd on the sly, Miss Bibbensack. No, don't bother to deny it; I've told you I know. If you
and your folks want your jobs with me, it had better stop. Boys like
Lloyd aren't for you and your kind."

Doodie at her interview had dripped with tears, Lloyd at his had
sworn that for money in hand each month he could be sober, indus-
trious and devoted to those engineering courses he was just beginning at the university. Evidences of change hadn't been any too plen-
tiful—Lloyd on allowance had seemed to get up as late, cut as many
classes, run up as many debts, and generally throw as much weight
around as ever.

"He came back to Meridian, did he? The minute my back was
turned." Anger merely stiffened a resolution which Frieda long—or
anyway for twelve months—had waited to put into practice. "I'll just
let Palmer take a hand with that young man, that's what I'll do.
Maybe he'll find out a few things he ought to know."

Such worries, however, could well be set aside until evening, when
she would see Lloyd for herself and find out what was up. What
had to occupy her in this present moment, just as it was occupying
Palmer, was the retaking of reins into her own good grasp. Balik's, as

soon was obvious, had thriven in her absence. Mr. Prenevost's phoned report, too, was good. Some little trouble with Lloyd and Idelle (goodness knew such things were not new in her life!) could be nothing to consternate a day such as this one, and nothing to stale, either, her snugged retentions of the month just past, in which she after all these long years had been married to Palmer, in which she had set off on the most fascinating of travels, in which she had taken nothing but the best train accommodations, stayed at nothing but the most swank hotels, in which she had risen late and leisurely of mornings, lunching in languor with memories of the night still strong, in which—clad elegantly and in no hurry—she had paraded parks, scenic wonders and stores, in which she had shopped desultorily and bought on whim, in which she had dined always amid palms, lights and music, departing in laughter and anticipation for that evening's play or movie, returning after a few drinks—and once more expectant—to their rooms. So close had this month come to fulfilling every dream she ever had had of wealth or enjoyment that she had told Palmer she couldn't have asked more. Prudence had set limits: a thousand from Palmer, a thousand from her; but prodigality so fenced had been prodigality made safe and therefore more savory. It wasn't, as she had told Palmer, as if, this once, they couldn't afford what they were doing; it wasn't as if they need suffer for it later.

From her marriages with Harry and Stillwell Kober—the other need hardly be reckoned in since she had never even used the *name*—she had expected transfiguration and gotten calamity; from her union with Palmer (this wasn't to be spoken aloud, of course) she had expected little beyond personal gratification, and been given a cup which for the time being, at least, seemed pressed down and running over. There were ways, of course, in which Palmer might have been a bit more *husbandly*. In Boston, it was true, Palmer might have taken her around to his Hake connections; in New York he might have visited with her at least a few dressmakers; at Atlantic City he need not so liquorishly have kept his eyes on those young women (hussies) who were going in *without stockings*. But these were sand grains beneath a sea of contentment. Once he had yielded to the idea of marriage, Palmer had come through with fair grace.

"Now you're a widow, I suppose what you're after is another wedding ring." The original opener, some two months after Stillwell Kober's death, had been a bit grim, but she had taken care of that.

"After what's happened, another marriage would be the last thing I could think of." Crushed still by her grieving, she had had to turn tremulously aside.

There was no getting away from it, losing a husband was a *terrible* experience for a woman. Those three weeks during which Stillwell had stayed around—well, those had been something to live through. And then when it happened, too—all the questions that doctor asked, when there couldn't be any question, goodness knew, but that Stillwell had gone *naturally*. Just the same, it had taken her a long time before she quit seeing him as he stood that day, there by the phonograph. And then when she found him that later day——

Only after Stillwell had been gone an entire six months (that impressed Palmer if nothing else did!) had she allowed herself to resume even the soberest social life. From then on, though, events had moved all in one line.

"Now aren't you sorry you didn't marry me when you should have, years ago?" she had dared to ask him, at a moment when he could scarcely say no.

"Don't be a fool, Frieda," Palmer had answered shortly. "Better let well enough alone." Which hadn't been what she had wanted, exactly, but she had been satisfied. Palmer had married her, and that was what counted.

"We'll keep our whole marriage just like this honeymoon," she had vowed tenderly as they neared Meridian on their return. "There's no reason on earth now why, with my credit, you can't build on twice the scale you have before. And with you to help me I'm going to pull in the rest of those mortgages so fast I can't even count 'em as they come in."

This far she had gone in honesty with Palmer: she hadn't even hidden from him that she had debts, how much or how many. Little was to be reserved this time, little hidden. That there could be slips between cup and lip she from the first did not doubt—who, with her experience of marriage, could think otherwise? With Palmer, however, she was prepared to be forthright—or almost forthright.

"I'm afraid I've got some bad news." When he called for her that night she brought up the rueful admission while he was still piling luggage into the Kisselkar, reclaimed from storage. "I suspect we won't have the flat to ourselves as we'd planned. I'm very much afraid Lloyd is there."

"Well, I guess I told you what I think of those brats of yours, Frieda." Palmer too was as frank with his answer as he was with the arm which, possessively, he threw about her while helping her into the car. "Having been a brat myself, though, I guess I can stand it."

"I've got to be cross, just the same, Palmer, and you'll have to help me. The idea of his coming back from West Haven to stay in that flat by himself!" Except in such minor matters as help in climbing stairs, or in getting her dress hooked, this was the first time she had asked his assistance, and the sensation spread like salve. When, a few minutes later, laden with groceries and luggage, they flung open their front-room door to confront not only Lloyd but also Idelle, both disposed crosswise in chairs, with magazines in their laps and the phonograph going full blast, she stepped forward ready and bastioned to meet them.

"Don't think that you're a surprise!" The opening salvo was hers. "I knew you were here. You might think, for once in your lives, that you could have let things be a bit easy for me, but not you. You couldn't stay——"

"It was too blasted dead." Riposte came from Lloyd. Obviously, this was intended to convey a negligent defiance, but it sounded, instead, weakly sullen, and the glance he for an instant swung toward her held something other than rebellion.

"You had to get out of that town yourself because you couldn't stand it." Idelle's contribution, too, was far from par. On coming in, Frieda had intended to push at once to an upshot. "You'll be packing and getting back to West Haven by tomorrow's train, that's what you'll be doing," she had meant to say, with Palmer coming in for a clincher: "And from now on, my young friends, you'll do as your mother says." At her instant recognition, however, that something here was seriously wrong, she flashed a "hold off" glance at Palmer, and about-faced.

"*This* is a nice home-coming for your new father, isn't it?" she asked bitterly. "Get up out of those chairs now, to help. We'll save this to talk over tomorrow."

"Sure, we're good sports." Both of them, as directed, got up to relieve Frieda of groceries, and to go with Palmer to the car for more luggage, but there was a weakness in their movements which could only increase the answering weakness in Frieda's knees.

"You had a nice trip, I hope?" Lloyd asked at the table from a gray politeness. "Bring us anything?"

"Yes, we had a nice trip, and we brought you something, though I'm not at all sure you're going to get it, the way things look now." Frieda carried through the amenities.

"You're right, they are brats," she had to say to Palmer at bedtime, with more bitterness. "People should never have children." She had rather forgotten, by that time, that Palmer had been supposed to take part in this too.

During the rush of getting Palmer off for work at six-thirty, little could be harbored beyond the scurry of packing a lunch, of cooking a breakfast—"Pork chops and fried potatoes, that's what sticks to a man's ribs." Even then, however, the emanations of something seriously wrong continued—Idelle, at that hour, got up to help, and as soon as the door had slammed behind the new master of the household, Lloyd too lounged out, blankly sullen, his puffed eye pouches and swollen lips showing the effects of far too little sleep.

In a pale green morning light which might have been that of sea bottom, neither Lloyd nor Idelle pretended eating, and their silence was defiant and entire.

I can just as well start in right now, Frieda's mind prodded, but instead, for an instant longer, forcing down coffee, she held back. It might be better, much better, if she got the two to her office, where she could be so much more surrounded by her authority and her success. Yet such a postponement, she knew, could be nothing but weakness; now Palmer was out of the flat, she must get at what had to be done.

"All right. Let's have it." Before weakness could re-enter, she set down her coffee cup, pushing it in its saucer toward the center of the table. "You two have been up to something. Out with it."

"Not we *two*, Mama." It was Idelle who answered, with a bright kind of malice.

"Oh no, you weren't in it, telling me to go ahead seeing her, no one could stop me if I wanted." Lloyd's voice tried to carry bravado and sarcasm, but with more weight carried sickness. "You weren't in it——"

"I was right, then. It's that girl." What Frieda intended in reply was a suitable harshness, but what she could not keep from feeling, immediately, was that same sick enervation displayed by Lloyd. "Out with it," she could again demand, though her lips were dry. "How bad is it?"

From the beginning Lloyd had slumped in his gray-painted kitchen chair, hands in pockets, dark hair tousled over his flushed and swollen face; his gaze resting nowhere. Yet he answered her straightly enough.

"I'll be married, I guess. I guess I got to."

It couldn't come as an unforeseen blow. Yesterday after the scene in the living room this was the worry that had made its entry; this was the worry which had filled her with foreboding all night. Yet even so much preparation could not soften the stated fact. This, her mind had said so far, is what must turn out not to be true.

After Lloyd had the words out, however, after she had crumbled like a masonry wall hit by a car, and then reassembled, what held her was no longer illness, but something more familiar.

"You're sure of what you're talking about."

"No one has to wonder if he's sure, Mama." Again reply came from Idelle's malice. "It's beginning to *show*. He might have been married before this, if I hadn't told him he couldn't before you got home. Doodie's folks have found out already, and they're hopping!"

Again illness threatened to wash up, but this time the more accustomed emotions were quicker to return. Ignoring Idelle entirely, she struck with closed fists on the table.

"You, Lloyd, my own son!" As the sound on her lips swelled to full diapason, she felt herself strong; bitter and deep reproach was what was called for here, and she could produce it. "When there's never been a stain on my name, never. When you, my first child, weren't born for three full years after your father and I married. If there was one thing I'd have thought you'd have learned from me, it was being decent; I don't see how you can sit there, barefaced, to let me know you've been so shameful. After I gave you an allowance, too, after you promised——"

In her wound, in her dignity, her voice broke; eyes streaming, she sat striking again at the table, seeking out her handkerchief to sob against that.

"I notice you got married." Lloyd offered a hardihood he must have planned, because it wasn't in him then. For once in his life he was cringing.

"*I* got married—as if you could compare my—my joining hands with a fine man like your new father to the—the ugliness you've got yourself into." Flashing indignation could invest this, anger so deep-felt that Lloyd once more cowered.

"The way I've worked, the years I've struggled to bring you up. The education you've had, the money I've given you, everything you've asked for, even to an allowance bigger than any other boy you know. And this is what you do. The first cheap chippy who comes along——"

Again Idelle cut in. "It's not exactly *Lloyd* who's in trouble, Mama." This time the interpolation could not be glossed over.

"Not *Lloyd* who's in trouble. Is that how you feel about it? One could almost think, the way you're talking, that you're enjoying this, Idelle; one could almost think you egged Lloyd on, on purpose. What's to be made of you? A girl so thoughtless, so heartless——"

Always, someway, it was easier to inveigh against Idelle. And

Idelle, having drawn the fire, sat in that smugness which suggested that, in becoming the center of attention, she was well enough pleased.

"Oh sure. Blame it on me, sure. Maybe you better read up a little physiology, Mama; maybe you think it's *I* got Doodie the way she is." Idelle had no decency.

"*Talking,* you know, isn't going to make much difference, Mama," she tossed in when, from pure lack of breath, Frieda began running down. "What I want to know is, what are you going to do?"

"There'll be no more allowances, that much I know," Frieda answered, but this, she knew as the children knew, was only a surface pronouncement, running on from before. Idelle's question had held the real point at issue.

"Outside of that," she went on, "we'll just see what will happen." Fireworks now were over; what must ensue next was action.

Doodie Bibbensack, in Frieda's office doorway, stood with her hand on the inner doorknob, not shrinking and not drawing back, but hesitating as if Frieda might have called her upstairs in error.

"You asked for me, Mrs. Hake?"

When Frieda looked up a ripple was passing down the girl's slim pale throat, but the thin voice was as guileless, the large eyes as mildly blue, as if neither voice nor eyes had anything from which to falter.

"Yes, I did ask for you. Come in and shut that door." The command was for immediate obedience, and Doodie, softly letting the door fall, scrupulously testing the catch of the latch, and then humbly trotting herself forward, showed no signs beyond a natural timidity of wanting to evade it. Yet, as Idelle had said, change in the girl's figure was already apparent, not so much in a thickening as in a pivoting just below the waistline, where the abdomen had contracted and drawn upward in first conscious carriage of what it held.

Since knowledge had first come that morning, floods of anger had flowed freely into Frieda's bloodstream; seeing the girl now in such meek effrontery before her, figure tricked out in schoolgirlish blue serge, face virginally artless, animus more than ever spurted. Years ago, at first sight of Doodie, she had—or so she now told herself— divined low cunning; today, for certain, she had to know that divination as only too justified. This little trollop, with baby-fine fair hair fluffed and drawn forward over cheeks and forehead, this wanton whose blue binding headband so carefully and exactly matched her eyes, this wench of pink bloom, was someone toward whom Lloyd even yet had hankerings. For that, as an end to her discoveries of the morning, was what had come out. Frightened as he was, stricken by his situation and by being caught, Lloyd had protested against Frieda's grim gathering determinations.

"Doodie won't like it," he had miserably muttered. "And her folks won't, either."

"Naturally they won't like it!" Frieda had repeated after him with crying-to-heaven patience. "Can't you see, you poor idiot, what they've been after from the first? My money, that's what they've been after. They've thought they could get set for life."

"She says I told her I'd marry her." Lloyd had kept up his mutter. "I guess I did tell her——"

Before he would give way, Frieda had had to outline what faced him.

"Look, Lloyd, you've lived a nice life, being my son. Money always in your pockets, nothing on your mind but fun. It won't be like that, I can tell you, if you marry Doodie. You'll be living with her and her folks then, in some smelly basement—not one of mine. You'll be working, that's what you'll be doing, sweating in some store or factory for enough to buy bread, coming home at night so tired you can't stand up, to dirt and diapers and a squally brat. Oh, go on, if you want to; I won't stop you. All I'm saying is this—marry her and you never get another cent from me."

Until she had said the last, until she had seen how it affected Lloyd, until she had glimpsed the approval, almost the applause, on Idelle's face, she hadn't herself realized what power she held. Accomplishment, success, possession—yes, her money had been all this, but never before had she had quite the tangible, close feel of power that she had then.

In the end Lloyd's capitulation had been so complete that she had been able to be gracious.

"I don't suppose we need upset ourselves too much over a thing like this; it isn't the first time a girl has gotten a young man into trouble. You'll have to pull yourself together, though, Lloyd, and take it for a lesson. I'll get on now to the office——"

"I can't see her." Lloyd had produced one more mumble.

"There's no reason why you should; I will." Already, on that, her mind had been busy.

"Oh yes, Mama." That had been Idelle again. "It's much better if you see her, Mama; Lloyd's *much* more apt to give in than you are." From first to last, Idelle's attitude had been something that would have to be dealt with later.

Right now, however, she had enough to occupy her.

"You need no longer be syrup and butter with me, Miss Bibbensack. I know the pretty pass things have got to between you and my son." That, according to plans made, was her opening gambit, and her dignity too was well planned, even if her voice did carry a tremor. The words sounded well, though, with a quaver—righteous and faced with iniquity, just as they should.

What happened to the girl before her when those words were spoken was not quite what it should have been. Some kind of shimmer seemed to pass over the guileless blue eyes, the pink cheeks, the round chin; the clasped hands lifted slightly and clasped tighter, the knuckles coming out creamy white and high. But after that movement had passed the girl didn't shrink; instead she stood if anything more tautly, her protruding eyes clear and bright.

"Lloyd's told you then—told you we're being married." If it was blurred and hasty, it also, in a way, sounded welcoming. "We intended we'd soon tell you——"

"You intended, did you? You intended." To Frieda, the girl was animal. This was the way a person spoke and looked, was it, when she tried to ruin all a mother's hopes; this was the way people could behave when they fell to the lowest contrivings any human could succumb to.

"You think you've been quite clever, don't you, Doodie? You think I can't do a thing now but sit back and let you get my boy—my money too."

Whatever happened to the girl before her, she, Frieda Hake—yes, that proud name was hers now!—must stay coolly calm, a figure of justice throned. Calm, however, was a hard state to keep. Syllables from Doodie—"Oh no, Mrs. Hake, that isn't it, really"—fell unheard; getting to her feet, she began to beat out a short path of fury, bringing up short at the filing cabinet only to fling herself once more about.

"Don't talk; I know you and your precious family; I was right there in West Haven when your father was caught stealing money from the man he worked for. You think you've got me in a corner, you think I'll have to set you and Lloyd up in a good flat, give you money to live on—that's what you've planned, isn't it, you and your folks?" The very idea, repeated in first one phrase, then another, was such that it sent her blood furiously pounding. Against the desk Doodie now stood quiet, blue-pale, but Frieda had little time to glance at her before she was lost in a fuller spate of words.

"Getting my boy to come to your house, leading him on until he didn't know what he was doing—that was your fancy scheme, wasn't it? Did you ever think that it might not work out? How would you like it if I told you right this minute that Lloyd won't be seeing you again; how would you like it if I told you that you're fired—you and your folks too? Because that's what you are, and that's all that you are. You can pack up, get out——"

For the first time since that morning, as she repeated, "Yes, you heard me, you can pack up, that's what you can do," anger halted its inflows, leaving a small shore of spent and almost satisfied exhaustion. She had, then, come to climax and an end. "Pack up, get out," she was telling Doodie, and there could be little more that needed adding.

Yet Doodie, when Frieda had turned, remained as she had been, uncrumpled.

"Lloyd wanted to marry me yesterday," she said.

"There's a phone right by you. Ask him how he feels today."

"If he's changed, you changed him." The girl made no motion toward the phone; she knew as well as Frieda that Lloyd, in this, was no more than a lay figure.

Breath, pushing its way through Frieda's nose, emerged as half laughter. The sweet surcease that follows storm was extending its small margin, so that in stateliness regained she could step—shaking only slightly from reaction—toward her desk chair, which she swung to seat herself.

"Do anything you damn please." What could ensue now was indifference. "Send your father to me—oh, by all means. Don't think you'll get any quiet money, either. Have your brat and raise it; maybe then you'll learn how it pays to be up to tricks."

Disdain—yes, the exactly right disdain, the feeling that she had done everything else, too, exactly right, struggled to establish itself, yet as more violent emotions drained off, she had again to sense that something somewhere was off-track. This girl who, during the one earlier instance in which she had been called to carpet, had dissolved immediately into a helpless sobbing, continued so exactly as she had been, body tight against the desk, face quiet. And as Frieda reached for her letter basket, signal that this episode, important as it might continue to be for Doodie, was over and done with for Lloyd's mother, who after all was an important person, with more demanding matters on hand, the quiet took on a quality of ordered waiting, in which, finally, it was Frieda who had to speak, this time in a way she had to know was weakly awkward.

"I said you could get out—why don't you? You wouldn't, I'm sure, want me to get girls who've been your friends up here to put you out. But that's what will happen if you don't get on your way."

"I don't really think you've meant all you've said, Mrs. Hake."
Gentleness, when Doodie answered, showed change only in increase.
"My folks and I"—the murmur here became confiding—"know a few
things about you too. If you think awhile, I'm sure you'll remember
there are things you might not like to have get out, Mrs. Hake."

CHAPTER XXXVIII

Doodie's blond head, swaying, might sooner have turned
flat and diamonded in dusty gray; the blue eyes, sooner, might have
squeezed flat and lidless; a slitted red tongue, flashing, might sooner
have forked lightninglike from Doodie's lips. On Frieda's facial exterior, which had been turned toward Doodie for final, chill dismissal,
eyebrows, after a while, became sensible as being held at much too
strained and high an angle, eyelids, perceptibly, ached from unnatural
quirking, beads, in a necklace pendant from her bosom, chattered to
the desk edge, her right hand, halfway across the desk with the letter
basket, remained momentarily where it was.

What caused such suspension was in no way fright—not then; who,
under heaven, could be frightened of a Bibbensack? Taken-aback
supefaction was what held her—did this mouse, this creeping, inconsiderable atom, actually think it dared strike back?

"To think," she said, "to think you'd have the nerve." But from
then on, speech had to seep from that distance to which her mind
clove itself, and from which it looked on with detachment. There, so
full, so assured, so substantial in her chair, sat Mrs. Frieda Hake, the
materials of her work and success before her, while the girl—she
hadn't realized, when she sat down, that Doodie was so near—was
motionlessly what she had been, not drawn up, not straight, but not
giving ground, either, by the desk.

"What do you mean," she had to echo, from her distance, "you
know something?" When, before, had she said something like this?
Yes, to that Swiss salesman! As her mind caught that similarity, it
returned to its proper position. This situation was something she had
handled before.

"I assure you, Miss Bibbensack, you can't bluff me. Anything you
know you can tell, Miss Bibbensack; I'll invite a crowd, if you like."
Her laugh came loudly; Doodie could hear from that how easy she
was to scare.

"You wouldn't really like it, though, if I talked; I think you haven't yet quite guessed what it is I know." The blue eyes, the voice, remained shyly soft. "There's no awful hurry, of course, Mrs. Hake; easily we can let you have a week to think it over."

What ensued then was again off key. What should have happened was that she, Frieda, take the girl like a stick to break, but that wasn't at all what was going on. As if she had come to happy end of an endeavor, Doodie, disorderingly, was now—not after ejection, but now, *now* leaving, detaching herself slowly from the desk edge, drifting across the floor toward the door.

"You get back here! I'll just teach you——" Speech was rasping to a throat shut tight, muscular motion had to be violent to pull her free of a chair which seemed to have raised arms, viselike, to hold and enclose.

"It wouldn't sound at all well if I screamed." That riposte, too, came gently before—at the door where there had been a figure and an opening—there was nothing.

"Why, that devil," Frieda whispered. "Why, that devil." For the moment there seemed nothing to do but sink back in one's chair and breathe. That a Bibbensack, one of those Bibbensacks—stupefaction still had to be stronger than any other emotion, but her whole body, she soon found, was perspiring. There couldn't *possibly* be anything important the girl knew, even if her bearing had suggested she had something to go on. What was there she could have got hold of? That marriage that nobody knew about? But that man was *Jewish!* And he hadn't wanted to go on with it either, any more than she had; there was no reason on earth why he should make trouble. Then that young Swiss salesman——

From her bosom the necklace once more chattered to the desk edge while her mind sought back. Of course, that salesman was it; George Bibbensack, always around, was just the person he would have talked to. Well, she had handled that business once and she could do it again; Palmer wouldn't like the story if he heard it; it might be just like Palmer to believe it, every word, no matter what denial she made. Forever, if that tale got to Palmer, it might be a sore spot for their marriage. But that was the worst that could happen. Palmer would never leave her because of any such thing, nor because he found out she'd had four marriages instead of three, either. Neither of these things could make her *change her mind*——

Composure was now so near at hand that she almost reached it. Why am I fussing? she asked herself. This whole thing doesn't amount to a row of pins. All I need do is forget it, put my mind to something else until I'm calmer, get some work done. But as she lifted an opened letter, its typed message grew indecipherable. Once more emotion swung her off.

All last night, and this morning, too, she had had a feeling of something old, much older than that Swiss salesman, or even that covered-over marriage, come back to haunt her. That night, that long-ago night in the grove, with Palmer. What must have happened between Lloyd and this girl was of course entirely different; she had felt things in a way that they hadn't; she had had to have Palmer, and there had been no stopping what occurred. Anyway, nothing had come of it; no one, ever, had been able to breathe so much as a word. Maybe that was what George Bibbensack thought he knew. Oh, that would be funny, wouldn't it, if George went to Palmer—"You may not know it, Mr. Hake, but your wife once went buggy riding——" How Palmer and she could laugh, together!

In the foretaste of that laughter she at last did reach calm, enough of it, anyway, so that matters assumed some proportion. Frieda Hake against Doodie Bibbensack—there could never be much question how a contest like that would come out!

With this more settled view of things, she was, at last, able to get down to the sewing room, where all the faces that belonged around the sewing table—except Doodie's—lifted careful, expectant, knowing eyes. At Doodie's place was empty table space, an empty chair—a fact which again was heartening. Doodie hadn't been so sure of herself, then, that she hadn't fled before Frieda could get at her again.

"I see," she told the girls austerely from the table head, "that I need not inform you of Miss Bibbensack's dismissal and disgrace. You may now take out her chair and fill up her place."

Two girls—those who had sat one on each side of Doodie—immediately did as they were bidden, pushing the chair back, covering the vacant table space with billows of finery. Like those of the other girls, their eyelids were now discreetly and demurely lowered; only Rozzie, at the back of the room, moved in dissent, starting toward Frieda. Frieda stopped her with a gesture.

"No, we won't talk of it. This subject isn't to be mentioned in my hearing again."

This, at least, was something to do savagely and finally. Unhalted, unimpeded, face lifted to air like a ship's prow, she returned upstairs majestic and alone.

"A summer camp, that's what you're bound for," she told Lloyd that evening. "I've made all the arrangements. And you, Idelle—back to West Haven by yourself, that's what's to become of you. No, I'll hear no arguments—all right, you'd rather go to a camp too, all right, what I'm doing for Lloyd will cost money. Don't think I'm forgetting how you encouraged him in what he did."

Such firm handling of the situation's minor facets quickly established her as once more ascendant, but she could not, entirely, relax. She had little worry, actually, that Doodie might seek Lloyd out again; Lloyd was no court of appeal, and Doodie knew it. Passively if sulkily Lloyd accepted what she decreed. Idelle, naturally, erupted into such a tantrum it drew laughing queries from Palmer:

"What were those two up to anyway, Frieda?"

None of these reactions, however, lay at the bottom of her well of worry. What existed there in the ooze came to the surface only when she slept.

Stillwell Kober. No sooner had her head touched a pillow than the name was thunder-loud in her ears. Suppose it was something about Stillwell Kober that the Bibbensacks had found out! Beside her, in the warm night, humped like a hedgehog beneath their common sheet, Palmer slept easily; *nothing* could touch her, not here beside Palmer. Beside, what was there to *find out* about Stillwell Kober? Hadn't she gone over that again and again? No one could have heard a few words spoken up in their own flat three weeks before Stillwell's death. Just suppose, though, that Stillwell hadn't shut the back door, that day when he came in with the record. Suppose that busybody downstairs was listening. Or suppose the milkman, the iceman—— No, it couldn't be anything like that; if it had been, she would have heard long before this. Anyway, what was there? All she had spoken was a half-dozen words. Nothing could be done to her because of a half-dozen words. It was Stillwell himself who had done—or neglected to do—the other thing. No one had *made* him.

"Whazz matter you?" Palmer muttered against her hair, disturbed by her tossings.

"Oh, trouble at the office again." Palmer was asleep before she could answer, but she answered anyway, just as she had answered, "Oh, nothing, really," when he asked about Lloyd and Idelle. Dragging Palmer into what was going on, when he could be of no possible use, could be only silly.

Daybreak brought with it new needs for action—the necessity for getting Palmer off to his work again, and Lloyd and Idelle to their respective trains. By the time she reached Balik's she was half recovered in her self-confidence. Handling Idelle, especially, had called for prodigies of deployment. Let those Bibbensacks come on, if they wanted to, she could handle them too! *Not knowing*—that was what caused all this upset; if Doodie had come straight out with whatever it was, the thing would have been well over by now.

Teasingly at the back of her mind as she worked there hovered a reminder—the Bibbensacks, all this time, were no farther away than across the street. When she left Balik's toward noon to make a quick trip to the bank and the Wells-West offices—think, this was only her third day back from her honeymoon—she indeed saw Flora, sweeping the front vestibule of the flats. Confident as she told herself she was, however, she did not cross the street to demand of Flora what it was they held over her. If it turned out they had nothing, if they were merely, for instance, trying to make her give herself away, then going to them was the last thing she should do. Only too likely, if she waited, she'd never hear another word.

That she would hear other words, however, she had to wait only until the week end to find out. Rozzie, on Saturday morning, knocked at the office door and came irresolutely in, much more apologetic than she usually was about such intrusions.

"You know how I must hate to bother you with anything like this." Even if with recoil, Rozzie pushed straight to the heart of her errand. "But Doodie—Doodie came over last night to ask me to—to intercede for her. She's not such a—not such a *terribly* bad girl, you know, Frieda——"

"This isn't to be mentioned in my hearing," Frieda had said in the sewing room, but by this time she was relieved to have the matter brought even in this way to the open.

"Not a *bad* girl?" she repeated. "Why, you yourself, Rozzie——"

"Oh, I know, Frieda," Rozzie agreed unhappily; for the last year or so Rozzie had been more quiet than usual. "I know I've always felt she was a little—well, sly. She isn't what you'd—she isn't what any mother would choose for a daughter-in-law, I guess. But human beings are never perfect, Frieda, and sometimes they get better. Maybe if Lloyd did marry her, maybe if she had something good to work for, maybe when she gets her baby——"

"You think I should throw my boy to those wolves, just so Doodie can have things all her way? You must know what she's after, Rozzie, what her folks are after——"

"Oh, I know," Rozzie again agreed, miserably. "It's only—well, it's that baby. If it gets born with no father—oh, I don't know, it just seems to me if it were mine, if it were a child coming of my flesh and blood——"

"Isn't it too bad it isn't? Isn't it too bad there's no one of your flesh and blood to get you in messes like this?" The necessity of hurting in return swept up over everything else. It was almost necessary, too, to go on from there: "Would you be begging for them this way," she would have liked to ask, "if you knew it was *blackmail* they were trying?" But at the threshold of disclosure she swiftly drew back. If Palmer couldn't be told, then Rozzie was no one to confide in.

Still subdued—"I'm no one to tell you what you should do, Frieda; it's only that I promised to say what I could"—Rozzie went off. And afterward Frieda found her area of fever inflamed rather than allayed. Talking should have helped, but it hadn't; all it had done was bring up the subject afresh. That, all too likely, was what Doodie had been up to in the first place, going to Rozzie; she had wanted to remind Frieda that the matter was not closed.

"Easily we can let you have a week to think it over." Leeway at first was an eternity in which to fret, and then, all too soon, an imminence of hours. The part-time honeymooning which, with Lloyd and Idelle out of the way, Palmer seemed to feel she expected, had to be, instead of the paradise it might have been, a chafing trial in which she had to assume glow and ardor—"I think of you and nothing else all day"—but in which her mind roamed, never at ease and often bitter. Here she was, after all these years, married to Palmer at last, and this was the way she had to feel about it.

When the day which ended Doodie's week dawned, finally, it was a termination to embrace. Packing Palmer swiftly off to work, she got to Balik's early; let the Bibbensacks bring in their little trumps; she was ready. As the day wore on, this denouement had to be postponed from hour to hour. Her front window gave full view of the flats, but they were flats from which no Bibbensack emerged.

"They've given up and gone," she began to say incredulously in late afternoon. "I was right; they didn't have a thing on me, really; they've skipped out, bag and baggage." Desire to see with her own eyes that empty janitor's flat in the basement grew so strong as to be almost insuperable, but she neither went nor questioned. "You don't know if the Bibbensacks have moved out, do you?" She could never put any such query to girls who already knew too much.

At five, almost stunned by release, she went home.

It was all a bluff, and she had called it.

Antiphonal answers—Don't be too sure of that; you can never be sure until you *know*—were something to be cast aside. When Palmer got home that night it was to reckless welcome.

"I'm celebrating tonight—don't ask me what. We're going out."

It was quite a night. But when she got to work next morning, late, George Bibbensack sat in her office.

George Bibbensack respectfully doffed his dirt-darkened cap, squeezing it close to his breast with both hands. George Bibbensack lumbered to humble feet when she walked in.

"We thought you might have been over to see us this past week, Mrs. Hake." What existed in flesh-buried voice and equally flesh-buried eyes was a soapy reproach. "We'd have taken it kindly if you had."

"Come to see you? Why on earth should I? Your daughter must have been able to bring you the news you were fired."

The moment she had opened the door to see him sitting, so flabbily slack, in a chair pulled, as for modesty's sake, to the opposite wall, the moment she saw him gather his loose bulk to rise, she had known what impended. Behind George's flabbiness, under his oleaginous respect, was no liquidity, any more than there had been real down under Doodie's softness. She had a feeling, before she stepped forward, of being, one instant, one person—one undefended, unorganized person, who rather blankly faced forward to no one knew what—and then, in the next breath, by infinite air gulped, by radical step taken, becoming a different and more habited person—a woman who could walk forward bluffly, shrugging from her light jacket (rain, toward morning, had been cooling), hanging that jacket with care on its hanger, lifting her hat at the mirror, settling it with delicacy in its box, and then returning to the mirror to fluff out her hair, to extract and replace hairpins, to turn her head for a final satisfied inspection from all sides, before swinging briskly about to her desk.

"Well now, Mrs. Hake, you know we've got a little else on our hands than my work." While her back was still turned to him, George earnestly, if with unabated mildness, went plodding on. "We've got our young people. There's a little something about our young people that we've got to settle."

"*You* may have something about *your* young people that you ought to settle." Established at her desk, Frieda could be unconcerned and gelid, with interest for little but her morning mail. "If it's any business of yours, my young people have been settled—good and settled. And that, if you please, will be all now. Unless you're here to tell me what day you'll be leaving my employ."

"It doesn't seem to me quite all, Mrs. Hake." Patent humility, a begging, almost, for forgiveness, did not alter. "I'm not sure—you may not know how serious things are, Mrs. Hake. My daughter Dorothy—it would never have entered my head, Mrs. Hake, that my daughter Dorothy could be so foolish—will be having a child whose father—and I'm sure he'll admit this readily, Mrs. Hake—is your son Lloyd. Now, you know we can't just let a situation like that go, Mrs. Hake."

Frieda had vigor for laughter; among the many ramifications she had considered was the one George might come to next.

"You'd sue, you mean? That's fine. That's just fine with me. Lloyd's barely twenty, you may have recalled that. Under age, and three years younger than Doodie. How would that sound to a judge? Lloyd won't be the only boy she's run with, either; I'm sure I can get witnesses to prove that."

"It happens Lloyd is the only boy she's been with lately." Even for insult as gross as this, George had none but the most patient answer. "But we aren't thinking of suing, Mrs. Hake; we're sure you could get any kind of witnesses you wanted. You can rest assured, we won't sue."

"Well, you seem to have some sense." At this point there should have been more to add, but from her position of frigid insouciance there wasn't too much to proffer. "If you'll leave me to my work now——"

"No, we won't sue." Going on from where he had left off, George followed what obviously was a set course. "We'll not bring any suit," he repeated, and as he did so Frieda's bosom jerked up; it was not difficult to hear, in this last repetition, the note of change. The cap maintained a slow revolution under fumbling thumbs, the body retained its hunched stance, but steel, of George's peculiar smooth kind, had crept into the voice, and within the small, overhung eyes appeared flickers of glancing light.

"It shouldn't be necessary, should it"—this was insinuating—"to do anything unfriendly, when things can so easily be fixed inside the family? I'll have to insist—surely you must see this—that my girl get married. But beyond that there's very little I'd ask."

When he said, "I'll have to insist," Frieda's breath audibly sucked in. This was the time for rising in one's might to ask, "Yes, let's just see what you'll do." But it was, also, a time for staying at one's mousehole, for maintaining an attitude of scorn. If she did this last, then George must come out with his cards, and those cards were something which, after a week of being on tenterhooks, she could not wait to see.

"You must know, Mrs. Hake"—when she didn't answer, George perforce, as she had foreseen, continued his oleaginous trail—"that we could—oh yes, in spite of your daughter—have forced through a marriage before you got home. But that wasn't our way, Mrs. Hake; we wanted things open and aboveboard. We're so sure you'll see reason."

He was putting out effort, all right; he was sweating. But, as she kept her head turned contemptuously aside, the parasite suckers of fear lay also on her own breast; in what he had just said George sounded very sure.

"You can imagine, Mrs. Hake, how I dislike bringing up any—unhappy facts." When she again didn't answer, he again had to stumble forward. "It's been very apparent, though, to my daughter Dorothy —it was apparent to Dorothy almost from the first——"

At that extreme edge, he for the first time stammered lamely— partly, it might have been, from self-doubt, but much more, it seemed likely, from craft. By hesitating he thought he could goad her from the redoubt of her calmness. But when she withstood him, when, coldly and scrupulously, she kept her glance on her work and did not reply, he at last—and this time it was his breath which came hard—took his plunge.

"It became obvious to Dorothy"—voice and glance here took on a quality flat, silvered, ribbonlike—"that Miss Balik wasn't getting anywhere near the share of Balik's she thought she was getting. Miss Balik is very free, you know, in talking about what she feels is Mrs. Hake's good treatment of her. But of course it was very easy for anyone with any business head at all—very easy—to see Miss Balik was being—some words are such strong words, aren't they? But only a strong word will do here, I'm afraid—cheated. Of course my daughter Dorothy had to make sure; it took my daughter Dorothy a good deal of trouble to get proofs—bills and invoices, you know, copies of pages from your records—you've been quite unreasonably careless, you know, Mrs. Hake, about leaving your office; much more careless than you'd ever have been, I'm sure, if you'd known we took an interest. But we have plenty of material on hand now—more than enough, I'm sure, for persuading Miss Balik."

No more than the one name, Rozzie's, had been needed to tell Frieda all that must follow; she would have said she heard nothing beyond that of what the flat voice uttered. Yet she sat without moving to let it proceed, while the blood from her arteries drained to the great recessed cradling veins of her abdomen.

Not anything to do with Stillwell Kober, not that night in the grove with Palmer or a later night with Harry, not the Swiss salesman, not her party marriage, not any of those other men she had known briefly during her first years in Meridian. But something she never in a hundred years would have picked on as a source of danger.

During the six years since the beginnings of her dealings with

Rozzie, those dealings had long ago become something to take for granted. When Idelle had had scarlet fever, and now recently for her honeymoon, she naturally had seen to it that Rozzie do no peeping, but that, especially in the later instance, had been explained as necessary because Rozzie hadn't the foggiest notions of bookkeeping; making Rozzie understand the accounts would be quite too tedious. Perhaps, way back, she had been a bit set up over her solving of a tight situation; in a way—a perfectly all-right, justifiable way—she had put one over on Rozzie. But gradually the piquancy of that glow had lessened; all she had been doing, after all, was see that the bulk of profit went where it should. Most of the time, and especially lately, when Rozzie's share often touched three hundred a month, she had felt herself ridiculous in paying it. Wasn't she carrying scruple too far? To have a charge of cheating Rozzie laid against her— Rozzie, to whom of all people she inordinately was generous!—was having denunciation strike at the heart of her virtue.

Yet righteous in this matter as she might be, she also had to know, immediately, how poisonously barbed and feathered was the little arrow George and his daughter had glued together from their guesses. No more now than at any other time could Rozzie, with her silly, incomprehending view of things, be expected to accept the facts with common sense. With measured deliberation, she essayed some speech at last.

"I would never," she said, "have suspected anyone of such underhanded and false dealing." Reproof, at a time like this, was ridiculous; no one knew this better than she. But before she could go anywhere or do anything, this boneless crawler who appeared before her, this creature of thick textureless white liquefactive flesh, whose blind, swaying, flattened head sought for those putrefactions which were its true food, must be forced to look at and agree to its uncleanness.

"Oh, I don't know, Mrs. Hake." Nowhere overtly on George appeared the stigmata of his debasement; if fat sluggishness such as his could be said to grow jaunty, his did; the cap which had revolved in two hands now twirled on one finger. "I don't see how you've much call to turn up your nose at me or my daughter, Mrs. Hake; we've done only what you'd have done in our place."

If he had taunted she would have been ready, if he had gone on to vision what would happen when—or if—Rozzie were confronted with the end products of his boring, if he had gone on to exorbitant demands—for any of these or for all of these she could have been armored. But that he should dare, *dare* liken himself to her; that he could suggest she, Frieda Hake, in all her probity, her unbroken respectability, her record of paying all debts, her reputation as a fine businesswoman, her being set up as an example, actually, for young women in their dreams to follow—that he could hint she was one with his kind—that made everything past bearing. Blood from its recesses slapped furiously upward; in the unexpanding arches of her cranium she felt the pressure of too much, too hot, too thick liquid, felt her face suffuse.

Maybe if what he offered had remained blackmail, only blackmail, she might have come to compromise and stipulation: "All right," she might have said, "in order to keep peace I'll let my boy marry your girl. But this far I'll go, and no further. There won't be any bonanza in this for you, Mr. Bibbensack; you'll stay where you are and you'll work as you've worked. I might allow you a trifle of money—say a ten-dollar raise. I'll see Lloyd and Doodie get some start—maybe a small business. But that will be all, Mr. Bibbensack."

She hadn't realized, during the long week of waiting, how in thought she had come so close, in fear of what she didn't know, toward giving in; she hadn't realized how busily, in some far corner of her mind, the terms were being set. But they were there now, as what she rejected. Those words, those terms, could only be something that she could never now give, no matter what the cost, because by so doing—this was obscure but ineluctable—she would intolerably be establishing the truth of what George said.

"Get out," she said. "Get out of here, or I'll kill you." By her desk was a statue of stone, a pillar of sitting salt, herself. George didn't know, didn't yet know, probably never would know, by what one false step, one error of judgment, by what he undoubtedly thought to be a soothing alleviation, he had destroyed his hopes and chances, ruined Doodie. Ducking, George stumbled ahead into sterile desert.

"It isn't so much we ask for, you know. Some help for the young folks, maybe a little help for us. You'd have nothing to worry over about your income, you know, if we shared in it. Take until five tonight to think it over; you can look me up then."

CHAPTER XXXIX

Poor fool, he thought he was turning another screw; poor fool, he thought he had her. When, scraping himself backward, dragging one leg like a decoying bird, he finally got himself away, it was only by herculean effort that she sat silent.

"You," she could have called after him, in what approached transport. "You. You ruined your own plan, yourself. I might have given in, too."

Slain, casketed and buried deep—so deep that only at very unusual occasions in her life was it ever to resurrect itself—George's comparison was already beyond touch or hearing. From then on it was to be approached only deviously—If George hadn't been so insulting, or if she just hadn't seen there was no other way. One thing only she knew: decision was irrevocable.

What confronted her as she sat on was need for immediate and slashing action. They can't go through with it, she told herself. After five o'clock they'll just give me more time—and then more time. What else can they do? Telling Rozzie can't get them anything. Rather than give up their hold, they'll just wait——

But no assurance lay beyond these denials. George's words had carried others, unvoiced. I've hated you, George's eyes might have said, by their glint. It was you who came, at Hake's, so busy with yourself you didn't even think what you did, to tell me I was caught, a thief. I've hated you, George's eyes might have gone on, working us like dogs, while you played the lady. It wasn't by our plan—no, don't think it was by our plan—that Doodie got the way she is; maybe that was part of her plan, maybe she was weak and foolish, but we can't bother over that, we can't much care. Because we can't fall much lower than we've fallen, Mrs. Hake, while you——

Two or three times, just after he left, she had sensations of hanging, giddy, over immense calling depths of space, sensations from which she had to shake herself, gasping. What actually would happen if Rozzie met George's facts? There'd be a bad time, no doubt of that, but even Rozzie couldn't be so idiotic—no, not even Rozzie!—as to want to break up Balik's just because of some little misunderstanding about *books!* The worst that could happen would be a quarrel, during which Rozzie might demand an accounting, might want money (each a possibility to be dealt with as best one could, giving way as little as one must, each time), might grow touchy and hard to handle. But this was the limit of what trouble could come to. Replies must be thought up, countercharges, sneers for anyone who'd listen to a worm like George—all that and more must be prepared well in advance.

What would be better, though, would be to think up something to stop George cold. Why had she kept books? Only because they were the business way of doing things, only because she so loved ordering and setting down the passages of money, only because she had thought those books a secret for herself alone. With an impulsiveness which at last gave motion to her body, her mind leaped to possibilities of destruction. A fire, either here or at home—that could take care of a lot of things. But brilliantly as this idea blazed, its blaze was brief—George said he had copies.

With the same denial she had had for Lloyd's trespass, she beat her fists against the bars of this newer necessity; somewhere in those bars must be breaks. All these years she had gone to such lengths to be amiable with Rozzie; Rozzie had had her own high hand about wages, about refurnishing bedrooms, about calling doctors when the girls got sick. If only Rozzie were a bit more sophisticated, a jolt would touch her less when it came.

"No one's ever had such a friend as I have in you, Frieda," Rozzie always insisted, or "Don't pretend you've no heart, Frieda; I know better."

Insipidities such as this now had to appear as the dangers they were. Thirty-seven years old as she was, Rozzie still held to the most ridiculous of childish loyalties. Suppose, though, she herself went to Rozzie——

"Can you imagine, Rozzie," she could ask, "what those Bibbensacks are trying to use against me, for blackmail? They've trumped up some idea that I've been cheating you, through the books. Can you imagine anything so farfetched? I hope, Rozzie, that if they come around you, you'll tell them off good and proper——"

Any such approach, or even one less explicit, could easily make Rozzie promise she'd not speak to the Bibbensacks. But even that, finally, might lead to danger. Rozzie could start thinking. George Bibbensack had no need of evidence, perhaps even he knew that. It was against her, Frieda, that he held his evidence, not against Rozzie. For Rozzie, thinking would be enough.

When noon came she was still at her desk as she had been, work undone. Through the afternoon, with urgency increasing as each hour ticked away, she stayed in her stalemate, body and mind both breaking into random, useless activity. Now she pushed strongly with her fists against the desk, now she rolled her head in close, holding arms, now she rose to pace shortly and erratically back and forth, now she took from a cabinet a glove of sand-colored kid—one whose mate had been lost only lately—and with careful fingers ripped it to fronds.

I've got Palmer—this was one nearly serviceable thought that came. Other wives were helped by their husbands; there was no reason why she couldn't be too. Palmer could beat George up, to a pulp.

Maybe then those people would find out how much blackmail paid.

"But what am I supposed to thrash him *for?*" Palmer would ask, inevitably. "I can't just thrash him for no reason." And while she could think up any number of reasons, the chances were—Doodie and Flora would see to this—that Palmer would find out what was up.

Why she should so shrink from having Palmer find out what was up, she didn't quite know. Palmer wasn't too squeamish; Palmer in his day had been in on a few fancy deals himself; Palmer would be the last person on earth to find fault—she had made money, hadn't she? She could not, however, see herself explaining her predicament to Palmer; Palmer hadn't even been told, yet, about Lloyd. Palmer, after all, had been married to her only a few *weeks.*

Beating up George, too, would be about the only thing Palmer would do, and where would that, actually, get her? Beaten, George would talk all the more; so would Doodie and Flora. The police might get into it. *Killed,* that's what they all ought to be, she thought, *killed.* As the thought came to her it seemed that she had with it, almost, the sensations of plunging a knife into George's soft body. Into that body, with her knife, she would strike again and again; her knife would come up again blood-clean and dripping, leaving gaping small mouths in the deep flesh through which it reached; she could strike until she was tired from striking, and until George's body, with all the life gone from it, would lie like a soft mass of dough on the floor. Flora and Doodie, she could kill them too; into their harder, more brittle flesh, the same knife could thrust——

The vision of carnage for a moment was so real that when she emerged from it she was panting and sweat-drenched, as if her muscles had put forth that tremendous effort. Weakly, a little dizzily, she reached her chair and sank down. No use having such ideas; *George was no Stillwell Kober.* Rather than that, she must confront what really faced her; she must prepare herself to pay Rozzie a full one third from now on, with restitutions.

Bleakly, with this prospect before her, she wondered what such restitution might amount to, although she went no further than admitting it might be thousands. Very carefully, all these years, she had never let herself know, actually, how much, under the rose, she had gained.

And then for an instant, as she sat there spent in both body and mind, she was visited by an aberrant impulse.

I could go to Rozzie right now, that impulse said; I could go to Rozzie and make a clean breast. That's the one real thing, that's the true thing, I could do. "I've cheated you, Rozzie," I could say with tears, and they would be real tears, because I have those tears here now, all ready to fall. "I've cheated you, Rozzie," I could say, "I'm sorry. I don't know how it happened. I beg your forgiveness." Rozzie would never be hard on me then. "I know you're sorry, Frieda," she'd say; "it will be all right." I'd have to pay her a third, then, from now on; I'd have to do that. But that, I think, would be all. And I could go to George, then, too. I could tell him his bolt was shot——

It was the true, one thing to do. Sitting, she knew it. But as the afternoon went on, she didn't move. Within a few minutes the idea of abasing herself before Rozzie had become, again, incredible. She, Frieda, couldn't tell Rozzie she had been wrong, when throughout there had been no real wrong (no, not really); she couldn't weep ignominiously before Rozzie. Whatever happened, she had to stand for herself, for her beliefs, for what she did.

Besides, she still had a chance to keep things as they were. George hadn't yet told; some miracle could still happen to keep George from telling. Some miracle could happen to keep Rozzie from listening. She hadn't for years thought of old Junius Hake, but somehow he was with her now, at her elbow. "Gamble," that's what Junius Hake would have said. "Play your game out to the end."

Before going home that night she did what she could. She stopped with a short set speech for Rozzie.

"Those Bibbensacks came out in their true colors today, all right. When George came over this morning he tried to blackmail me— yes, that's right, Rozzie, *blackmail* me—into letting that marriage go through. He even threatened to come to you with some trumped-up story. You'll know better, I hope, than to listen to him."

"Why, Frieda!" Rozzie rose aghast from her sewing machine. "That seems just impossible. *Blackmail!* But of course you know I'd never listen."

When Frieda returned to Balik's in the morning, however—drawn there, repelled from there—she could not be surprised. Rozzie had been got to listen.

"Miss Balik isn't feeling well." One of the girls was waiting for Frieda just inside the front door. The girl's face was colorless, her glance did not rise. She too, all too likely, knew. That was a contingency not to be foreseen, but to be accepted now. The sewing girls, too, knew.

"Miss Balik wondered," the girl went on, "if you'd see her, in her room."

"I'm so sorry, Frieda." What Rozzie spoke in was a pleading whisper.

When Frieda entered, Rozzie had been at her one window, standing with bowed head as if looking down; Rozzie continued with her back to Frieda, and for an instant it seemed to Frieda she was having a hallucination. This was not Rozzie's dark little bedroom to which she had come, but another room, a kitchen, with someone standing, back toward her, at a sink, while two other women, one dropping cut chicken into a kettle on a stove, the other rolling out noodles on a table near by, turned to fix her with unnatural and hating eyes. Just as she had stood alone in the kitchen, so she had to stand alone here too, very starkly alone, with nothing to hold to but her handbag.

But then Rozzie turned, and the room took on at least some of its ordinary aspects; it acquired a bed, dresser, chairs, with Rozzie at one side of them, and Frieda at the other. "I'm so sorry," Rozzie repeated in her whisper. The dress Rozzie was wearing was the same dress she had had on yesterday when she rose from the sewing machine, her wound braids were disordered, her face swollen from weeping. Rozzie looked as if she hadn't been to bed all night.

"If it makes you feel any better," Frieda threw in, "I didn't rest last night either. I was pretty certain you'd get upset."

"Frieda," Rozzie went on as if she didn't hear, moving forward until her hand found the footrail of her bed, "it wasn't one of the Bibbensacks came to me, I want you to know that. It was the girls, all the girls, up here in my room. We were talking—I had no way of knowing what was coming, Frieda—they were just all around me at once. They said so many things, Frieda; things I've tried to forget. I shut my ears to them, I scolded and sent them away——"

Other people held hands before their faces when they wept; other people at least kept handkerchiefs against their noses, but Rozzie stood by her footrail in gray morning light making no effort to conceal either her misshapenness or her misery, raising a handkerchief to blow her nose, but then letting it fall to expose a distorted and wet face.

"The trouble was, it was too late, Frieda." Before Frieda could form any answer, Rozzie had gone wretchedly on. "They didn't have anything to tell me, really. I've known—I suppose I must have known —for a long time. I've just—refused thinking. I didn't want to believe, so I didn't."

"It wouldn't have been possible," Frieda asked then, "for you to have any belief in me; it wouldn't have been possible for you to come to me instead of pussyfooting and suspecting."

She still stood unsupported, and not reaching for support. Two things only she knew: one that whatever happened she couldn't buckle, the other that in this present encounter she had only her own personal skills to support her. From Rozzie's first "I'm so sorry, Frieda," she had drawn almost hilarious wild hope; could it be, could it possibly be, that by one of those queer twists of which Rozzie so entirely was capable, Rozzie was blaming not Frieda but herself? As Rozzie next spoke that glimmer had had to die quickly; what she had looked for then was some opening, any opening, through which she could take the offensive.

"Since you're doing so much listening and thinking," she struck forward boldly, "maybe it's time you listened to me. When George Bibbensack came in with his story yesterday—you'll remember, I hope, that this is all his scheme, his filthy, lying scheme for getting even with me—I knew then there'd be a fuss if it got to you; I was hoping, last night when I warned you, that you could be spared it."

So far she had scarcely known, from one phrase to another, where she was heading, but flickeringly, now, she got a sense of direction. If she wasn't to bow down, then there was only one other hand she could take—the high hand. At least Rozzie's bolt was now shot. Quiescent, face painfully averted, Rozzie would now have to listen. And so authoritatively, so confidently did her own words ring that she felt she must, somehow, arrive at something that would be convincing. As faith in herself gathered, she too moved, not forward but sideward, until she reached the one stuffed chair, to whose arm she dropped. The very act of sitting down in this informal fashion worked, she felt, in her favor; there she sat, with one foot free—surely Rozzie could see this was no position she would have taken if she were really worried.

"It never entered your head, I'm sure—I know it didn't enter George's head, and I don't suppose those girls could think it out either—that there might be a great many more expenses to running a business than anyone who isn't on the inside knows."

For the fraction of a second she considered leaving the matter there; perhaps if, on this, she stood up and swept out, Rozzie would be forced to take it. Almost immediately, however, from the mute refusal on Rozzie's face, she had to know this wouldn't suffice.

"Did you and your precious girls ever add up house payments, repairs, taxes, interest on mortgage? Did they count in those eternal groceries I buy? Did they include coal, lights, gas, ashes to haul, sidewalks to shovel, George Bibbensack's pay and the furnace to clean and repair and the windows to wash and the plumbing I fix?

Did you ever sit down to add up what wages around here have got to, and that interest should be paid on capital investment, and that perhaps we wouldn't do so well if we got caught without a single penny in the bank, or that you couldn't always demand this and that and get it—new sewing machines, new dress forms, bureaus for the girls' rooms—if I didn't have a little reserve? Oh, I'm sure you, *and* the girls, *and* George Bibbensack"—there could be real sarcasm for this; she didn't have to simulate it—"are certain you know all there is to know about business, but maybe if you'd think twice you'd realize you're not such experts. Maybe if you——"

"It's no use, Frieda," Rozzie said from lips so swollen and tremulous they seemed almost incapable of speech at all. "I've had a whole night of—seeing."

"You've had a whole night of seeing." First scorn for this, then question. "And what, if I might ask, did you see?"

"I saw—there must have been—somewhere between five and ten thousand dollars every year—that never was accounted for at all."

The words dropped slowly, torturously, but Frieda heard no overtones; the words themselves were enough. Five to ten thousand every year—could there have been that much? *Oh no, surely not that much!* That money was gone now, gone with most of the rest of her income, into stores, flats, houses; mortgages had fallen to her hands like grapes, but she couldn't have used up that much money; she just couldn't. At the same time, curiously, she knew how close Rozzie had come. Around five thousand those first years—yes, that must have been it. And nearer ten thousand these last years. Almost a thousand dollars every month.

As if this accuracy ballooned Rozzie, she saw Rozzie looming near her footrail, larger, sharper, more dangerously an adversary.

"After all I've said," she asked harshly, "you still think so?"

"I'm afraid—yes, Frieda." The reply was despairing but unmoved.

"All right. Look, Rozzie." Where an avenue should have opened there now appeared only a blank wall, so that in order to go on at all she was forced to veer sharply. "Look. All these years you've been with me, have you felt you weren't getting money enough? Is that how you've been feeling? Have you felt you could better yourself——"

"You know it's not that." Interruption was waited for, and came at last. "I've been getting more here than I ever expected——"

"Then what's all the fuss about? You——"

"Wait, Frieda, you're deliberately not understanding." The hands that had been worrying a handkerchief fell to Rozzie's sides, and she bit down hard on her lower lip. Then her eyes looked straight toward Frieda, dark, damp, but steady. Her voice too was steadier, low at first, but rising to a kind of cry. "It's you, Frieda. Maybe you aren't going to understand what I mean, but I'll have to say it. Ever since we were girls—can you remember that Sunday, Frieda, when you asked me to go with you to look at those other people at that church? I saw you then, that day, Frieda; I saw how you ached for what those other people had. I ached for something too, Frieda; it was different than the things you ached for, but I had an ache too. I'd have done anything for you, Frieda; I did do all I could; I don't suppose you felt anything but that I was useful, but those first dresses I sewed for you—that was love I sewed into those dresses; it was love made me see, always, just how a dress should be for you. You're a part of what's made me what I am, because so often when I haven't been able to think what to do with a dress, I have thought to myself, Now, if this were for Frieda—and then I know. You were so beautiful when you were seventeen, Frieda, so straight, so slim—as I never could be; when people began saying harsh things of you I wouldn't listen; I couldn't believe you took Harry away from Schatzi; I couldn't believe you were horrid to him and his folks. I knew how you wanted things but I couldn't believe you were cruel and grasping, because for me you were my only one true friend; any crumb you could give me I was glad for. Then when Balik's happened—it was wonderful, wasn't it? Wasn't it, Frieda?—too wonderful to be true; every minute of six years, Frieda, all too wonderful to be true. That's why I'm crying, Frieda, for everything gone——"

Rozzie's tears could never have been said to cease, but they now flowed more swiftly down already runneled cheeks, mouth and voice neared uncontrol, but managed always to go on. She raised trembling, ineffectual hands to her nose, to her streaming eyes, she seemed ready to throw herself forward on Frieda, begging, but managed to maintain herself where she was.

Against the long outpouring Frieda at first had felt mostly discomfited—this was the sort of thing, wasn't it, that Rozzie would go in for, talking, of all things, about *love,* as if any such thing existed or could possibly be decent between women. But somewhere in midcourse she found herself standing, chair against the backs of her legs, in a kind of terror.

"What do you mean," she asked thickly, "everything gone? You can't mean that, Rozzie——"

"Yes," Rozzie said. "I'm afraid I mean it, Frieda." In abrupt contrast to everything she had been before, Rozzie now stood quiet, the twist of her mouth that of a bitter, dry humor. "This is a day when

I might take a look at myself, I guess. I've been willing enough to keep my eyes closed while you cheated—and took things away from other people, but I can't do the same thing—not forever—when it comes to me."

Against the scarifying determination in this statement and in Rozzie's bearing, Frieda threw herself forward until she had Rozzie by one shoulder. "You can't mean that, Rozzie," she denied, once more in the grip of horror. "You can't mean that. Look, Rozzie——"

Yesterday, after George Bibbensack had left her, this possibility of which Rozzie was speaking with such terrible certainty had occurred to her, but she had thrust it away; Rozzie, she had said then, could never be so foolish. Rozzie, though, was being so foolish, and something must at once be said, something be done, to blast her from the position she was taking. No more than when she came in could she grovel—that was the one impossibility—but now matters had come to this pass she might have to explain.

"Look, Rozzie," she repeated, over a tongue and lips of sandstone. "I admit—I admit maybe I should have let you know, always, where all money went. But what happened was so gradual—there never was a time, and I swear this, Rozzie, when anything was wrong. One of the things I planned from the first, one of my highest hopes, was that you'd be rewarded richly for the work you did here. A little meant so much in those days—can't you remember, Rozzie? Twelve dollars a week—I knew that was what you'd been getting at Pomeroy's, but I used to dream; perhaps with me, I thought, Rozzie might get so she'd make a hundred dollars a month, or two hundred. You can't say that was niggardly of me, Rozzie; it was the biggest hope I had for myself."

In the pause Rozzie said gently, "I know, Frieda."

"It took more capital for getting started, Rozzie, than I'd ever dreamed it would." This had best be hurried. "But I put it in—put in everything I had. And at first every penny had to be held tight —it took hard work, often, to squeeze out what I thought you should get; I dipped into my own share, sometimes, to make sure you got it."

Rozzie's eyes were so steady that she must surely be believing every word of what she heard.

"But later, after we got going, after the debts were paid up, I admit there was a little extra. I increased what you got generously, Rozzie; you can't say I didn't. But after a while I began paying some small interest too—much less than any other business head would have done —on the capital I put in."

She hadn't thought, when she started, that interpretation would take as much time or as many words as it was taking, or that it would make breathing so difficult, or that a feeling of being strangled would grow so tightly at her throat. Against Rozzie's silence, however, she had to keep talking.

"Gradually I built up a little reserve; gradually I got us solid. You can't blame me for doing those things, Rozzie; they're the very things that mean a difference, often, between success and disaster. You say yourself you were getting enough; you were giving it away, throwing it away, sometimes—you know, as well as I, that often when you've helped those girls or their families it hasn't been strictly necessary. But I didn't let that stop me. I've paid over to you, always, more than any other dressmaker in Meridian makes or ever will make."

Again, against no reply, she had to continue, although by this time she felt empty.

"That's the story, Rozzie. Sometimes, and I'll admit it freely, the interest I've paid on our debt has been generous. But you can't—no one can—say it's been any more than fair, in return for the gamble I took in the first place. That's one thing you might remember. You, when you went into this business, put in nothing but your time and effort. I put in money."

What she had to do now was stand waiting, her hand still on Rozzie's shoulder. And when she first stopped it seemed Rozzie must have been won; Rozzie was no longer crying; Rozzie's eyes were now large, clear and gentle, as if during Frieda's long pleading she had felt each beat of Frieda's heart.

"You needn't explain to me, Frieda; I know how it was." The voice too was so gentle that in Frieda hope leaped like a salmon, silver and flashing. "When an investment is one's own, it's quite in order, isn't it, to pay interest of a hundred or two hundred per cent every year, or even five hundred? There's nothing in business—is there?—to say one shouldn't."

Pushed thus to a wall, there was only one answer for Frieda to make; only one answer that in probity she could make.

"No, there isn't."

"It's all right, Frieda," Rozzie repeated, with more of the gentleness. "I won't ask for anything—no share of the business, I mean, and no more income. You can get a fine woman, a designer, for much less than you're paying me; two hundred a month is the most anyone would expect. And I'll stay a month, anyway, to get that new woman broken in; I'll never wish you anything but the best."

"Rozzie." What now was being outlined could not be faced. Rozzie somehow must see reason. "Where can you hope to do better than you do here? Where can you hope, even, to do anywhere near as well? You know it's hard for me to speak out"—this took swallowing—"but our partnership has meant things to me too. If what you want is that I quit paying interest on investment—well, I can still manage; you'll get——"

Rozzie's head was shaking. "Don't expect me to be sensible, Frieda; this hasn't got much to do with being sensible. It isn't just that you've cheated me, Frieda, can't you see that? It's that you've *wanted* to cheat me, while I—well, I haven't wanted to cheat you, Frieda; I've —there've been ways I held myself back, to make sure you got what you wanted. But you'd always go on as you are; you can't help it. Right now, you're being as dishonest with me as you can."

"Can't you see that's not true?" So far it had been possible to keep at least some semblance of order, but at this indication that all the effort she had just put forth had been for nothing, that Rozzie still stood exactly where she had stood, a final anchor gave way. What she herself meant or didn't mean, what she should tell and what she shouldn't, no longer meant anything against the catastrophe that she must somehow, anyhow, prevent.

"If nothing else means anything to you, Rozzie, can't you think of *me?* Can't you think of what you'd be doing to *me* if you left? Not anything else I own, not any of the houses, not Palmer or Lloyd or Idelle—not all of them together mean as much to me as Balik's; Balik's is something I've *made,* out of my mind, out of nothing, out of everything I'd hoped or dreamed, out of you, out of me, out of years I spent hunting and crawling, out of money I saved up in pennies, every penny black with the dirt I dug to get it. I gave up everything for that money, my brothers left home for it, I let someone or anyone raise my children for it, Harry died for it, I married old Stillwell Kober——"

"Frieda!" The voice that struck in was a whip, back-coiling. "Remember yourself! Don't tell me things you'll be sorry for!"

Up to that moment Frieda had allowed herself no actual possibility of failure. But at Rozzie's abhorring and yet pitying command, as she had to realize what she herself had said, she shrank back, her hand at last dropping from Rozzie's shoulder. There was no changing, now, how things were. Under a great tidal wave of despair, she turned aside.

"You mean it. You really mean it," she accepted, while the wave was over her. But that was the nadir. Long before the curling white crests had broken or given up their grip of her, long before her feet had again touched ground, she was reaching out for such jetsam of pride as there might be.

"I've done my best to make you be reasonable, but I see I can't." What she thought to attain was a sorrowful benignity, but it turned, as soon as she touched it, to something else.

"All right, go on, leave me, we'll see who gets hurt. You were right in one thing—I can get somebody to take your place for half the money. Just remember what you had here, that's all I say—remember it when you're tacking up hems in some back room for ten dollars a week. You were a nobody in West Haven when I took you; it was I made you into Mme. Balik, but I might know this is the thanks I'd get."

Behind her, just as she swept out, was a glimmer of motion which might have been Rozzie extending a hand. But it was a hand held out not in change of purpose but in pain; there was nothing in it to draw Frieda back.

CHAPTER XL

Again, at a wall, she struck out as she could.

Of the dozens of dressworkers met on her recent trip East, one had been a Miss Vivienne Glix, a suave and blonde underdesigner who had piloted her through fabulous Jackman's, in New York.

"See that gown?" Miss Glix had asked lightly, pausing to flip the lace sleeve of a dress on a dummy. "That's mine. But you'll scarcely see my name as designer. Oh no. It's not the people who do the work get the credit—or the money. Odd, isn't it?"

Because of this glimpsed little scorch, and because, too, the dress on the dummy had been an eye-catcher, it was to Miss Glix that, in her extremity, Frieda's fevered thoughts fled. Any Meridian dress-maker in Rozzie's place would be the same as throwing up one's hands. But someone from Jackman's——

And in this much, at least, she was to be successful. Ten days after the breakup with Rozzie, Miss Glix, in an orchid, a long linen duster and a smother of veils, stepped down from a cross-country train.

"Just too, too, incredible," cooed Miss Glix, adjusting her orchid. "Really, Mrs. Hake, all the most incredible adventure——"

Condescension as supreme as that of Miss Glix, Frieda told herself feverishly, must truly be based on real worth. "This, I presume, is your business district?" Miss Glix asked in the taxi, gazing out with raised brows at Frigman's and Westermarck's, and, when the taxi stopped, "Oh, is this the place? But it's not a bad old house, not bad at all!"

From then on, too, most omens continued favorable. After Miss Glix had met Rozzie and the girls, after she had been taken upstairs to a refurnished bedroom, after she had been conducted on a tour of the fitting and sewing rooms, and after, especially, she had been shown a few gowns, Miss Glix displayed the exactly right change of attitude. She did not in the least descend, but she allowed Frieda and Rozzie to rise.

"These gowns could have come right out of one of the best New York houses," she informed them graciously.

As time wore on, also, Miss Glix showed the most entire knowledge of dressmaking. Miss Glix at her drawing board (Rozzie sketched anywhere, but Miss Glix got the proper impedimenta) turned out long, slinky designs that anyone could see were original and startling; with only a few hints from Rozzie Miss Glix took over the scissors; Miss Glix supervised fittings—"Perhaps a *wee* bit more ease at the hips, Miss Balik."

In some ways, in fact, things went on so smoothly that it was almost impossible to believe an upheaval impended. Rozzie moved past with eyes lowered, not speaking, Rozzie continued to look worn and disordered, but customers streamed in as usual for fittings. At the news, true, most customers turned aghast—"Mme. Balik is *leaving?* But she *can't!* No one else on this earth understands my figure." The eyes they turned to Miss Glix were none too friendly—"From Jackman's, you say, in New York?" The name Jackman, however, had to give them pause; the name Jackman was magic. "H'm. Well, we'll see"—this was the conclusion to which most of the eyes came—but wasn't that all that Frieda and Miss Glix asked? Frieda and Miss Glix would make them see.

The girls too—those girls who should every one of them have been cleared out for the traitorous part they had played, if it hadn't been that one could hardly fire one's whole staff at once—were acting nicely toward Miss Glix. Some of those girls—Grace Adams, for instance, and Theresa and May Fisko—girls who had been there almost from the beginning, might think they were quite friends of Rozzie's. By this time, though, maybe they were beginning to remember on which side their bread was buttered.

Uplifting as were these portents, however, and uplifted as Frieda tried to be by them, there still had to be times when, willy-nilly, she dropped into her pit.

This *can't* all be happening, she told herself then. It's just a bad dream. The next time I see Rozzie she'll be cozy and chattering. She'll beg to come back. The customers will start saying they like Miss Glix much better than Rozzie—we'll be the biggest dressmakers this side of Chicago. Or I'll get out of this whole thing entirely—get into something so much bigger Balik's will look like toothpicks. That trouble with Lloyd, that trouble with Doodie, that business with George—that didn't all *happen*—I'll wake up in a minute so I can stretch and laugh.

The one really bright spot—the one she could put her finger on as being surely and inalterably bright—was the departure of the Bibben-sacks. On the day after they had loosed the hounds of their vengeance their flat was empty. In what mood they went she did not ask herself; she did not wonder what would become of Doodie, or Doodie's child. The Bibbensacks had cut themselves off completely.

For half a day, too, another star shone out, more brightly if more briefly. Rozzie, on request from Miss Glix—"I *should* get the time, you know, since these customers are all so new to me—a new kind of woman, really"—rather quietly consented to stay on another two weeks. Discretion might have warned that, at this point, hands had better be kept off, but overpowering necessity thrust Frieda into cornering Rozzie one night in the sewing room.

"I *hope* your staying on means you're being more sensible about things, Rozzie." It wasn't the first time she had reopened, or tried to reopen, her pleadings, but it was the first time any augury hinted of possible success. "You know I don't *want* you to leave, Rozzie; if you like Miss Glix—well, I'm sure we could get enough new business to keep her on too, beside you. *Do* say you're going to be reasonable, Rozzie; don't leave me."

"You'll still have your flats and your houses," Rozzie threw back, in a tone so unlike herself—so inflexible—that nothing could follow but a helpless turning aside. And from then on, there could be only unalleviated melancholy—"Even if I do get on all right with Miss Glix, it can never be the same"—and unalleviated waiting for what was to come.

When the day of conclusion did arrive, she had all she could do to maintain a decent magnanimity before Miss Glix and the girls.

"I do hope you'll be happy in New York, since you insist on going there," she managed, "but I hope you'll remember, too, the good days you had here."

"Of course I will, Frieda, of course I'll remember." No longer inflexible now, Rozzie stood in the downstairs hallway with her hat and coat on, already looking alien and unfamiliar, smiling, wiping at her eyes with a fast-crumpling handkerchief. "I wish you well too, Frieda; you know I do. But then I don't need to; you'll always do well."

From then on the leave-taking became one of such hubbub that Frieda was forced to stand back. "I'll never know anybody like you again, Miss Balik," some girl wailed; Miss Glix clung to Rozzie as if she too, of all people, could scarcely bear the division, while each girl returned so many times for embraces that Rozzie, laughing as she wept, had to pull herself free.

"You can all help get my luggage out, girls, if you want to," she said damply. "There, that's my last bossing." Inside seconds, whizzing, straining, unbelievably short seconds, she was inside the taxi and away.

"Good-by, Miss Balik; good-by, oh, good-by——" Frieda herself could never have taken part in that tear-thickened cry, although, when she came to her senses, she too, like the others, stood out on the side-walk, cheeks wet and handkerchief waving toward that other limp white fragment which fluttered from the departing taxi window.

"That will be all now, girls," she was able to say. "We have lost a friend." During the entire remainder of that day it was impossible—after a few feeble efforts in that direction she no longer tried to make it be possible—to be anything but depressed.

"Miss Balik is gone, then, she's actually gone." Customers who came in used the hushed tones of condolence. Quiet, for once, reigned in the sewing room. Miss Glix, who, during the weeks just past, had not only taken on Rozzie's crown-of-braids hairdress, but had also added something to her sinuous glide that was almost a limp, relapsed from suavity to a sharpness which at any other time might have had the whole house by the ears. After a little exposure to this general prostra-tion, Frieda retired to her office, where she could wallow in private. If anyone on earth could have prevented what had just taken place she would have; no one had a better right to be temporarily overcome by the perversities of human nature and of fate.

By the next day, as she told herself firmly, she would, of course, begin feeling differently. When that morrow came, however, she found that it too brought little to console.

Arriving at Balik's early (an example would have to be set, now, of hearty pitching in!), newspaper neatly under arm (not that the paper that day was worth reading; just more trouble in Europe), she found the front door locked.

When she had sifted through her handbag's contents for the key, too, and finally wrestled the heavy lock into turning, it was only to meet new evidences of change. No sooner was she in the entrance hall than that hall seemed to lengthen and expand to twice any size it latterly had owned; any reason for such unnatural expansion she at first couldn't grasp, but then did—*Balik's, at this hour, was silent!* From above, where by this time there should be a dish-and-silver din, there came no slightest whisper, no young heels clattered on the stairs, from the back issued no whirr of sewing machines, no murmur of words spoken past thumbs moistened for the threading of needles, no stir and rustle and dulcet tune of Balik's getting ready for another day of work.

Immediately seized by dreads too unformed yet for sorting, she ran down the long hall, throwing open side doors as she went upon rooms which, except for their emptiness, were exactly as they had been left the night before. Upstairs she burst first into the dining room where startled figures should have leapt from a disordered table at her step, but where now she met only a naped white expanse unsurrounded by anything save its twelve chairs. In the kitchen beyond there was only the stove, vacantly polished and cold, unyielding of that fragrant coffee steam, that hiss and splatter of frying eggs and bacon, that sweetness of toast, which for years it had so expensively sent up. Door after bedroom door she then flung open, on nothing but cleared dresser tops and undisturbed beds. Not until—gasping, by that time, moving on only by automatic impulse—she erupted into the chamber so lately taken over by Miss Glix did any sign of life assert itself.

That one room was more as it should have been; it was dark, and at her abrupt entry a form stirred on the bed, a head and a blurred voice lifted.

"That you, Fisko? I'll be right up; thanks for waking me."

"I'm not May Fisko," Frieda got out, roughly. "What's going on here? Where are the others? What are you doing in bed, at this hour?"

"Mrs. Hake? Gracious, is that *you,* Mrs. Hake?" Movement followed this, genteel movement, but vigorous enough to get Miss Glix sitting up in bed, long blond braids tossed back. "I just can't understand it. That girl swore—positively she swore—that she'd call me. After what went on yesterday I took a sleeping powder. In just two minutes, Mrs. Hake——" She was scrambling into a robe.

"Gone," Frieda managed. So far it had been possible, by fending off any thought at all, to keep the truth at bay. But somehow the sight of Miss Glix, struggling into her robe there in the sea of bedclothes, broke any self-defense that could form.

"Gone," she repeated through her stiff, lost lips. "Every one of those girls, cleared out. Rozzie would never have done this to me; they must have planned it themselves. They're all gone."

Like a mother with a threatened child, she had so far mixed determination with despair; whatever happened, she could not give up. Standing alone with Miss Glix, however, in that great vacant house which only yesterday, or so it seemed, had so ebulliently throbbed with life, she had to face facts as they were.

"Those girls *can't* be all gone. They just *can't.*" Pausing to stare and tremble, as she slung herself (not so suave now) into clothes, Miss Glix bleated blank protests. "We've forty-three orders in this house right this minute, Mrs. Hake; I can't possibly——"

Turning away from this stay to her miseries, Frieda walked away. Balik's could no more be gotten together again than Humpty Dumpty, but out of pride, out of need for cover, out of old habit too well established to be given over, she had to go through the motions.

"Mrs. Opperheim?" she asked at her phone, from a file she had never expected to use. "This is Balik's——"

By noon four women had joined Miss Glix in the sewing room; by night it was nine; the next day fourteen. Miss Glix, by that second night, breathed flaccid fire—"We'll pull out of this, Mrs. Hake; you just watch us." But at that chill distance which now seemed immovably her home, Frieda still knew what she had. The old Balik's had been quick and animated; the old Balik's had been strong. Whatever the chatter, the babble, the laughter of Balik's had been on the surface, underneath there had been but one current, one love, one power. Today, that current said, we are sewing the most delicious, the most ravishing gowns that ever walked this earth on women. And the fun of doing this is the most exciting fun that ever goes on in the world. That was what Rozzie had thought, and so that was what the girls had thought too.

But no such infection touched these newer workers. "Oh yes, I quite understand, Miss Glix," they said comfortably. "You want this tunic shirred by hand to this lace panel." But they knew that the work they so tranquilly did with their hands was the sewing of winding sheets. How could they escape it, in a house which so smelled of death?

As long as gowns being delivered had been fitted and ready, except for minor finishing, before Rozzie left, customers retained their affability. "This place just isn't the same, though," they sighed, "with Mme. Balik gone." It was at later fittings that real trouble began.

"This skirt," Mrs. Houghtaling asked, pivoting to frown at her mirrored rear quarters. "Is that the way it's supposed to be—that queer bunching effect?"

"Gracious," came from young Mrs. Wendt, "that bone there on my hip—I never knew, before, that I had it!"

"This isn't a *Balik* dress, is it really?" Mrs. McFee asked sweetly, Mrs. McFee, who owed favors from away back at Frigman's.

"You *know* that panel has to be tucked in." Suavity entirely gone now, Miss Glix darted in, perspiring and harried, to snap orders at Mrs. Opperheim, the most capable of the new workers. "No, no, not *out; in,* I said, Mrs. Opperheim; can't you ever do anything right? And this gore—yes, it must be this gore—needs some easing—no, no, Mrs. Opperheim! Not so much! Can't you tell what's a *little?*"

After a few days Miss Glix was shrill not only at the girls but at the customers. "Maybe if you stood still we might get something done," she would say. Dresses that for Rozzie would have smoothed themselves in an instant grew instead bunchier, irreparably wrong.

"I'm afraid this is what you'd call a botched job, isn't it, Mrs. Hake?" At a seventh fitting on one dress, Mrs. Houghtaling lost patience. Mrs. Houghtaling not only made it plain that she was not taking the dress in question, but that it was extremely unlikely she would ever darken Balik doors again.

Up to this point Frieda had maintained her ice-fastness. Patiently she had encouraged—"You know you can do this, Miss Glix, if you take time. Use Mrs. Opperheim, try not to be fretted——"

Having Mrs. Houghtaling direct blame at her, *at her,* though, was too much.

"You're the great New York designer." Before Mrs. Houghtaling was out of the fitting room—let Mrs. Houghtaling know where the blame really lay—she had rounded on Glix. "You're the one who's work was so high-style; you're the one who was going to revolutionize dressmaking in the Midwest!"

Shattering of the ice in which she for days had been held was so sudden a shock that she herself stood dazed by it, feeling the release, the great, upspringing violence of being at last about to let go, of being at last able to vent all her injury, her outrage.

"You, you filthy blond shikepoke, trying to make me think you were such a noise—you, you slinking long weasel——" One's voice could rise on epithets such as this; one's voice could strike out not only against Miss Glix, but against all the other staring new workers, too, who came rushing in such fright to the door.

"I know it; I can't do skirts." Broken completely, backing swiftly from Frieda toward the group in the doorway, Miss Glix sobbed confession and self-defense. "At Jackman's I never had to do fitting; design, that was all I had to do; they were glad to work my things over; you can't expect me to design and cut and do fitting too—no one on this earth could do it—no one but Miss Balik!"

Over this squealing trickle thundered the jagged blocks of Frieda's broken floe.

"If you'd been even half a dressmaker—that's all I'd have asked you to be, *half* a dressmaker—I could have kept this business going. But no, you've got to be *nothing!* Dressmaking, God knows, is simple enough; you've worked at it half of your lifetime, but you can't put even a straight seam together. I'd be doing this world a favor if I rid it of a half-blind dribbling fool like you; that's what I should do, too; I should cut you in ribbons——"

Not only Miss Glix moved, but she too. Hindering motion came, also, but that was later; in between there was a time when she had her hands on Miss Glix (Or was it Rozzie? Or was it George Bibbensack?); she got those Rozzie braids down, she sank her nails deep into flesh.

"Let's see you get any money out of me, that's all I say; let's see you get paid——" By that time she was no longer moving, and Miss Glix had vanished from her hands, Miss Glix had drowned backward in women.

"All right, maybe I am making an exhibition of myself; maybe I am making a scene." This too was said sometime, in answer to something. "But no one can say that Glix doesn't have it coming; no one can say I haven't stood more than flesh can bear."

After that, either a long or a short time after that, she sat alone in her office. About her, from the hall outside, beyond the closed door, existed a stealthy palpitation, as if some of her workers still loitered there, whispering. Well, let them. She had given them a tidbit to last them awhile.

Toward those loiterers, toward Miss Glix, toward the clients, toward Rozzie, all she could feel now was a great aloofness, a great casting off. Anger, struggle, defeat, all were done. As soon as her voice could be steadied, she reached for her phone.

"Mlle. Henriette?" she asked of that dressmaker who, in Meridian, had usually been considered as second to Balik's. "This is Mrs. Hake. . . . Yes, that's right, of Balik's. You may recall—yes, I'm so glad you remember—you came once to see me; you made an offer for Balik's. I'm still not interested in selling, really, but——"

Too much play existed in muscles about her mouth, too much vibration in her throat. But the necessary words got said.

CHAPTER XLI

For two weeks the pall stayed upon her.

Anger during those two weeks was absent, recrimination spent. Although her thoughts stayed fast to their treadmill, she herself knew there was no use in looking at what might have been; no use in saying she should never have hired George Bibbensack when in principle that hiring remained so good; no use in saying she should have gotten Lloyd away from Doodie somehow when she had bent every effort— hadn't she?—to that end; no use in saying that perhaps she should have given in to George, when George himself (no need to recall how) had made giving in impossible; no use in wondering if there was any other pressure she could have used on Rozzie.

Through its very strength, Balik's had grown to be a boat, a cradle, a river, which she had thought must carry her forever. Anything else might go, she had thought, but not Balik's. Now, however, she had to see Balik's too, like any other entity, take on dimensions in time. Just as it had had its beginnings in a moment when she sat alone on a bedside in a horrible two-room dingy flat, with a shirtwaist of treachery close to her bosom, so it also had had an end, in a moment when a red-wigged, lance-eyed old harridan—no businesswoman, but just a worker who herself did sewing—had snapped out decision.

"No use showing me fancy books, my lady; I've heard what's gone on here. You've neither a customer nor a shred of good will left. The house is still good, though, and the site and the stock. I'll offer you eight thousand, cash."

Eight thousand, cash. One niggardly, laughable entry in her bank-book, Miss Glix melted away between night and morning (not, as it turned out, payless—receipts proved that), the temporary workers once more scattered. When Frieda walked into Balik's on the second morning after abdication the house already was no longer hers; an unfamiliar horde stirred through the sewing rooms, unfamiliar workmen scraped at the window lettering, unfamiliar moving men strained under boxes. In her very office upstairs Mlle. Henriette bustled.

"I know you won't mind my taking right over," Mlle. Henriette hinted. "You can't have so much more to take out."

No. Not much more, by that time, to take out. Ledgers and files, a few personal items.

"The furnace leaks smoke, a little; I thought I'd let you know."

Then, for a last time, in bright merciless sunlight, she was pushing her chair from the desk, for a last time adjusting her hat at the pier glass (forgotten, but no matter; let it stay here in what had been its true home); there was a last issuing from what had been sanctum and sanctity, a last trailing descent of the stairs, a last march down the long hall, with the familiar rooms on either side pushing their remembrance to her sight. Handkerchiefs had waved at the last for Rozzie, but no white waved for her; when her taxi drove off it left behind nothing but bare blank desolation.

In addition to what she was suffering at the office at this period, she was also having to endure a defection from Palmer. Two days before Rozzie's departure, there had been a scribbled note in her mirror.

"Called West Haven—explain I get back."

Almost, before seeing that note, she had been ready to shift to Palmer a little of the weight of her wrongs; surely, if ever, this was a time to draw from Palmer some of that understanding and compassion, that sharing of calamity, which he must have for her. Finding the note was one more gash in a world of gashes. Lloyd was back from his camp but off again with his friend Jack Bucklin; Idelle had been told, by letter, that she could now come home, but perversely and inexplicably she was choosing to stay on in West Haven until school opened. At every point of her life, therefore, Frieda found herself alone.

As long as she rose each morning to go to Balik's, it was only during the measureless, neither long nor short night hours that she lay too crowded by emotion for sleeping. When all necessity for rising had ended, however, she got up only when hunger or other instincts urged. Let Prenevost look after the properties, let the rents slide. She was equal to nothing but a constant staring at one panorama.

So short a time ago there had been Balik's and herself at Balik's; she had been busy, happy in her happy busyness each day and all day, buying how many thousand yards of fabrics from how many salesmen, running her hands over grained or crisp or satiny or ribbed rich surfaces, raising the swatches toward light, rubbing, comparing, making decisions on which hung livelihoods and breath. A dozen times each day there had been Rozzie. "Mrs. Hormanbutt wants a tunic, but what she ought to have really—that *bustle* of hers, you know, Frieda—is a long side drapery." Lines, such sure, right lines, had sprung from Rozzie's pencil. A dozen times each day, too, there had been a progress through the sewing rooms. "Move those machines apart, there; what we need is more sewing and less talking." "That's hardly Balik stitching; Balik stitching can't be seen." At least a half-dozen fittings each day. "Don't look at those sleeves, Mrs. Rebedoux, they're being done over." That was the most one had to say, ever.

All this had been so sweet and so right, so exactly as it should be, even if over and above all this there had not also been that other activity which transcended them all—the getting of money. Always, from the very beginning, that had been what was best; that had been the end for which Balik's was contrived and created: that she sit daily at a desk, with mail before her, and that from that mail issue money. There had been women for whom credit was an error, but not many; Balik's had made money, lots of money, and that money could never flow for her again.

Six years—that was all Balik's had lasted. Six years—so short a time to hold the core of one's life.

Beneath these griefs there were other thoughts, struggling; thoughts which touched that cry of Rozzie's—"I ached for something too, Frieda; it was different than the things you ached for, but I had an ache too." Somehow it was impossible to face that cry of Rozzie's; somehow, whenever that cry reawoke in her mind, some other part of her mind thrust it swiftly aside.

But if she believed she could so by-pass an attack on her basic thinking, if she believed that fate, having crowded its blows, must now for a while let her alone to recover, she was to find otherwise. Palmer, when he came back from West Haven after two weeks of absence, did not come unaccompanied.

At the moment of Palmer's return, as it happened, she was in the kitchen buttering an indifferent sandwich for her supper. It was by that time perhaps nine o'clock; in the stricken numbness of the days just past she had not bothered with clocks or her watch. But at already unfamiliar sounds on the front porch downstairs, at the click of a door lock, the murmur of voices, the muffled fall of footsteps on carpeted stairs, she roused enough to notice it must be dark outside; she had a light on.

"Anyone home here?" Palmer's voice, the thump of suitcases, the snap of living-room lights going on, preceded his person.

"I must say you were gone awhile." The beginnings of petulance underlay her own greeting; during a time such as the one she had been having, the least Palmer might have done was be on hand. But as she turned to catch sight of him in the kitchen doorway she had to experience a swift ebbing of some of her long self-immersion; temporarily she forgot about Balik's, forgot her long illness of loss. Palmer looked as if it were he who had been shaken; Palmer looked as if he too had been assaulted and bereft. Only after this eyewink of perception did she grow aware of the two who were with him. Not only Idelle—a well-focused, Cheshire-cat Idelle—but a small girl that he held by one hand.

"Hello, there, Mama! Just look who's turned up!" A greeting issued from Idelle, but Frieda did not hear.

"Who's that?" Her own query rose loudly, protesting. She had very well guessed, by the time that she asked, who the child was, but her question had still to be put.

"This is Amiot. My little girl, Amiot," Palmer replied from that same oppressed gravity which had been so immediately discernible. "Amiot will stay with me here, for a while. She's tired—*Frieda, I'll speak with you later*—if Lloyd's not at home, we can sleep in his room. Come along, Amiot, you can see the whole place, so you'll know what's around. Then to bed——"

His entire anxiety, all his solicitude, was for his daughter; except for the one interpolation he might scarcely have realized Frieda existed. He had not really greeted her, not as a husband; he had not asked if she had been ill, or if anything was the matter. Idelle too was intent upon the small intruder; when Palmer turned she also turned, glancing down as if the pale, silent child were a freak.

"Sure, she'll see everything. She's just too cute, isn't she, Mama?"

"Well!" Still near the kitchen table, Frieda fought down emotion. *If there was one thing Palmer had promised her*—what was this, another blow falling? She had trouble, she found, in drawing herself upright, trouble in breathing evenly, trouble in leaving the table to which her hands clung. Distraction, the long dulling hold of her grief over Balik's, was being sloughed off in large sections, but what came to replace it was mainly a different blankness. That human fragment now drifting so quietly on beside Palmer might appear to be any moppet of five in a long-outgrown navy-blue coat and knee-wrinkled white stockings, but she couldn't be only that, come with Palmer. Old Thomas Amiot, Lord of West Haven, who so ostentatiously parted his coattails before sitting down, seal-sacqued Mrs. Amiot—"But, Cecilia, foreigners, too, are people", Cecilia herself, in her rustling cool silks and disdain, Jessie Drake, Mrs. Drake, Dr. Watts, dinner parties, Fred, Bink, Mr. Orcutt, a front pew in church, eager friendship, acceptance—of that whole West Haven escalade from which Frieda so rudely had been rebuffed, this small girl had to be not only in name (that linking name, Amiot) but in other ways, too, a continuance. More than that, though, and much worse than that—she was Palmer's daughter, and it didn't take percipience to see how the charge of his daughter was affecting Palmer.

Almost unaware of what she did, but beginning to be impelled, too, by deep necessities—no matter what happened, this child couldn't be allowed to come *between* herself and Palmer—she dragged on to the dining room, through which Palmer was now lugging suitcases.

"Would she like some milk, do you think? Or a sandwich?" The offer had to be laggard, but still might have gained more response than it got.

"No, thank you, Frieda; we've eaten." As aloofly as if she were no more than an innkeeper, and he the most transient of guests, he shut himself away with his daughter.

"Well!" Frieda once more allowed herself the small expletive. Idelle, as she soon saw, was bursting to be the deliverer of news; Idelle, as she drew nearer to Frieda, showed all the stigmata of almost incredible tidings.

"That kid, Mama, if you can imagine it—*lived all alone, with her grandmother dead in the house, for three days.* Think of that! No one knew till the kid told a neighbor—said her grandmother slept all the time, on the floor."

Frieda turned aside. She knew then, or at least in a way she knew, what she could expect.

She could do no less for herself, however, than go through with the motions. When Palmer emerged from Lloyd's room, toward nine the next morning, she was up, bathed and dressed, the right words on her tongue.

"Idelle's told me." She moved to him, hushed. "I—it's no use my saying anything, Palmer; you know how I sympathize. How is she this morning?"

He paused, letting her hand rest on his arm.

"That's kind of you, Frieda; she's asleep now; it was late before she dropped off last night. I hope she'll be all right; she's sound underneath."

He breakfasted, sitting across from her in the intimate small kitchen, breaking his meal to tiptoe back to the door of Lloyd's room, eating little, speaking distantly.

"Good of you to stay home today, Frieda." He offered more of his sober gratitude. This might have been her opportunity to tell him that she no longer had anything from which to stay home, but the moment slipped by. "I've got to do some tall thinking." He again was speaking. "Amiot's not going to those half uncles in Boston, that's one thing I've made up my mind to."

Some quarrel, deduced Frieda swiftly; a fight, no doubt, about Amiot money. It might be interesting to know how much—but that could not be important, not to her, right then.

"I don't expect you to take care of Amiot; I know that's impossible. She's too young for school—I just haven't seen my out yet. I ought to get around to the yard, too. I've been gone too long now."

"Oh nonsense," she reassured him. "Of course I'll take care of Amiot, for a while anyway; it can't hurt me a bit to be home for a change." By that time she had seen—she had thoroughly seen—what her one course must be. "I've got your lunch all packed; you go right on. This won't be the first time, you might remember, that I've handled a child; I'm sure I can get on with her."

Even with such a promise, however, he insisted on waiting until Amiot woke. Still big-eyed, almost rigid, Amiot nodded her head to indicate yes, she was willing to remain with Frieda; docilely she raised her arms for the removing of a ruffled white gown, docilely went off by herself in her slip to the bathroom, docilely waited while Frieda bent over stubborn small buttons and garters. But not until he saw his child take a small bite from the toast Frieda gave her would Palmer acknowledge himself even temporarily satisfied.

"Remember"—even then he went only with warning—"I'll be right there at the yard; you can call me if she gets upset. I'll drop by often too." Only when his car door slammed did Frieda really believe he would go.

"There! We're better off by ourselves, aren't we, Amiot?" She had to speak some relief. "What shall we do next? Hunt up paper dolls?"

Through all the rest of that day, as she religiously thought up amusements, she had to sense that what she was doing was, indeed, ironic; here she was, she, Frieda Schlempke—no, she, Frieda Hake—going to all this trouble for Cecilia Amiot's child. No awareness of irony, however, could lessen necessity; Palmer was not Harry Gurney, he was not Stillwell Kober, he was her wanted husband, and she had to keep in with him. What she felt about Amiot, what she felt about what she was doing, could have little import; all that mattered was that each time Palmer came home she should be able to report new progress.

"Now, Palmer, aren't we getting on nicely? Show him your whole box of paper dolls, Amiot; show him the new shawl we found for your doll. You can smile for him, too, can't you, Amiot? You've been smiling so nicely for me. If you're going anywhere near the park, Palmer, you might drop us off; I promised we'd visit the swans."

All this Palmer accepted, but without relaxing. "I'll be by again," he promised mistrustfully. "Don't ever leave her with Idelle, now," he warned, "and she's never to be by herself."

That night again he retired with his daughter, so weary he scarcely answered when Frieda bade him good night. All of her effort, as she well knew by that evening, was gaining her no more than a breathing space; Palmer still remained as cut off from her as he had been on his return, and she hadn't told him of Balik's. In the very absence of any other tack to take, however, she next morning took up where she had left off, once more sending him to his work, once more coaxing Amiot to eat, cutting puzzles from pictures in magazines, taking her to the park.

"I can't remember you putting in all this work on *me*," Idelle was moved to remark by that second day. "Mostly, as I remember, you left me to myself."

"Probably I was out earning your living," rejoined Frieda, but without real tartness. In that medium in which she now moved—that all too familiar feeling of imminence and waiting—it was almost impossible to take up those facets of her life that had gone untended. Like Palmer, she had to realize, she had been gone too long from her yard; Idelle, for one thing, needed taking in hand; Idelle, during her weeks of absence, had taken on more of that characteristic insolence which was at once so flaunting and so sly; Idelle spent the greater part of her time in covert, long telephone conversations, in running out to meet girl friends, in hanging about for the postman. Idelle, it grew more and more obvious, was holding other suppressions than what she had known of Amiot. Lloyd too had to be located and ordered home; Jack Bucklin was all right as a convenience, but no person for Lloyd to be with forever. Prenevost, also, must want to see her; her flats and her stores and her houses, after all, were her *property,* they were what she still had and would have; she couldn't neglect them.

Yet any such return to normal living could only take place in a vacuum; too much had still to happen, too much must be settled, before her life could reach anything like balance. All I need do is tell Palmer about Balik's and get it over, she urged herself. It isn't as if he had any true right to *object;* it isn't as if I'm left penniless; I still have a good income each month! She had only to think of telling him, however, to feel all through her body that cold hungry licking which is the tongue-imprint of fear; through all the time of their second courtship, as she now had to see mercilessly, through the brief two months they had had of marriage, she had been the rich sun-glowing Frieda of Balik's; there could be no telling how Palmer would take it when he found out she could fail. To have on her hands at the same time, too, all this business of Amiot——

Through four days, four whole days, she kept things as they were. Then on the fourth evening Palmer let her know the direction his thinking about Amiot had taken him, and she could continue postponement no longer.

Lloyd, on that fourth day, had come home as commanded, and Amiot and Palmer had been moved to the porch room. Amiot, found sitting dreamily in the porch-room bed after her afternoon nap, whispered shyly that now she was a caterpillar, up in a tree.

"There! Doesn't that sound as if she's coming along?" Frieda took occasion to ask that evening, as soon as Lloyd and Idelle had gone out. "I'm sure, Palmer, that Idelle would be willing to take Amiot in her bed; after all, Palmer, you can't——"

"No, thanks." To any suggested companionship between his daughter and Idelle, Palmer remained inflexibly obdurate. "When I'm home I'll take over myself."

He was, when this exchange took place, already on his way toward the porch room, where Amiot for only an hour or so had been asleep. Every night since his return he had continued this practice of early retirement, partly, as Frieda guessed, from real, accumulated weariness, but also partly because he too had something to be postponed. When he crossed the living room he had already washed for the night, so that his suit coat was over his arm and his necktie loosened; seeing him thus, so familiar and yet so cut off from her, Frieda, although she knew the danger (again, that cold hungry licking), could not hold back an impulse. There was, after all, one strong link——

"Are things—are things going on this way forever?" She didn't actually make her query with hope; she only knew it was impossible to remain at her distance.

"I can't tell you that, Frieda." He did pause at her question, but his troubled and uncertain gaze, although it swung toward her, did not rise above the newspaper she held in her lap. "I've thought—well, I've got to get, first, to some kind of decision. I guess I don't have to tell you I'm not too happy over what's come up; you can see I'm not happy. I've thought—well, if I could find the right kind of woman, someone who'd take Amiot in as if she were her own daughter, a woman who'd be near enough so I could drop in often——"

She had been sitting in a chair, while she waited, but as he struggled with his answer she rose to step toward him.

"That's a good idea, of course, but need we hurry it? After all, she's been doing so well here——"

"Yes, she has, Frieda. She's been doing better than I ever expected. You've been nicer to her, Frieda"—recognition had an effect of being wrung from him—"than I'd ever have thought possible. That doesn't keep me from knowing, though, that things can't go on this way forever; you've got your own affairs, you've got your business; you can't be tied to Amiot. Besides—well"—once more his speaking slowed and grew difficult—"well, I may just as well take this up with you, Frieda, because I suppose I'll need your consent. The person I've thought of is Rozzie Balik. It could never be in Rozzie Balik, I've thought, to be anything but good to a child. Amiot could play around there, near the girls, she could eat when the girls do, and sleep with Miss Balik——"

The newspaper must have come with Frieda when she stood up, because suddenly she was aware of it crumpled in her hands; she was aware of its clammy, wet stickiness in her icy, damp hands.

"Palmer," she whispered, "you don't know. That's impossible." This, then, was it; this was it; he would have to know now, and *this too she had lost*—the one perfect solution, the way she so easily could have had her life as it was. She backed away from him, then again stepped forward; she forced her mouth open, an effort taking inestimable time, inestimable strength, an effort she could feel to its uttermost limits, through the muscles of her jaw, down her neck, through her shoulders. "You don't know," she said once more. "That's impossible."

"I don't see what real objection you can have to it." Palmer, from her weak and wild protest, was taking a contrary meaning; Palmer, thinking she opposed him, was turning obstinate. "I'd pay, naturally, for all Amiot's keep; there'd be no expense to you. She'd be less trouble there than she——"

"You don't understand, Palmer." Before she could go on she must, it seemed, go through a tremendous lifting of herself, a lifting for which she had no power to call upon except that integral and final power which held together her inner being. On such precious and vital strength she had to rise higher and higher, desperate and panting with the spending of what couldn't be spent. "You don't understand," she repeated finally, then. "Rozzie's gone. You can't take Amiot there, not to Balik's. It's sold."

Her voice drifted out, drifted down. It was thin.

"You sold Balik's?" What came back to her, from Palmer, was an

equally thin incredulity. "You don't know what you're saying. You're just—what do you mean, you've sold Balik's?"

"Just what I've said, that's all."

"But why would you do it—a thing like that?" Still incredulity, but sharpening, the wide jaw jutting forward, the lower lids creeping up over eyes that were direct enough now. "You said yourself that that place was a gold mine. You said you were taking out——"

Even as high up as she was—as uncertainly, teeteringly high—a shrug must be managed.

"I got my price, so I sold."

"Oh, you got your price." He seemed closer to her, not as if he stepped closer, but as if he rose toward her height. "What price?"

"Shouldn't that be my business?"

"I'm not too sure it's your business." The taller Palmer bore an attitude almost of menace. "Where's Miss Balik gone to?"

One more shrug. "She went East, I believe; somewhere East. That, as far as I'm concerned, is all her affair."

The two eyes against her were knives to cut down her defenses.

"You quarreled—that's it, then. She left you, and you had to sell."

She said stonily, "It can't be the first time, I suppose, that partners have broken up."

He said, "You needn't try deceiving me, Frieda. I saw what you had there; I knew Rozzie Balik. The only reason she'd ever have left you was that you were crooked with her." What followed was slow, spaced, inexorable. "That was it, wasn't it? You had a setup like that one, you had a friend like Rozzie. But you couldn't hold yourself. You could take in a few extra dollars, so you had to cheat her."

She had no sense of falling—or did she? She cried wildly, "You've no right whatsoever to say things like that to me; no right whatsoever. Every dealing I had with Rozzie was the most——"

"No front for me, Frieda. You forget—I know you." What struck at her then was a settled weariness, a cold harsh finality. "It was the first thing I realized when I took over Amiot—I couldn't let you be in charge of her. You're no mother for Amiot."

She looked at him, stared at him.

He said, "If you could cheat Rozzie, you'd have to cheat Amiot, and me. Not right away, maybe, but sometime. We'll make plans to leave here as soon as we can."

CHAPTER XLII

She still could only stare at him.

"Palmer," she got out then, finally. Her feet were affixed, now, her feet brought her down from all space to the room where the two of them stood: he, loosening his necktie as if everything had been said and he should get to bed, she wringing her newspaper, crumpled and clubbed, in her hands. "Palmer, you don't mean that. You know that what we've had together is something you wanted. Our honeymoon—our *honeymoon,* Palmer—you can't deny that you wanted it. We'll have more times like that, Palmer, we've got a whole life together——"

It was no longer the newspaper she held; she had stepped to him; she had his arms. "Just because you've got a daughter, you can't give up our marriage——"

Echoes, the echoes of useless, lost pleading, seemed to ring with her words; this was—or wasn't it?—the same pleading she had done for Rozzie, but this was different; this was Palmer, her husband, of whom she pleaded; this was Palmer, the boy who had run down the balcony stairs, Palmer who had caught at her, asking, "Say, where did you come from?"; this was Palmer—oh, memory which was bliss and life, no matter what its agonies might be—this was Palmer with whom she had gone riding long ago through deep summer nights; this was Palmer who had lain with her in the grove; this was Palmer who alone in his essence, his being, could hold all she had asked and wanted of life.

"Oh, I know I've had other husbands"—at a time such as this everything must be dared—"but you know that no other man ever meant anything, Palmer—you know this is my one true marriage——"

He asked heavily, his head turned away from her, "Is it? I've sometimes wondered, even apart from Amiot. It's——"

"Palmer, you——"

"No, you'll have to wait, Frieda; I'm not as quick as you are; you'll have to let me talk as I can." Head still aside, he stood breathing laboriously, and there was something about him, his figure, his face, to choke off her wild rush of pleading. "When I remember—I guess you're doing that too—when I remember when we were young—it's hard to say, but there are ways you're right for me, Frieda; when I'm with you I don't have to worry; I don't have to live up to anything; I can let myself go. I guess that's why I gave up and married you; I said, 'Ah, what the hell,' that's what I said to myself, 'there's not much in living but money and a woman like Frieda.'"

Again he paused, and this time she knew what he was like; he was like a crunching slow juggernaut.

"All my life, I guess," he went on, "I've been mostly one kind of person. I've seen there were other things, sometimes I've tried to reach other things; maybe I'll always blunder—that's something I can't tell. All I know is, I've got to make myself over, from a man who can be a fit husband for you to a man who can be a fit father for Amiot."

Once more the juggernaut halted, before it took up its difficult progress. "You've got to see, Frieda, this is no place for Amiot; there's no air here for her; she can't take you to live by. And I won't have her spoiled rotten, the way Lloyd and Idelle are."

Against all of this assault she had let him take his way, but at this last she must gasp out denial. "You can't say a thing like that; Lloyd and Idelle are as——"

So far he had been in some ways dispassionate, but when she argued against him he turned on her, and there then was a quality of cruelty in him, as if, having hurt her, he could now only want to hurt more.

"You can't really have thought, can you, Frieda, that I've lived in this flat these two months, without knowing what's been going on? You didn't think I'd be put off with your 'no, nothing's wrong'? I've got eyes and ears, Frieda; I may know what you don't. Do you know, for instance, what Idelle was up to in West Haven this summer? If I'm not mistaken, you'll soon find that out. Do you know why Lloyd was kicked out of his classes last spring? You may soon wish you'd let Lloyd marry that girl of his; he'll be into worse trouble."

"You don't know what you're saying." For this, at least, she must have breath and voice. And then, a dam broken, she had voice for more.

"You who know everything, you who're a judge for me—would you like to know more? It was that girl of Lloyd's, as you call her, it was that girl and her father who blackmailed me, who went with their lies to Rozzie, who made me lose Balik's. Yet you can stand there to tell me——"

"Blackmail," he repeated, and now he was smiling, he was cruelly, successfully smiling. "That's all of a piece, isn't it, Frieda? Exactly the game that you might have gone in for, if you'd stood in their place."

"Don't say that!" Explosion must rip past her teeth. Who else had said that? At what other time had she fought down this tentacled octopus? She could cry, "When I've been the most honorable——" But like eyes brightly winking at night, here, there, everywhere, tiny curtains flew up. Schatzi at a sink. Mrs. Gurney, a helpless and paralyzed rabbit. Harry in his coffin—no, she hadn't looked, but she knew. Eddie Noble at the foot of the hardware-store stairs. Stillwell Kober——

"You yourself, Frieda," Palmer said then, with more quietness, "all these last days, you've known the whole thing was impossible; you've known it couldn't last."

At a breaking point, because this, surely *this* was the cruellest, that he should ask her to confirm him, that he should ask her to acknowledge that cold licking fear, she came to her own quietness.

She said, "I don't suppose you feel it's at all important to know what you'll be leaving me for, since you can't get at Rozzie."

He said, "No, I don't think it's too important—I still think I'll find Rozzie Balik. I can sell this lumberyard."

Once more she stared at him; for a hung, flickering second she had a sensation as if the walls of the room about her flew away from her, widely, and then closed back in.

She said, "Palmer, you aren't by any means thinking, are you, that you might someday *marry Rozzie?*"

He said, "I don't suppose she'd have me, but I could make a damn good try."

The humility was new. But the set of the jaw—that was old. Very old.

She sat in her chair, the same chair in which she had been sitting when Palmer came through the living room. She sat in her chair, without knowing exactly what position her body took; all she knew was that she felt tight and drawn in; she might have been rolled in a ball. This was what happened, this was the state one was left in, when all one's strength and one's faculties had to be centered on keeping life in one's body.

Rozzie. Palmer, in a way, was leaving her for Rozzie. Oh, it was impossible that Palmer should marry Rozzie; impossible to think Rozzie would ever take Palmer; Rozzie had not been meant to marry; Rozzie had been born to sew dresses. But it couldn't be hard to know how Rozzie would take to Amiot. "If it were a child of mine, Frieda——"

Once, long ago, when she had had strength for such walking, she could have risen, to pace back and forth. Once, long ago, she would have had violence to vent. But as she sat now, what seemed to possess her was bleakness, a vast desert bleakness. Only one wall, one thin wall, shut away Palmer's person; there he lay in a bed less than fifteen feet from her, but already he might have been his thousand miles distant; already he might have asked for, and gotten, divorce. Palmer might change in some ways, but he always would hold to a course he had chosen.

"No, no, no; no, no no," her lips said. Was this all she was to have of her marriage with Palmer—two months? There remained yet so much that she was to have had from this marriage, so much of living and loving and making and spending; not she and Lloyd, never she and Idelle, but *she and Palmer* were to have sought out together those Edens where living was palmiest; "Oh yes," she and Palmer were to have said, at some time in the future, as so often her clients at Balik's had said, "thirty-six dollars a day, but of course we were right on the ocean." "Yes, alcohol's a good cleaner for diamonds, but I never take chances; I always send mine to a jeweler's." "It never pays to buy anything, I always say, if it isn't the best." In the seats of observation cars, in the fine big lobbies of fine big hotels, these were the laurels that they should have tossed to each other. But there was more than this too. Sometime in the future, oh, far in the future, perhaps when he was old, she was to have had revenges on Palmer, revenge because she was a woman, revenge for the baiting, the taunting, of his second courtship, revenge for his spoken and unspoken censuring, revenge for her wrong marriages, revenge for her loss of Hake's, revenge for his jilting, revenge—yes, revenge for Shindy Day.

She stayed fast in her chair, but once again, just as at Harry's death, the jolting of Shindy Day was what she experienced; hands tossed her from one rough repulse to another. All that, all hope of getting even, must be forgone now; Palmer had once more cast her off, not for Cecilia, not for anyone like Cecilia, but for Rozzie, whom all her life she had scorned.

She turned a little, resting her cheek against the back of the chair, and as she did so that motion too was familiar. "I think I want to be a nun," she had said, resting her cheek against the shelf of Father Doern's confessional. So too she could now have collapsed and broken. "I've seen other things," Palmer said. "Sometimes I've tried to reach them." "I ached for something too," Rozzie said. "It was different than the things you ached for——"

All her life, ever since that night of beginning when Mr. Hake had thrown his money, she had seen her one goal and held to it. "Did you ever think, Miss Schlempke"—that was what Mr. Hake had said, turning on the balcony to swing his long shadow until it covered them both—"that it might someday be yours?" Yet Mr. Hake himself—and this was something she now had to see with an all too clear vision—had owned a different goal that he held to; Mr. Hake had wanted to make money, yes, but what he had really held as attainment had been something inside himself; he had wanted to rise cool and superior above any wealth or the lack of it; he had wanted to make money or lose it with equal disdain. The Gurneys too, even the Gurneys, had had their different goal. "For us," Mr. Gurney once said, "with our ideals of plain living and high thinking——" It was hard, even now, sitting in the pitiless white light in which she must now sit, to see what the Gurneys had lived by, exactly, but it had been something. Then Rozzie——

Those other people, who had other goals, did they find in their lives a real richness? Did they never have to see themselves cut down and wounded, as she sat wounded now? "What else could you come to, Frieda?" Was it Harry who asked that, or Palmer? Harry—or Palmer; yes, there was a link there; many times, not just at Harry's death, but in a smaller way, many times, she had sat as she was sitting now. Between Harry and Palmer her life had a pattern: always there had been something for which she reached, something for which she worked, something of which she dreamed, but always, even when she had seemed to achieve what she wanted, some circumstance had robbed her of fruition. Never had this circumstance been of her making; had it been her fault, years ago, when all she had asked of the world was a dress, that her mother couldn't sew? Had it been her fault, in this last reversal, that Palmer had begotten a daughter? Not she but accident, *the way life was,* that was what had robbed and despoiled her.

She sat in her chair, arms not locked now, but clasped over her abdomen. Is that true? Is that true? Within the darkness around her she saw all the faces, the old, well-known faces, trying to force from her some different conclusion. It couldn't be, no, it couldn't be, that it was her dream of possession which in itself was corrupting; it couldn't be her hunger to own which had seemed to rot everything human with which she came in touch. Suppose, just suppose, she had turned to those other doors which had always stood open beside the doors she chose: suppose she had said, "I can't take Harry, he's Schatzi's"; suppose she had said, "I may lose it, but I'll let Harry have my money for bicycles"; suppose she had said, "I must stay home to tend Lloyd and Idelle myself." Would things then have been different, would she herself have been different, would she *want* to be different?

That was the crucial question, that last, and time seemed to wait while she answered. If she could say yes, then maybe like Palmer she could change, maybe she could get him back, maybe she too could be different. She sat trying to will herself toward that difference, but even as she did so she knew that she would never reach it; maybe once, when she was younger, but not now. She could never say to herself honestly, If I could do it over, if I could have Lloyd and Idelle the way they should be, if I could be the kind of a woman that Palmer would want as a mother for Amiot, I'd be willing to give up the rest that I had—I'd be willing to give up having had Balik's and all that lovely profit, I'd be willing to give up what I still own. She could never say, Take all my property, I don't really want it; I don't care about being a person of property, my real wants lie elsewhere.

She sat long, she sat late. Sometimes from outside she heard cars passing, she heard swift, late-going footsteps clacking against cement, she heard the sudden swelling and receding rush of late streetcars Idelle and Lloyd, before the night was quite gone, would be home; she would hear their feet stealthy on the porch downstairs, she would hear the lock stealthily turned, she would hear the stealthy fumbling while they took off their shoes before beginning a stealthy ascent of the stairs. When that happened she would have to stand up. "What's this I hear of you?" she would have to ask; she would have to keep on in the road she had chosen, even though she knew about the corruption, even if she had to accept that Lloyd and Idelle forever must be what they were now. She had made her choice, and her choice was what she had.

She moved forward slightly in her chair, rocking, her hands clasped over her abdomen. She was no woman for feeling any kind of dissolution in herself, but she might, then, have felt life as draining away from her; she might have seen what her future must be. She was no woman for crying, but she might have whimpered.